About the A

Cursed with a poor sense of d
to read, **Annie Claydon** spent much of her childhood
lost in books. A degree in English Literature followed
by a career in computing didn't lead directly to her
perfect job – writing romance for Mills & Boon – but
she has no regrets in taking the scenic route. She lives
in London: a city where getting lost can be a joy.

Kate Hewitt has worked a variety of different jobs, from
drama teacher to editorial assistant to youth worker, but
writing romance is the best one yet. She also writes
women's fiction and all her stories celebrate the healing
and redemptive power of love. Kate lives in a tiny village
in the English Cotswolds with her husband, five children,
and an overly affectionate Golden Retriever.

Rebecca Winters lives in Salt Lake City, Utah. With
canyons and high alpine meadows full of wildflowers,
she never runs out of places to explore. They, plus her
favourite holiday spots in Europe, often end up as
backgrounds for her romance novels because writing is
her passion, along with her family and church. Rebecca
loves to hear from readers. If you wish to email her,
please visit her website at: cleanromances.net

Princess Brides

Princess Brides: Friends to Lovers

ANNIE CLAYDON

KATE HEWITT

REBECCA WINTERS

MILLS & BOON

First Published in Great Britain 2025
by Mills & Boon, an imprint of HarperCollins*Publishers* Ltd
1 London Bridge Street, London, SE1 9GF

www.harpercollins.co.uk

HarperCollins*Publishers*
Macken House, 39/40 Mayor Street Upper,
Dublin 1, D01 C9W8, Ireland

ISBN: 978-0-263-41717-3

This book contains FSC™ certified paper and other controlled sources to ensure responsible forest management.

For more information visit: www.harpercollins.co.uk/green

Printed and Bound in the UK using 100% Renewable Electricity at CPI Group (UK) Ltd, Croydon, CR0 4YY

BEST FRIEND TO ROYAL BRIDE

ANNIE CLAYDON

CHAPTER ONE

The first Friday in February

THE EVENING OF the first Friday in February had been marked out as *'busy'* in Marie's calendar for the last twelve years. As she looked around the table, stacked with food and wine, twelve people all talking at once, she could only hope that it would be booked for the next twelve years.

During her final year at medical school there had been one class that was special. A tight-knit group who had laughed together and shared the ups and downs of their studies. Since then they'd graduated and gone their separate ways, but one evening every year still belonged to them.

Sunita was passing her phone around so that everyone could see the pictures of her new baby. Will was just back from America, and Rae had stories to tell about Africa. Nate was having relationship problems, and was talking intently to David, who was nodding thoughtfully. When she got the chance, Marie would change seats and offer what support she could.

And Alex…

Marie didn't like to admit it, but she looked forward to seeing him the most. He had been the golden boy of the class, managing to combine a carefree love of life and a wicked sense of fun with academic brilliance. He and

Marie had struck up an especially close friendship and, in truth, if you were looking for anything long-term with Alex, then friendship was the way to go. He was seldom without a girlfriend, but those relationships never lasted very long.

Tonight he looked as if he had things on his mind. He'd flipped through Sunita's photographs, grinning and saying all the right things, but when he'd passed the phone on he'd gone back to playing with his food and staring abstractedly into space.

Marie leaned over, feeling the softness of his cashmere sweater as she brushed her fingers against his arm to get his attention. 'What's going on, Alex?'

'I'm...coasting at the moment. One hand on the driving wheel with the wind in my hair.' He shrugged, smiling suddenly. Those long-lashed grey eyes were still the same, and so was his mop of dark hair, shorter now but still as thick.

The memory was as fresh as if it had been yesterday. Alex pulling up outside her student digs, the soft top of his car pulled back, saying he just wanted to feel the warm breeze on his face and would Marie like to keep him company? It was a world away from the worries that seemed to be lingering behind his smile now.

'And you're still moving mountains?'

Marie laughed. 'I'm still shovelling, if that's what you mean.'

'Moving mountains one shovelful at a time. That's your speciality.'

He made it sound like a good thing. Something that was fine and virtuous, and not just a fact of life. Her life, anyway.

Alex had never had to worry about money, and had received a generous allowance from his family. Marie had gone to medical school knowing that her family needed her help rather than the other way around. Hand to mouth, taking each day as it came. Mostly she'd had enough to eat and cover her rent, but sometimes it had been a struggle. She'd made it through, one shovelful at a time.

On the other side of the restaurant a waiter was bringing a cake, flaming with candles, to a table of six young women. He started to sing 'Happy Birthday' and the tune was taken up around all the tables. Alex was watching, singing quietly, and Marie wondered whether he had any wishes tonight.

The birthday girl stood up, leaning over the cake. And suddenly Alex was moving, ducking adroitly past a couple of waiters and making his way towards her. It wasn't until Marie was on her feet that she saw what the matter was. The girl was waving her arm, which only fanned the flames licking at her sleeve.

Stop, drop and roll. She hadn't done the first, and it looked as if she wasn't going to do the second or the third either. Alex reached her just as she started to panic, grabbing her arm and deftly catching up a pitcher of water from the table.

Suddenly the restaurant was deathly quiet, the girl's keening sobs the only sound. Alex had his arm tightly around her and he flashed Marie a glance, to check that she would stay with the other young women at the table, before hurrying their injured friend towards the ladies' restroom.

'Where are they going? We'll go with her...'

One of the party rose from her seat and Marie motioned to her to sit down again. She knew Alex had this under control, and if he'd needed any help he would have left no one in any doubt about what he wanted them to do.

'It's okay, we're doctors. The burn should be cooled straight away and that's what my colleague has gone to do. It's best that we stay here.'

Alex would be checking for signs of shock, and being surrounded by people wasn't going to help.

'But…is she going to be all right? She was on fire…' Another of the friends spoke up.

Things could have been a lot worse. It had looked as if her blouse was cotton, not a man-made fabric, and the flames had spread relatively slowly. If Alex hadn't acted so quickly precious minutes would have been lost…

'The fire was extinguished very quickly. I'll go and check on her.'

Marie turned towards her own table, where everyone was watchful but still in their seats, trusting that Marie or Alex would call them if they were needed. She beckoned to Sunita, who rose from her seat, weaving her way past the tables towards them, and asked her to stay with the group of friends.

A waiter was standing outside the restroom and let Marie through. Inside, Alex had sat the young woman by a basin and was gently supporting her arm under a stream of lukewarm water. He was smiling, his voice gentle and relaxed as he chatted to her quietly.

'How many candles on that cake, Laura?'

'Eighteen. It's my eighteenth birthday tomorrow. I'm having a party.' Laura turned the corners of her mouth down.

'You'll be fine. This is a first-degree burn, which is the least severe. It's going to hurt for a little while, but it won't leave a scar. You're going to have a great birthday.' He glanced up at Marie. 'This is my friend, Marie. She's a doctor too, so she can't help poking her nose in and making sure I'm doing everything right.'

Alex shot her a delicious smile, the kind that reminded Marie of when they'd been young doctors together in A&E. Laura turned towards Marie, and Alex steadied her arm under the water.

'He's doing pretty well.'

'Glad to hear it. What about you? How are you doing?'

'I'm all right. Where is everyone? Are they eating my cake?'

'They sent me to find out how you were. They're not eating the cake.'

Alex had done a great job of keeping Laura calm if her main concern was cake.

'That's a relief,' Alex broke in. 'Laura's promised me a slice. Not for another ten minutes, though. We need to keep cooling the burn. Then I think we'll send you off home, with a list of instructions.'

'Oh, you're going to write a list of *instructions*?' Marie grinned conspiratorially at Laura. 'Watch out for those.'

Alex chuckled. 'First on the list is to have a very happy birthday...'

Things might have been so different. Laura's eighteenth birthday could have been spent in a burns unit, with a prognosis of skin grafts and a great deal of pain. But she was going home with her friends, a little wet from the pitcher of water that Alex had poured on her arm to extinguish the flames, and with a couple of miraculously minor burns. Whatever future she wanted for herself was still waiting for her.

Alex spent another half an hour making sure she was all right, and advising her on how to care for the burns. Sunita had persuaded Laura's friends to come over and sit with her, and the cake was being divided into portions and wrapped. The low hum of chatter in the restaurant indicated that the incident was already largely forgotten, cleared away along with the debris from Laura's table.

Alex had gone outside to see Laura and her friends into a taxi, and Marie saw him turn, leaning back against the railings that separated the pavement from the front of the restaurant, staring up at the scrap of sky that showed between the tops of the buildings. It appeared that his easy, relaxed air had been all for Laura's sake.

Whatever the last year of medical school had thrown at them, Alex had always bounced back, but now he seemed brooding, almost heartbroken. There was definitely something wrong.

Maybe she could help. Maybe he'd stayed outside hoping she'd join him. It wouldn't be the first time they'd confided in each other, and Marie had always wanted him to feel he could talk to her about anything.

She picked up Alex's jacket from the back of his chair and slipped away from the table.

Alex had been looking forward to seeing Marie again. He'd wondered whether he should confide in her, and now that he'd sent Laura safely on her way the yearning to do so reasserted itself. He knew he wouldn't, though. Marie normally understood everything, but she wouldn't be able to understand how difficult the last few months had been. She'd struggled for everything she had, and it felt somehow wrong to confide his pain and dismay at finding he had much more than enough of everything.

'Aren't you cold?'

When he heard her voice it didn't come as much of a surprise. Maybe that was what he was doing out here, shivering under the street lamps: waiting for Marie to come and find him.

'Not really.' He took his jacket from her, wrapping it around her shoulders. The pleasure he got from the gesture seemed way out of proportion to its true worth.

'That was a bit like old times.'

She turned her gaze on him and suddenly it felt a lot like old times.

'Yes. I'm glad Laura's okay.'

'She has you to thank for that. So, since we seem to be

out here, and your jacket's nice and warm...' Marie gave him an impish smile. 'You can tell me what the matter is.'

It was tempting. Alex had never been able to resist her eyes. Almost violet in the sunlight and deep blue in the shade. She wore her dark hair in a shining pixie cut, and Alex always thought of mischief and magic when he looked at her.

'I'm fine...just tired. You remember tired?' He smiled at her.

She chuckled. 'Remember that time you came round to my place and I'd been up all night working on abstracts?'

'I've never seen anyone actually fall asleep *while* they're drinking coffee before. Particularly since I'd made it so strong...'

Marie had got a job writing abstracts for scientific papers, which had been more lucrative than waitressing and had fitted around their busy study schedule better. Working and studying at the same time had been a struggle for her, but Alex had learned early in their friendship that she never took help from anyone.

Suddenly he was back in that time when he'd first felt completely free. Marie's two shabby rooms, right at the top of a multiple-occupancy house, had been as clean as one pair of hands could scrub them, and full of outrageous low-cost colour.

'Funny thing about that...' Marie gave him a knowing look. 'When I woke up you were gone, but I sat down to review my abstracts and found they were all perfect. Not a spelling or grammar mistake in any of them.'

Alex had reckoned he'd got away with that. He'd tried to make Marie stand up but she'd slumped against him, still asleep, so he'd had to practically carry her into the bedroom. He'd taken off her cardigan and shoes and decided to stop there, covering her up with the brightly patterned quilt. He'd sometimes imagined their two bodies naked together under that quilt. But Marie was far too good a friend, too good a person, to contemplate having a throwaway romance with her.

Alex had glanced at the document that was open on her laptop, meaning to close it down. He'd seen a mistake in the text, and had sat down and worked through everything, correcting the slips that fatigue had forced upon her.

'You must do your best work when you're flying on autopilot.' He tried to maintain a straight face.

'I suppose I must. Apparently I also spell synthesise with a *z*.'

'Really? There must be a study in there somewhere. How fatigue alters your spelling choices.' Alex shrugged guiltily. 'They're both correct, according the dictionary.'

'Yes, they are. Although I imagine that "ize" as a verb ending is considered either an anachronism or an American spelling these days.' She smirked at him.

'You can mock if you want. Just because I went to a school that prided itself on having been the same for the last few hundred years…' Alex had hated school. It had been only slightly less snobby and suffocating than his parents' home.

'I'm not mocking; I thought it was very sweet of you.' She took a step towards him. 'Along with all those expensive textbooks you used to lend me. And dropping round to pick me up so I didn't have to take the bus.'

'Why bring that up all of a sudden? Just to let me know I'm not as tactful as I thought I was?' Alex wondered if he was in for a lecture about how she could have managed perfectly well on her own.

Marie shook her head. 'You were *very* tactful. I hardly even noticed what you were doing most of the time. And you were my friend and you helped me. That's something that goes both ways.'

He knew that. But he couldn't talk to Marie about this. 'I'm fine. Really. And I appreciate your concern.'

'Just as long as you know that I'm always here for you.'

She reached out, touching his arm, and Alex almost flinched. All his senses were crying out for comfort, and yet he just couldn't bring himself to ask. Was this the way she'd felt, despite all her self-sufficiency?

'I know. Thank you.'

He'd meant to give her a basic friendly hug, the kind he'd given her so many times before. But when he felt her body against his he couldn't let her go. Marie seemed to be the one thing in his life that wasn't tainted right now.

He leaned down to kiss her cheek. But she turned her head and his lips brushed hers. Before he could tear himself away her gaze met his, her eyes midnight-blue in the darkness.

What if…?

What if...?

What if he could turn his back on the vision of his parents' unhappy marriage and sustain a relationship for more than a few months? What if he could trust himself to get involved with the one person he cared about the most, even knowing he might break her heart and his? And what if everything he'd sought to escape hadn't just caught him again in its iron clutches?

They were all serious questions that needed to be asked and answered before he took the step of kissing her. But then he felt her lips touch his and he was lost. Or maybe this was exactly what it was like to find himself. Alex wasn't sure.

She was soft and sweet, and when he kissed her again she responded. Maybe it lasted a moment and maybe an hour. All Alex knew was that it was impossible to attach a time frame to something that was complete and perfect.

Even the way she drew away from him was perfect. A little sigh of regret, her eyes masked by her eyelashes.

He'd always supposed that kissing Marie was the one thing he mustn't do. The one thing he wouldn't be able to come back from. But in a sudden moment of clarity he realised that kissing her had only made him more determined that he couldn't do it. Marie wasn't just another pretty face he could walk away from without looking back. She was his friend, and he wanted her for a lifetime, not just a few months.

'Do you want to go back in?' If it meant keeping her then he had to let her go.

She still wouldn't look at him. 'Yes...'

He felt her move in his arms and let her go. Marie looked up at him for a moment, and he almost forgot that this had been a very bad idea that had the power to spoil something that had been good for years. Then suddenly she was gone, back into the restaurant to take her seat at the table again.

Alex waited, knowing the group always swapped places between courses, so everyone got to speak to everyone else. When he went back inside there was a free seat for him at the other end of the table from Marie. Alex sat down without looking at her, and was immediately involved in the heated debate about football which was going on between Emily and Will.

She didn't meet his gaze until the restaurant closed and a waitress pointedly fetched everyone's coats. Then, suddenly, he found himself standing next to her. He automatically helped her on with her coat and Marie smiled up at him.

'I'll see you next year. Be well, Alex.'

'Yes. Next year...'

He'd scarcely got the words out before she was gone. Marie had made her meaning clear. They were friends, and nothing was going to spoil that. Not fire, nor flood, nor even an amazing, heart-shaking kiss. By next year it would be forgotten, and he and Marie would continue the way they always had.

The thought that he wouldn't see her again until next February seemed more heart-rending than any of the other challenges he'd faced in the last six months.

CHAPTER TWO

The first Friday in May

IT WAS ONLY four stops on the Tube from the central London hospital where Marie worked, but shining architecture and trendy bars had given way to high-rise flats, corner shops and families with every kind of problem imaginable.

Marie knew about some of those problems first-hand. She'd grown up fifteen minutes' walk away from the address that Alex had given her. Her father had left when she was ten, and her mother had retreated into a world of her own. Four miserable months in foster care had seen Marie separated from her three younger brothers, and when the family had got back together again she'd resolved that she'd keep it that way.

It had cost Marie her childhood. Looking after her brothers while her mother had worked long hours to keep them afloat financially. She'd learned how to shop and cook, and at the weekends she'd helped out by taking her brothers to the park, reading her schoolbooks while they played.

It had been hard. And lonely. After she'd left home she'd had a few relationships, but knowing exactly what it meant to be abandoned had made her cautious. She'd never found the kind of love that struck like a bolt of lightning, dispelling all doubts and fears, and the continuing need to look after her family didn't give her too much time for regrets.

When she reached the Victorian building it looked just as ominous as she remembered it, its bricks stained with grime and three floors towering above her like a dark shadow in the evening sunshine. The high cast-iron gates creaked as Marie pulled them open, leaving flakes of paint on her hands.

'This had better not be a joke…'

It wasn't a joke. Alex's practical jokes were usually a lot more imaginative than this. And when he'd called her it had sounded important. He'd made a coded reference to their kiss, saying that he wanted her to come as a professional favour to a friend, which told Marie that he'd done exactly as she'd hoped and moved past it. That was both a relief and a disappointment.

She pushed the thought of his touch to the back of her mind and made her way across the cracked asphalt in front of the building. There was a notice taped to the main door that advertised that this was the 'Living Well Clinic'. Marie made a face at the incongruous nature of the name and pressed the buzzer, wondering if it was going to work.

The door creaked open almost immediately.

'Hi. Thanks so much for coming.' Alex was looking unusually tense.

'My pleasure. What's all this about, Alex?'

'Come and see.' He stood back from the doorway and Marie stepped inside, trying not to flinch as the door banged shut behind them.

'Oh! This is a bit different from how I remember it.'

At the other end of the small lobby was an arch, which had been sandblasted back to the original brick, its colour and texture contrasting with the two glass doors that now filled the arch. As Marie approached them they swished back, allowing her into a large bright reception space, which had once been dingy cloakrooms.

And it wasn't finished yet. Cabling hung from the ceiling and the walls had obviously been re-plastered recently, with dark spots showing where they were still drying out. One of the curved-top windows had been replaced, and the many layers of paint on the others had been sanded back, leaving the space ready for new decoration.

'You know this place?'

'Yes, I went to school here.'

'Did you?' He grinned awkwardly. 'I wish I'd known. I would have looked for your name carved on one of the desks.'

'You wouldn't have found it.'

'Too busy studying?'

'Something like that.'

Leaving her name in this place might have signified that she would look back on her schooldays with a measure of nostalgia, when they'd been no more than a means to an end. They'd been something she'd had to do so she could move on and leave them behind. Just like she'd left that kiss behind. The one she couldn't stop thinking about...

'What's going on, Alex? Are you working here now or is this something you're involved with in your spare time?'

'I don't have spare time any more. I'm here full-time; I gave up working with the practice.'

Alex had always said he'd do something like this, and now he'd actually done it. The next logical step from his job as a GP in a leafy London suburb would have been to go into private practice, and Alex had the contacts and the reputation to make the transition easy. But he'd given all that up to come and work here, in a community where his expertise was most sorely needed.

'And you'll be seeing patients here?'

'As soon as we don't have to supply them with hard

hats.' He bent, picking up two safety helmets and handing her one. 'Come and see what's been going on.'

As he showed her around, the scale of the project became obvious. Some of the classrooms had been divided into two to make treatment rooms, with high ceilings and plenty of light from the arched windows. A state-of-the-art exercise suite was planned for the ground floor, which would be staffed by physiotherapists and personal trainers, and the old school hall was being converted into a coffee shop and communal area. Upstairs there was provision for dieticians and other health advisors, along with a counselling suite and rooms for self-help groups of all kinds.

'We'll have facilities for DEXA scanning in here...' He opened the door of one of the old science labs, which had now been reduced to a shell. 'Along with other diagnostic equipment. There's a space for the mobile breast-screening unit to park at the side of the building, and when the clinic's finished it'll be part of its regular route. We'll be able to undertake general health screening as well.'

'It's wonderful, Alex. Everything under one roof.'

The project was ambitious and imaginative, and would be of huge benefit to the local community.

'That's the idea. It's a kind of one-stop shop, and although it'll cater for complex medical needs it's also going to be for people who just want a healthier lifestyle.'

'What's going to happen with the courtyards?'

They were walking along a corridor that looked out onto one of the two central light wells. They were one of the few things that remained unchanged, and the dingy concrete floors were a reminder of what this place had once been like.

Alex shrugged. 'There are no plans for them just yet. Some planting might be nice.'

'And what about the old gym?' The annexe at the back

of the school was enormous, and it seemed a waste not to use it for something.

'We made a discovery. Come and see.'

He led the way to the large double doors that opened onto the gym and Marie gasped. The folding seats had been taken out and light from windows on three sides flooded into the space. Instead of sprung wooden floors there was a large concrete-sided hole.

'That's not...not a swimming pool, is it?'

He nodded. 'When we looked at the plans we found that this annexe was built in the nineteen-thirties as a full-sized swimming pool. Later on it was made into a gym, but when we took up the floors we found that the pool had just been filled in with hardcore and the foundations were still there and solid enough to use. There's room for a hydrotherapy pool, as well as the main pool.'

Alex seemed less excited about this than he should be. Maybe he was about to tell her that they'd run out of money, or had found some catastrophic problem with the building's structure and it was all about to fall down.

'This is marvellous. Are the pool and gym just for patients or are they available to the whole community?'

'There'll be a nominal charge, well below the usual rates. Anyone who's referred by a doctor or one of the medical staff here won't have to pay anything.' Alex was suddenly still, looking at her thoughtfully. 'What about you? Would you be interested in being part of it all?'

That sounded a bit like the stuff that fairy tales were made of. A gloomy old castle brought to life and transformed. Alex would fit in there quite nicely as the handsome Prince. But something about the quiet certainty in his manner stopped Marie from brushing the suggestion off.

'You'd put in a good word with the boss for me?'

'It's more a matter of putting a good word in with you. We'd be lucky to get you.'

Excitement trickled down Marie's spine. This was real. In that case, Marie needed to ask a few real questions.

'What exactly is your role here, Alex?'

He frowned, as if that might be a problem. 'It's rather a long story… Why don't you come to my office and we'll have some coffee?'

Marie followed him to a small suite of offices situated at the front of the building, off the main reception area. From here it would be possible to see all the comings and goings, and Marie guessed that Alex would have had a hand in the location of his office. He always liked to be in the thick of things.

His office was one of the few rooms in the building that was finished, but it didn't seem much like the kind of place the Alex she remembered would like. The cream walls and tall windows lent themselves to minimalism, but Alex didn't.

'How long have you been here, Alex?'

'A couple of months.' He looked around at the sleek wooden desk that stood at one end of the room and the comfortable easy chairs grouped around a coffee table at the other end. 'Why?'

Alex had been here for two months? And he hadn't yet covered the walls with pictures and stamped his own personality on the space? That wasn't like him at all. Perhaps the clinic had some kind of rule about that.

'It just seems a bit…unlived-in.' Marie looked around for something, anything, to comment on, instead of asking whether all that light and clear space hurt his eyes. She nodded towards the stylish chair behind his desk. 'I like your chair.'

'I reckoned I'd be sitting in it for enough hours, so I wanted something that was comfortable. Give it a try.'

He walked over to the wood-framed cupboards that

lined one wall, opening one of the doors to reveal a coffee machine and a small sink unit.

The chair was great—comfortable and supportive—and when Marie leaned back the backrest tipped gently with her movement. She started to work her way around all the levers and knobs under the seat.

'I love this. It's got more controls than my first car.'

She got to her feet as Alex brought the coffee and he motioned her to sit again, smiling as if it hurt his face to do so.

'You've missed a few of the adjustments. The knob on the left lets you tip the seat forward.' He sat down in one of the chairs on the other side of the desk.

'Oh!' Marie tried it, almost skinning her knuckles on the stiff lever. 'Nice one. I'm glad to see the clinic practises what it preaches and looks after its staff.'

She was just talking. Saying things that might fill the space between them and hoping to provoke a reaction. She'd never seen Alex look so worried before.

Not worried…

Burdened.

It was time to grasp the nettle and find out what was going on. She leaned forward, putting her elbows on the desk as if she were about to interview him. 'So what's the story then, Alex? I'm intrigued, so start right at the beginning.'

He paused, staring into his mug, as if that would tell him exactly where the beginning was.

'A hundred and ten years ago…'

'What? Really?'

He gave her a strained smile and Marie regretted the interruption. Whatever had happened a hundred and ten years ago must be more important than it sounded.

'You said start at the beginning.'

'I did. Sorry...' She waved him on and there was silence for a moment. Then he spoke again.

'A hundred and ten years ago the King of Belkraine was deposed and his family fled to London. They brought with them a lot of very valuable jewels, the title deeds to property in this country, and what was literally a king's ransom in investments. His eldest son was my grandfather.'

Marie stared at him.

She'd thought that she and Alex had shared most of their secrets over the years but he'd obviously been holding back. Marie wasn't entirely sure how she felt about that.

'So you're...a prince?'

He gave her a pained look. 'Belkraine no longer exists as a separate country. I'm not sure how you can be a prince of something that doesn't exist.'

He was missing the point. The role of many monarchies had changed in the last hundred years, but privilege and money was something that didn't change.

'A prince in exile, then?'

'Strictly speaking a king...in exile. My father died in June last year.'

'Alex, I'm so sorry.'

'Thank you. But it's... We'd been estranged for some years. Ever since I first went to medical school.'

'But—'

Marie bit her tongue. He'd never spoken much about his family, but she knew that he was an only child and that his parents lived in a big house in the country somewhere. There hadn't ever been any mention of an estrangement, and Marie had always assumed he came from a normal happy family.

Now wasn't the time to mention that this was what Alex had allowed everyone to believe. He had no chance to make things right with his father now.

'That must have hurt you a great deal.'

He shrugged. 'That door closed a long time ago. I came to terms with it.'

There were too many questions, piling up on top of each other like grains of sand in an hourglass. What was Alex doing here? Why had he never said anything about this before?

Maybe she should just stay silent and listen.

Alex glanced at her uncertainly and Marie motioned for him to keep talking.

'I didn't expect that my father would leave me anything, let alone his whole estate. But he did. I find that I have more money than I know what to do with.'

'How much…?'

It wasn't good manners to ask, but money had never bothered Alex all that much. If this was a life-changing amount, then that was both good news and bad. Good, because he could do the things he'd always wanted to. Bad, because he seemed so burdened by it.

'If you include all the assets and property then it runs into something more than two billion. Less than three.'

She stared at him. That was the kind of number that Marie would never get her head around, so it was probably better not to even try.

'And this… *You've* done all this?' She waved her finger in a wild circle.

'My ancestors viewed wealth as a way to gain power and more wealth. I want to spend the money a little more wisely than that.'

It was worthy. Altruistic. Right now it was about all she recognised of the Alex that she knew. The smiling, carefree soul who was in the habit of taking one day at a time had gone.

'Wait a minute…' A thought struck her. Had Alex been hiding all this in plain sight? 'Alex *King*?'

'Dr Alex King is who I really am. But my birth certifi-
cate says Rudolf Aloysius Alexander König.'

Suddenly she couldn't bear it. She hadn't even known
his *name*? The man she'd thought of as her friend, whom
she'd dared to kiss and had loved every minute of it…

Marie sprang from her seat, marching over to the window and staring out at the street. Maybe that would anchor
her down, keep her feet firmly on the ground, and then she
could begin to address the question of whether this really
was Alex any more, or just a stranger who looked like him.

Marie wasn't taking this well. It was almost a relief. The
small number of other people he'd had to tell about this
had congratulated him on his sudden and immense wealth
and started to treat him as if he was suddenly something
different. It was typical of Marie that her objection to the
whole thing wasn't what he'd expected. She brushed aside
the money and his royal status as if they didn't exist. All
she cared about was that she hadn't known his name.

'King is a translation of König. Alex is my middle
name…' He ventured an explanation.

She shook her head. 'I thought I knew you, Alex…'

There was no point in telling her that a lot of people
changed their names, or that a lot of people came from
unhappy families. Marie was hurt that he'd never told her
about any of it before. Maybe if she'd known his father she
would have understood a little better.

'Rudolf König was the name my father gave to me to
remind everyone who my family was. I wanted to make
my own way in life, Marie, and to be measured by what
I've done.'

'Yeah. I see that.' She was staring fixedly out of the
window and didn't turn to face him.

'Then…?'

'Give me a minute. I'm processing.'

Okay. Processing didn't sound so terrible. If Marie could come to any conclusions then he'd like to hear them, because all he'd felt since he'd heard about his father's will was that he was being dragged back into a life from which he'd previously torn himself. Money and status had soured his parents' lives, and it already felt like it was slowly squeezing all the joy out of his.

She turned slowly, leaning back against the windowsill and regarding him thoughtfully.

'So…it's still Alex, is it?' Not *Your Majesty*…?'

'You don't need to rub it in, Marie. Who the hell else do you think I know how to be?'

Her face softened and she almost smiled. It was one step towards the warmth that he craved.

'Sorry.' She pressed her lips together in thought. 'Who knows about this?'

'A few people that I know from school. No one here. But it's not a secret. I just don't talk about it.'

She turned to face him, her eyes full of violet fire. 'Isn't that what secrets are? Things you keep from your friends?'

'I *never* lied.' He heard himself snap, and took a breath. 'I want the clinic to be about the work and not about me.'

'It *is* about you, though. You built it.'

'I facilitated it. I want people to talk about the things we do here, and talking about who I am is only going to divert attention away from that.'

Alex decided to leave aside the fact that he really didn't want to talk about who he was, because that would be a matter of reopening old wounds.

Marie was nodding slowly. It was time to take a risk.

'If you're not interested in a job here you can always just walk away.'

She pursed her lips. 'I never said I wasn't interested.'

Good. That was a start. He knew she'd seen the possibilities that the clinic offered, and maybe it was a matter of getting her to look at those and not at him. Not at the friend who'd broken the rules and kissed her. The friend who'd never told her about where he came from.

'This is the deal, then. This clinic is a flagship development, which is funded and run entirely by a trust I've set up with part of my inheritance. I don't want it to be the only one of its kind; it's intended that what we do here will be a model for future clinics all over the country. In order to achieve that we'll need to attract extra funding from outside sources.'

'You always did think big, Alex.'

He saw a flicker of excitement in her eyes. That was exactly the way *he* wanted to feel.

'I want you to share that vision with me as my co-director for the whole project. This clinic and future developments as well. You'll be able to dictate policy and do things on your own terms.'

She stared at him. 'Me? You want *me* to do that?'

Marie hadn't said no yet. He resisted the impulse to laugh and tell her that she could do anything she set her mind to doing. He was offering her the job on purely business grounds and he had to treat this conversation in that light.

'Your professional experience in A&E and diagnostic wards makes you ideally suited to the work here, where we're suggesting effective therapies and ways forward for patients. And you're not afraid of a challenge.' Alex allowed himself the smallest of smiles. 'That's one thing I happen to know about you.'

'This would be the first time I've taken on a management role.' Marie gave a little frown, obviously annoyed that she'd betrayed a little too much interest. 'If I decide to take the job, that is.'

'We already have a practice manager on board. She's very experienced and can advise on the practical aspects.

It's your vision that matters, and your knowledge of what this community needs.'

'Is that your way of saying that you don't understand "poor people" and I do?'

She crooked two fingers to indicate quotation marks. There was a touch of defiance in her tone, and it would be very easy for Alex to say that the thought had never occurred to him.

'I think you understand some of the issues that people who live in this neighbourhood face. I want to formulate policies that are appropriate and which are going to work. If you want to boil that down to understanding poor people then be my guest.'

She grinned. He hadn't given her the expected answer, but it had been the right one.

'I think I *could* help…'

'I don't want you to *help*. This is a full partnership and I expect you to tell me what's wrong with my thinking.' He could trust Marie to do that. Their friendship was founded on it.

'It's a big step for me, Alex. I need to think about it.'

'Of course. Take as long as you like.'

Alex knew that Marie wouldn't take too long; she was nothing if not decisive. If she said no then that would be the end of it. But if she said yes then maybe, just maybe, she'd save him from being the man his father had wanted him to be and make him into the one *he* wanted to be.

By the time she got home Alex's email was already in her inbox, with a full job description and a detailed brief of his plans for the clinic appended. It took a while to read through it all, and Marie didn't finish until the early hours. She decided to sleep on it.

But sleeping on it didn't help, and neither did extending her usual running route around the park to almost

twice the distance. Neither did staring at the wall or surf-
ing the internet.

She wanted the job—very badly. It would give her a
chance to shape policy and to be part of a bold initiative
that promised to be a real force in helping people to live
fuller and better lives.

But Alex…

Before she'd kissed him, before she'd known that he
wasn't who he'd said he was…

That wasn't entirely fair. Thinking back, he'd never
actually said anything about who he was. If it hadn't occurred to her to ask if his father was an immeasurably
rich king in exile then maybe that was a lapse in imagi-
nation on her part.

But it still felt as if she'd kissed a man she didn't really
know at all and had let herself fall a little in love with him.
A future working closely with Alex seemed fraught with
the dangerous unknown.

By Sunday evening she'd distilled it all down. There
was no doubt in her mind that this was her dream job, but
there were three things she wanted to know from Alex.
Could he forget the kiss? Why hadn't he told her who he
was? And what did the clinic really mean to him?

They were tricky questions. She had to find a way of
asking indirectly, and after an hour of scribbling and cross-
ing out she had three questions that might or might not
elicit the information she wanted.

Marie picked up her phone and typed a text.

Are you still awake? I have some questions.

Nothing. Maybe he'd taken the evening off and gone out
somewhere. Or maybe he was asleep already. As Marie put
her phone down on the bed beside her, it rang.

'Hi, Alex…' She panicked suddenly and her mind went blank.

'Hi. Fire away, then.'

She'd rather hoped that she might ask by text, as that would give her a chance to carefully edit what she intended to say.

'Um…okay. Have you interviewed anyone else for this post?' That was the closest she could get to asking about the kiss.

'Nope.'

Marie rolled her eyes. 'That's not much help, so I'm going for a supplementary question. Why not?'

He chuckled 'You're asking if I offered you the job because we're friends? The answer's no. I need people around me who I trust and who are the best at what they do. If I wanted to meet up with you I'd call and ask if you were free for lunch.'

Okay. That sounded promising. Alex had drawn the line between professional and personal, and if he could take the kiss out of the equation then so could she.

'Next?'

Marie squeezed her eyes closed and recited the next question. 'That Christmas, at medical school, when we all went home for the holidays, what did you do?'

He was silent for so long that Marie began to wonder whether he'd hung up on her. She wondered if he knew how much this mattered, and why.

'Okay. I'll play. I stayed in my flat and watched TV all day.'

Marie caught her breath. He knew, and he'd answered honestly. 'You could have come to ours. You just had to say you were on your own.'

'You're *really* going to take that route, Marie? You'd have been too proud to let me bring as much as a box of mince pies with me. And you're wondering why I was too proud to admit that I was going to be on my own?'

Marie could understand that, even if she was sorry that he'd felt that way.

'Next question. And tell me you're not going to let me down by making this an easy one.'

Marie felt her ears start to burn. But that was Alex all over. He could be confrontational, but there was always that note of self-deprecatory laughter in his tone that made it all right.

'Do you think the clinic's going to save you, Alex?'

He was silent for a moment.

'Nice one. Those aren't the words I'd have used... But the inheritance is a responsibility, and I know from bitter experience that it's the kind of thing that can subsume a person. I want to hold on to who I am. So, yes, I guess I am hoping that the clinic will save me.'

These were the answers she'd wanted. And there was only one thing more to say.

'It's a great project, Alex. And, yes, I'd really like to take the job.'

CHAPTER THREE

THE MONTH'S NOTICE Marie had given at her old job had seemed like an age. She'd received daily email updates about what was going on at the clinic, and she'd spent many evenings and most of her weekends replying to Alex. If their exchanges seemed more businesslike than friendly, then that was all good. They needed to start as they meant to go on, and Marie was ready to begin work in earnest.

She knew what had been done, but that didn't match the effect of seeing it for herself. The facade of the building had been cleaned, exposing the soft yellow of the brick and the red terracotta detailing around the windows and door. The railings had been sanded and painted, and the old Tarmac playground was now a paved area, dotted with saplings that would soften the space as they grew. The main door had been stripped and varnished, and the dents from being kicked a thousand times as pupils had passed this way only added to its character.

The bell was new as well, and when she pressed it Alex appeared at the door, looking far less formal than his emails had been, and suspiciously like the man she'd dared to kiss. Maybe seeing him every day would quash that reaction.

Marie smiled nervously as he led her through the glass lobby doors. 'This is amazing!'

Everything was neat and tidy, with cream-painted walls

and comfortable seating. Marie knew that the large curved barrier between the receptionist and the public space had been designed to protect the staff by stopping anyone from climbing across, but the sloping front looked like a thing of beauty and not a defence mechanism.

'I'm pleased with the way it's turned out.' Alex looked around as if this was the first time he'd seen the space. 'You didn't have to start until Monday, you know. How was your leaving party last night?'

Marie rolled her eyes. 'Long. We had too much cake, and then we went to the pub. I cried. I need something to do today to work off all the calories and the emotion.'

'You're not regretting this, are you?' He frowned.

'No. Looking forward to what's next doesn't mean I can't miss my old job a bit as well.'

He quirked his lips down, as if missing the past was something he'd been struggling with, and then smiled suddenly in an indication that he wasn't about to dwell on that.

'You want to see your new office?'

'Yes, please.'

Alex had suggested that she take the office next to his, but Marie wanted to be close to the two practice nurses and the health visitor who comprised their medical support team, and who would be located on the first floor. The problem had been solved by giving her an office that was directly above his and connected by a narrow private staircase.

'What do you think?'

Cream walls, lots of light and plenty of space. That was standard issue here, but no doubt she could inject a little colour of her own. Marie had chosen a light-framed wooden desk, and behind it was an identical chair to Alex's.

'You got me one of these!' Marie had wanted one, but hadn't wanted to ask.

'Yes. Call it an investment. I don't want you taking any time off sick with a bad back.'

Marie grinned at him and sat down, feeling the chair respond to her weight. 'I'll just take two days off to adjust it, shall I?'

'Mine took a week. The instructions are in your top drawer. Would you like to offer me some coffee?'

'Have I got any?'

Actually, Marie could do with some coffee. The combination of cake and beer last night had left her feeling a little fuzzy this morning.

'Behind you.'

He indicated a door at the far end of the cupboards that lined one wall, and sat down in one of the chairs on the other side of the desk. Marie went to look and found that the door concealed a neat worktop with a coffee machine and supplies. A splash of colour next to the line of cream mugs caught her eye.

'You got me a mug!' She took the bright pink mug down from the shelf and examined it. 'With a flying pig! You remembered!'

'You always used to say that you wanted an office with a sofa, and time to sit and talk with your patients.'

The informal seating area in his office contained four easy chairs, covered in a chocolate-coloured fabric, but for Marie he had chosen a sofa and two chairs in a lighter cappuccino colour.

'And when you said that nothing was impossible, I told you that pigs might fly...' It had been a joke between them. 'Thank you, Alex.'

He seemed pleased with her reaction, but there was still a hint of reticence about his manner. The man Marie knew would have seen only exciting new opportunities, but Alex seemed burdened by his responsibilities.

He'd come round. The clinic would be opening next

week, and as soon as it started to fill with people he'd respond to that. He was going to have to if this place was to reach its full potential. Alex had so much more than money to give, and it needed his creative enthusiasm to thrive.

Marie switched on the coffee machine, running her finger along the selection of different capsules. 'I'm going to have to try all of these, you know. I'll work from left to right.'

'I'd expect nothing less of you.'

When she put his cup down in front of him, he nodded a thank-you and pushed a manila envelope towards her. Marie opened it, tipping the contents out onto her desk.

'These are yours. The credit card is for any purchases you need to make, and the key card opens every door inside the clinic. Those two keys are for the main door, and the other one is the main override for the alarm system. The car keys are for the practice's vehicles.'

Marie laid the keys and cards out in front of her on the desk. This was the start of it all…

'The IT guy will be coming in on Monday to set up your computer. Let me know if there's anything else you need.' Alex got to his feet, picking up his mug. 'I'll leave you to settle in, if that's okay. I have a few things to do.'

Marie had wanted to share all this. Unpacking the bag she'd brought with her and taking a tour of the clinic to see all the work that she and Alex had been discussing for the last month. But Alex was already halfway out of the door.

'Yes, okay. Maybe we can sit down together later today to go through some things?'

'That would be great.' He flashed her a sudden smile. 'You like your office?'

'It's better than I could have imagined. Thank you so much, Alex.'

'My pleasure.' He turned, closing the door behind him.

Marie leaned back in her chair, listening to the silence. There was a lot to do here. A whole community of health professionals to build. There were mountains to move, and the most stubborn of them had just walked downstairs. Alex had built his dream, and although he had a fierce determination to see it thrive, Marie sensed he couldn't love it.

That was going to have to change.

After Saturday's quiet solitude, most of which Alex had spent closeted in his office, the bustle of workmen and staff on Monday morning was a welcome relief. Marie spent two days with Sofia Costa, the practice manager, interviewing the shortlisted candidates for the medical support team, and on Wednesday morning picked up the flowering plant she'd brought from home and went down to Alex's office.

She'd wondered if his subdued manner was a reaction to their kiss, part of some kind of attempt to keep things professional, but he was like that with everyone. Thoughtful, smiling, but without the spark that made him Alex. In one way it was a relief to find that it wasn't just her, but it was clear that the change in Alex's life and the months spent developing this place had taken their toll on him. He normally thrived on hard work, but this was different. It seemed to be draining all the life out of him.

'The interviews went well?' He looked up from the pile of paperwork on his desk.

'Very well. It was difficult to decide, as they were all good candidates. But Sofia and I have chosen three who are excellent. I've emailed their CVs to you so you can take a look at them.'

She put the Busy Lizzie plant down on his desk and Alex picked it up, examining the bright red flowers. 'Is this a subtle hint that my office could do with brightening up?'

'No, I don't do subtle. It's more in the way of a brazen, in-your-face hint.'

Alex smiled, walking over to the windowsill and putting the pot at the centre. He moved it to one side and then the other, finding the place he wanted it.

'I don't suppose you have any more of these, do you?'

Marie hid her smile. The old Alex was still there—he just needed a bit of coaxing out. If he wanted more plants she'd fill his windowsill with colour.

'I've got loads at home. I took some cuttings from my mum's. I'll bring you more tomorrow.'

'Thanks.'

'I've got an idea.' She sat down in one of the chairs on the other side of his desk.

'Fire away.'

His lips curved a little. Alex clearly hadn't lost his penchant for ideas of all shapes and sizes.

'The light wells. They're pretty awful as they are, and I'd like to turn them into gardens. I spoke to Jim Armitage and he says that there are some brick pavers that were taken up from around the gym and he saved because they were still good. He reckons they should be fine on top of the concrete, but he needs to get out there to check everything. The key card lock disengages, but there's an original lock still on the door. Jim was going to climb out of the window, but I persuaded him not to.'

The foreman of works was a portly man approaching retirement, and Marie had feared he'd either get stuck while climbing out or not be able to get back in again. The same thing had obviously occurred to Alex, because one of those flashes of humour that reminded Marie so painfully of the man he'd once been lit his face.

'Good call. I might have the key somewhere...' He opened the bottom drawer of his desk, producing a large cardboard box full of keys of all shapes and sizes.

'So you'll come and have a look with me?'

If Alex was going to tell her that she was quite capable of doing this alone, then she was going to have to argue with him. She was capable, but that wasn't the point.

'I have a few things to do…'

'This is much more important, Alex. As your co-director, I'm telling you that you need to come.'

He grinned suddenly and stood up.

Step one accomplished. Step two might be a bit trickier…

Marie never had been much good at hiding the motives behind her actions. It was something Alex wished he hadn't had to learn how to do. She'd decided to get him out of his office and there was no point in arguing that he had work to do when Marie was determined. And when Alex thought about it, he didn't really want to argue.

He'd missed this. Marie had brought colour to a life that had become suffused by restful cream walls and spaces that were fit for purpose. He followed her along the corridor that ran parallel to one of the light wells, holding the box of keys.

She took her key card from her pocket, swiping it to disengage the main lock, and then started to fish around in the box for keys that looked as if they might fit the older one. It took a few tries to find one that fitted, but finally Alex heard a click as the key turned in the lock.

She rattled the handle of the door. 'It's still stuck…'

Alex tried the door. 'Looks as if it's been painted shut—no one ever goes out there. You want me to open it?'

She gave him a beatific smile. 'Yes, please.'

He put his shoulder to the door, and there was a cracking sound as it opened. Marie picked up a plastic bag, which had been sitting on one of the windowsills, and stepped out into the courtyard.

'Right. We need to check the height of the pavers…'

She produced a brick from the bag, wedging it under the bottom of the doorframe. 'That looks okay to me. And Jim says there's drainage, so we'll be fine there...'

She pulled a folded A2 sheet from the bag, spreading it out on the stained concrete. Marie was nothing if not prepared, and Alex was getting the feeling that he'd been set up. But Marie did it so delightfully.

'I reckon seats there...and planters in groups here and here... Perhaps a small water feature in the centre? What do you think?'

'I think that's great. Do we have the budget for it?'

'Yes, if we don't go overboard with things and we use the resources that we already have. Jim says that one of his guys will take me to the garden centre to get what we need.'

'Fine.' But something told Alex that his agreement to the plan wasn't enough. Marie wanted more.

She turned to him, her eyes dancing with violet shards in the sunlight. 'What do you say, Alex? Do you want to make a garden with me?'

Suddenly the one thing that Alex wanted was to make a garden, but there were more pressing things on his agenda.

'Do you think that's the best use of our time? We're opening in six days.'

'And the clinic's ready. You're not, though. You've been stuck in your office, working seven days a week, for months. You need a break before we open, and since I doubt you'll go home and take one this is a good second-best.'

This. This was why he'd wanted Marie to be his co-director. For moments like now, when she glared at him and told him exactly what he was doing wrong. He'd hoped she might come up with a plan, and that it might not just be for the clinic but for him as well.

'Well?' She put her hands on her hips.

She was unstoppable, and Alex did need a break. Something to refill the well that felt in imminent danger of running dry.

'Okay. I'm in your hands. What do you want me to do?'

'I'll go and get what we need for this courtyard, and we can store it all in the other one and start planting everything up. I'll ask Jim exactly when he can lay the paving; he said he'd probably be able to fit it in this week.'

'Maybe I can help with that. I could do with the exercise.' The waistband of his trousers was slightly tighter than usual, and Alex reckoned that he really needed to get to the gym.

'I wasn't going to mention that.'

Her gaze fell to his stomach, and Alex instinctively sucked in a breath. He hadn't thought he was *that* out of shape.

'It's nothing a little sunshine and activity won't fix.'

'What? You're my personal trainer now?'

'Someone has to do it, Alex. What are friends for?

This was exactly what friends were for. Crashing into your day like a shaft of light, slicing through the cobwebs. Doing something unexpected that turned an average working week into an adventure.

Alex dismissed the thought that it was also what lovers were for. He'd never had a lover who meant as much to him as his friend Marie. He doubted he ever would. He'd seen the way his father had reduced his mother to a sad, silent ghost. Alex had decided a long time ago that he would concentrate on making the best of every other aspect of his life and pass on marriage and a family.

He caught her just as she was leaving the clinic with Eammon, one of Jim Armitage's builders. 'Don't worry about the budget on this. Get whatever you want. I'll cover it.'

Marie shook her head. 'We have the money to buy a few planters and grow things. It's better that way.'

He'd said the wrong thing again. It would mean nothing to him to buy up a whole garden centre. It occurred to Alex that he was becoming used to throwing money at any problem that presented itself, because that meant much less to him than his time. He hadn't realised he'd lost so much of himself.

'Okay, well…' He'd play it her way. 'Let me know when you get back and I'll help unload the van.'

'Great. Thanks.' She gifted him with an irrepressible smile and turned, hurrying across to the front gates, her red dress swirling around her legs.

As she climbed up into the front seat of the builder's van that was parked outside the gates, Alex couldn't help smiling. Marie always looked gorgeous, but somehow she seemed even more so now, rushing towards a future that held only excitement for her and looking oddly pristine in the dusty, battered vehicle.

She'd be a couple of hours at least. Alex turned back to his office, feeling suddenly that those two hours were going to drag a little, with only a desk full of paperwork to amuse him.

When Marie returned, Alex had already found the key to the other courtyard and opened it up, then changed into the jeans and work boots that he kept in the office for inspecting the works in progress with Jim.

The van pulled into the car park, and Marie climbed down from the front seat, cheeks flushed with excitement.

'You got everything?'

'Yes, we've got some small shrubs and loads of seeds, along with planters and growing compost. I came in two pounds under budget.'

'And you didn't buy yourself an ice cream?' Alex

walked to the back of the van, waiting for Eammon to open the doors.

'*I* bought her an ice cream.'

Eammon grinned, and Alex wished suddenly that he'd volunteered to drive. He'd missed his chance to play the gentleman.

He started to haul one of the heavy bags of compost out of the back of the van, finding that it was more effort than he'd expected to throw it over his shoulder. He and Eammon stacked the bags in the courtyard while Marie unloaded the planters from the van.

'What do you think? I was hoping that less might be more.'

She'd arranged some of the planters in a group and was surveying them thoughtfully. There was a mix of colours and styles. Some large clay pots, a few blue-glazed ones, which were obviously the most expensive, and some recycled plant tubs, which were mostly grey but contained random swirls of colour. Each brought out the best in the others.

'They're going to look great.'

Alex picked up two of the heavier clay pots and Eammon took the pot that Marie had picked up, telling her to bring the lighter plastic tubs through.

Another opportunity for gallantry missed. Alex had carefully avoided any such gestures, reckoning that they might be construed as being the result of the kiss that they'd both decided to ignore, but he reckoned if they were okay for Eammon then they were probably permissible for him, too.

Alex was clearly struggling with his role at the clinic. If he'd worked for this then he would have seen it as the re-alisation of a lifetime's ambition, but it had all fallen so easily into his lap. The inheritance had left him without anything to strive for and it was destroying him.

Marie's ambitions had always been small: helping her mother cope with the pressures of four young children and a job, then making a life for herself and keeping an eye on her younger brothers. But at least they were simple and relatively easily fulfilled.

After they'd unloaded the van, carrying everything through to the courtyard and stacking it neatly, Alex seemed in no particular hurry to get back to his office. Marie asked him if he wanted to help and he nodded quietly.

She set out the seed trays, filling them with compost, and Alex sorted through the packets. Then they got to work, sitting on a pair of upturned crates that Alex had fetched.

'So…tell me again what country your great-grandfather was the king of?'

They'd worked in near silence for over an hour, and now that everyone had gone home for the evening they were alone. Marie had been regretting her reaction to Alex's disclosure about his family, and the subject had become a bit of a no-go area between them.

Alex looked up at her questioningly. 'It doesn't matter. It doesn't exist any more.'

'I'm just curious. And… I feel sorry about giving you a hard time when you told me about it.'

'It's nothing.' He puffed out breath and then relented. 'Belkraine. My great-grandfather was Rudolf the Most Excellent and Magnificent, King of Belkraine. Modesty doesn't run in the family.'

'I guess if you've got a few squillion in cash and a palace then you don't need to be modest…' She paused. 'Did he have a palace?'

'Why stop at one when you can have several? The old

Summer Palace still exists; it's near the border between Austria and Italy.'

'Have you ever been there?'

His lip curled slightly. 'It was my father's idea of a summer holiday. We'd go there every year, for a tour of what was supposed to be our birthright. It was excruciating.'

Alex sounded bitter. He wasn't a man who held on to bad feelings, so this must be something that ran deep with him.

'I'd be interested to see where my ancestors lived. Although I can say pretty definitely that it wasn't in a palace.'

'I guess it's an interesting place. It's been restored now, and it's very much the way it was when my great-grandparents lived there. Unfortunately my father used to insist on pointing at everything and telling my mother and me in a very loud voice that all this was really ours and that we'd been exiled to a life of poverty.'

'Ouch.'

Marie pulled a face and his lips twitched into something that resembled a smile.

'Yes, ouch. Even though my great-grandfather brought a fair bit of the family's wealth with him—and we had more than enough—my father used to reckon that he was poor because he didn't have everything he thought he should. He had no idea what real poverty is. It was just… embarrassing.'

'Is that why you never said anything about it?' Marie was beginning to understand that this hadn't been a wish to deceive, but something that had hurt him very badly.

'That and a few hundred other things. Like having to wear a version of the Crown Prince's military uniform at the annual party he gave on the anniversary of our family ascending the throne in 1432. After a particularly bloody series of wars, I might add. My family took the kingdom from someone else, so I never could see how having it taken from us was any cause for complaint.'

He ripped open a seed packet as if he was trying to chop its head off. Seeds scattered all over the concrete and Alex shook his head in frustration, cursing under his breath.

Marie swallowed down the temptation to tell him that it was okay, that they could pick them up again. This wasn't about the seeds, and he'd obviously not had much chance to get it out of his system. The idea that it had been nagging at him for so many years, concealed beneath the carefree face he'd shown to the world, was unbearably sad.

She bent down, picking the seeds up one by one. 'Good thing these aren't begonias. We'd never be able to pick up those tiny seeds.'

He laughed, his resentment seeming to disappear suddenly. Marie would rather he held on to it. His feelings were shut away now, under lock and key, and when he'd tipped the last of the seeds back into the packet, he stood.

'I've a few things that I really need to do. Do you mind if we start again in the morning?'

'Of course not. Anything I can give you a hand with?'

'No, stay here. We really need a garden. It will give people hope.'

Would it give *him* hope? Or just other people?

Marie decided not to ask, because Alex was already opening the door that led back into the building, and she doubted whether he would have answered anyway.

CHAPTER FOUR

WAS THIS REALLY what Marie wanted to know about him? That he was the great-grandson of a tyrant king? Alex decided he was overreacting, and that it was just natural curiosity. *He'd* be curious about the mechanics of the thing if he'd suddenly found out that Marie was a fairy princess. But then that wouldn't come as much of a surprise—he'd always rather suspected that she was.

He waited until he heard the main doors close and then threw down his pen. The table of dependencies he'd been sketching out for Jim Armitage wasn't working anyway, and he should probably just tell him what needed to be finished before the clinic opened, and leave him to work it out. There was such a thing as being too hands-on. And he couldn't leave without taking a look...

Marie had moved some of the planters, obviously having changed her mind on how best to group them. The shrubs were arranged under a makeshift plastic canopy to protect them from the weather, along with the seed trays that they'd filled.

Alex sat down on the upturned crate he'd occupied earlier. It occurred to him that this was the first garden he'd ever really had a hand in. His parents' garden had been designed to be looked at, preferably from a distance, and hadn't really been the kind of place for a child who might disturb its well-ordered beauty. When he'd left home, the

indoor plants he'd bought to brighten up his flat had generally died from neglect, and Alex had decided that his
contribution to the environment was to leave them in the
shop and let them go to someone who would remember
to water them.

But this time the idea of creating something from
scratch and tending it over time was something he very
much wanted to be a part of. And so what if Marie had
asked him about the one thing he always shrank from discussing? She wanted to know about the Kings of Belkraine
because she wanted to know about him. If she had any
questions tomorrow, he'd answer them.

When he arrived at the clinic the next morning, Marie was
already sitting on her crate, wearing a T-shirt and jeans.
His crate had been left in exactly the same place it had
occupied last night, in mute invitation.

Alex opened the door of the courtyard and went to sit
opposite her.

'Morning.'

She gave him a bright smile. Her cheeks were still a
little red from where the sun had kissed them yesterday.

Alex nodded and sat down, reaching for an empty seed
tray from the pile. He filled the tray with compost and
opened one of the seed packets, letting the cool quiet of
the hour before everyone else arrived for work seep into
him for a while before he spoke.

'I argued with my father and he threw me out of the
house when I was eighteen.'

She looked up at him, her lip quivering. 'That's a hard
thing to have to bear, Alex.'

He shook his head. Marie knew far more about hardship
than he did. 'Your father left when you were ten.'

'It's not a competition, Alex. You don't have to keep
quiet about what happened to you because you think what

happened to me might have been worse—it doesn't work that way. Anyway, my father left because of what happened between my mum and him. She told us that. It's different.'

Alex wondered how different it really was. Marie had worked so hard to help support her brothers, and he'd always had a sense that she felt somehow responsible for her father leaving.

But this wasn't about probing her; Marie had never made any secret of her childhood. He'd hidden his past out of a wish to leave it behind. Now, for the sake of the friendship that was so precious to him, he had to put that right.

'What did you argue about?' Marie had clearly been waiting for him to go on, and finally she asked the question.

'My father was an embittered man. He had everything money could buy, but he considered that our family had been deprived of its birthright. He insisted that we live as if we *were* royal, but I wanted more from life than that. I wanted to make my own choices. I wanted to be a doctor. He told me that if I went to medical school he'd disinherit me, and I told him to go ahead and do it.'

A faint smile hovered at Marie's lips. 'I wouldn't have expected you to do anything else. Didn't he ever see what you'd achieved and come around?'

'No, he never accepted what I wanted to do. The money that took me through medical school was from a trust that my grandfather had set up for me. He knew what my father was like, and he locked the trust in an ironclad agreement so my father couldn't get his hands on it.'

'Would he have tried? It sounds as if he had enough already.' Marie's eyebrows shot up.

'My father didn't care about the money; he thought it a paltry amount. He wanted control over me. I got to do what I wanted when I was eighteen because of that trust.'

'So being disinherited…that was a good thing in a way. Your father couldn't force you into his mould.'

'I felt as if I was free.'

She chuckled, picking up another seed tray. 'Free was how you seemed then. I used to envy you for it, but I didn't know what you'd had to go through to get your freedom. Did you never reconcile with your father?'

'I didn't want to. He was never a good husband; he hurt my mother very badly. I couldn't forgive him for that.'

There was nothing like telling a story to find out which parts of it really hurt. Alex could feel his chest tightening from the pain.

'Alex…?'

Marie was leaning forward now, concern registering on her face. Maybe she knew that this was what he really needed to say.

'He had mistresses. Lots of them. He used to spend a couple of nights a week in London, and my mother always seemed so sad. When I was little I thought she must miss him, but by the time I was fifteen I knew what was going on. He didn't go to much trouble to hide it.'

Marie's hand flew to her mouth. 'Your poor mother…'

'She just accepted it. That was the thing that hurt the most. She grew thinner and sadder every year, until finally she just seemed to fade away. She died five years ago.'

'And you never got to see her?'

'I used to visit her all the time. I'd call her, and she'd tell me when my father would be out of the house and I could come. It was the only thing she ever defied him over and she used to love hearing about what I was doing as a doctor. She knew that she always had a home with me, but she'd never leave him.'

'People…they make their own decisions. Parents included.' Marie shot him a wry smile.

'Yeah.'

Alex had made his decision too. However much the idea of a wife and a family might appeal to him in theory, his parents' unhappy marriage had always made him balk at the prospect of commitment. His father's money and title were new reasons to make him wary. Alex didn't know how he was going to cope with that yet, and the last thing he wanted to do was inflict his own struggle on anyone else.

'I did try to speak to my father once—at my mother's funeral. It was a very lavish affair, and after the way he'd treated her it made me feel sick. But I decided that it was what she would have wanted, and so I went up to him to shake his hand. He turned his back on me. I'll never know why he changed his mind about leaving me his money and I wish he hadn't.'

Marie frowned at him suddenly. 'It sounds as if he did the right thing, for once.'

'What? You think I'm *better* as a billionaire king in exile?'

'No, I think you're pretty rubbish at it, actually.'

The tension in his shoulders began to dissolve and Alex grinned at her. 'That's one of the things I like about you. That you don't think it's a good thing.'

'I didn't say it wasn't a good thing. I said you were rubbish at it. Look around you and tell me it's not a good thing.'

'Point taken. So the clinic's a good thing and I'm a rubbish king. Is that right?'

She nodded. 'You can write your own script, Alex. If you let the money and the title define you then maybe that's what your father wanted. But if you define it, then you can do anything. Things ordinary people only dream of.'

As usual, Marie was right. He'd been letting the money and the title define him a little too much recently, and the idea that he could become anything he wanted lifted a weight from his shoulders. And right now he wanted to be a gardener.

Marie had finished planting three seed trays and they were lined up on one side of her. He hadn't completed any yet. Alex picked up his tray.

'I was wondering if you'd cover for me in the office. Today and tomorrow.' He finished planting the tray and laid it down next to hers.

'Yes, of course. You're going out?'

'No, I spoke with Jim Armitage and he's given me the go-ahead to lay the pavers. I've never done anything like that before, but...' He shrugged.

'You can learn. I don't think it's that difficult.' Marie's sudden smile told him what she thought of the idea.

'You don't mind, then?'

It had been Marie's idea for him to get involved with the garden, and now he was going one better.

'Mind?' Marie laughed, a clear happy sound that echoed slightly against the walls that surrounded them. 'Do I mind you getting covered in brick dust and sand while I sit in a nice comfortable office? Nah, I don't mind that at all.'

Marie had spent most of the morning in her office, trying to find things to do. When three-thirty came around and the stream of mothers walking past the clinic from the school began to start she fetched the printed leaflets which detailed the services the clinic had to offer from the stockroom, along with one of the chairs from the café, and went to sit out in the sun by the main gates.

It would be one thing if Alex had changed over a few years—everyone changed. But he'd always carried this burden. The pressure of inheriting the money after his father's death had just made him less adept at hiding it.

And she'd never noticed. Caught up in her own work

and looking after her family, she'd seen Alex as some-one she wished she could be. A golden dream that she'd held on to, wanting to believe that work and responsibility weren't the only things in life. But now she'd seen a new Alex, challenging and complicated, and she couldn't help loving him better for it.

The stream of parents and kids had lessened now, and she'd given away almost all her leaflets. She'd catch the two young mums who were dawdling down the road to-wards her, plastic bags hanging from the arms of their pushchairs, and then she'd call it a day.

'Hi. May I give you a leaflet, please? About what we're doing here...'

One of them nodded, taking the leaflet and stuffing it into one of her shopping bags. The other took hers, and started to read it.

'I was wondering what was happening with this place. I used to go to school here...'

'Me too.' Marie grinned. 'Looks a lot better now.'

'Tell me about it. It was a real dump when I came here. We transferred over to the new school after a year.'

'We're opening next week. You're welcome to come and have a look around, see how it's changed.'

'I don't know...' The woman shook her head.

'You don't have to sign up for anything. Just look. There's a café.' Marie fished in her pocket for one of the printed vouchers. 'And this is for a free coffee.'

The woman took the voucher, stowing it away in her purse. 'Okay, thanks. What do you think, Nisha?'

Marie offered a second voucher and Nisha took it. Now that she had a conversation going, Marie decided that she should capitalise on it.

'I don't suppose you'd like a few extra leaflets, would you? To give to your friends? We have a range of services.' Marie pointed to the list on the leaflet. 'There's going to be a gym and a swimming pool, and they'll be open seven days a week. There's a nominal charge for those, but we've tried to keep it affordable.'

'I used to like swimming. The pool over on Stratton Road closed down, you know.'

Two pairs of eyes suddenly focussed away from her and over her left shoulder. Marie turned and saw Alex, wheeling a barrow full of bricks around the side of the building.

'That's the director of the clinic.'

Nisha's eyebrows shot up and the other woman choked with laughter. 'Really? Doesn't mind getting his hands dirty, then?'

'When he's not laying bricks he's a doctor. But we don't just tackle specific medical problems—it's all about living well.'

'And what do you do here?'

'I'm a doctor too.'

'Neesh…?'

The other woman nudged her companion, but Nisha shook her head. A sixth sense pricked at the back of Marie's neck. This was just the kind of thing the clinic was here for—the problems that people didn't want to talk about.

'Take my card.' Marie offered one of the cards that had been printed with her name. 'If there's ever anything I can help with, just ask for me.'

Nisha nodded, taking the card. She looked at it, glanced at Marie, and then unzipped her handbag, putting the card inside. Maybe she'd take the offer up, but Marie knew from experience that she needed to let her think about it. Pushing now would only elicit a *no*.

'My name's Marie.' She turned to the other woman.

'Carol. Do you do mother-and-toddler swimming classes?'

'Yes—you can sign up for them next week, when the clinic opens.'

'I'll definitely do that. We come past here every day. We might get another eyeful of that director of yours...' Carol laughed as Nisha raised her eyebrows. 'Only joking, Neesh.'

The toddler in Carol's pushchair started to fret. 'Yeah, all right, Georgie. We'll be home soon, and then we're going to the park. It was nice to meet you, Marie.'

'You too. Hope I'll see you again soon.'

The two women started to walk again, chatting companionably. Marie heard footsteps behind her and turned to see Alex, holding two glasses of lemonade. He handed her one.

'Thanks, I could do with that. I've talked my head off, given out a whole handful of leaflets and also some free coffee vouchers. How are you doing?'

Alex grinned, leaning towards her as if he was about to impart something highly confidential. 'Rather well, I think.'

'Can I see it?'

'No. The courtyards are my territory for the next couple of days. You can have the offices and the front gates. I'll water the seeds for you.'

'You won't forget? You know how bad you are at watering plants.' Marie shot him an imploring look.

'That's reassuring. I'm expecting people to put their lives in my hands, and you can't trust me with a few seed trays.'

It was nice to see Alex teasing again. Marie had missed that, and it seemed that a little practical work had lifted some of the weight from his shoulders. He was looking a lot more like the relaxed and cheerful Alex that she'd known before all this had happened.

Alex nodded at the pavement behind her and Marie

saw Carol hurrying towards them. It looked as if she had something on her mind.

'Hey, Carol. This is Alex, our director.'

'Pleased to meet you.'

Alex wiped his hand on his jeans and held it out. Carol shook it, nodding at him quickly, and then turned to Marie.

'Did you mean what you said? To Nisha?'

'About coming to see me? Of course. Is there something wrong?'

Carol nodded, tight-lipped.

'Do you want to come inside and talk?'

Perhaps it was something Carol didn't want to say in front of Alex.

'No. No, that's all right. I've got to get home—this one's going to start playing up in a minute.' She gestured down at Georgie, who was wriggling in the pushchair, clearly cross that the park was on hold for the moment.

Alex squatted down on his heels and poked his tongue out at the toddler. Their game of pulling faces seemed to be keeping them both occupied for a moment, which left Carol free to talk with Marie.

'Is there something Nisha needs? Something we can help with?'

'Yeah. Look, I can't really talk about it…'

Carol was almost whispering now, and Marie lowered her voice too.

'That's okay. Has she been to see her GP?'

'No, she won't. This place looks…' Carol shrugged. 'She might come here. I could get her to come. But you will see her, won't you? I don't know that it's a strictly medical thing.'

'If it's not a medical problem I'll refer her to someone who can help her. The whole point of this place is to find whatever answer is appropriate.'

'Right. Thanks. When are you opening? For…um… whatever… Appointments?'

'Next week. But Nisha doesn't need an appointment— she can come at any time. All you need to do is get her here and I'll make time to see her.'

'Great. Thanks.' Carol looked down at Georgie, who was laughing and trying to reproduce the faces Alex was making. 'I'd better get back. I told Nisha I was just popping back for something at the shops and I'd meet her in the park.'

'All right. But, Carol…' Marie caught Carol's arm before she could leave. 'This is important. If you think Nisha's in danger in any way you must get her to call someone. Or bring her here.'

'No, it's nothing like that. Her husband's a good man. It's just…embarrassing. You know?'

'Okay. I can do embarrassing. Get her to come and see me—you can come with her if that helps.' She glanced down at Alex, raising her voice to catch his attention. 'I don't think Alex's quite used up his stock of funny faces.'

Alex grinned up at Carol, getting to his feet. 'He's a great little chap.'

'Thanks. He can be a bit of a handful.' Carol was smiling now. 'I'll see you, then…?'

'I hope so.' Alex gave her a smile and Carol turned and hurried away.

'What was all that about?'

Marie shrugged. 'I don't know. Something about the friend she was with a moment ago. She wouldn't say.'

'You think she's in any danger?' Alex's first question was the same as Marie's had been. It was always their first question.

'No, Carol says it's embarrassing.'

He nodded, tipping his glass towards hers. 'Here's to

your first patient, then. Congratulations, you've pipped me to the post. I haven't got any yet.'

'Thank you. I dare say that'll change, but I'm quietly triumphant over having beaten my excellent and glorious co-director.'

Marie took a sip of her lemonade and saw the corners of Alex's mouth quirk downwards. Maybe the joke was a little too close to the mark for him.

'All right. Never say that again.' His face was serious for a moment, and then he smiled, knowing he'd fooled her. 'I might consign you to the dungeons.'

'How about Your Majesty? I suppose that's out as well?'

He chuckled. 'Definitely. That's a throwing-from-the-battlements thing…'

'Get back to work, Alex.' Marie drained her glass, handing it back to him.

CHAPTER FIVE

MARIE HAD MADE no secret of the fact that staying away from the courtyards was driving her insane with curiosity. Alex had escorted her off the premises at five o'clock and gone back to work, sorting out the best of the bricks and discarding those that were damaged.

The second day of Alex's practical introduction to laying pavers had involved an early start and a concentrated burst of work, but by the afternoon he was surveying the newly swept paving with Charlie, the lad Jim Armitage had sent to help him. Alex suspected Charlie had also been instructed to report back to Jim if it looked as if he was about to make a complete mess of things, and it was a matter of some pride to him that Charlie hadn't gone to seek out his boss at any point.

'What do you think, Charlie?'

Charlie nodded sagely. 'Nice job. Are we going to lay out the planters now?'

'Yes, I think so. Then we can show it to Marie.'

'She can put her flowers in. She'll like that.'

Charlie spoke with the certainty of all his nineteen years, and Alex smiled. The warm colours of the brick had made all the difference to the space.

'Yes, I think she will. Thanks for all your hard work.'

Charlie nodded, obviously pleased.

They set out the planters from the chart Marie had given them, and Alex left Charlie to bring some of the shrubs through from the other courtyard while he went to find Marie.

She was sitting in the reception area, where she could keep an eye out for anyone whose curiosity had brought them to the door, staring at the screen of her laptop.

As soon as she saw him she jumped to her feet. 'Is it finished?'

'Yes. You want to come and see it?'

'There are a few things I have to do, but I'll have a look later on...' Alex's face must have shown his dismay and she laughed. 'Of *course* I want to come and see it!'

'Okay.' From his pocket he produced the extra-large handkerchief he'd brought from home that morning, brushing a speck of brick dust from it. 'Stand still for a moment.'

'You're going to blindfold me? Seriously?'

'Charlie's worked hard on this. I think it deserves a little bit of a ceremony, don't you?'

The blindfold was nothing to do with Charlie. Alex just wanted to see the look on Marie's face when she saw the paved courtyard.

'Yes, okay, then. Hurry up!'

He tied the blindfold carefully over her eyes, trying not to breathe in the scent of her hair. Then, just for good measure, he turned her around a couple of times. Marie flung out her hand, her fingers brushing his chest, before they found a secure hold on the sleeve of his T-shirt. Alex shivered as tingles pulsed down his spine. They were almost in an embrace.

'Enough, Alex! Take me there or else!'

'Okay. Hold my arm.'

She clung on to him as he walked her slowly along the corridor. When the idea of blindfolding her had occurred to him this morning Alex hadn't taken into consideration how good it would feel to have her walking so close, hanging on to him. He was glad he hadn't foreseen it, because if he had he might have thought better of the idea. And it would have been a shame to miss this moment.

Charlie opened the door for them, standing back with a huge grin on his face.

'The step's right in front of you…' Alex held her arm firmly so she couldn't fall, and Marie extended her foot. 'That's it. A little further.'

When her foot hit the surface of the bricks she gave a shiver of anticipation, her fingers tightening around his arm. Alex's knees almost gave way, and then suddenly his body was taut and strong again, ready to catch her if she fell.

Marie stepped out into the courtyard carefully, letting him lead her into its centre.

'You can take the blindfold off now.' He heard his voice catch on the lump in his throat and knew he dared not do it for her. If he touched her hair again he might forget himself.

Marie reached up, fumbling a little with the knot. She was silent for a moment, her hand to her mouth as she looked around.

'Herringbone! I didn't expect that!'

Alex and Charlie exchanged smug looks. The herringbone pattern meant that there had been extra work in cutting the bricks at the edges, but they'd both agreed it would be worth it. Now, it was definitely worth it.

'This is *beautiful*. It's perfect. Charlie, you must have worked so hard…'

It was just like Marie to praise the younger member of the team first. Charlie had worked hard, he'd made sure everything was exactly right, and he deserved it. Alex smiled as Charlie's cheeks began to redden.

'And you've set out all my planters as well. Thank you so much.'

Charlie nodded. 'Would you like to see the drainage gulley?'

'Yes, please.'

Alex watched as Charlie led her to one corner of the courtyard, showing her where excess rainfall would drain away from the surface and into a waste pipe.

'You've made such a good job of it. When we put some flowers and seating out here it's going to be a lovely place for people to sit.'

Charlie was grinning from ear to ear, and had obviously taken about as much praise as one young man could stand from a beautiful woman. He muttered something about having to report back to Jim, and made his escape. Then Marie turned her gaze onto Alex.

No words. Just a smile. But Alex felt just as pleased with her reaction as Charlie had obviously been.

'You like it?'

'You really need to ask, Alex? I love it.'

Alex nodded. This was everything he needed. It was well worth the hard manual labour, the aching muscles and the scraped fingers.

'Our garden...' Marie turned around as if she could see it right now. Flowers and seating—everything as it would be when it was finished.

'Yes. I like the sound of that.'

'Me too. I could really, really hug you. If you weren't so dirty.'

He could really, really hug her too, and love every second of it. It was just as well that he was covered in grime, with streaks of adhesive all over his jeans.

'I think I'll go and give the showers in the gym changing rooms a trial run. Then I'll go to my office.'

'This has been keeping you from your other work...' Marie shot him a guilty look.

'There's nothing so urgent that it won't wait until tomorrow. I just really need to sit down.'

'Then come out here. I'll fetch you a chair and a cold drink, and you can sit and watch me work.'

The idea was much more enchanting than it should be. He could survey his handiwork with a sense of pride at something started and finished amongst a list of tasks that never seemed to end. Better still, he could watch Marie. Her dress brought a splash of colour to the monotonous pale walls of the clinic, and the way she moved injected life and fluidity. He loved the way the light glinted in her hair and—

Enough. He should confine himself to appreciating the colours of the brick. He might even allow himself a moment of self-congratulation that all that tapping with a mallet had borne fruit and they were perfectly level.

'I'll be back in ten minutes.'

He grinned at her, leaving her standing in the middle of the courtyard, still looking around, while he headed for the shower.

Marie couldn't wait to get started. By the time Alex had returned she'd brought the rest of the pots and seed trays through from the other courtyard and was shifting the planters around into different configurations.

'Stop!' Alex was leaning back in his seat, drinking lemonade. 'That's the one I like.'

Marie stood back. 'Yes, me too. Then there's space for some seating.'

Alex nodded. 'Where are you thinking of getting that from?'

Now or never... The idea had occurred to her yesterday, and since then Marie hadn't been able to stop thinking about it. 'I had my eye on some old garden benches I saw in a junk shop. They'd scrub up nicely. But...'

Suddenly she felt as if it was too much to ask. As if this little garden with its recycled pots and bedding plants grown from seed wasn't really good enough.

'But what?'

Marie must have shown her embarrassment, because Alex was suddenly still, looking at her thoughtfully. There was no way out now...

'I thought... Did your mother like flowers?'

He raised his eyebrows in surprise. The question had come so much out of the blue.

'She loved her garden. She was always out there, planting things and helping the gardener. Whenever my father wasn't around, that is. He reckoned she shouldn't get involved with any actual work.'

'I thought... Well, I know this garden's never going to make the Chelsea Flower Show, but you made it... And you know how they have seats in the park with people's names on them...?'

She couldn't quite say it, but Alex had caught her meaning and was nodding slowly. Marie held her breath, hoping Alex wouldn't take offence at the suggestion.

'My mother would have loved this garden. And I'd like to buy something for it in memory of her.'

Marie let out a sigh of relief. 'You're sure, Alex? I know it can't do your feelings for her justice.'

He shook his head. 'My father thought cut flowers and ostentatious wreaths did her justice. I hated her funeral and I wanted to go away and do something simple for her on my own, but I never could find the right thing. *This* is the right thing. You said you wanted a water feature?'

'Yes? Do you think that would be better than seating?'

'Much better. She liked the sound of water; she used to

say it was soothing.' Alex thought for a moment. 'No brass plates with her name, though. I don't want that.'

His obvious approval for the idea gave Marie the courage to suggest another. 'What was her name?'

Hopefully it wasn't something too long…

'Elise.'

Perfect. 'If you wanted we might spell her name out? With the plants we choose to put around the water feature?'

He smiled suddenly. 'I'd love that. Thank you for thinking of her, Marie. She'd be so pleased to be part of this garden.'

'Good.' Marie's heart was beginning to return to something that resembled a normal pace. She felt almost lightheaded.

'As this is Friday, and we'll be opening on Monday, I'll have to go to the garden centre this weekend. I don't suppose you could spare a couple of hours to help me choose?'

Marie rolled her eyes. 'Where else did you think I was going to be this weekend? Yes, of course I'll help you.'

They'd worked hard at the weekend. Alex had chosen an old millstone, with water bubbling from the centre of it, which was a great deal heavier and more expensive than Marie had envisaged. Jim was going to have to construct a base for it, and install the motor and drainage tank, but Alex and Marie had heaved the millstone into the place reserved for it in the courtyard, and it already looked stunning.

She hadn't stopped Alex from buying plants, some more planters for them, and four wooden benches. This was a labour of love, and the look in his eyes when they'd hauled the first of the planters through into the garden, filled it with compost and arranged echinacea and lavender in it had told her that it meant a great deal more to him than anything money could buy.

On Monday morning everything was ready. Tina, the receptionist, was at her post, and Alex and Marie were sitting in the chairs at the far end of the reception area, along with one of the counsellors, a physiotherapist, and therapists from the pool and the gym. Tina would welcome visitors and summon the relevant person to talk to them.

'You're sure we shouldn't be next to Tina? She looks a bit on her own.' Alex waved across to Tina, who waved cheerily back.

'No. We don't want to frighten anyone away with a horde of therapists waiting to pounce.'

'But I *want* to pounce. Actually, I want to go out onto the street and kidnap anyone who walks by.' Alex was looking a little like a caged lion at the moment.

'Well you can't. We're supposed to be friendly and non-intimidating. We wait, Alex. We've got some groups coming soon. Before you know it you'll have more people than you can cope with.'

'I hope so…' He caught his breath, stiffening suddenly as a shadow fell across the entrance. 'Aren't they the women you were talking to the other day?'

Carol and Nisha had manoeuvred their pushchairs into the lobby and were standing by the door, looking around. They moved forward to let a group of young mums past, who had obviously just dropped their children off at school.

'Yes.' Marie smirked at him. 'They're mine, Alex. You can wait here until Tina calls you…'

He grinned at her, obviously relieved that the reception area was beginning to fill up. 'No one likes an overachiever, Marie.'

'Too bad. I'm still first.'

She stood up, walking across to where Carol and Nisha were standing.

'Hi, Marie.' Carol saw her first, and gave her a wave. 'We've come to check out the mum-and-baby swimming classes.'

'That's great. I'll get you signed up… Would you like to come and see the pool first? It's in the old gym.'

'The gym?' Carol rolled her eyes. 'That I'd love to see.'

Marie led the way. Both women had been to school here, and by the time they got to the swimming pool the three of them were swapping memories of their years spent here.

'You've worked wonders with it all, that's for sure.' Carol nodded her head in approval of the changing rooms and showers, and then stopped short when Marie opened the door that led through to the pool area. 'Wow! This is a bit different!'

The aqua blues and greens of the tiles and the light playing across the water made this one of Marie's favourite parts of the clinic. 'This is the main exercise pool. The hydrotherapy pool is where we're holding the mum-and-baby classes.'

'Does it matter if I can't swim?' Nisha was looking uncertainly at the pool.

'No, the hydrotherapy pool is much shallower than this one. You'll be able to stand up in it. It's kept at a warmer temperature, which makes it more suitable for babies and children.'

Marie led the way through to the smaller pool, where the same blue-and-green tones lent a more restful, intimate atmosphere. Georgie whooped with joy and started to wriggle in his pushchair, obviously keen to try it out straight away.

'I think that's one taker!' Carol grinned, taking him out of the pushchair and keeping a tight hold on him in case he decided to try and jump in. 'What do you think, Nisha?'

'Yes, definitely.'

The matter was settled. Marie had filled two places on the mother-and-baby swimming course, and maybe she'd get a chance to talk a bit more to Nisha.

'Would you like to come to the cafeteria for some coffee?'

'That would be nice. There was something I wanted to ask…' Nisha smiled hesitantly.

'Oh. Yes—good idea. I'll leave you to it, then. See you tomorrow, Nisha. Thanks for the tour, Marie.'

Georgie's protests went unheard as Carol put him back into the pushchair and hurried away, giving them both a wave.

Marie turned to Nisha, who was grinning broadly at her friend's receding figure. 'If there's something you want to talk about we could have coffee in my office.'

'It might not be anything at all. I'm probably just being silly…' Nisha twisted her mouth into a grimace.

'If it matters to you then it's something. The one thing I'm *not* going to do is tell you that you're being silly. You're the one who tells me what's important.'

Nisha nodded. 'It *is* important to me. I wish you could help me…'

Half an hour later Marie walked Nisha through to the reception area, which was now buzzing with activity. Nisha was grinning, clutching the information pack and the appointment card Marie had given her. Alex was nowhere to be seen, and it was another half hour before he appeared again.

'Everything okay with Nisha and Carol?'

'Yes, it's all good.'

She nodded towards his office, and by silent agreement they walked away from the bustle of people. Alex closed the door.

'I had a talk with Nisha; she says she hasn't felt right about sex since having her baby. She's worried about her relationship with her husband.'

He nodded. 'So what did you both decide?'

'Nisha's coming back to see me tomorrow. I'll examine her, and she's given me permission to write to her doctor so he can send her for some tests. Once we've ruled anything physical out we can discuss relationship therapy here.'

'She looked as if she was happy about that?'

'Yes—she said she'd get her husband to come with her tomorrow. He's tried to talk to her about it, but she says she panics and shuts him down.'

'Just talking about it helps.' He threw himself into his chair, staring at the ceiling. 'Of course, I'm a proven expert on talking about things.'

The heavy irony in his tone set off an alarm bell. Something was up with Alex. His hand was shaking, and it didn't seem that hopeful nerves about their opening day was the cause.

'What's up?' She sat down.

'It's…' He waved his hand dismissively. 'Telling you it's nothing and that we should be getting back isn't going to wash, is it?'

'No. There are plenty of people out there to greet visitors, and we're confident the staff here can manage without us for ten minutes. Aren't we, Alex?'

'Yes. Absolutely.' He puffed out a breath. 'In that case… I had a boy who came in to ask about bodybuilding classes. He's only ten. I talked to him a bit, and told him that he'd have to bring one of his parents with him before he could sign up for any kind of exercise class with us.'

'Why did he want to do bodybuilding?' she asked, knowing Alex must have had the same instinct she did.

'It turned out that he'd skipped off school, so I got Tina

to phone the school and they sent a teacher down to fetch him. He's being bullied.'

'Poor kid. And he wants to be able to fight back?'

'Yes. His teacher's going to talk to the parents, and I told her we would enrol him in our anti-bullying programme. He's a little overweight, so if he wants to do exercises then I'll get Mike to devise an exercise programme that suits his age and build.'

'That makes sense.'

'Yeah… But when he realised I wasn't just going to sign him up for bodybuilding he threw a tantrum and then… started to cry—' Alex's voice broke, suddenly.

'That's good, Alex. You got through to him. He must have a lot of negative emotion bottled up.'

Alex was committed to setting up a programme for both kids and adults who were being bullied. He'd applied his customary insight and thoroughness and then left it to a specialist.

Marie had supposed that someone with Alex's charm and natural leadership ability couldn't possibly have first-hand knowledge of being bullied, so he'd left the finer points to the experts he'd recruited. But she'd based her supposition on what she'd thought she knew about Alex. The happy childhood she'd imagined for him.

'You know, I always wanted you to have been happy as a child.'

He looked up at her. 'Yeah? That's nice.'

'Not really. I just wanted to know someone who'd grown up normally. It made me feel better—as if that was something I could shoot for.'

'Ah. Sorry to disappoint you, then.' He turned the corners of his mouth down.

'But, thinking about it, I guess it might have been a bit difficult to make friends when you were little.'

He was gazing at his desk, as if something there might

provide an answer. 'My father didn't think I should play with any of the kids who lived nearby because I was a prince. I was taught at home until it came time for me to be packed off to an exclusive boarding school. I was a shy kid, with a name that invited a thousand jokes. Of course I got bullied.'

And so he'd become the student who everyone liked. He'd listened to what people said and charmed them all. Marie had never looked past that.

'I wasn't much of a friend, was I?'

His eyebrows shot up. 'What? You were kind and honest. You brought me colour, and you showed me that however hard things are there's always time to celebrate the good things. I wanted...'

He fell silent suddenly, and in the warmth of his gaze Marie knew what he'd wanted. He'd wanted *her*. She'd wanted him too. Honesty was good—but this was one place they couldn't go.

'I wanted to be like you.'

His smooth refusal to face that particular fact was a relief, because Marie couldn't face it either. She'd never really moved on from wanting Alex.

'Will you do me a favour?' she asked.

'Anything.'

The look in his eyes told her he meant it.

'You've got a lot you can give to the anti-bullying programme. All those feelings and the things no one ever said. I want you to get more involved with it.'

He laughed suddenly. 'Don't underestimate me by giving me the easy option, will you.'

'You *want* me to underestimate you?'

'No, not really. Keeping me honest is what you do best.' He held his hands up in a gesture of smiling surrender. 'Yes, I'll do it. And now we really should be getting back to our visitors.'

CHAPTER SIX

YESTERDAY HAD BEEN a success. The flood of people who'd wanted to be first to explore the new clinic had subsided into a steady but satisfying trickle. Alex had received a couple of calls from local doctors, enquiring about referring patients to the clinic, and he'd shown a consultant from the nearby hospital around. She had a young patient whose family were currently travelling an hour each way to get to a hydrotherapy pool, and was pleased to find a closer facility that would meet the girl's needs.

Today there was a new challenge.

Alex assumed his best trust-me-I'm-a-doctor smile, and when he looked down at Marie he saw a similar one plastered uneasily across her face.

'Oh, really, Alex.' Sonya Graham-Hall flapped her hand at the photographer from the local paper, indicating that he was to stand down while she gave her clients a good talking-to. 'Can you try not to look as if you've eaten something that doesn't agree with you? You're supposed to be welcoming. And stand a little closer to Marie. You're a team…'

Marie was looking a little overawed by Sonya. Alex took a step towards her, feeling the inevitable thrill as her shoulder touched his arm. He bent towards her, whispering an old joke from medical school, and she suppressed a laugh. He couldn't help smiling, and heard the camera click rapidly.

'Wonderful!'

Sonya beamed at everyone, and Alex stepped forward to shake the photographer's hand and thank him. Then Sonya marched across the reception area to where the local reporter was standing, leading him towards the front doors.

'What's she doing?' Marie looked up at him. 'Can't he find his own way?'

'It's Sonya's modus operandi. She's making sure he knows what he's meant to write. Although he probably won't realise that's what she's done until after he's filed his story.'

Alex knew Sonya's husband from school, and knew she was the best PR representative in London. She was so much in demand that it was usual for her to interview clients, rather than the other way round. Alex had been lucky, though, and a phone call had not only managed to secure Sonya's services, but they were on a pro bono basis, because she loved the idea of the clinic. There was something to be said for the public school network.

'She's formidable, isn't she?' Marie's smile indicated that she thought formidable was a really good thing. 'I'm a little scared of her.'

Alex couldn't fathom what Marie would have to be scared about. If he'd been asked to define 'formidable', the first person who would have come to mind was Marie. But not quite in the same way as Sonya, who relied on killer heels, designer jackets and an upper-class accent that would have sliced through concrete.

'She knows so many important people...'

'It's her job to know people. Anyway, don't we prefer to think of *everyone* as important?'

Marie frowned, nudging him with her elbow. 'Of course we do. You know what I mean.'

Alex knew. Marie had already told him that she felt like a fish out of water with the great and the good, but they were exactly the kind of people who had the money and influence to help them make this project grow into a whole chain of clinics in different parts of the country. He wished Marie would stop thinking of them as somehow out of her league, because she was just as good as any of them.

'Right, then.' Sonya returned, beaming. 'I think he's on track. While I'm here, perhaps we can review where we are with everything else.'

'Thanks, Sonya. My office?'

Alex led the way, hearing Sonya chatting brightly to Marie, and Marie's awkward, awestruck replies.

Sonya plumped herself into one of the easy chairs, drawing a slim tablet out of her handbag. In Sonya's eyes, paper was messy, and she didn't do mess.

'Ooh, look. I love these. Such lovely colours. Can I have one?'

She leaned forward towards the coffee table, catching up the sheet of brightly coloured stickers that Marie had presented him with this morning. They had the name of the clinic on them, along with the main telephone number and website address, but Alex suspected that their real intent was to bring yet another much-needed shot of colour into his office.

'Help yourself. Marie has had a few printed. Shall we get some more?' Marie was already squirming in her seat, and Alex decided to embarrass her a little more.

'Definitely. This is just the kind of fun thing we want. Something to get away from the boring medical image.'

Alex felt his eyebrows shoot up.

'You know what I mean, Alex. Of course the medical part is the most important, but we want people to feel that you're approachable and not a stuffy old doctor.'

'Yes, we do.' Marie spoke up, reddening slightly at her audacity, and Sonya nodded.

'Now. I have the local radio interview set up—you're on your own with that one, Alex.'

'I can handle it.' Alex reckoned he could talk for ten minutes about the clinic easily enough.

'I'm sure you can. But I'm sending you a list of keywords and I want you to memorise them.'

Sonya swiped her finger across her tablet, and Alex heard a ding from the other side of the room as his desktop computer signalled that he had mail.

'Really? Keywords?'

'Yes, of course, darling. Think of it as like...' Sonya waved her hand in the air, groping for the right words.

'Like talking to a patient? Sometimes you have to emphasise what's important without confusing them with a load of irrelevant detail,' Marie ventured.

'Yes, exactly.'

Sonya gave Marie a conspiratorial smile, indicating she was pleased to see that at least one of them was on track, and Marie reddened again.

'I'm still working on the TV appearance, and there are a couple of functions that I'd like you to go to if I can get you an invitation.' Sonya leaned forward in her seat. 'You still have reservations about promoting the royal aspect in the media?'

Alex felt the side of his jaw twitch. 'If by *reservations* you mean that I'm absolutely sure that I don't want any of that in the media, then, yes, I'm still absolutely sure.'

'But it's such a good story, Alex. It would catch people's imaginations. It doesn't get much hotter than this—you're a doctor, very rich, royal, and to top it off a handsome bachelor.'

Alex shook his head, and then Marie spoke. Like an angel coming to rescue him.

'We've agreed a policy about this.'

'Ah… Yes?'

Sonya turned to Marie, clearly wanting her to elaborate. And Alex wanted to know what policy he'd agreed, as well.

'The compelling nature of Alex's story is the problem— it could quite easily prompt a media circus. Our values are that the clinic is the one and only important thing. Once it's a bit more established we could look at it again, but now's not the right time.'

Nicely said. Alex shot Marie a thankful look and she received it with the quiet graciousness of a queen.

Sonya nodded. 'Yes, that makes sense. Why didn't you say that before, Alex?'

'Marie sums it up a great deal better than I can.'

Sonya flashed him a look that told him she agreed entirely with the sentiment, and then moved on. 'Now, I'm rather hoping you have something presentable to wear, Alex.'

'I have a suit…' Just the one. It was the suit he wore for job interviews, and he hoped it still fitted.

'All right. I'll send you the names of a few good tailors, just in case.'

Alex's computer dinged again and Sonya swiped her finger across her screen, in clear indication that she'd ticked that particular item off her list.

'I'm very pleased with the website—are you getting anything via the enquiries page?'

'Yes, quite a few things. Sofia's coordinating that.'

'Good. She seems very efficient. And the mural for your reception area? There are lots of possibilities there. How ever did you find these people? I've had a look at their previous work and it's stunning. Inspirational, even.'

'That was Marie's idea.'

'Of course…' Sonya's questioning gaze swept towards Marie.

'Oh. Yes, well… They're a group of artists who do wall

art for charities and public spaces like hospitals and libraries. They choose the organisations they want to be involved with and work for free—we just pay for their materials.'

'And who's in charge?' Sonya enquired.

'Corinne Riley's their coordinator. She's about as much in charge as anyone is. She's an artist, and works part-time as an art therapist. Her husband, Tom, is head of Paediatrics at the hospital where I used to work.'

'And would they consider a magazine article, or even a short TV piece featuring their work here?'

Marie shrugged. 'I could ask. I know Corinne's very interested in spreading the word about how art can change spaces and involve people.'

'It's fascinating…' Sonya's mind was obviously hard at work on the possibilities. 'Yes, please. And I'd love an introduction if you feel that's appropriate?'

Alex smirked, wondering if Marie was taking notice of the fact that Sonya had just asked her for an introduction. It seemed she was, because she smiled suddenly.

'I'll email Corinne today and get back to you. Do you have any particular time in mind?'

'If she sends me a couple of dates which suit her I'll fit in with them.'

Sonya swiped again, and Alex braced himself for the next item on her agenda.

'You do have a suit, don't you?'

Now that Sonya had left, Alex's office seemed a little quiet. Marie had waited to ask the awkward question.

'Somewhere. Unless I left it at the dry cleaner's…'

Marie frowned at him. 'It's not that suit you bought for your job interviews, is it?'

'What's wrong with that one?'

'It's not going to fit you any more.'

Alex put his hand on his stomach, sucking it in, and Marie laughed.

'I meant across the shoulders. You've lost those few extra pounds you were carrying.'

So she'd noticed. Alex couldn't help smirking. 'You think I've lost a bit of weight?'

She made a thing of eying him up and down. She was teasing, but her gaze made his stomach tighten with apprehension. When she grinned, it felt as if a warm wave was washing over him.

'You're in good shape, Alex. But you'll probably need a proper suit for these functions that Sonya was talking about.'

Alex sighed. 'Yes. Probably.'

'How many suits did you have when you were a child?' Marie homed in unerringly on the exact reason why Alex never wore a suit.

'Oh, about a dozen, all told. New ones each year.'

'That sounds excruciating.'

'It was.'

But he was doing things on his own terms now. Marie had told him that, and she wasn't going to underestimate him by reminding him again. In the silence he could feel her presence pushing the memories back and turning his gaze forward.

'You're right. I'll order two new suits; that old one probably doesn't fit me any more.'

She nodded. 'You'll be your own kind of excellent and glorious. What about some striped socks to match?'

Alex chuckled. His father would have blown a gasket at the thought of his wearing striped socks with a suit. Or with anything else, for that matter. Having to be excellent and glorious suddenly didn't seem so bad.

'Okay. Striped socks it is. You can choose them.'

* * *

The clinic's first week was reassuringly busy. Marie and Alex had agreed on a 'walking around' approach, to see how things were going and to iron out any teething problems, and they took turns with it. One dealt with patients and any urgent paperwork, and the other simply walked around the clinic, visiting all the different departments and talking to people.

It was working well—the staff were encouraged to talk about any difficulties they had, and the clinic's clients were beginning to know that either Marie or Alex would always be somewhere in the building if they wanted to chat.

'Hi, Terri. How are things going?' Marie saw a young mother with whom Alex had been working approaching her.

Terri's older child had been born with spina bifida, and although surgery had closed the opening in her spine, the little girl had been left with weakness in her legs and needed a specialist exercise regime.

'Good, thanks. This place is an absolute godsend.' Terri beamed at her. 'All that travelling we used to do to get to a hydrotherapy pool for Amy, and now we can just walk around the corner.'

'You're enjoying your swimming?' Marie grinned down at Terri's eight-year-old daughter and Amy nodded.

'*I'm* going to swim too.' Five-year-old Sam had been walking next to his sister's wheelchair, hanging obediently onto the side of it. 'I'm going to be a really good swimmer, and then I can help Amy.'

Terri grinned. 'It's great for both of them. We couldn't afford the time to take Sam to a class as well, but the hydrotherapist says she'll book Amy's sessions at the same time as the junior swim class, so Sam can swim too. Usually he just has to sit with me by the pool.'

'That's great.'

It was exactly what the clinic was for. Helping whole families to cope. Terri was looking less tired than she had when Marie had first met her.

'What's that?' Sam had left his sister's side and was standing on his toes, peering through the window into the courtyard.

'It's our garden. If you've got time, you can come and have a look.'

Marie shot a questioning look at Terri and she nodded. Opening the door, Marie let Sam into the courtyard and he started to run around, stopping in front of each planter to look at the flowers.

Terri parked Amy's wheelchair next to the water feature, so she could reach out to touch the plants around it. Then she sank down onto a nearby bench.

'This is lovely. I could stay here all day.'

Sam and Amy were amusing each other, and Terri gave a satisfied smile.

'Hello, Amy.' A woman stopped in the corridor by the open door. 'How are you, dear?'

'Very well, thank you, Miss Fletcher.' Amy sat a little straighter in her wheelchair and Marie suppressed a smile.

Jennifer Fletcher had been one of the first people through the doors when the clinic had opened. A retired primary school teacher, she seemed to know every child in the district, and had taught a number of their parents as well.

'This is lovely.' Jennifer craned her neck to see the garden, obviously hesitant to inspect it more closely without being asked.

'Come and join us, Miss Fletcher.' Terri grinned at her.

'It's about time you called me Jennifer.'

Miss Fletcher walked slowly across to the bench and Marie moved to make room for her.

'What brings you here…um…Jennifer?' Terri was

clearly reticent about calling her old schoolteacher by her first name.

'I've been having a few aches and pains since I retired last spring, so I decided to come along and see if I could join an exercise class. I had a full physical, and the doctors have found I have an inflammation in my right hip.'

Jennifer beamed at Marie. She'd had the distinction of being the first patient to try out the new MRI scanner, and it had shown that, instead of a touch of arthritis, the bursa in her right hip was inflamed. Jennifer had professed delight at the thought that this could be rectified, and was already seeing the clinic's physiotherapist.

'I've got a full exercise programme and I think I'm doing rather well. It's early days, of course, but the physiotherapist here says that core strength is important as you enter your seventies.' Jennifer looked around the garden. 'You'll be adding a few bedding plants?'

'It's a work in progress. We've planted some seeds, and we have some cuttings over there in the corner.' Marie pointed to the yoghurt pots, full of water, where the cuttings were beginning to grow roots.

She saw Amy's head turn, and the little girl leaned over to see. 'I don't suppose you'd like to help us plant some, would you, Amy?'

'Mum…?' Amy turned to Terri.

'Of course. But we mustn't take up Dr Davies's time.' Terri flashed Marie an apologetic look.

'That's all right. If Amy would like to help with the garden—'

'Well, I would, too…' Jennifer spoke up.

It seemed that the garden had just acquired its first few volunteers.

Marie brought some of the pots over, moving a table so that Jennifer and Amy could work together, planting the

Busy Lizzies. Sam had taken a couple of action figures from his mother's handbag, and he was playing with them.

'Would you like a drink? I'll pop over to the café.'

Everyone else was occupied and Terri deserved a break.

'You know what…?' Terri gave her a wry smile. 'I'd like to just stroll over there and get something. On my own. If you or Jennifer don't mind staying here with the kids, that is…?'

Marie knew the feeling well. Terri craved a moment to herself, so she could do something ordinary. She'd felt like that when she was a teenager. Wanting just five minutes that she could call her own, without one or other of her brothers wanting something.

'Of course. We'll be another half an hour with this, if you want to sit in the café?'

'No, that's okay. Can I get you something?' Terri pulled her purse out of her bag. 'My treat.'

If Marie wanted coffee, she had the lovely machine in her office. But that wasn't the point. It was clearly important to Terri that she get it, and she should accept the offer.

'A cup of tea would be nice. Thank you.'

Terri grinned, turning to Jennifer. 'Would you like a drink?'

Fifteen minutes later she saw Terri strolling back towards them, chatting to Alex. He was carrying a tray with four cups and a couple of child-sized boxes of juice, and when he'd handed the drinks around and stopped to find out how Jennifer and Amy were he strolled over to Sam to deliver his drink.

'They never quite grow up, do they?' Terri was drinking her coffee, watching Alex and Sam. The little boy had shown Alex his action figures, and the two were now busily engaged in making them jump from one planter to another. Sam jumped his onto the water feature with a splash and Alex followed with his, and the two figures started to fight in the swirling water.

By the time Terri said that they should go home, Alex's shirt was dappled with water. The pots were gathered up and labelled as Amy's, so that she could watch her plants grow and transfer them to the planters when they were big enough. Sam said goodbye to Alex, promising that they would continue their fight the next time he was here, and Alex thanked him gravely.

'I'm hoping your mother wouldn't have minded too much...' Marie nodded towards the water feature.

'Mind? She'd have loved it.' Alex grinned at her, coming to sit down on the bench.

'Good. And of course all that splashing about was entirely for Sam's benefit?'

It had occurred to Marie that Alex's love of silly games was because he'd never got the chance to play them when he was a child.

'Of course.' Alex brushed at his shirt, as if he'd only just noticed the water. 'I have absolutely no idea why you should think otherwise. Ooh—I had a call from Sonya.'

'What does she want us to do now?'

Sonya's calls generally meant smiling for one camera or another, but every time they did it Sofia Costa received a fresh wave of enquiries.

'It's an evening do at the Institute of Business. They throw a very select party once in a while, so their members can meet people who are doing groundbreaking work in various charitable and medical fields. Most big businesses like to have their names associated with a few good causes, and making those contacts now will help us in the future.'

Even the scale of Alex's wealth wasn't going to finance his dreams of creating and running a chain of clinics all over the country. This was about the future—one that Alex was going to build for himself.

'That sounds great. Does Sonya know someone at the Institute?'

'No, but it turns out that a couple of the Institute's board of directors went to my school and they vaguely remember me. Sonya's managed to swing a couple of invitations.'

'So Sonya's going with you?' That would be good. She'd keep Alex in line and on message.

'No, she's going with her husband. The second invitation is for you.'

'What?' All the quiet peace of the garden suddenly evaporated. 'Tell me you're joking, Alex.'

'Why would I be? You have as much to say about the clinic as me.'

He leaned forward, his eyes betraying the touch of mischief that Marie loved so much. At any other time than this.

'And the whole point of a man's dinner suit is to show off a woman's dress.'

Suddenly she felt sick. 'I can't hobnob with the rich and famous, Alex. I don't know how to talk with these people, or how to act.'

'How about just the same as you always do?'

There was a trace of hurt in his voice. *He* was rich. And it was only a matter of time before he'd be famous. She knew Alex was under no illusions that he could keep his royal status under wraps indefinitely—he just wanted to put the moment off for as long as he could.

'I can't, Alex. I just…can't.'

He thought for a moment, his face grave. 'Okay. If you can't do it, then you can't. I'm not going to tell you that the clinic needs you, or that I need you, because that wouldn't give you any choice. You're always there for the people who need you.'

'What do you mean?' The lump in Marie's throat betrayed her. She knew exactly what he meant.

'You've always been there for your mother and brothers.

Don't get me wrong—that's a fine thing, and I envy you it. I'd have done anything for my mother to need me a bit more. But I know it's not been easy for you; it never is for people who care for the people they love.'

She'd been thinking the same about Terri, just moments ago. He was right, but Marie dismissed the thought. It was too awkward.

'So you're telling me I don't have to go?'

'Of course. You don't *have* to do anything. I'd really like you to go, because I think you're selling yourself short. And because a very wise person once told me that I needed to accept who I am and write my own script. I'd like you to accept who I am and come with me, as my friend.'

Dammit. Saying he needed her would have been easy compared to this. Alex was reaching out, asking her to step out of her comfort zone and meet him halfway.

'So when is this reception?'

'Next month. I could go dress-shopping with you…?'

He looked as if he'd enjoy that far too much.

'No, that's fine. I can handle that.'

'Then you're coming?'

'Yes, all right. I'll come.'

At least it would serve as a reminder to her that she and Alex came from different worlds. That they could be friends, but anything more was unthinkable. It had always been unthinkable, but it was doubly so now that they were working together.

He grinned. 'Great. I'll let Sonya know. Should I quit while I'm winning?'

She could never resist his smile. 'Yes. Please do that, Alex.'

CHAPTER SEVEN

MARIE HAD BOUGHT Alex an action figure. She reckoned it was what every boy needed, in case someone turned up in his office needing to play, and Alex had arranged the jointed arms and legs so that the figure leant nonchalantly against one of the plant pots on his windowsill.

She tried to repress a yawn, failing miserably. Jennifer Fletcher had expressed enthusiasm over an idea for a carers' support group for mums like Terri, and said that she had another couple of friends who might be interested in helping. They were having to sort out all the relevant statutory checks for the volunteers who were going to be working with children, and assess the needs of the kids so that the clinic could provide the professional staff that would be required. It was going to take a couple of hours.

'Why don't we finish for the evening? This can wait,' said Alex.

'It can't, Alex. We've both got a full day tomorrow.'

And Marie had left work at five o'clock sharp for the last couple of evenings. She was feeling guilty about having left Alex alone working, but her mother was having one of her crises and Marie had been up late, talking her down.

He opened his mouth, obviously about to protest, but the sound of the front gates rattling silenced him.

Alex went to the window, and then turned. 'Nisha's outside. You don't have an appointment with her, do you?'

'No, all her medical tests came back okay, so I referred her to our relationship counsellor...'

Marie followed Alex outside and saw that Nisha was walking away from the gates now. He hurried to unlock them.

'I'm sorry...' Nisha turned back to him, tears streaming down her face. 'I shouldn't have come...'

'That's all right. Come inside and tell us what the matter is.'

Alex's question provoked more tears. 'When I spoke to Anita at the clinic she said that we didn't have to have sex...we could just spend time together. But one thing led to another...'

It was a measure of her distress that Nisha had forgotten all her reticence in talking about the problem.

'Okay, well, come inside.'

Alex glanced at Marie. He had no hesitation in talking to patients about sexual matters, but he was clearly wondering if Nisha wouldn't feel more comfortable discussing this with Marie.

'We had such a lovely time. But now it hurts to pee, and I'm passing blood. Carol says it's cystitis. What am I going to tell my husband?'

Alex frowned, clearly wondering whether Nisha wanted him to respond or not.

Marie decided to put him out of his misery. 'Let's go inside, eh? Alex, why don't you take the pushchair?'

'I'm so sorry. It's later than I thought—you must be closed by now...'

'That's okay. I'm glad you came.'

That was almost the truth. Marie *was* glad Nisha had asked for help—she just wished she'd needed it on another evening, when she wasn't so tired. But when she took Nisha's hand she felt it warm and trembling in hers and forgot all about that.

Nisha was running a fever, and clearly not at all well. After Marie had tested a sample of her urine, to confirm Carol's diagnosis, she curled up on the examination couch, shivering and crying.

'Can we call your husband? I think it would be best if he came and picked you up.'

Nisha nodded. 'I'm so disappointed. I thought we were doing everything right, at last…'

'I know it's easy to feel it is, but this is not your fault. Recovery isn't always a straight line; it's sometimes two steps forward and one step back. But this is an infection and we can deal with it. You'll feel a lot better when the antibiotics start to take effect.'

'Sorry…'

Marie smiled at Nisha. 'And stop apologising, will you? This is what we're here for.'

'I'm so glad you *are* here. Thank you.'

Nisha's husband arrived—a quiet, smiling man, who made sure that the first thing he did was hug his wife.

Prompted by Marie, Nisha told him what had happened and he nodded. 'I'll stay home from work tomorrow to look after you.'

'No. You don't need to…'

But Nisha obviously wanted him to, and Marie guessed it wouldn't take much before she gave in and accepted his offer.

'Give us a call if there's anything we can help with.' She handed Nisha's husband her card. 'If the clinic's closed, you can use the out-of-hours number; there will be someone on hand to advise you.'

'Thank you—for everything. I'll take good care of her.' Nisha's husband helped her down from the couch, putting his arm around her protectively.

Alex opened the gates and bade the couple goodbye, reserving a special smile for the child in the pushchair, who had slept soundly through the whole thing.

Then he turned, walking back to his office, where Marie was waiting for him. He picked up her laptop and papers, tucking them under his arm. 'We're going back to mine. We'll get a takeaway.'

Just like the old days. When he'd brook none of her arguments about needing to work and insist she take a break for just one evening. That had usually involved food, as well, and the tradition had persisted. His flat was on her way home, and after a day spent at the clinic it would be nice to talk over a meal.

'It's my turn to get the takeaway, isn't it? Shall we go for Thai this time?' Marie's resources stretched to taking her turn in paying for the food now.

He shrugged, picking up his car keys. 'That sounds great.'

Alex's flat was on the top floor of a mansion block in Hampstead. Quiet and secluded, but just moments away from a parade of artisan food shops and cafés, and little boutiques that sold clothes with hefty price tags.

Inside, it reeked of quiet quality. Large rooms with high ceilings, and a hallway that was built to accommodate cupboards and storage and still give more than enough space. Alex might have rejected his father's lifestyle, but he'd absorbed an appreciation for nice things, and he always bought the best he could afford. The sofas were the same ones he'd had in medical school, but they were still as comfortable and looked as good. If you could afford it, there was economy in that.

'You order. I'll put some music on. What do you fancy? A little late-night jazz?'

The sitting room was lined with cabinets that housed Alex's extensive books and music collection. Marie had never hesitated in sharing his music with him—it was one of those things that cost nothing and brought them both joy.

But it wasn't late-night yet, even though Marie felt tired enough. 'Late-night jazz is going to send me to sleep.'

'Right. Driving music?'

'No, that's a bit too wakey-uppy. Have you got a soul mix?'

It was a rhetorical question. Alex chuckled. There was a pause while he decided which soul mix fitted the occasion best, and then a muted beat began to fill the room.

They began to work, spreading their papers out on the large glass-topped coffee table. When the food came they added a couple of plates and a jumble of takeaway cartons. Ideas came more easily in this setting, and by the time they were ready for coffee they were finished.

He stood, stretching his limbs with satisfaction. Marie leant forward to gather up the plates and he batted her hand away.

'Leave it, will you? Try relaxing for a few minutes.'

It was impossible not to, in the heat of his smile and the rhythm of the music.

'I'll take a hot towel for my face while you're there...' she called after him as he made his way to the kitchen, laden down with the remnants of their meal.

'Sorry, ma'am, we're fresh out of hot towels. Coffee will have to do.'

Marie rolled her eyes, teasing him. 'No hot towels? What kind of service is this? I'm not coming back here again!'

'I've got a dark roast arabica...' he shouted through from the kitchen, and Marie chuckled. Alex always served good coffee.

'You're almost forgiven,' she shouted back.

He returned with two cups of black coffee, with a thick foamy crema on top. Even the smell of it was gorgeous.

'That's it. This is definitely a five-star establishment.'

'It can't possibly be. I'm not done yet.' He grinned at her, catching her hand. 'I've got moves.'

Another one of those old jokes that had stood the test of time. They both loved to dance, and Alex's grinning query as to whether *she* had moves, and his promise that he had a few of his own, would often prompt them to dance until they were exhausted. Marie had often wondered whether it was a substitute for sex, but had decided not to think too deeply on the question.

'My moves are already asleep. I will be too, as soon as I get home.'

Alex was far too tempting at the moment. Too delicious and complicated. She'd never wanted to be one of those women who went out with Alex for a few months only to see him walk away without looking back.

'Are you sure? You're tapping your foot.'

He turned the music up, trying to tempt her, but when Marie laughed and shook her head, he turned it back down again.

'Okay, your loss. It means you'll just have to tell me what the matter is.'

'Nothing. I'm just tired…'

How many times had Alex heard Marie say that nothing was the matter? How many times had he asked and felt shut out when she wouldn't talk about it? He'd accepted it once, but it was becoming more and more difficult to take what she said at face value and turn away from her.

'I can wait you out.' He sat down, taking a sip of his coffee.

Marie smiled. How she managed to do that, when she was so tired she could hardly keep her eyes open and clearly worried about something, was beyond him.

'Great coffee.'

'Yes, it's a good blend.' Alex decided that Marie's diversionary tactics weren't going to work on him any more. 'I'm still waiting.'

She puffed out a breath. 'It's nothing, really. I just... I was up a bit late last night, talking to my mum. She's worried about my youngest brother.'

'What about you? Are you worried about him?'

She gave a frustrated shrug. 'I'm *always* worried about Zack.'

This was something new. Alex knew Marie had always supported her younger brothers, but she'd never really said much about the day-to-day process of that. Just that her mum often found that three boys could be hard to handle on her own and needed a bit of help. Alex had assumed that Marie helped out financially, but it seemed there was more to it than that.

'What's the problem?'

Perhaps he'd remind her that they'd been friends for a long time. Maybe he'd even mention that Marie had given him a hard time over the secrets he'd kept.

'You know... He's twenty...'

'He's having difficulty finding time to study and check out all the bands he needs to see?'

She laughed suddenly. 'No, Alex. He's not like *you* when you were twenty. Anyway, you never seemed to have much difficulty keeping up.'

'Yeah. It was easy. You managed your studies, as many jobs as you could find, *and* about five minutes per day for recreation. So what's Zack not managing to do?'

She shrugged, reaching for her coffee cup. That was a sure signal that she was done talking.

They'd been through a lot together over the years. Studying, dancing, working until they were too tired even to speak. He'd carried her into her bedroom once and then turned his back, walking away, because the one thing Alex had always known for sure was that he couldn't take things any further with Marie.

He'd rejected the idea that he'd always loved her and instead he'd asked her to help him build a clinic. But he *had* always loved her, and when she turned her gaze on him, her eyes dark in the approaching dusk, he knew he wasn't going to flinch from this.

'What is Zack not managing to do?' he repeated. He heard the quiet demand in his tone and saw surprise on Marie's face.

For a moment he thought she would get up and leave, but then she spoke.

'At the moment he's not managing to do anything very much. He did well with his A levels, but decided he wanted to take a year out before university. I think it was just that he couldn't get motivated to choose a course. I got all the prospectuses and sat down with him, but he wasn't very enthusiastic about it.'

'So he's working?'

'No. He had a few jobs, but couldn't stick at any of them. He's been unemployed for the last six months, and increasingly he's staying up all night and sleeping all day. Mum doesn't know what to do with him. A few days ago he took money from her purse and went out. He came back the following afternoon, went straight upstairs and slept for fourteen hours. She's worried he might have been taking drugs, but I took a look at him and didn't see any signs of it.'

'How much money did he take?' Alex felt a cold weight settle in his chest. This wasn't fair...

'Two hundred pounds. She'd just gone to the bank to get the money for her main monthly food shop. She can't afford that; she's already keeping him in food and clothes.'

'So you gave her the money?'

Marie rolled her eyes. 'What else was I supposed to

do? I told Zack this was absolutely the last time, and that I wasn't going to bale him out again.'

'Did he listen?'

'Yes, he listened. Listening's not the problem with Zack. He'll hear what you have to say, and tell you all the things he thinks you want to hear. Then he'll ignore it all and do exactly as he likes. Mum knows he's got to change, but she makes excuses for him. About how he's never had a strong father figure, and how she's not been able to give him enough time because she's at work.'

The words came out in a rush of frustration. Then Marie reddened a little, as if she'd made a faux pas by admitting that there was something she couldn't manage on her own. He wasn't going to give up on her now.

'What about your other brothers?' He knew that both of Marie's other brothers had been to university and had good jobs.

'Dan's washed his hands of him completely—he says Zack needs to pull himself together. And Pete lives up in Sunderland. He tried talking to him last time he was down on a visit, but Zack just gave him that lovely smile of his and told him everything will work out.'

'And your mother?'

'She's…she does her best. Mum's fragile. She had a breakdown when my dad left, and we were all put into foster homes for a while. It was awful.'

Alex nodded. Marie had told him, years ago, how all she'd wanted when she was a kid was to have her family back together and to keep it that way. At the time he'd almost envied her for having something she cared about so much.

'It never was your fault, Marie. You didn't have to be the one to put things right.'

A single tear rolled down her cheek. Suddenly the room was far too big and the distance between them too great.

He couldn't reach for her and comfort her, and if he moved she'd only shoo him away and tell him that she was okay.

'In a way, it was my fault. My dad left because a wife and four children was too much for him. He couldn't deal with it. My mum broke down over it...'

'You were ten years old.' The impulse to hold her and comfort her was wearing him down fast. 'You were trying to clear up a mess that adults had made.'

'Families, huh? Who'd have them?' She brushed away the tears and gave him a smile.

Was he supposed to empathise with that? Alex reckoned so. And Marie was only telling him what he already knew. He couldn't contemplate having a family of his own because he'd lived with the consequences of failure and seen what they had done to his mother. Marie had lived with the consequences of failure as well, and she needed someone who would be there for her.

Maybe that was why he'd always maintained his distance. He'd helped her as much as she would let him in practical terms, but always shied away from the emotional. It was time to redraw the boundaries.

'What do you need?'

She shrugged, shaking her head. 'I've had a takeaway and some music. Now an early night.'

She obviously wasn't going to discuss the matter any further, and Alex needed a plan. Something with no loose ends, that she wouldn't be able to argue with or reject out of hand. Something that was going to work and maybe change things in the long term.

'I'll take you home, then.'

'That's okay. It's early enough to take the Tube.'

Alex got to his feet. 'You can take the Tube, then, and I'll drive over to your place. I'll see you there.'

The expected smile almost tore his heart in two.

'Since you're going my way, I suppose I *could* ask you to drop me off, then.'

He walked through into the hall, picking up his car keys and waiting for her there. Marie appeared, her bag slung across her shoulder, but before he could reach for the latch on the front door she suddenly flung her arms around his waist.

'Uh!' He allowed his hands to move slowly towards her back, returning her hug as impersonally as he could. 'What was that for?'

'For being my best friend. And for listening to me blather on.'

She hugged him tight, and then let him go, stepping back. Alex's knees almost gave way.

'This is just between you and me, right?'

She saw everyone else's needs and yet treated her own as weakness. And she was clearly regretting saying as much as she had.

'Of course. What are friends for?'

The look on her face seemed a lot like relief that he'd decided to drop the subject. For once, Marie had misread him. Alex wasn't going to back off and if she put up a fight then so be it.

He'd fight her back.

A good night's sleep had applied some perspective to the matter. Marie would deal with Zack, and she'd deal with her mum the way she always had. Alex couldn't help her with this.

She retreated to her office, and then spent most of the day showing a few local GPs and hospital doctors around the clinic while Alex saw patients. Working together with other health professionals, becoming one of their options when they thought about what their patients needed, was a must if the clinic was going to reach its full potential for helping the community.

When Alex appeared in the doorway she couldn't help starting. Last night had lit a slow-burning fuse, which had been fizzling all day. Sometimes it seemed to go out, but that was just an illusion. The spark never quite died.

'How was your day?'

His question was much the same as it usually was when they'd been working on separate things and hadn't seen much of each other.

'Good, thanks. They all seemed impressed with what we had to offer, and a couple of them have said that they already have patients on their books they'd like to refer.'

'That sounds great.'

He dipped his hand into his pocket and put a small box on her desk. Marie looked inside, finding a tangle of pink paper clips, and when she tipped some of them out she saw that they were in different animal shapes.

'They're wonderful—thank you. Where do you get all this crazy stuff?' Marie already had a collection of unusually shaped, brightly coloured things on her desk, which Alex had bought for her.

'That's my secret. If you knew, you wouldn't need me to feed your stationery habit. And, by the way, I saw Anita just now. She popped in to see Nisha today.'

'Yes? How is she?'

Alex had clearly decided to forget her show of emotion last night, and they were back to business as usual. If he could do it, then so could she.

'Feeling much better.' He grinned. 'I'm going to stick with that blanket assurance and leave the details to you and Anita. I imagine that Nisha will be more comfortable with that.'

'Good move.'

Marie bit her tongue. She didn't need to be thinking about Alex's moves—or hers. Last night was last night.

Alex seemed to be loitering, neither sitting down to talk nor about to leave. Suddenly he planted his hands on her desk, leaning forward towards her.

'I want Zack.'

'You…want Zack?'

Marie felt her jaw harden. Alex obviously thought he could solve this problem, but he didn't know Zack.

'What for? There's nothing you can do, Alex.'

'Why on earth not? We're friends, Marie. Heaven forbid we'd actually try to help each other with our problems.'

All right. He had her there.

'I can deal with it. I appreciate the offer, but—'

'It's not an offer. You can't deal with this on your own, and I can help. You told me I had to accept what I've been given and do the right thing with it. I'm just following your advice.'

'Well…what are you going to do with him?'

Alex was clearly on a mission. If she wasn't so cross with her brother for treating their mum so badly Marie might have felt sorry for Zack.

Alex straightened up. He suddenly seemed very tall, his determination filling the room. 'He's going to work here. I've had a word with Sofia, and there are a lot of things she can get him to do, so he'll be working hard. He'll need to, because he's going to have to pay you back the two hundred pounds he took.'

'That doesn't matter, Alex. It's done now.'

'It matters. This isn't about the money. It's about how he treats people. I need you to take the two hundred pounds and for your mother to accept something from him for his bed and board. Everything else I'll deal with. He'll work a full day and he'll pull his weight. If he turns up here with a hangover I'll find a job for him that'll make a cracking headache even worse. And if I see any evidence of drug-taking I'll test him myself and put him into our drug rehab programme.'

It was exactly what Zack needed. But Alex shouldn't have to do this.

'The clinic can't afford it, Alex. We have budgets and that money could be spent elsewhere.'

'Yes, but it appears that I have a small inheritance on my hands, and my income is embarrassing enough to be able to pay Zack without even noticing the difference. My real problem is *you*. Which I guess makes you Zack's real problem as well.'

Marie felt herself redden. Alex was right—she was standing between Zack and an amazing opportunity.

'He does need something like this. Zack's just so charming that he thinks that everyone will forgive him anything. He's right, and I'm just as much at fault as anyone in falling for his promises...'

Alex chuckled, finally sitting down. '*I* can be charming, can't I? You never have any problem resisting that.'

'That's different. I respect you.'

'Okay. I'm not sure how that works, but I'll take it. Can you get your mother on board?' Alex finally sat down.

'Yes. That won't be a problem.'

Alex had come up with a plan that would make a real difference for Zack. Marie had to acknowledge that with good grace.

'Thank you, Alex. It would do him a lot of good, and I really appreciate your help. If you're willing to take him on for a couple of weeks, that would be great.'

He smiled. If he was about to make some comment about how that hadn't been so difficult to agree to, then she was going to throw him out of her office.

'I want him for more than a couple of weeks. I reckon it'll take him a little while to earn enough to pay you, and he's going to have to do all the boring jobs that no one else wants. When he's earned it, he'll get the chance to choose something that interests him. I'll be reviewing things with him every month, and if he decides on a study path then we'll support him in that. If he wants to look for employment then he'll get the experience he needs, and I'll write him a great reference.'

'This is too much, Alex.' Marie couldn't think of a reason why it was too much, just knew that it was.

'That's what I'm offering. Take it or leave it, Marie. But know this—I'll think less of you if you turn down an opportunity for Zack just because of your own pride.'

She felt herself redden. Alex had just stripped her of all her excuses, and the loss of that armour made her want to shiver. If it had been anyone else she wouldn't have been able to countenance it.

'I'll take it. Thank you, Alex.'

'It's my pleasure. Is tomorrow too early for an interview? Or do you need a bit more time to convince your mother and Zack?'

'Tomorrow's great.' Marie frowned. 'He won't be wearing a suit, though…'

Alex chuckled. 'Good—neither will I. Will nine o'clock suit him?'

'He'll be there.'

'Right, then.' Alex looked at his watch. 'It's nearly five o'clock now and I guess you'll be needing to go.'

It would have been nice to stay a little longer. Zack was difficult to contend with at the moment, and Marie wanted Alex's company. She loved the give and take that had developed between them, which made her feel that it was possible to step into new territory.

But she did need to speak to her mother, and to Zack. If he was going to make the best of this opportunity she needed to prepare him, convince him that this was an opportunity and not a punishment.

'Yes, thanks. I'll…um…see you tomorrow, then. With Zack.'

'You will.' He got to his feet, a satisfied smile on his face. 'You're doing the right thing, Marie.'

'Yes, I know…'

She wanted to hug him again. For caring and for being the tower of strength that had given her a way to really help her brother. Alex had been a true friend.

'You were right. Thank you.'

He narrowed his eyes. 'I think we'll never mention that again.'

Alex's dry humour always made her laugh. 'Yes, okay. It'll be our secret.'

CHAPTER EIGHT

MARIE HAD DONE her part. She'd convinced her mother that this was exactly what Zack needed, and then the two of them had hauled him out of his room and given him little choice but to accept the plan. Zack, as always, had been accommodating and cheerful at the prospect of working for his keep and paying back the money he'd taken. Whether he would stick with it for more than a week would be the real test.

She'd called round to her mother's house at seven-thirty the next morning and found Zack sorting through shirts, throwing them onto the bed. Marie gathered them up, putting them back onto their hangers.

'Mum's ironed all these.'

Sometimes she felt like a broken record, nagging Zack about everything. Like the grumpy big sister who squeezed all the joy out of his life.

'Sorry, sis.' Zack gave her a winning smile. 'I just want to make a good impression. I don't want to let you down.'

'I'm not your problem.' Zack knew she loved him, even though he did make her want to scream at times. 'This is about not letting yourself down.'

'Okay…' Zack frowned at the line of shirts that Marie had put back into the wardrobe and then whipped out a checked shirt with a plain tie that matched one of the colours. 'What about this?'

'Perfect. My handsome little brother.'

'I don't want to look handsome. I want to look...contrite. Hard-working. That kind of thing.' He pulled a face that indicated deep sorrow.

Marie rolled her eyes. 'Don't pull that one with me, Zack. I'm not Mum. You're going to look nice because this is an interview, but just turning up and saying the right things isn't going to get you off the hook. Afterwards is when you get to prove whether or not you're contrite and hard-working.'

She got yet another of Zack's dazzling smiles. That was his trouble; he never took anything too seriously. She was going to have to keep a close watch on him if he came to work at the clinic.

'All right. Half an hour to get washed and dressed and have a shave. Then we're leaving.'

Getting Zack to the clinic was a bit like getting a recalcitrant six-year-old to school. But at least he straightened up a bit and smiled cheerfully when Alex came out of his office and greeted him.

Alex whisked Zack and Sofia into his office, shutting the door firmly behind them. It wouldn't do to listen at the door, so Marie returned to her office and frowned at the wall, fiddling with a pink paper clip.

After an hour, she called down to Reception, asking Tina to give her a buzz as soon as Alex was free. Zack might be blissfully free from interview nerves, but Marie couldn't help worrying about him.

Zack was a graceful, engaging youth, with a ready smile. He declared himself ready for all kinds of hard work, and was excited at the prospect of earning the opportunities that Alex and Sofia outlined. Yes, he wanted to study. And, yes, he wanted to take responsibility for all the jobs in the clinic that no one else wanted to do. He wanted to show that he could take on the outreach tasks that Sonya had outlined as well. But if he could manage to do all that, he'd be working for more hours than Marie had at his age, and that wasn't really possible.

Despite himself, Alex liked the kid. He was charming and intelligent and he reminded him of Marie. And there was something in those heavy-lashed blue eyes that made Alex feel the boy might just have the same grit as his sister, if it were only possible to bring it out in him.

After they'd shown Zack around Alex left him in Sofia's care. Then he returned to his office and waited.

He didn't have to wait long. Marie appeared in the doorway, clearly trying to give the impression that she'd just happened to walk past on her way somewhere else. She put a large piece of card face down on his desk and sat down. They'd fallen into the habit of bringing things for each other's offices—unusual stationery or pictures for the walls—and he turned the card over, wondering what she'd found this time.

'Oh! That's wonderful. Where shall I put it?'

His wall was filling up now, and he'd brought some pictures and vintage record covers from home to go with the various prints Marie had given him. This one was an old photograph she'd got from somewhere, which reeked of late nights and the blues, showing a drink propped on top of a piano and one of his favourite artists, shirtsleeves rolled up and eyes closed as he played.

'You're beginning to run out of space.' Marie surveyed the wall.

'Not for this one.'

It was clearly something Marie had gone out of her way to get, and an image that Alex hadn't seen before. He took one of the framed pictures off its hook, and started to prise open the back of it, so he could replace it with the photograph and put it in pride of place.

Marie obviously wasn't going to ask, so he told her anyway. 'Zack seems…unrealistically enthusiastic.'

Marie laughed. 'Yes, that's him all over.'

'Maybe an eight-hour day will slake his zeal a little.'

'He'll be here before nine o'clock tomorrow morning. I promise.'

Marie flashed him that intent look that he'd seen so many times before. When she took on the troubles of the world and tried to work her way through them. She usually succeeded, but Alex had seen the toll it had taken.

'Will you do me a favour? Don't go round to your mother's every morning and chivvy him.'

'He told you about that?' Marie looked a little as if she'd been found out.

'No, I guessed. You have enough to do here, without running around after Zack.'

Alex could see that this wasn't reason enough for Marie and decided she needed a bit more persuasion.

'I've told him that he'll work eight hours, with an hour's lunch break every day. If he's late then he can work an extra hour in the evening, but he's not to stay here after six o'clock. If he gets here after ten in the morning I'll dock his pay.'

'That's very generous. He really should be here at nine every day.'

'Flexible hours work for us. But he needs to take responsibility for himself. I'm hoping your mother won't decide to give him spending money for the weekend if he finds his pay has been docked at the end of the week.'

Marie shook her head. 'No, she'll do whatever you ask; she's really grateful that you're taking Zack on. I'll mention it to her, though.'

She seemed a little unhappy with the arrangement, and Alex answered the question that she hadn't asked but which was clearly bothering her.

'You won't be helping him, Marie. Let him suffer the consequences if he can't get here on time. If he needs to be told to buck his ideas up, let Sofia and me do it.'

She saw the sense in it and nodded.

'I rather wish I had brothers or sisters.' Alex leaned back in his chair. It would have been nice to have someone to care about so ferociously. Someone for whom he'd do anything.

'Sometimes they're a pain in the neck.'

'You wouldn't be without them, though.'

'No. I wouldn't. Even Zack.'

She loved her little brother. He was driving her to distraction at the moment, but she loved him all the same. And she'd given him to Alex, trusting that he'd do the right thing. Alex felt a little unequal to the prospect, but it warmed him all the same.

'So...' All that was better left unsaid. 'Anything you want to discuss?'

'I've got the ideas for the mural in Reception back. Would you like to see them?'

'Not really.'

Marie's eyebrows shot up.

'Surprise me.'

She did that all the time, and it was always fantastic. Alex wondered vaguely what he'd do if Marie ever left the clinic. Left *him*.

But that wasn't going to happen. He wouldn't let it.

Alex had stayed out of the way while the artists took over the reception area. He had a final fitting for his dinner suit, and a few other errands to run, and although he'd spent most of the day itching to see what Marie was doing he'd decided that this was her project and she should be allowed to enjoy it alone.

Zack had expressed a fervent desire to come in on Saturday and help, and since he'd managed to turn up on time for nine of the last ten working days Sofia had allowed it.

When he'd arrived at two in the afternoon one day he'd been abject in his apologies. Alex had smilingly shrugged them off and simply docked his pay. After that, Zack had made sure he wasn't late again.

Alex arrived at the clinic at four o'clock and saw a dark-haired man walking across the courtyard, pushing a buggy and talking to the small boy who walked beside it. Alex caught him up. He introduced himself and they shook hands.

'I'm Tom Riley—Corinne's husband. That's Matthew, and this is Chloe…' He bent down to the pushchair, taking the little girl out of it and letting her stagger uncertainly towards her brother.

'We really appreciate this, Tom. I know your wife has a waiting list for this kind of thing.'

Tom chuckled. 'I get to spend a day with the kids, and Cori gets to cover herself with paint. What's not to like about that—particularly when it's for a project as exciting as this one? Although I'm still cross with you for poaching Marie away from the hospital.'

'I needed someone who's the best at what they do.'

Alex shot Tom an apologetic look and he laughed.

'Then you made the right choice. I'm interested to see what you're doing here; some of my patients' families live in this borough.' Tom swung round, calling to Matthew. 'Leave the tree alone, son. I don't think digging around it is going to do it any good.'

'I'll give you the tour. And if Matthew would like to plant something we have a garden. There are some bedding plants that need to be put into planters.'

'Thank you.' Tom grinned down at his son. 'Hear that, Matthew? We can help with the garden.'

The pushchair was manoeuvred up the ramp and into

the reception area. Tom was greeted with an excited cry from a woman in dungarees spattered with paint, some of which had made its way into her red curls. As she hurried towards him Tom backed away, a look of mock horror on his face, and she laughed, leaning forward to kiss him without allowing any of her paint-spattered clothes to touch his. She greeted Matthew and Chloe similarly, making a show of not getting any paint on them.

It was the picture of a happy, relaxed family. Secure in each other and the obvious love that bound them together. Alex felt a pang of loss. It was all that he hadn't had, and probably never would have. He couldn't imagine ever trusting himself enough to believe that his were a safe pair of hands which could hold such precious gifts as Tom had.

The reception area was full. Artists were working with people from the clinic, who'd come in to help. Sonya was deep in conversation with one of the film crew who were packing up in one corner. From her paint-spattered hands, and the marks on her designer jeans, she'd obviously been tempted into ruining her manicure by picking up a paint brush.

Zack had obviously torn himself away from painting duties and was working his way round with a large tray, distributing cups of tea. A sudden warmth at his side told him that Marie had seen him and come over to greet him.

No kiss. However much it would have made the moment complete. But Marie was grinning from ear to ear, and that was a very good second-best. She had a smudge of paint on her nose and wore a baggy T-shirt and a pair of frayed jeans. Diamonds couldn't have outshone her.

'What do you think?'

Alex tore his eyes away from her, scanning the mural. A black-and-white line-drawn representation of the clinic building was in the middle, surrounded by colour. There was a blue sky, a sparkling rainbow and, at the bottom in freehand writing, the words *Living well at our clinic*, followed by a list of all the clinic's services. When he looked more closely, the cloud that floated across the otherwise clear sky was made up of the word *Welcome* in many different languages.

'It's fantastic. Way beyond anything I could have dreamed of.'

The mural brought life and colour into the otherwise bland reception space.

'Those are mine...' Marie pointed to a group of people depicted outside the clinic doors. 'I didn't draw them; Cori did the outlines and I filled them in. I like people best...'

Of course she did. And Marie was right—the people made the picture. Doctors and nurses, a fitness instructor in gym wear, mothers with babies, old people, young people, people of different colours, sizes and cultures, talking together in groups or walking past. There were animals as well. A family of foxes trekked in a line at one side of the building, and birds flew in the sky, eyed by a lazy cat curled up on the roof of one of the clinic's cars.

'It's breathtaking. It'll take me a few hours just to look at it all. I think your people are the best, though.'

She gave a little snort of laughter, but was obviously pleased. 'Cori suggested that we have some extra seating over there, all in different colours.' She waved her hand towards the space opposite the mural. 'Just to balance things up a bit.'

'Good idea. And were you talking about painting in some of the other areas, as well?'

'We were, and Cori's offered to do something for the children's areas. But she's got some stencils and pictures to work from, so I said we could give that a go ourselves. I said that we were looking for paintings from local artists to hang in the café and communal areas, and she's given me the names of a few people.'

'That's perfect.'

'You're happy with it all?'

His opinion seemed to mean a lot to Marie.

'More than I can say. It's fabulous.'

He'd planned and built this place, but it had been bland and devoid of any personality. Marie had brought life to it in a way he never could have done alone. She'd made him bring a little of himself as well, and now he felt at home here.

'There's still lots to do. Would you like to help?'

He'd resolved to step back and let Marie see this through on her own, but that was all forgotten now.

'Try and stop me...'

CHAPTER NINE

Last week had been all about getting paint in his hair and under his fingernails. After work every day Alex had donned a pair of overalls and laboriously filled one of the walls in the children's playroom, using the stencils Cori had given them. Zack had been allowed to help too, on account of being on time each day, and doing every job that Sofia gave him cheerfully and well. He was showing real artistic flair, bringing life to Alex's rather flat representations with a just a few extra brushstrokes.

This weekend was entirely different. Alex had picked up his evening suit from the tailor and gone to the bank to open his safety deposit box. He'd scrubbed every trace of paint off under the shower, and while he towelled himself dry he regarded the suit that was hanging on the door of the wardrobe.

He sat down on the bed. He'd actually rather go naked tonight than pull that dark jacket on over a crisp white shirt. And the bow tie? He had a step-by-step diagram, downloaded from the internet, but he'd never tied a bow tie himself. His mother had always done that for him, brushing specks of dust from his jacket and telling him he looked every inch a prince.

Suddenly he missed her very much. Planting the flowers that spelt out her name and switching on the water feature in the garden had felt like his own very personal goodbye. It had awakened feelings that Alex had tried hard to repress.

Would his mother have loved the clinic the way he did, and allowed it to bring some colour into her life? Or would she have stubbornly clung to his father, fading into his shadow?

But thinking about that now would only make it harder to put the suit on, and there was no way he could answer the door to Marie in this state of undress. Alex pulled the white shirt across his shoulders, looking at the full-length mirror in the corner of the room as he did so. He'd lost all the extra weight he'd put on and felt better for it.

He picked up the pair of striped socks Marie had added to his ensemble and smiled. He was ready for anything now.

Almost anything.

When the doorbell rang he wasn't ready for Marie.

She smiled at him, stepping into the hallway. 'Where's your tie?'

'Uh?'

She was wearing a pair of high-heeled black court shoes, which made her legs look even longer than usual. She had a dark green brocade coat on, fitted at the waist, and her hair was sleek and shining. She looked stunning.

'Alex!' She snapped her fingers in front of his face. 'Earth to Alex!'

'Yes. Nearly ready.'

That was about all he could manage in the way of communication at that moment. He just wanted to drink her in.

She put a small black clutch bag down on the hall table and started to unbutton her coat.

Where were his manners?

Alex helped her out of the coat, admiring the shape of her arms and the silky softness of her skin. The plain, sleeveless green dress was perfect, because it didn't draw any attention away from her beauty. It was flattering, slim at the waist to show the curve of her hips and breasts.

Alex decided not to think the word 'breasts' again tonight; it would be sure to get him in trouble.

'Please tell me you didn't forget to get a tie.' She was looking at him quizzically. 'I'm not sure I can manage a late-night mercy dash to your tailor in these heels.'

'I've got a tie. And some instructions.'

She turned the corner of her mouth down in a look of resigned humour. 'You want me to give it a go?'

'Yes. Please.'

He went to retrieve the tie and found her sitting in the lounge, perched on the edge of a chair, her legs folded neatly in front of her. He was beginning to revise his opinion of formal dress.

'Let's give it a go, then.' She took the instructions from his hand and studied them carefully. 'I haven't done this before, but it doesn't look so difficult…'

She got to her feet again, reaching up to button his collar. The touch of her fingers against his neck made him feel a little dizzy.

Consulting the diagram every now and then, she went through each step carefully. She was concentrating too hard on getting the tie right to be as aware as he was of how close they were.

'That's okay.' He glanced at his reflection in the mirror over the fireplace. The tie was slightly crooked, but it was a big improvement on any of his efforts.

'No, it isn't—it's lopsided. Come here, I'll give it another go.'

Marie untied the bowtie and Alex stared at the ceiling, glad that he didn't have to look her in the eye. He could feel the brush of her body against his, and reminded himself yet again that breasts were a forbidden thought.

'I think that's it.' She stood back to survey her handiwork and gave a little nod. Alex looked in the mirror.

'That's perfect. Thanks.'

'Okay, now the jacket.'

They'd said they would stick together tonight, and Marie was making his dislike of dressing up much easier to bear. Alex fetched his jacket, and handed her the pocket handkerchief. She folded it carefully and brushed a speck of dust from his shoulder. Then she tucked the handkerchief into his top pocket and Alex buttoned his jacket.

'Let me look at you.' She stepped back for a moment, looking him up and down. 'That's great, Alex. You've scrubbed up *very* nicely.'

'You...' Alex realised suddenly that he hadn't told her how wonderful she looked, and that he really should make some effort to do her justice. 'You've scrubbed up really well too.'

It was a paltry kind of compliment, but Marie was still pleased with it. 'Are we ready to go, then?'

Not quite.

He went to his bedroom to fetch the velvet-covered box he'd taken from the bank that morning. 'I thought... I mean, I'd be very honoured if you would wear this.'

She stared at him. Maybe this hadn't been such a good idea after all. Alex knew Marie was nervous about tonight, and he'd reckoned this would maybe give her confidence. It was a bauble that would outshine anything that any of the society women might wear.

He'd committed himself now, though. He opened the box, taking out the exquisitely crafted platinum-and-gold chain, the delicate filigree strands of which were deceptively strong. They had to be, to support the large diamond that hung from it.

Marie backed away from him. 'That must be... That's... How big is it?'

'Um...around twenty carats, I think.' Thirty-one, actually.

'It's got to be worth an absolute fortune. Alex, I can't wear this. We're going to be asking people for money.'

'That's not really how it works. I couldn't sell the Crown Jewels to raise funds for the clinic even if I wanted to. They're held in trust.'

Marie shook her head, tears welling in her eyes. She blinked them away furiously, trying not to spoil her make-up, and Alex regretted his gesture immediately.

'Marie, I'm sorry...'

His apology seemed to upset her even more, and a tear rolled down her cheek, leaving a thin trail of mascara.

'You don't have to be sorry, Alex. I just... I can't wear this. It's too good for me.'

'Oh, no. I'm not having that. Nothing's too good for you, Marie.'

She sniffed and he handed her his handkerchief. She dabbed at her eyes, trying to smile.

'Alex, I really appreciate this; it's a generous and kind gesture. But I'm not someone who wears diamonds. I can't meet the people who are going to be there tonight on their terms, and you told me it was okay to meet them on mine.'

That was the crux of it all. Marie saw them as being stranded on opposite ends of a spectrum—so much so that she couldn't even accept the loan of a necklace for the evening. Maybe she was right. Maybe asking her to fit in with the kind of people he'd known all his life made him just as bad as his father, demanding that Alex's mother fit in with his grand aspirations.

'Let's forget about all this, eh? Go to the bathroom and fix your make-up and we'll start again, shall we?'

She nodded, blowing her nose and then frowning at the handkerchief.

'Don't worry about that. They come in packs of two. I have another one.'

He propelled her out into the hallway, where she grabbed her bag and made for the bathroom.

She was back in less time than he'd thought, her make-up reapplied and flawless. Alex was standing in front of the mirror, trying to retie his bow tie after he'd pulled at it to loosen his collar a little.

'Let me do that. I think I have the knack now.'

She got the bow tie right first time, and folded the new handkerchief, putting it into his top pocket. A second chance to do things right. Alex picked up the velvet box, ready to put it back in the safe in his bedroom.

'Alex, would you mind...? Would you be able to perhaps lend me just the chain to wear? It's so pretty.'

She was meeting him halfway. Alex decided this wasn't the time to tell her that the workmanship on the chain was of such quality that it was considered a work of art just by itself.

'I'd like that very much. I think it's the better choice with that dress.'

He could go halfway too. Maybe that would be enough to breach the gaping chasm that seemed to have opened up between them.

He unclipped the fabulous stone from its place on the necklace, and then carefully fastened the chain around Marie's neck. 'There. What do you think?'

She walked over to the mirror. In Alex's experience, women didn't usually look this grave when trying on jewellery.

'I really like it. I'd love to wear it...just for tonight...'

Marie turned to him, smiling. And suddenly all Alex had wanted in having her wear the diamond was turning out better than expected. In choosing just to wear the chain Marie had made a powerful statement. She could take or leave one of the best-known stones in the world, but she still wanted to wear something of his.

'Tonight's going to be a little weird for both of us. We'll stick together, eh?'

She nodded. Alex stepped forward, catching her hand in his and pressing it to his lips. Not actually a kiss, it was the kind of thing his father had taught him that a gentleman would do. A royal kiss for the hand of a beautiful woman. But the sudden warmth in her eyes made the hollow gesture into something that lived and breathed.

'You look gorgeous.'

Finally Alex got to deliver the compliment he should have given when he'd first laid eyes on her. And, better still, she accepted it.

'Thank you. Shall we go?'

Marie was *very* nervous. But Alex seemed determined to get her through this one way or another. The diamond had been too much of a gesture, and the panic she'd felt when she saw it had only driven home the sinking feeling that she could never fit into his world. The kind of woman who should be on Alex's arm would have accepted the loan and given him the pleasure of seeing her wear it.

But they'd worked it out. The chain was delicate and very pretty, with silver-and-gold tendrils that made it seem as if it were almost floating around her neck. And when Alex relaxed into the back seat of the taxi and started to talk about the everyday matters that took their attention in the clinic she felt a little calmer.

The taxi took them right to the door, stopping outside the wide portico that stretched out to touch the gravel drive. The mansion was in one of the many secluded streets in central London, just moments away from the noise and bustle but surprisingly quiet. This was the territory of the rich, living cheek by jowl with everyone else, but separated by privilege and heavy closed doors.

This door was open, though. Perfume from the flowering shrubs that bordered the portico lay heavy in the air. And when she took Alex's arm, walking into the spacious lobby, the scent of wealth was all around her: beautifully waxed wooden panelling, and the smell of the fuel for the flares burning at the doorway, in the heat of the early evening.

He solved the question of when exactly she should take her coat off by stopping and helping her out of it himself, handing it to a porter. Then he made an almost imperceptible gesture and a waiter materialised with two glasses of champagne.

'Ah. There's Sonya...'

He shepherded Marie across the crowded ballroom, smiling and nodding as he went, without allowing himself to be diverted from his intended trajectory.

When Sonya saw them she waved wildly.

As always, Sonya looked as if she'd just stepped out of the fashion pages of a magazine. She wore a bright red look-at-me dress that Marie would have loved to have had the confidence to wear, with just one heavy diamond bracelet. She flung her arms around Alex's neck, air-kissing his cheeks, and then it was Marie's turn.

'You look *wonderful*!' Sonya loudly confided this information to Marie. 'I see you've managed to shoehorn Alex into looking respectable too.'

He didn't look at all respectable to Marie. She'd heard the adage that women had the same reaction to a man in a really good suit as men did to a woman in fine lingerie, and she hadn't given it much credit before now. But that exact reaction had been fizzling away inside her for a while now. Alex looked meltingly gorgeous, and the feelings that he engendered in her were anything *but* respectable.

'I'm always respectable,' Alex protested, and Sonya laughed.

'Yes, I know you are, darling, but sometimes running

around saving people's lives leaves you dishevelled. You know that as well as I do.'

She turned to Marie, rolling her eyes, and Marie grinned, feeling some of the tension slip away.

Sonya took her arm. 'I suppose we'd better get to work, then. I have some very interesting people I'd like you both to meet...'

Sonya had oiled the wheels and she was making things easy. But Marie couldn't have got through it without Alex. His glances that were just for her. The way he steered the conversation, always asking first about the other person's interests without indulging his own. And when anyone asked why he was there, he spoke about the clinic, effortlessly including Marie in the conversation.

Chandeliers glinted above their heads as Marie talked about the issues that ordinary people faced, and how the clinic was being set up to address them. Under the stern eye of the lords and ladies looking down from the oil paintings on the wall, she spoke of inclusivity and the modern art that adorned the wall of the reception area, feeling the words flow naturally from her lips. And when someone who knew Alex's family asked about his plans, now that he had inherited his father's title, he said that he was taking his family traditions into new and exciting areas and left it at that.

'Did you see Sir Richard's face?' Sonya whispered in her ear as they returned together from the ladies' restroom. 'He was so impressed with everything you said, and I'd be very surprised if he doesn't want to know more. He's very influential, you know... Oh, no! You just have to leave them alone for one minute!'

Sonya came to a sudden halt, staring across the room. When Marie followed the line of her gaze she saw Alex approaching a dark-haired man in an impeccable dinner suit.

'What's the matter?'

'I didn't know Mark was going to be here. Where's Andrew?' Sonya stood on her toes, looking around for her husband.

'I can't see him. What's going on?'

Sonya puffed out an exasperated breath. 'Mark was at school with Andrew and Alex. You know that Alex was bullied?'

Marie nodded. 'Are you saying that man was the bully?'

'Yes—him and some of the other boys. Andrew told me some of the things they used to do to him and it made my toes curl. Oh, dear... I hope Alex doesn't hit him or something...'

Alex was the taller and broader of the two. One blow from him would fell the other man.

'No. It's okay, Sonya. He's not going to hit him.'

It was almost as if he'd heard her. The two men exchanged a few words, and then Alex held his hand out to Mark.

'Oh, thank goodness.' Sonya whispered the words as the two men shook hands.

Marie felt her head begin to swim. Alex must have known that this man might be here, and he'd never said a word. He was making his way back across the ballroom now, and as soon as he got within touching distance she took his arm, holding on tight.

She looked for Sonya, but she'd melted away into the crowd. She could let this go but... No. Actually, she couldn't let this go. She needed to tell Alex how proud she was of him.

'Sonya told me that man was one of those who bullied you at school.' She stretched up onto her toes, murmuring into his ear.

Alex nodded, guiding her towards the back of the ballroom, where large doors opened out onto a terrace edged by stone balustrades. As they walked down the shallow steps to one side, into a secluded garden, she clung tight to his arm.

'You did just shake his hand, right? That wasn't some kind of death grip and he's going to fall over any minute now and need urgent resuscitation?'

Alex chuckled. 'No, it wasn't a death grip. I shook his hand.'

'It was a generous act. Sonya was afraid you were going to hit him.'

'And you?'

'For a moment, maybe, but then I realised you're a lot braver than that.'

The lights of the city were beginning to brighten in the growing dusk. Here, in the quiet darkness, it felt as if they were all for her. Marie could be a queen tonight but, like Cinderella, it was only for one night. Tomorrow she'd have to give up the glass slippers and get back to work.

He let out a sigh. 'It didn't feel… When I saw him, and decided what I was going to do, I thought it might be one of those cathartic moments that changes everything. But it was a bit of an anticlimax. He seems like just an ordinary guy now.'

'Perhaps that's the whole point.'

Marie reached up, brushing her fingertips against his cheek. He wrapped his fingers around hers, pressing her hand to his chest. Everything else seemed to take a step back, the chatter of the city and the noise of the party diplomatically turning their backs on them to give them one moment alone.

'I'm so proud of you, Alex.'

The extra height her heels gave her meant that Marie didn't have to stand on her toes to kiss his cheek.

'I'm proud of you, too. I know it wasn't easy for you to come here.'

Marie shivered as she felt his lips brush her cheek in return.

Slowly he propelled her away from the path and into the dark shade of an enormous spreading tree. Marie could feel the rise and fall of his chest against hers, and as her eyes adjusted to the darkness she saw tenderness in his face.

Marie couldn't help herself. She heard his sharp intake of breath as she moved against him, brushing her lips against his. He put his arms around her, steadying her on the uneven ground, and then he kissed her.

Careful and tentative turned to demanding as a ferocious wave of pent-up desire washed over her. And Alex was already there, holding her tightly against his body as if somehow they could melt into each other and become one being.

His kiss was one that wanted it all. Everything that Marie wanted to give him.

This couldn't last. Maybe that was why it was so exciting. They both knew that these moments were stolen, and that real life would take them back soon enough.

He held her tenderly, his breath caressing her ear as he murmured words she couldn't help wanting to hear. That she was beautiful. How much he adored kissing her on a moonlit summer's night.

'So a tent in Siberia doesn't push any of your buttons?' She smiled up at him.

'You can organise the tent and I'll get the plane tickets. We'll find out.'

He obviously found the thought as interesting as she did, but she knew they could talk this way because they both knew they'd never do it. They had something that was much too important to both of them to contemplate anything more than a forbidden fantasy.

'Or we could go to Egypt. Ride out into the desert on camels… Or to Paris and climb the Eiffel Tower…'

'We could. And there's always Camden. Hoxton. Maida Vale…'

The familiar names sounded suddenly exotic on his lips. Alex would make anywhere exciting, and his kiss would be equally intoxicating.

'Or we could go back inside. Finish off the job we came to do.'

'That would be good, too. In a completely different way.'

Alex's arms loosened around her waist. They both knew this had to end, and that they'd never go to Siberia or Egypt or Paris together. That Camden, Hoxton and Maida Vale would seem perfectly ordinary in the morning.

He was the one who had the strength to move, to take the first step back. Marie had his arm, but when they emerged from the shadows she stopped.

'Lipstick.' She pointed to her own mouth, to indicate where the smear was on his, and then pulled the handkerchief from his pocket, shaking out the folds and giving him the end that would be hidden when it was refolded.

'Did I get it all?'

'Bit more.' Marie took the handkerchief and wiped tiny smudge from the side of his mouth.

'Thanks. You've got some…er…' He waved his finger in a circle, pointing at his own face.

That wasn't a lot of help. Marie was sure she didn't have lipstick in her eyebrows. She wiped her lips, deciding she would go straight to the ladies' room and repair the rest of the damage.

'Okay?'

He nodded, offering his arm again. Marie took it and they walked together back up the steps to the terrace. They had a job to do, and it didn't involve kissing.

CHAPTER TEN

LAST NIGHT HAD been a mixture of emotions: wanting to protect Marie and the horrible suspicion that one of the things he needed to protect her against was him; meeting Mark and finding that he was an ordinary man and not an ogre; the feeling that if Sonya made any more introductions he was going to go out onto the terrace and yell for mercy.

And also sheer, unthinking delight.

Alex had tried to convince himself that their kiss was something that happened between friends. Out of curiosity. Like the way that, as boys, he and Andrew had kissed the backs of their own hands, to practise what it might be like to kiss a girl.

But kissing Marie had been nothing like kissing the back of his hand.

He felt a little less awkward at seeing Marie again than he might have done. She'd made it easy—going back to the party with him, slipping her hand into the crook of his arm just as she had before. They'd talked about the evening in the taxi together without mentioning the kissing part. And then they'd said their goodnights and he'd watched her to her door.

It was over. Done. And even if it couldn't be forgotten they'd both put it behind them because it was impossible to do anything different.

He saw Marie strolling across the front courtyard now,

chatting to Zack. She seemed happy, smiling in the late-morning sunshine.

Alex quickly got the papers he was supposed to be working on out of his briefcase and laid them on his desk to make it look as if he had actually been doing something. He heard a knock on his door and then Zack entered, leaving a respectful distance between himself and the desk.

'Is it okay if I help Marie, please? She's going to do some more wall-painting.'

'Yes, of course, Zack. Thank you very much.'

Alex wondered whether Marie would decide to do all her communicating with him via her brother today. It was a possibility.

But as Zack turned to go Marie popped into the doorway. 'Charlie and a couple of the other guys are here. They've come to help for a few hours.'

'That's nice of them. Tell Charlie I'll be along soon.'

'I'm sure he could do with a hand from his number one apprentice.' Marie grinned.

'Yep. As soon as I've checked the accounts I'll be there.'

Alex could almost manage to look at her without thinking about last night. The softness of her lips...

'Here...'

She had something in her hand, and she tossed it towards him. Alex caught it, opening his fist to see what it was.

'That's exactly what I need. Thank you.' She'd brought him an eraser in the shape of a dinosaur.

Then she was gone. Alex congratulated himself on not embarrassing either her or himself, and turned his attention to the papers in front of him.

Half an hour later, he scribbled his signature on the last page, and was about to write a note to the accounts manager, when Zack came bursting into his office.

'Come and help... Marie...'

Panic and breathlessness had rendered Zack capable of alarming Alex, but not able to tell him where he needed to be.

'Zack!' Alex stood up taking him by the shoulders. 'What's happened? Where's Marie?'

'Over the road—at the site office. Charlie went over there for something and didn't come back. Marie and I went to find him...'

That was enough for the time being.

Jim knew the letting agent for the small row of shops across the road, and he'd negotiated the use of an empty one as office space and storage while the works at the clinic were being carried out.

'We called him but he didn't answer...we looked through the front window and his hat was there...we banged on the door... Marie broke in...'

Zack was breathlessly recounting the story, running behind him as Alex crossed the road. He didn't need to know any of that. Just that Marie and Charlie were all right.

The door of the shop was open, and there was a bent piece of wire that Marie must have shoved through the letterbox to flip the lock. Alex cursed under his breath. Why hadn't she come to fetch him?

Because she could do it herself.

The warm, pliable woman who had clung to his arm last night, to balance herself over the uneven ground in her high heels, was more than capable of doing what needed to be done this morning. That was what he loved about Marie...

There was no time to consider his use of the word *love*. Alex noticed Charlie's bright red baseball cap, propped on one of the drawing boards by the window, and hurried past the desks and storage boxes to the open door at the back, which led to the stairs. He could hear sounds of effort, followed by a loud crack, and then a clatter.

He ran headlong down the stairs. At the bottom he saw Marie's face, shining up at him.

'Alex. Thank goodness!'

He resisted the impulse to hug her. 'Are you all right? Where's Charlie?'

'Inside. I heard him.' She gestured towards the door that led into the basement. 'But I can't get the door open— there's a pile of stuff behind it.'

She'd made a good start. The door stood open a few inches, and the light was on inside. Alex could see a mess of plaster from a broken sack and pieces of wood piled against the other side of the door, which stopped it from opening any further. Marie had found a crowbar from somewhere, and had managed to lever the bottom hinge away from the doorframe.

She wasn't tall enough to get good leverage on the top hinge, and nor was she strong enough to move the heavy door, which was now hanging on just one hinge. Alex took the crowbar, inserting it as far as it would go between the door and the jamb.

'Hold that in place.'

Marie stretched up to grip the crowbar, and Alex felt Zack jostling at his back.

'Zack, get out of the way, will you?'

Zack jumped back, giving them some room. Alex jerked the door closed, bracing his foot against the door, and holding on to the handle.

'A bit further…'

When he pushed the door open again he could see that the hinge had given a little. Marie slid the crowbar further into the gap and he pulled again. This time it gave, and he grabbed the other side of the door before it fell forward.

'Zack, mind out.'

Marie stepped back, taking Zack with her as Alex tipped the door forward, turning it slightly so that it would fit through the frame and then backing with it into the lobby.

Before he could stop her Marie had slipped past him and into the basement, climbing over the sacks of concrete mix that had slipped from a pile further inside the room and blocked the door. Dust hung heavy in the air, and there was a mess of spilt paint cans, brushes and other supplies, which had come from the heavy timber shelves that had once lined the wall. The shelves must have collapsed, because there was splintered wood everywhere.

'Charlie!'

She picked her way across the debris to where Alex could see Charlie's red T-shirt and fell to her knees.

'He's hurt, Alex. We're going to need an ambulance.'

Zack was ready to pile into the room and help, but Alex pulled him back. 'Go upstairs, Zack. Call an ambulance and tell them there's been an accident and to hurry. When you've done that, I want you to fetch the medical kit from the urgent care room in the clinic and bring it down to us.'

'But... Marie...' Zack's eyes were full of frantic tears for his sister.

'Do you want me to stand here arguing with you, or shall I go and help her?'

Zack nodded, pulling himself together suddenly. 'Look after them, Alex.' He threw the order over his shoulder as he ran up the stairs.

He would. Both Marie and Charlie.

Marie was vaguely aware that Alex was making his way across the piles of debris towards her. She'd heard Charlie crying out when she'd first reached the door that led into the basement, but now he was still and unresponsive, the lower half of his body pinned down under a pile of rubble.

'Airway?' Alex was there beside her.

'He's breathing and his airways are clear. I don't see any

major bleeding…' She leaned forward, finding Charlie's wrist. 'And his pulse is surprisingly steady.'

'Okay, stay with him, and I'll move some of this wood away from his legs.'

Marie nodded. She'd known that she couldn't get the door open by herself and had hoped that Zack would find Alex quickly. Together they would be able to help Charlie, and now they'd fallen automatically back into the habit of depending on each other to get the job done.

'Glad you're here.'

'Yeah. Glad *you're* here.'

Alex set to work, clearing the mess of paint cans and smaller pieces of wood from around Charlie's legs. Charlie was alive. All they had to do now was keep him that way.

Marie bent over him, smoothing his hair from his brow and tapping his cheek with her finger. 'Charlie! Charlie, can you hear me?'

Charlie moaned, moving his arms as if to push whatever was holding him down away. Marie caught his hand, holding it tightly in hers.

'Charlie. It's Marie. Look at me.'

As Charlie opened his eyes he let out a long, keening cry of distress.

'Charlie, I want you to stay still, if you can. Just look at me.' Marie clung to his hand, trying to calm him.

'I can see his legs,' said Alex. 'The right one looks okay…'

Which meant that the left one didn't. But Alex would tell her if he needed her, and Marie concentrated on Charlie's pulse, beating beneath her fingers.

'It hurts…'

'I know. We'll have you out of here soon, Charlie. You're doing really well—just hold my hand.'

'Yeah. Hold on.' Charlie groaned as Alex carefully lifted the piece of wood that was lying across his leg.

One more piece to go, and then Alex would be able to see better. It was a big piece, though—one of the shelves that had fallen from the wall. Marie glanced up at Alex and he nodded.

'Charlie, Alex is going to move the last piece of wood. It's going to hurt, so hang on to me.' She bent over Charlie, so he wouldn't see what Alex was doing.

Alex positioned himself in order to take the strain, and carefully lifted the heavy shelf. Charlie howled in pain, his fingers digging into Marie's arms.

'Okay. Okay, we're done. That's the worst bit over, Charlie.'

She could see his left leg now, twisted and certainly broken. Blood was pluming out over his jeans and dripping onto the concrete beneath him.

Alex leaned forward, gripping the top of Charlie's leg, putting pressure on the main artery to stanch the flow. His other hand found Charlie's, gripping it just as tight.

'Where's the medical kit?' Alex muttered the words, looking up as movement in the doorway indicated that Zack was back.

Marie broke free from Charlie and picked her way across to Zack. He was standing staring at Charlie's leg, and looked as if he was about to faint.

Marie grabbed the medical bag from his hand. 'Is the ambulance on its way? Zack!'

'Yes… I told them to hurry.'

'Good. Well done. Now, go back upstairs and wait for them outside. Got it?'

'Yes. Yes, I can do that.'

Zack straightened suddenly, and Marie turned him around, pushing him towards the door. Her little brother had been thrown in at the deep end, but he was doing fine.

She opened the medical kit, sorting through the contents of the bag to find a pair of surgical gloves and scissors. Alex was talking to Charlie, trying to reassure him while he did what he could to slow the bleeding. Carefully cutting Charlie's jeans, Marie exposed the wound on his lower leg.

The broken bone was sticking through his flesh, blood pumping out around it. There was no way that Alex could put any pressure on the wound to stop the bleeding.

'Tourniquet?'

Alex nodded. Marie took the tourniquet from the bag, looking at her watch and writing the time on the tab.

'Let go of Alex, Charlie. Hold *my* hand.'

As soon as Alex was free to work he wrapped the tourniquet around Charlie's leg. The bleeding slowed and then stopped, and Alex turned his attention to check that there was no other bleeding.

By the time the ambulance crew arrived they were ready to move their patient. Alex helped them to carry Charlie through to the small goods lift at the back of the building, and he was transferred into the ambulance.

'I'll go with him.' Alex moved towards the back of the ambulance.

Marie caught his arm. 'You're sure?' She knew the ambulance paramedics could be trusted to look after Charlie.

'He's my responsibility.' Alex's jaw was set firm.

It was a bit of a stretch to feel that any of this was Alex's responsibility, but there was no talking him out of it. He and Charlie had struck up an unlikely friendship, and Alex wouldn't let him go to the hospital alone.

'Okay. I'll call Jim and get him to contact Charlie's family. When you're done, give me a call; you can't walk back looking like that.' She nodded towards the blood on Alex's jeans.

He looked down, seeming to see it for the first time. 'Yeah, okay. Thanks. Zack did well. Don't forget to tell him that.'

'I won't.'

Zack had been frightened, but he'd done everything he'd been asked. Marie wondered whether her little brother would have been able to do that before he'd come to work here, and was proud of how far he'd come.

She watched as Alex spoke to the paramedic and then got into the back of the vehicle. The doors closed and the driver climbed into her seat. There was a short pause, and then the ambulance drew away from the kerb.

Jim had arrived at the hospital with Charlie's parents. About ten minutes later Charlie's older brother and his wife had come bursting through the doors of the waiting room.

Alex had sat them all down and explained what had happened, and the surgeon's prognosis. Charlie would need an operation to set his leg, and he'd be in hospital for a few days, but he had no other major injuries. The bruise on his face looked distressing, but it would heal.

When Charlie's mother saw her son her hand flew to her mouth, but she steadied herself and walked over to his bed, kissing him. Charlie's father shook his hand and thanked him, and Alex knew that it was time for him to leave.

He called Marie and then sat on a bench outside the A&E department, adrenaline and concern for Charlie still thrumming in his veins. All he wanted to do was hug Marie—but he saw Zack walking towards him from the direction of the car park.

'I said I'd come. Marie needed to wrap things up at the clinic.' Zack settled himself down on the bench next to him, asking the obvious question. 'How's Charlie?'

'They'll need to set the leg, and that means—'

'An operation and he'll be here for a few days. Yeah, Marie told me. They didn't find anything else?'

'No. He's got lots of cuts and bruises, but he'll be fine.'

Alex grinned. Marie had obviously talked everything

through with Zack and he seemed to be taking it all in his stride.

'When can we go and see him?' Zack peered at the doors of the A&E unit, obviously wondering if he might go in and see Charlie now.

'His family are with him, and we shouldn't interrupt. I'll call tomorrow, and you can take some time off in the afternoon if he's up to having visitors.'

'Great. Thanks. I'll make the time up.'

'That's okay. I think it counts as official clinic business. Charlie's one of ours.'

Zack nodded, his face suddenly thoughtful.

'What, Zack?' Alex leaned back on the bench, ready to listen to whatever Zack had to say.

'It's nothing really. I just...' Zack turned the corners of his mouth down. 'I didn't know what to do.'

'Your sister's a doctor. She's been trained to know what to do.'

Zack nodded. 'Yeah, I know. But... I was afraid. I said we should phone someone to come and let us in. If we'd done that Charlie might have bled to death. She was so brave the whole time, and nothing stopped her. I didn't know she knew about breaking and entering.'

'The coat hanger trick?' Alex grinned again. Marie hadn't actually used a coat hanger, but she'd found a piece of wire that had done just as well. 'I taught her that years ago.'

'Really?' Zack gave him a searching look. 'It was *you* that led her astray, then?'

Not really. Getting Marie into her student flat—when he could have asked her back to his place for the night— could be construed as *not* leading either of them astray. But Zack didn't need to know that.

'You did well, Zack. You did what we needed you to do and let us work.' Alex held out his hand, reckoning that

Zack needed something a little more definite than words. 'I'm proud of you.'

'Thanks.' Zack brightened suddenly, shaking Alex's hand. 'You know, Marie's always looked after me... Mum too. A bit too much sometimes.'

That was Alex's opinion, too. But he had no business saying it.

'I'm going to take more responsibility for things. I'll pay her back every penny of the money I took. I want to make a difference, the way she does.'

Alex laid his hand on Zack's shoulder. 'You made me proud today, Zack, and I'm sure your sister feels the same way. And, yes, you *are* going to keep working until you pay her back.'

Zack nodded, getting to his feet. 'She'll be wondering where we are. I'll drive.'

Marie's jeans were still spattered with blood, but she'd washed the grime from her face and hair, and cheered up considerably when Alex gave her the exact details of Charlie's condition.

'He was lucky. How on earth do you think it happened? Everything coming down on top of him like that?'

'Jim told me that he caught him climbing up those shelves the other day, to get something at the top. He gave him a dressing down—told him it was dangerous and said he should use the stepladder. But I guess Charlie didn't listen.'

Marie quirked her lips. She knew as well as Alex did that there was no saving people from themselves. 'What about the mess? Should we go and clear up a bit?'

'That's okay. Jim's been on the phone to a couple of his guys and they'll take care of it. I think we're done for today.'

Neither Marie nor Zack argued. Alex claimed the car

keys from Zack, saying that they'd drop him home, and Marie directed him to a neat two-up, two-down terraced house with a riot of colourful plants in the front garden.

'I'll come in with you…' Marie went to get out of the car but Zack reached forward from the back seat, grabbing her.

'I'll deal with Mum.'

Marie frowned. 'Are you sure? You can't just tell her about it and then disappear up into your bedroom. You know she worries.'

'I'll make her a cup of tea and talk to her. You're not the only one who knows how to do that, you know.'

'No, I know.' Marie grinned suddenly. 'Okay, then, Zack. See you tomorrow?'

'Yep. Bright and early.'

Zack shot Alex a grin and then got out of the car, loping up the front path and turning to give them his characteristically ebullient wave.

Alex put the car into Drive and accelerated away before Marie could change her mind.

'He did well today.'

Marie didn't ask where they were going, and Alex decided to head for his flat. Maybe he could make her lunch.

'Yes. He told me he wanted to make the kind of difference that you make.'

'That's nice.' She smiled. 'Mum tells me that he's got a severe case of hero-worship. "Dr King says this…" "Dr King did that…"'

She was twisting her fingers in her lap, clearly thinking about something. Alex wondered if it was the kiss, and hoped not. In between dealing with Charlie, he'd been thinking about it enough for both of them.

'I was wrong.'

'Were you?' In his view Marie was perfect. 'What about?'

'I thought that if I worked hard enough then I could fix

things. I could pay Mum back myself and persuade Zack to buck his ideas up. But I couldn't. I had to stand back.'

'That's the most difficult thing sometimes. Not that I'd know—I don't have a great deal of experience with families...'

Marie was so involved with her family. That might have its difficulties, but she felt a part of them. Indissolubly linked. Alex had worked for most of his life to distance himself from his family.

'You know people, though.' She reached forward, pulling her phone out of her handbag. 'Mum hasn't called me yet. I suppose that's a good sign...'

'Put it away, Marie. Give Zack a chance to deal with things. I know you've always been there for him, ever since he was little, but maybe it's time to let go now.' Alex ventured it as a suggestion.

'What? And have a life of my own?'

She made it sound like a joke, but Alex knew she'd got his point, and that she was thinking about it.

He shrugged. 'Funnier things have happened.'

'Yes, they have.' She gave a little sigh. 'I couldn't do what you did, Alex—taking Zack on like that and giving him direction. Thank you.'

A warm feeling spread through Alex's veins, making his hand shake a little on the wheel. He felt as if he'd been part of something good, and in his experience good things didn't happen in families.

Suddenly the idea of driving Marie home and leaving her there seemed impossible.

'It's Sunday afternoon. Would you like to go for a late lunch somewhere?'

'Like we used to?' Marie smiled.

'Yes.'

Driving out into the country would be good. He'd lost something from those days and he wanted it back.

'I can't go anywhere like this.' She pointed to the grime and blood on her jeans.

'We could drop in to your place.' Or, better still, he could avoid Marie's flat entirely so she didn't get a chance to change her mind. 'Or I could lend you a pair…?'

Apparently they called the style 'boyfriend jeans'— rolled up at the bottom and cinched tight at the waist. But Alex decided that he didn't need to be her boyfriend to lend Marie a pair of jeans, and that plenty of women wore the manufactured version.

'You've got diamond-encrusted jeans?'

Marie giggled suddenly, and Alex realised she was teasing him. 'Yeah. It was all the rage in eighteenth-century Belkraine.'

'This I have to see…'

CHAPTER ELEVEN

THE NEEDLESSNESS OF Charlie's accident, the repeated wish that he'd applied a bit of common sense, or a least listened to what Jim had told him, was beginning to be set aside now, along with her worry about Zack and her mother. This afternoon there was just Alex—and he was irresistible.

There had been a bit of awkwardness about who should go where to get changed, which Alex had solved by laying out a pair of jeans for her in his bedroom and then going to get changed and take a shower in the bathroom.

She could hear the sound of water running, and tried not to think about the inevitable consequence of that. Alex… soaking wet and naked.

Resisting Alex had always been hard, but she'd grown used to it. Now that she'd felt his touch it was a whole new ball game. And now that some of the responsibility for Zack and her mum had been lifted from her shoulders there might be time to indulge her fantasies.

But it was too risky. They were friends and colleagues and they were both at turning points in their lives. Anything could happen and they would smash all that they'd built together.

She rolled up the legs of the jeans, cinching the waist tight. They didn't look so bad with her flat canvas shoes, which had thankfully escaped any specks of blood. Her lace-edged sleeveless shirt was fine on its own, and now that the sun had burned away the early-morning cloud she didn't need the zipped hoodie she'd been wearing.

She walked back into the sitting room. Perhaps Alex had always looked her up and down like that but she'd never noticed, and it made her heart jump. His smile was even better.

'Diamonds really suit you.'

She laughed, and the joke loosened the tension between them. Alex picked up his car keys, hooking his sunglasses onto the front of his shirt, and Marie put her purse in her pocket. They were ready to go, travelling light the way they'd used to do. Just the open road and what they could carry in their pockets.

He left the clinic's car to charge in the basement garage under the flats and they took his car. With the top rolled back, raw power purring from the engine and a warm breeze caressing her skin, this felt a lot like sex. Although she reckoned that sex with Alex would be a lot better.

After a drive that was enough to blow the most stubborn of cobwebs away they found a picturesque pub in a picturesque village and ordered lunch to eat in the garden. The artisan burgers weren't quite as nice as they'd looked on the menu, but it didn't matter. They were taking the world as it came.

'Careful...' said Alex.

Marie had slipped off her shoes, putting her feet up on one of the plastic chairs, and luxuriating in the sun. 'Careful of what?' She opened one of her eyes, shading her face so she could see him.

'You'll catch the sun. Might even look as if you've been on holiday...' He smirked at her.

The last holiday she'd been on had been the summer before her father had left. Since then, the only thing that had seemed remotely like getting away from it all had been the times when Alex had persuaded her away from her books and out into the sunshine.

'We can't have that, can we?' She wrinkled her nose at him.

He chuckled. 'Too late. I think I see a touch of pink on your shoulder.'

'Oh, no!' Marie pretended to brush it off and Alex laughed.

'Do you want to tell me about your plans for the open day? It's only two weeks away.'

'Not right now.' Marie stifled a yawn. 'This is our afternoon off. We can go through them tomorrow.'

'I never thought I'd hear you say that. *Mañana* has never been your thing.'

Marie let the idea roll for a moment. *Mañana* never *had* been her thing, but that was because there'd always seemed to be so much to do.

'I might take it up. Take a break once every month or so.'

'Yeah... I wouldn't overdo it—you might find it becomes a habit. *Then* where would you be?'

If all her breaks were like this one she would be... happy. Marie dismissed the thought. However alluring it was, it was a fantasy.

They spent another hour in the sun together, and then Alex suggested that a film might fill the evening nicely. But after they'd driven back to his place and consulted the listings they found there was nothing that either of them particularly wanted to see.

'Shall we download something to watch?'

'That would mean making a decision, wouldn't it?' Marie was too relaxed to move.

'Yep. Good point.' He grinned, reaching for the remote for the sound system and switching it on. 'Random will do...'

'Random' did very nicely. Some soul, some rock and roll—a bit of everything.

Marie's foot started to tap against the leg of the coffee table and suddenly Alex was on his feet, catching her hand.

'You want to dance?'

She hesitated, and he shot her an imploring look. He picked up the remote and suddenly the sound swelled and the beat became irresistible.

Alex was irresistible.

Marie stood up and he swung her round, away from the sofas and towards the clear space to one side.

Alex was a great dancer. He had always moved well, and he danced without any of the tense awkwardness that made sitting it out the best choice with some partners. They seemed to fit together, anticipating each other's next steps, and by the time the rock and roll track was finished she was out of breath, falling laughingly into his arms.

There was a moment of silence in which she looked up at him, felt his body against hers, her chest rising and falling with excitement. And then the next track started.

'I love this one...'

'Me too.'

He wrapped his arms around her and they started to sway slowly to the music. Each movement was perfect. There was nothing more that she needed.

Then she felt his lips brush the side of her forehead, and realised there *was* something more she needed. She tipped her face up towards his, stretching her arms around his neck.

This was better than last night. They were truly alone, without having to worry about lipstick or someone strolling into the garden and discovering them. She could feel his body, hard against hers, still swaying to the music. But now there was another, more insistent rhythm, which gradually began to take over.

'Alex...'

He moved from her mouth to her neck, and she felt herself shudder with pleasure. Pulling at the buttons of his shirt, she slid her hand across his chest, feeling muscle move under soft skin.

They were breathing together now. He gasped as she tucked one finger under the buckle of his belt, knowing that this was a statement of intent. She intended to make him feel everything that she did.

Suddenly he lifted her off her feet. Marie wrapped her legs around his waist, feeling the hot surge of desire suddenly let loose after far too long spent denying it. He took a step and she felt her back against the wall, his hand curling protectively around her head.

'Alex...' She fumbled for the heavy belt around her jeans, trying to pull it off. 'Now. Please...*now*.'

It had to be now. While she was still lost in the powerful force of trembling expectation.

Suddenly he stilled. And as he let her gently down onto her feet he planted a tender kiss on her brow.

It was gone. The moment was gone.

'We can't, Marie. Not like this.'

One of his arms was braced against the wall above her shoulder. He seemed to be pushing himself back, away from her.

What did he mean? Not like *how*? Marie stared up at him, frustrated longing bringing tears to her eyes. She was too scared to say anything.

He picked up her hand, pressing it to his lips. 'I want to make love to you, Marie. But if we rush at it before we have a chance to think and change our minds... I need to know that you're not going to regret this when you do get a chance to think about it.'

He'd known her haste was borne of uncertainty. That

they had a lot to lose. A friendship that had lasted for years. Their work together.

He turned away from her suddenly and flipped the remote. Silence. Picking up the keys of the clinic's electric car from the coffee table and then putting them into her hand, he closed her fingers around them.

Alex wouldn't tell her to go. He didn't want her to go— she could see that in his eyes. But if she stayed, it had to be a real decision. They couldn't just let themselves be carried away by insistent desire.

They could go back now. Pick up on Monday morning and keep working together. Working together was their strength and anything else was a weakness. They could stick with what they were good at or...

They could want more.

Suddenly, she knew. Marie put the car keys down onto the coffee table. 'Alex, you're my friend, right?'

'Always. You know that, Marie...'

'We both have regrets about the past. You wish your mother had left, and I wish my father had stayed. And although we're so different we've always talked about things. I feel that whatever happens we can work it out.'

He didn't move. 'Is that a yes?'

'I trust you, Alex. It's a yes.'

The heat of his gaze was more exciting than the heavy beat of the music had been. More arousing even than his touch.

'I trust you too. My answer's yes.'

Marie stepped forward, undoing the buttons of his shirt that she hadn't already torn open. He didn't move, letting her slip it from his shoulders. When she ran her fingers across his chest he caught his breath, stifling a groan.

He reached for her, pulling her vest over her head in one swift movement that made her gasp. He traced the edge of her bra with his finger, bending to kiss her neck, and Marie felt her knees start to shake.

'Alex…?'

Just moments ago this had been unthinking desire, but now it was a true connection. If he severed it now she didn't know how she would survive.

'I've got you.'

He understood everything. He understood all her fears. And she understood his, and they'd face them together.

Alex picked her up in his arms, carrying her along the hallway and kicking the bedroom door open.

They undressed each other. Alex had thought about this so many times before, but never dared go there. He wasn't in the habit of sleeping with girlfriends on a first date, but he'd never known someone so well. The challenge was so much greater, and yet the rewards might be equally so.

It would be all right. He'd dreamed his dreams, and now that Marie held them in her hands he knew that they were safe there.

'I never imagined you'd be so exquisite.'

He'd lingered over taking off her underwear and they were both trembling now. She flushed with pleasure. Her fingertips were exploring his body, her gaze fixed on his. This was the first time he'd made love to a woman who really knew him.

'You're the only one, Marie, who knows who I am.'

'I'm not going to call you Rudolf.' She whispered the words. 'I prefer Alex.'

'So do I.'

He lifted her up, feeling the friction of their bodies healing him. He knew exactly what to do now. When he tipped her back onto the bed she gave a little cry of joy that made him feel like a king. A *real* one.

She was reaching back, her hand feeling behind her to

the curved wooden headboard. Alex grinned, warming to the task of making it as hard as possible for her to concentrate on anything but him, and she moaned, her body arching beneath his.

Long minutes of teasing ensued, but finally she managed to do what she'd set her mind on. Marie knew that about him too. She hadn't forgotten that late-night conversation between five young doctors during which Alex had declared that the best place to keep condoms was taped to the back of the headboard. Always handy to reach, and never in the way.

She pressed the packet into his hand. He wouldn't normally reach for them so soon, but he knew they were both ready now. They'd waited for this for years, and there was no denying it any more.

'I can't wait any longer, Alex. We've waited too long already...'

CHAPTER TWELVE

ALEX WAS THE kind of guy who liked to talk. Marie liked that, because he knew what to say and he also knew exactly when to stop talking.

The first time, he'd been as careful and tender as any new lover should be. It might have lasted hours if it hadn't been for the groundswell of emotion making every gesture into something that had taken them both to the very edge. When he'd pushed gently inside her they'd both known there was no going back. And when the moment had come it had gripped them both with the same splintering, tearing pleasure, ripping the world as they'd known it apart. Marie could pretend all she wanted, but things were never, ever going to be the same again.

He'd held her in much the same way as he was holding her now—curling his body around her as if she were finally truly his. They should have drifted off to sleep, but it had still been early, and light had been streaming in through the windows. Marie had felt more awake than she'd ever felt, and Alex had murmured comfortable words until shared jokes and whispered tenderness had become spiked again with longing.

That seemed like a very long time ago now. They'd made love and slept in equal measure for hours, and now it felt as if his body and hers belonged together.

'You're awake?' Marie shifted slightly in his arms as he spoke.

'I'm too comfortable to open my eyes. What's the time?'

She heard him chuckle and felt the brush of his lips against her cheek. 'Four o'clock. We don't have to get up yet.'

'Hmm... Good.' They'd been in bed for ten hours already, but Marie didn't want to move. Not yet.

'I really liked ten o'clock...'

Marie opened one eye. 'You were looking at the time?'

'You're not going to tell me that you didn't hear the clock chiming in the other room, are you?'

'Yes, I heard it. Was that ten?'

'I counted ten. Did you lose count?'

The innocence in his tone made her smile. As the clock had chimed ten she'd been astride him, and he'd taken hold of her hips, moving suddenly in the same rhythm as the sound. Marie had got to three and then lost count. A couple more thrusts and she'd started to come so hard that ten hadn't even existed.

Alex knew how to break her, and he knew how to be broken. Marie had always felt that was what sex must be all about, but this was the first time she'd allowed it to happen with anyone. He knew how to make her beg, but he had no hesitation in putting himself at the mercy of her touch.

'So what's four o'clock going to be?'

She snuggled against him, dropping a kiss onto his lips. They really shouldn't be doing this. They should both be considering the benefits of an IV drip to combat exhaustion by now.

'I can't imagine.'

The glint in Alex's eye told her that he probably could imagine and that he was doing so right now.

Marie closed her eyes again. 'Surprise me.'

His arms tightened around her and he pulled her back

against his chest. Already desire was beginning to make her tremble.

'You like this...?'

One of his hands had covered her breast and the other was moving downward, nudging her legs apart. He held her tight, dropping kisses onto her neck.

'Yes, Alex!'

She wriggled, trying to make his fingers move a little faster, and heard his low chuckle.

'Four o'clock is all for you...'

At six in the morning there was the smell of coffee. Alex had left two cups on the table beside the bed, and was gently kissing her awake. They wished each other a drowsy good morning, and Marie reached for a cup.

'Mmm. That's better.' Neither of them spoke again until the caffeine began to kick in. Then she said, 'I should be going soon.'

Alex turned the corners of his mouth down. His expression of regret was just what Marie wanted to see.

'I've got to go home for a change of clothes and a shower.'

She didn't want to go either, but the idea of turning up to work in Alex's jeans was impossible. The dress code at the clinic was relaxed, but that was a little too relaxed, and someone was sure to notice.

'You won't shower with me?'

Tempting. 'We could try to leave *one* thing for next time.'

Voicing that fantasy had prompted a slip of the tongue and turned into a suggestion that there *would* be a next time. Neither of them had broached the subject; last night had been an exercise in the here and now, and no forward planning had seemed necessary.

He grinned suddenly. 'I'm hoping that means you're not

going to break my heart and tell me that this is the first and last time this is going to happen.'

Break his heart? Marie left the thought where it belonged, along with all the other professions of love spoken in the heat of the moment.

'I want a next time, Alex.'

'Me too.' He gathered the scattered pillows and leaned back against them, putting his arm around her. 'It's not going to be easy to keep everyone from noticing at work today.'

'We could just stay in our offices.'

Marie didn't really care if everyone knew, but it was common sense not to advertise the fact when you were sleeping with someone you worked with—especially not until you knew exactly where the relationship was going.

'Nah. That's not going to work. When two people suddenly start avoiding each other at work, the first thing everyone thinks is that they're sleeping together.'

'Hmm. True. How about being so busy that we don't have time to think too much about it?'

'Might work.'

He thought for the moment. 'Although I'm not sure I can sustain that level of busy for more than a couple of hours. I guess we'll just have to wing it.'

He took the cup from her hand, putting it down on the table.

'Alex! Not again!'

'We have time. You could be half an hour late for work, couldn't you?'

'No, I couldn't. And neither could you. What kind of example is that?'

He chuckled. 'It's a dreadful example. We shouldn't do it...' His eyes flashed with boyish mischief as he raised her hand to his lips.

'There you go, then.'

She really wanted to stay…just for another fifteen minutes. But temptation was there to be resisted.

Marie pushed him away, and he flopped back onto the pillows, laughing.

'Can I at least watch you dress? Crumbs to a starving man…?' She was picking her clothes up from the floor.

'You are *not* starving, Alex.'

He couldn't possibly be—not after last night. She pulled on her underwear, and then his jeans, belting them tight around her waist. Then she crawled onto the bed, keeping the crumpled duvet between his body and hers.

'One kiss.'

'Just a kiss?' He grinned at her.

'Yes. No cheating, Alex…'

He held his hands up in a gesture of surrender. Those hands were his most potent weapon. She dipped down, planting one kiss on his lips, thrilling at his sigh of disappointment as she left him, hurrying into the sitting room to find her top and shoes.

She drove home in the clinic's electric car, with the radio playing and Alex's scent still on her body. Even after she'd showered it felt like she was still his. He'd claimed her, and she couldn't escape by merely being apart from him.

She dressed, drying her hair in front of the mirror. There was something different…something she couldn't quite put her finger on. Her expression made her look like the cat that had got the cream, and try as she might she couldn't persuade her face to assume her usual smile.

But Marie need not have worried. When she saw Alex at the clinic, he smiled his usual greeting. He made the Monday morning meeting easy, not seeking out her gaze but not afraid to meet it. He acted as if last night had never happened. If anyone should divine that something earth-shaking had happened to her over the weekend, they never would have connected Alex with it.

It was slightly unnerving. Marie didn't want anyone to know any more than he did, but her vanity felt he might have made this appear a little more difficult.

But it was just the way Alex was. He was protecting his privacy and hers. He'd grown up learning to maintain a face for the world that didn't show any of his true feelings, and it had become a matter of habit for him. She shouldn't confuse that with the real Alex. The one who'd made love to her last night, who'd listened to her heart calling him, and whose heart had replied so eloquently.

Alex had phoned the hospital and the news was good. Charlie's leg had been operated on yesterday afternoon and he was recovering well. Zack was eager to visit him, and Alex had said he'd go too. Marie had decided that three around his bed might be a little too much for Charlie, so she contented herself with packing a bag full of things he might need, along with a few treats, and had given it to Zack to take in.

'So how is he?' When Alex walked into her office later, she breathed a sigh of relief that she no longer had to pretend to work while she waited for them to get back.

'He's okay.' Alex closed the door behind him and sat down. 'He's pretty sore and he's got a real shiner. But I spoke to his surgeon and he'll mend.'

'Great. That's good.'

Marie wondered if she was supposed to keep the pretence up now that they were alone. Perhaps the rule was that they only referred to last night when they were off clinic premises.

'I saw his mother as well. I told her we'll provide whatever Charlie needs in the way of rehab and that either you or I will personally oversee his case.'

'Good. Thanks. She's happy with that?'

Knowing what to do with her hands was a problem. She'd known exactly what to do with them last night, but that wasn't appropriate here.

'She asked me to thank you for everything you did yesterday. Charlie might well have bled to death if it hadn't been for your decisive action.'

Marie's heart was beating even faster than it had been. Rolling a pencil round and round in her fingers took the edge off the tension a little. 'It's...you know...'

He grinned. 'Yes, I know. All in a day's work.'

So far there was nothing. Not even any of the in-jokes that they cracked all the time. Marie could do this. She just wished that there was one hint from Alex that he hadn't already left last night behind. That he didn't regret it.

'I've sent Zack out to get an MP3 player and a decent pair of headphones. Charlie's phone got smashed in the accident and the hospital radio doesn't play his kind of thing.'

Marie frowned. 'What is his kind of thing?'

'I'm not completely sure. Zack's going to help me with that; we'll download some music for him after work. You want to join us?'

Something sparked in his eyes. Maybe it was just the mention of music, and the prospect of exploring a few new artists. But even if it was just that, the thought of spending a few hours with two of her favourite people was incredibly tempting.

'I can't—sorry. I'd like to, but I promised I'd call round and see Mum after work. She wants a chat.'

A crease formed on Alex's brow. 'Okay.'

It wasn't okay with Marie. She wished now that she'd asked her mother whether it really needed to be tonight, instead of just automatically acquiescing. But that was what she'd always done before.

'We'll miss you.'

What would have happened if he'd said that before? All

the times when their friends at medical school had gone
to play softball in the park, or gone to the pub to talk out
a long day's work.

Marie dismissed the idea. She'd always tried not to
think about the things she was missing out on, and concentrate on the things she needed to do instead.

Suddenly he got to his feet, leaning across the desk
towards her. Meeting Alex's gaze was hard, because his
grey eyes held all of the promise of last night. It wasn't
over between them.

'Could I persuade you to come back to mine after
you've seen your mother?'

The pencil snapped suddenly in her fingers. Marie
jumped, dropping it onto the desk, and saw the edge of
Alex's mouth curve.

'Yes. That was what I had in mind, too.'

'You want to snap pencils with me?'

'All night.'

'I might be late… I won't get away from Mum's before
about nine.'

'I'll wait. I have a spare door key downstairs; you can
let yourself in. And take one of the clinic cars—you'll get
back to me sooner…'

'It's an emergency?'

'Yes.'

He brushed a kiss on her lips and her whole body went
into overdrive. Definitely an emergency…

It was ten o'clock before Alex heard the key turning in
the door of his flat. He'd decided to go to bed and allow
himself to doze a little before Marie arrived. She'd know
where he was.

She did. He heard her footsteps in the hallway and the
light outside being flipped off. The warm glow of the

lamp in the corner of the bedroom threw shadows across the floor.

Alex watched as she took her clothes off. No words. She knew he couldn't take his eyes off her, and it seemed that her movements were slower and more deliberate than usual. She took the time to hang her dress carefully across the back of the easy chair that stood next to the lamp, and he devoured the shadows that played across her body.

When she was naked, she walked over to the bed. She hesitated, as if she'd forgotten something, and then ran her fingers across one breast and down towards her stomach. The sudden urgent wish to take her now crashed over him, but he resisted it. Waiting would make the having so much better.

'Get into bed...'

His words sounded suspiciously like an order, which made Marie smile. Her movements seemed to slow even more and Alex grinned. She knew exactly how to tease him.

When she slipped under the duvet he moved towards her, wrapping his arms around her but keeping thick layers of down between them. He could tease too.

Alex leaned forward, planting a kiss on her mouth, and she let out a gasp.

'Everything okay?' He smiled innocently at her.

'Yes. Mum just wanted to say how pleased she was about Zack.' She turned the corners of her mouth down. 'She could have said that when she called me.'

Alex resisted the temptation to agree. He loved the way that Marie was so close to her family, and wished he could have had a measure of that himself. It was hypocritical to say that he wished they'd give her a bit more time to herself. Because what he really meant was that *he* wanted her time.

'We've got a few hours to catch up on...' she said, disentangling her arm from the duvet, caressing the side of his face.

'Hey... You know I don't mind if you've got something else to do.' Tearing Marie in two wasn't going to solve the problem—it would only make things worse.

'I know you don't. But *I* mind.'

The thought shattered the last of his self-control—that Marie had wanted to give up the responsibilities that she clung to so ferociously in favour of this.

He pulled the duvet away from them and rolled her over onto her back, covering her body with his. She could see and feel how much he wanted her.

'Where do you most want to be now?'

He wanted to hear it. If she screamed it out, then all the better. He wanted every moment she spent with him to be time that she didn't want to be anywhere else.

Her eyes darkened suddenly, the light playing that trick he loved so much and turning them to midnight blue. Marie reached behind her, giving an impatient huff when she remembered that they'd used all the condoms taped to his headboard last night. Her fingers searched the surface of the bedside table until she found the packet he'd bought on his way home.

He gritted his teeth, waiting while she fumbled with the wrappings. Then she reached down, and he felt his blood begin to boil as she carefully rolled the condom into place.

When she took him inside her it felt as if he was coming home after a long journey. He stared into her eyes, watching every small movement, listening to the way her breathing started to quicken and match his as he pushed deeper.

One moment of stillness.

They spent it wisely, feeling the warm sensations of being together at last.

Then Marie's lips parted. 'Here, Alex. I want to be right here.'

CHAPTER THIRTEEN

ALEX HAD ENVISAGED a rather sedate affair for the clinic's open day—a Saturday afternoon spent coaxing people in with the promise of free coffee and then showing them around to give them an idea of what the clinic could offer to the community.

Marie had dismissed that idea with a wave of her hand and started to search the internet for someone who could supply bunting.

Alex knew that Marie thrived on organising this kind of thing and he'd passed the preparations to her, taking over her clinic caseload for a week while she appeared and disappeared, off on various missions to secure the things that they simply couldn't do without. When they were alone at night he got her undivided attention. Alex had always reckoned that sex was a pleasant addition to a relationship, but when he had Marie in his arms it was more important than breathing.

He arrived at eight in the morning the day of the open day, six hours before the doors were due to open, and found that a bouncy castle was already being set up on the grassy area at the back of the clinic. When he walked into the café, he found Marie supervising a couple of Jim Armitage's men, who were manoeuvring a piano into place.

'Where did you get this?' Alex ran his finger over the

wooden frame. It was a good one, and had clearly been
polished recently.

'I found it in the outhouse where Jim puts all the things
you ask him to get rid of.' She tapped her nose, in the way
that Jim did when he was about to impart a pearl of wis-
dom. 'You never know what might come in handy.'

'I thought it was just old pieces of wood. What else is
in there?'

'Loads of stuff. I found one of those old-style black-
boards, with a wooden stand. You should go and take a
look sometime. This was from the school music room.' She
opened the lid that covered the keyboard. 'I had it tuned.'

Alex hadn't seen or heard the coming or the going of
a piano tuner. Marie's innocent look indicated that she'd
probably kept that activity well away from his notice.

'What are you going to do with it?'

Alex supposed it might make a nice piece of furniture
for the café. Marie had added a few things in there to make
the clean lines into a more welcoming area.

'Well, we could always play it. We've got some people
coming to sing this afternoon; I thought it might help break
down a few barriers.'

'So that's where you and Zack disappeared off to the
other evening. Auditions?'

Marie nodded. 'I've got an a capella group. A few of
them are backing singers for other bands, and they look
and sound marvellous.'

'Great.' Alex had no doubt he'd approve of her choice.

'Why don't you try it out?'

She opened the lid that covered the piano keys and Alex
reluctantly jabbed a couple of notes with his finger.

'Sounds as if it has a good tone.'

Marie rolled her eyes. 'Come on, Alex, I know you
can play.'

Long hours at the piano when he was a child had seen

to that. But Alex didn't play any more. Apart from just that one time…

'I don't think Christmas carols are going to be appropriate for today.'

She rolled her eyes. 'I don't know all that much about music, but I know that anyone who can play Christmas carols with the kind of tempo that gets a whole ward full of kids singing along can play pretty much anything.'

That had been a good evening. A Father Christmas had turned up from a local charity, but no one had admitted to being able to play the piano that had stood in the corner of the family room on the children's ward. Alex had sat down, and the kids' faces had made him forget for a while that all the piano meant to him was rapped knuckles.

'I haven't played for years.'

She flashed him an imploring smile. 'It's like riding a bike, isn't it? Do you know this one?'

She started to sing, her voice wavering up and down, somehow managing to hit every note but the right one. He grinned. Marie had never been able to carry a tune, and it was yet another thing that was perfect about her. But he could recognise which song she meant from the words and he picked it out with one finger.

'That's the one.' She gave him a thumbs-up.

He'd do anything to make Marie happy—even this. So Alex sat down, trying a few chords and then moving down a key. That was better. He was rusty, but he could still play.

Alex operated the volume pedal and added a little oomph to the tune, gratified at the way she smiled, moving to the music. He improvised, adding a few extra choruses. He was enjoying watching her.

When he'd finished, a muffled round of applause came from the kitchen.

Marie shot him an I-told-you-so look. 'That's great. I wish you'd play more.'

Alex was almost tempted. But in a world where everything seemed to be changing he had to hang on to a few of the rules he'd made for himself when he'd left home.

'I don't have good memories of playing the piano. You wouldn't either if you'd been at one of my father's music evenings. Twenty adults, all staring at you, just waiting for you to make a slip.'

'It sounds awful, Alex. But you love music—you always have. You have a talent, and you can't let anything take that away from you. And...well, the a capella band did tell me they have a couple of numbers that they usually sing with backing tracks...'

'Even if I wanted to, I can't just sit down and play for them. There's such a thing as rehearsal.'

Marie shrugged awkwardly. 'They'll be here soon to set up their equipment. There's plenty of time before we open the gates to the public.'

Alex sighed. 'Have I just been set up?'

She capitulated so suddenly that he almost hugged her. Marie was the one person he couldn't resist, and her transparency made her all the more seductive.

'No. Well...yes. But not really. The band have a recorded backing track they can use.'

'So that's not quite a yes. But it's not a no, either.'

She gave him an agonised look. 'I always wondered why you didn't play—you're so good. When you told me about your father I put two and two together. But this is...it's *your* place. You should fill it with your sound. Of course, if you really don't want to...'

He held up his hand and Marie fell silent. 'Send them through when they arrive. I'll help them set up their equipment.'

'So that's a yes?'

'Not quite. But it's not a no, either.'

'Okay. Good.'

She gave him a ravishing smile and hurried away.

Marie could have made more of a mess of that, but she wasn't sure how. Although Alex hadn't seemed too cross, and he was at least going to talk to the a capella band.

There was plenty left to do. She had to make sure all the examination rooms were locked, and call Sonya to check that she had their special guests in hand. Then rescue Zack before he got himself completely buried under piles of bunting, and make sure the cafeteria staff had everything they needed…

The bouncy castle was inflating nicely, and when the band arrived she sent them through to the cafeteria. Zack appeared, red-faced and grinning, declaring that the bunting was finally all under control.

'Who's playing the piano?'

Soft strains of music were floating through into the reception area. A few chords, and then a woman's voice, singing a few bars and then stopping as player and singer began to adjust to each other.

'Um… Alex, probably.'

'He plays?' Zack took a few steps in the direction of the music. 'I've got to see this.'

'No, I need you here.' Marie frowned at her brother.

'But…'

'Help me get these display boards up.'

This was something Alex needed to do on his own for a while. The woman's voice had begun to swell, more powerful now, and she could hear Alex beginning to follow her lead. They didn't need any interruptions.

Zack pulled a face. 'Okay, where do you want them…'

The countdown seemed to fly by. Sonya arrived, along

with the special guests she'd promised to bring—a foot-baller and a runner—who ceremonially opened the gates at two o'clock to let the small crowd that had gathered in.

The sun shone, and more people came. The sound of voices and music echoed through from the cafeteria, and the two celebrities set up shop in the reception area to sign autographs and smile for an endless number of photographs.

The clinic staff were all busy showing small groups around and answering questions, the café was packed, and the bouncy castle was a big hit with the children. People were sitting out on the grass at the back of the clinic, just enjoying the sun. Sonya had the reception area well under control, and Alex was nowhere to be seen.

When she heard the singers stop for a break, and the strains of the piano drifted through from the cafeteria, Marie smiled. Finally she felt that she might join him.

The lead singer of the a capella group, a shy woman who suddenly became a force of nature when she opened her mouth to sing, was standing by the piano, tapping her foot and drinking a glass of lemonade. When she put her glass down and nodded to Alex, he smiled, working the music around to what seemed to be an agreed point, when the woman started to sing.

It was breathtaking. Full of energy and soul. And both of them were clearly enjoying themselves.

Marie sat down in the corner of the cafeteria and Zack hurried up, putting a cappuccino down on the table in front of her before turning to help the serving staff. Everything was under control.

This was what the clinic was all about. A community helping each other. It was about Alex too. She'd asked him if he thought that the clinic would save him. Watching him here, it seemed that it just might.

* * *

Saturday had been great. Sunday had been delicious and lazy. Monday was nerve-racking.

'Are you nervous?' she asked.

Alex didn't look a bit nervous; he looked handsome and dapper in his dark blue suit.

'Terrified. You?' He shot her a smile across the bedroom.

'I don't think this dress is right. And my jacket's far too bright...' Her make-up was probably wrong as well, for a TV appearance, and Marie hoped that part of the reason they had to be at the studio hours before their scheduled appearance was because they would fix that.

'You look gorgeous. Anyway, the whole purpose of a dark suit is to show off the woman next to you.'

Marie wasn't sure that made her feel any better. She'd rather fade into the background and have Alex take the glare of the attention they were hoping to generate.

'I'm a doctor, Alex. Not a mannequin.'

'Who says you can't be a stunningly beautiful doctor? The two aren't mutually exclusive.'

'Stop.' She held her hand up. 'I know you mean well, but you're not making this any easier.'

'Does this?'

He walked around the bed, enveloping her in the kind of careful hug that was designed not to crease their jackets, but still felt warm and reassuring.

'What happened to being able to do anything together?'

'It's live TV, Alex!'

'We've built a clinic and we can do this.'

Marie nodded, disentangling herself from his arms and smoothing the front of his jacket. He was steady and secure, like a rock. She just had to remember not to hang on to him too much in public, however much she might want to. She knew Alex wasn't ready to let that mask of his slip yet. He guarded his private life fiercely.

The car arrived to take them to the TV studio and they drove through clear streets, bathed in early-morning light. She slipped her hand into his, knowing that this was breaking all their rules about keeping their relationship strictly behind closed doors, but not really caring. Alex's touch might be subtle, and he didn't kiss her fingers the way he had before they'd left his flat, but it was enough to keep her from panicking and trying to jump out of the car when it stopped at a red light.

A cheery make-up girl applied lipstick in a shade that seemed too bold for Marie, explaining that it would look much the same as her normal colour under the lights of the studio. They were shuffled from one place to another by various production assistants, and finally they walked onto the set.

Alex was standing to one side, to let her go first, but still keeping protectively close. The presenters of the morning show beamed at them, murmuring a few words of encouragement. They were clearly used to dealing with nervous guests.

First there was a short film about the clinic that had been made earlier in the week. Sonya had picked out all the elements which were most important in the accompanying press release, and the questions were easy enough. Alex answered his with exactly the kind of friendly approachability that they wanted to be the hallmark of the clinic, and Marie managed to get through hers without stumbling.

It was going well. She kept her gaze on the two presenters, trying not to look at Alex. She knew he was there with her, and that gave her courage.

Then the female presenter leaned forward, smiling at Alex. 'I believe that it's your inheritance that has made the clinic possible, Alex?'

Too close for comfort. But Alex's face didn't show any of the dismay that Marie felt.

'I count myself fortunate in having been able to use it to do so.'

'And as you've also inherited a royal title...' the presenter paused for effect '...I think we can all agree that you're one of London's most eligible bachelors now. Is there any chance that we have a royal wedding to look forward to?'

The woman was being deliberately challenging. Marie wondered whether strangling her on live TV would be considered an appropriate response, and glanced up at Alex.

His smile didn't change. 'I'd far rather everyone saw me as a doctor. One who's working a little too hard to contemplate romance at the moment.'

'You're sure...?'

The male presenter shot a pointed look at Marie, and she wondered whether her body language had given her away. She'd been so frightened that maybe she'd unconsciously sat a little too close to Alex on the sofa.

'I'd love to think that there's a woman out there who could put up with me.' Alex's tone took on an appropriately rueful note. 'But I'm still waiting to find her.'

The female presenter laughed, looking quickly at the overhead screen. 'Well, I think we have a few offers coming in already on our social media feeds. Thank you, Alex and Marie, for being with us this morning.'

A new topic was started, and the programme cut to a filmed report. The two presenters thanked them again, and they were hurried off the set. Marie's heart was beating so fast she could hardly breathe.

As soon as they left the glare of the cameras Alex's face turned ashen. Marie grabbed his arm. 'Not a word...' she said. Not until they could talk privately.

He nodded down at her. The kind of decision-making that had seen them through so many medical emergencies would get them through this one.

They walked back to the small dressing room where they'd left their things, and quietly managed to elude anyone who might stop them. The receptionist called after them, asking if they were going to wait for their taxi there, and Marie gave a smiling shake of her head while Alex kept walking. As soon as they were on the pavement he hailed a taxi, and to Marie's relief the driver saw him and stopped to pick them up.

'I suppose it was going to happen sooner or later. I'll speak to Sonya,' Alex said. His whole body was tense, as if he was waiting for some new blow to appear from somewhere. 'It can't hurt the clinic so much now. We've started to establish ourselves in the community and people know what we're about. We just have to hold on to our values and try to keep the press away.'

Clinic first. Always. But this had to hurt Alex. He'd spent so much time leaving his past behind, and now it had come back to haunt him in the most public way possible.

'My father would have *loved* this.' There was a trace of bitterness in his voice. 'Just think—all he had to do was one good deed and the press would have come snapping at his heels.'

'He missed a trick there.' Marie tried to lighten the mood between them, and Alex smiled grimly.

They both knew that with a little careful management this wouldn't compromise their work at the clinic, but it had raised a question that neither of them wanted to answer just yet. If Alex was going to be caught in the media's spotlight, what would happen to their relationship?

Alex fell silent, his face clouded with worry. When the cab drew up outside his mansion block he paid the cabbie and wished him a good day. He didn't say another word until they were inside his front door.

'I'll protect you. I'll make sure none of this touches you,' he said.

Marie suppressed the urge to shake him. 'What if I don't want you to protect me?'

'This isn't the time, Marie. I know you can do everything by yourself, but things would be a lot easier if you'd let me help.'

Her face was itching from the heavy make-up and suddenly all Marie wanted was to be alone. 'I'm going to wash my face…'

He nodded, and she escaped to the bathroom, washing her face and splashing it with cold water.

Sonya had been right. Alex's royal heritage and his determination to do something good with it was a great story. He was one of the most eligible bachelors in London, and of course there would be interest in his love life. What had she been thinking when she'd got involved with him?

She'd been thinking about his touch. About how they got each other, as best friends *and* as lovers. She hadn't been thinking about the practicalities, about how when the news became public she'd be standing with him in the glare. About how she'd cope with navigating his world when she had no compass.

She wanted to get out of these clothes. She went to the bedroom, changed into a pair of comfortable trousers and a shirt. She heard the phone ring and the low resonance of his voice.

'No. No comment… You can speak to Sonya Graham-Hall about any publicity matters to do with the clinic. You have her number… No, I really don't have anything else to say…'

When she went back into the sitting room the jack for

the landline lay unplugged on the floor and he was holding his mobile against his ear.

One minute...

He mouthed the words, holding up his finger to indicate that the call wouldn't last long, and then spoke into the phone.

'Hi, Sonya. Did you see it?'

Suddenly Marie didn't want to listen to this. She went into the kitchen and set the kettle to boil, making two mugs of tea. When she heard Alex stop talking, she walked back into the sitting room.

'Thanks.' Alex was in full damage-control mode now. He took the tea, putting it down on the coffee table in front of him. 'I've spoken to Sonya, and she's going to field all the press enquiries for now. We don't answer any questions from anyone.'

'Okay.' That sounded sensible enough. 'So what do you think we should do?'

He pressed his lips together. 'I don't see that we have much choice. We don't see each other for a while—until this all blows over.'

'I have a choice. I can stand by you.'

'You don't want this, Marie. You've told me yourself that you're not comfortable with my royal status, and it's about to get a whole lot worse.'

'I never said that!' Marie reddened. She'd demonstrated it, though, by refusing to wear the diamond. Actions spoke louder than words.

'Are you going to tell me you'd be happy with that kind of notoriety?'

'No. But I don't have to be happy with it, Alex. If it's who you are then that's what I'll be.'

'That's...'

His gaze softened for a moment, and Marie though he was about to relent. Then steel showed in his eyes again.

'I've seen the damage that can do, and I won't let you do it, Marie.'

'But I *want* to do it. I don't want to be the kind of person who thinks the best thing to do when things get tough is to walk away. My father did that, and I've been dealing with the consequences ever since.'

That was the difference between them. It wasn't just a matter of lifestyle—although it terrified Marie to think she might be catapulted into a world where she felt like a fish out of water. They'd both lived through different versions of an unhappy childhood, and they'd always have different solutions for life's problems.

Tears suddenly blurred her vision, burning like acid. Maybe the answer to this was that there *was* no answer. That there was nothing either of them could do to make it right.

He got to his feet. 'Perhaps we should talk about this later. I have to go over to see Sonya, to work up a press release. Just the basic facts; she reckons that'll give us some breathing space.'

That was probably wise. It would give them both a little time to cool off. Although in truth Alex looked perfectly cool now. He'd switched off, retreating behind the mask he'd worn all his life—the one he'd hidden behind as a child, which had protected him from his past ever since.

'Yes, okay. You'll go back to the clinic?'

'Yes, I'll see you there.'

He turned away. When Marie heard the front door close it sounded just the same as it always did. She'd almost prefer that he'd slammed it—at least it would have given some hint of what was going on in his head.

She should go to work. By the time Alex returned to the clinic she'd be calm. And when they came back here they'd go to the bedroom and forget all about their differences.

Maybe.

Marie picked up the overnight bag into which she'd folded her dress and jacket, collecting up the other odds and ends that had found their way here and putting them into it too. A comb and a tub of moisturiser. A book that she was only halfway through, which lay on the kitchen table. The pages were creased at one corner from where it had been dropped on the floor, discarded when Alex had leaned over to kiss her and passion had made her forget everything else. Tears pricked at the corners of her eyes and she stuffed it quickly into her bag.

She didn't need to do this. Gathering up her things seemed so final…as if a decision had been made. People argued all the time…

But Marie couldn't see the way back from this. As she closed his front door behind her the click of the latch seemed to mark an ending.

Alex's meeting with Sonya lasted half an hour. She'd seen that he couldn't concentrate, and had kept it short and simple. 'Just tell me what you want and I'll handle it,' had just about covered it.

He took a taxi back to his flat, but Marie was already gone. That at least gave him some time alone, to think. He just wanted to take shelter from a world that wanted to know nothing about *him* and everything about his royal connections.

Running to the comfort of Marie's arms would ease his pain, but it was the same as hiding inside the walls of the clinic. If he was going to protect them—Marie and the clinic—he had to distance himself from them both for a little while.

Sonya would manage things, and a few well-chosen media releases and interviews would draw the press away from the gates of the clinic, so their patients didn't have to run the gauntlet of photographers. It would draw them away from Marie, as well, so she didn't have to face the bright glare of publicity.

Marie would never forgive him if he walked away. She'd told him already that she would stand by him, but he'd never forgive himself if her commitment to the job, to the clinic, to his dream, meant she had to change in an attempt to fit in with what she thought was expected of her.

If he stayed he'd lose her completely, but if he left there was a chance that their friendship might survive.

For the last few weeks he'd been beyond happy, and he'd allowed himself to think that maybe he did know how to make a relationship different from his parents' marriage. But he'd fallen at the first hurdle.

When he finally made a move, changing out of his crumpled suit and making his way back to the clinic, he knew what he had to do. Marie was in a staff meeting that was due to last for the rest of the afternoon, and he waited until Tina, the receptionist, popped her head around his office door.

'Everyone's gone for the evening. It's just you and Marie.'

'Thanks, Tina. Have a good evening.'

'You too. Are you okay…?'

Tina shot him a puzzled look, and Alex nodded and smiled back at her. The last thing he wanted was to make his relationship troubles the talk of the clinic.

He heard the front doors open and then slam shut again. He had to do it now. Before his courage failed him and wanting Marie took over, driving everything else from his mind.

Alex walked upstairs, feeling his burden increase with every step. Marie's office door was open and he stopped in the doorway, afraid that if he went in and sat down he wouldn't be able to do this.

She looked up from the papers in front of her and her

eyes seemed suddenly hollow, as if she hadn't slept for a week. 'You're back.'

'Yes.'

No invitation to come in and sit down. It seemed Marie had nothing to say to him—which was fair enough because he had nothing to say to her. They'd always understood each other, and they understood this as well.

He took a breath. 'I think we should stop. For good. We'll tear each other to pieces if we don't.'

She nodded. 'Yes. I think so too.'

That was the most difficult part and it had been achieved in a matter of a few words. Alex bit back the temptation to fall on his knees and beg her to fight him. That would just prolong the agony, because he and Marie had never been meant to be together.

'I'm going to bring forward my trip,' he said.

The trip had been planned for him to scout out sites for new clinics around the country. It was an ideal excuse to get him away from London for a couple of weeks.

'After that I'll be concentrating on development, so I'll be working from home most of the time.'

'But… No… I'll clear out my things. There are plenty of jobs for qualified doctors in London. I'll just call an agency and I'll have another job by the weekend.'

She was regarding him steadily, her lip trembling and her eyes filling with tears. This wasn't what he'd meant to happen at all.

'What? No, Marie. We always kept our private lives separate from our work before. You can't leave.'

He knew he was in no position to tell her what she could or couldn't do. Thankfully Marie overlooked that.

'I'm not sure I can stay, either.'

Alex thought fast. It was beyond unfair that a broken relationship meant Marie felt she had to walk away from her job. If she decided to leave he'd make sure she was paid until the end of the year, but that wasn't the point. She'd put her heart into this place and given it life. It was as much hers as it was his, and she'd see that once the initial shock of their parting had subsided.

'Stay for a couple of weeks at least. I need you to be here while I'm away. We can talk again when I get back.'

She nodded. 'All right. Just until then, Alex.'

It was almost a relief to walk away from her, so he could no longer see the pain in her beautiful eyes. He'd never wanted to hurt Marie, but all he'd brought her was sorrow. He'd come to love this place, but he'd give it up a thousand times over if it meant she would stay.

He needed her in his life, and he hoped desperately that in time they'd learn to be friends again, but he was beginning to doubt that. There was no coming back from this.

CHAPTER FOURTEEN

IT HAD BEEN ten days since she'd seen Alex. He'd walked out of the clinic that evening and Marie had been able to hold back her tears only just long enough to hear the main doors close downstairs. Then she'd got unsteadily out of her chair and walked over to the corner of her office. Sliding down the wall, she'd curled up on the floor, sobbing.

But they'd done the right thing. They needed completely different things from a relationship, and it never could have worked. That didn't mean it hurt any less.

The emails had started the following day. Alex's first one had been short and polite, and Marie had replied in the same vein. They'd loosened up a little as the days went by and his itinerary took him further and further away from London. Maybe after a year or so one of them might crack a joke.

She missed him so much. Her head wanted him and her body ached for him. Sofia Costa had asked if she was coming down with something, and Zack had noticed too.

'What's up, sis?' He wandered into her office now, carrying a packet of sandwiches, and plumped himself down, offering her one.

Marie took it, wondering whether he'd made extra this morning just for the purpose of sharing.

'What's this?' She peeled one of the slices of bread up. 'Ah…cream cheese and cucumber. Thanks.'

Zack nodded. He knew that was one of her favourites. 'I've made egg and bacon as well.'

Zack was definitely on a mission to spoil her. Marie smiled at him, grateful for both the sandwiches and his concern. Her little brother had come a long way in the last few months.

'Is something going on? Between you and Alex?' he asked.

'What…?' Marie almost choked on her sandwich. 'What makes you think that?'

'Well, he's never around any more. You know that's always a sign there's something going on…when two people start avoiding each other at work.' Zack nodded sagely.

'Where did you get that from?' Clearly not from his own experience; Zack hadn't managed to hold a job down for more than a week before he came here. Marie wondered if people at the clinic were talking.

'It was in a film on TV. Two people started an affair and all the people at work knew because they suddenly started being really horrible to each other.'

'Well, I'm not having an affair with Alex.' That was strictly true—she wasn't having one with him any more. And she wouldn't be having one with him in the future, either. 'And he's not been around because he's in Edinburgh at the moment, talking to people about possible sites for a new clinic.'

'Only half an hour away by air… You were looking pretty tired on Monday—'

'Stop!' Marie brought her hand down onto her desk and Zack jumped. 'I haven't been sleeping so well recently.'

Zack frowned. 'So what is it, then?'

'Nothing. Really.' Marie decided this was as good a time as any to tell Zack. 'I'm going to be leaving the clinic.'

Zack's eyes widened in shock. 'But why? You love it here.'

'It's…not what I thought it would be. I'm not with the patients as much as when I was working at the hospital.'

'I thought you liked it? You know…developing stuff. Finding solutions.'

She did. But it was the only reason that Marie had been able to think of which didn't involve talking about her split with Alex. She wasn't able to do that just yet without dissolving into tears.

'It's a lot of paperwork. But, Zack, this won't affect your job here. That's between you and Alex, and my going won't make any difference.' Marie knew Alex would honour his agreement with Zack, whatever happened.

Zack thought for a moment. 'I want to stay. I like it here.'

And Zack had been more than pulling his weight. He'd turned into an asset for the clinic, and people were beginning to depend on him.

'Like I said, my leaving doesn't make any difference to your position here.'

'Okay. Thanks.' Zack was obviously a little unhappy with this, but he'd run out of questions to ask. Instead he offered her another sandwich. 'Bacon and egg?'

'Thanks. I'll keep it for later, if you don't mind.'

Their email conversation hadn't been an easy one, but Marie had been determined. She couldn't stay at the clinic. Even when Alex wasn't there everything about it reminded her of him. She had to make a clean break. And it wasn't fair that he was staying away, because she knew he loved the place. He'd built it and she wanted him to have it.

He'd protested, but she'd stood firm, because she knew it was the best thing for both of them. They'd agreed that she should stay on for another week, until he was back, and that he'd take on her current medical and management duties after that.

It was where he was supposed to be. It was where he'd always intended to be, and Marie was just making things right.

She cleared out her office, trying not to cry over the box of pink paper clips and the lava lamp that Alex had given her. Then she said her goodbyes to everyone and left. Alex would be coming to the clinic tomorrow, and she wouldn't even lay eyes on him.

The next two weeks were hard. She missed Alex every day. She missed the clinic every day. But she kept going, cleaning her flat from top to bottom and applying for jobs. Running in the park, with the express purpose of exhausting herself so that she'd sleep. Sometimes it worked and sometimes it didn't.

But today was a good day. There were two emails asking her to job interviews. The sun was shining. She still missed Alex, but even that was beginning to subside from a sharp, insistent pain to a dull ache. Her life would never be the same without him, but it could still mean something. She could still make a difference.

She replied to both the emails, saying she'd be there at the times stated, and sorted through her wardrobe to find a suitable outfit. Her red jacket might go nicely with a plain dress, but that was still in her overnight bag, creased and crumpled. Marie hadn't been able to bear opening it to go through all the things that had once been at Alex's flat.

The doorbell rang and she pressed the Entryphone. That would be Zack. She opened the front door of her flat and went into the kitchen to put the kettle on. She heard footsteps on the stairs, and then a quiet knock on the door.

'Come *in*, Zack.' Why was he messing around knocking at the door?

'It's not Zack.'

Marie froze. Alex's voice. When she looked out into the hallway she could see him, standing outside the open door.

He looked tall, tired and handsome. Marie swallowed down the lump in her throat, willing her heart to slow down, but it ignored her.

'Alex… I'm sorry, I was expecting Zack.'

Polite was the way to go. They'd been ruthlessly polite in their emails and that had worked. Perhaps it would work in person, too.

'I wanted to talk to you. I asked Zack if he knew whether you'd be at home this morning.'

Light suddenly dawned. Zack had called her, asking if she'd be in, because he had something for her. It was Alex. Seeing Alex again was what Zack had for her. She was going to kill him.

'Well, come in.' She switched on a smile that didn't feel even vaguely natural. 'I dare say I've got things mixed up.'

He was holding the soft leather briefcase that he used for his laptop and papers. Perhaps he needed to speak to her about something to do with the clinic, in which case she was going to be professional. She wouldn't cry, and she wouldn't hold on to him, begging him to stay.

'Thanks.' He stepped into her hallway, closing the door behind him. They were standing twenty feet away from each other, but suddenly he seemed very close.

'I'll make coffee. Go and sit down.'

She motioned him towards the sitting room and he nodded a thank-you. Good. Two minutes to breathe deeply and try to recover her composure.

By the time she carried the coffee into the sitting room she was feeling a little giddy. Maybe the deep breathing had been a bad idea.

'What can I do for you?' She didn't dare say his name. Not after she'd whispered it so many times to herself in the dark hours of the night. 'Something to do with the clinic?'

'No.'

He opened his briefcase, reaching inside and producing a large thick book, bound with an elastic closure. He put it down on the coffee table, laying his hand on it as if he were about to swear an oath on it. Whatever the oath was, it seemed to be a matter of some importance to him; he was looking unbearably tense.

'This is my life. Everything about me. It's for you.'

She stared at him. Perhaps he'd been in therapy and this was his homework. If that was the case, she wished it hadn't brought him here to seek closure.

'The final pages are blank…'

'Alex, I'm not sure this is a good idea.' Closure was going to take a little longer than this for her. Her whole life, if the last few weeks were anything to go by.

'They're blank because I want you to write them with me. We both want the same things, but we've both struggled with a way to find those things. I love you, and I believe we can find a way together.'

It was as if the sun had just emerged from behind a cloud. Light streamed into a very dark place.

'You love me?'

'Yes, I do. Tell me now if you don't feel—'

'I love you too, Alex.' Now wasn't the time to listen to him work his way through any of the other options. 'I always have.'

He leaned forward, stretching out his hand. Reaching for her across the chasm that divided them.

'I've always loved you too, Marie. I couldn't put the past behind me, and that broke us apart. But I want to make this work and I'll do anything to be the man you want. I'll stick by you always, whatever happens.'

Marie reached for him, putting her hand in his. 'And I'll never give in to you. You'll never make me into someone that I'm not.'

He grinned suddenly. 'I know. I shouldn't have underestimated you.'

She could feel herself trembling. All she had to do was give herself to him, and it was the only thing she wanted to do. She and Alex could do anything they wanted…

'I only want you, Alex. Just as you are.'

The urgency of her need to be close to him took him by surprise. Marie bolted across the top of the coffee table and fell into his arms, kissing him. He caught his breath and then kissed her back with the same hunger that she felt.

'Just as I am? Crown and all?' His lips curved into a delicious smile. 'You're sure about that, now?'

'I'm sure.'

When he kissed her again, it all seemed wonderfully simple.

It was the best day of Alex's life. They were both finally free.

Marie had reached for the book he'd been labouring over for the past couple of weeks, pulling it onto her lap, but they hadn't been able to stop kissing each other. It had slipped unnoticed to the floor when he lifted her up to carry her to her bedroom. She'd practically torn off his clothes, and he'd been just as eager. If this was what commitment was like, then he was its new biggest fan.

'What do you want to do? Apart from spending the rest of your life with me…?' he asked. Marie had told him that already, and he'd voiced his own pledge. He belonged to her, and he always would.

'Mmm…' She stretched in his arms. 'I want to shower with you and then look at my book.'

Her book. It was her book now. His memories, his life, were all hers.

Alex loved it that Marie found it important enough to choose a bright summer dress from her wardrobe and apply a little make-up, just to look at it. It gave it a sense of occasion.

She laid the book on the small dining table at one end

of her sitting room, along with a couple of photograph albums from her own shelves. Then she sat down, opening the first page of the book.

'Oh! I think you might just be the cutest baby I've ever seen!' Marie reached forward, flipping over the cover of one of her own albums. 'That's me.'

'So you were born adorable, then…?'

It took hours to go through everything. But it felt as if they were slowly taking possession of each other. As if Marie was saving him, and he could save her.

'Are you hungry?' By the time they finished it was late in the afternoon.

She nodded. 'Why don't we go out somewhere and eat? Anywhere. Then we could go to the seaside.'

'We'll drive down to the coast and find somewhere to stay for the night.' Alex grinned. Just the two of them. No baggage, just his car keys and his credit card, and maybe a change of clothes. 'There's something I want to do first, though.'

He went to fetch the velvet-covered box from his briefcase, putting it in front of her on the table. She recognised it immediately, and raised her eyebrows quizzically.

'I didn't tell you all you should know about this.'

He opened the box and the large diamond glinted in the sunshine that filtered through the window.

'Go on.'

'This diamond is called Amour de Coeur.'

'It has a name?'

'Most large and well-known diamonds do. It was given by one of the more enlightened Kings of Belkraine to his wife, a few hundred years ago. They were very famously in love, at a time when a king's marriage wasn't really about love. And although she had her pick of all the other royal jewels, she only ever wore this one.'

'It's a beautiful story.'

'Will you dare to wear it, Marie?'

Alex could hear his own heart beating. She caught her breath, and then she smiled.

'I'd be proud to. It's a part of your heritage so it's a part of me, now.'

She reached forward, running one finger over the large diamond and the beautiful filigree chain. Suddenly the jewels of Belkraine and Marie's smile—which outshone them all—seemed to go naturally together.

'I have one more diamond for you.'

He got up from his seat, falling to his knees before her and taking her hand in his.

She let out a gasp, knowing exactly what this was.

'Alex!' Tears began to roll down her cheeks.

'Will you marry me, Marie?'

'Yes!' She flung her arms around his neck, forgetting all about the diamonds.

The ring had been burning a hole in his pocket, but it wasn't the thing that sealed their loving covenant. It was Marie's kiss.

'Will you let me go?' He finally managed to tear his lips away from hers.

'No. Never.'

He chuckled. 'Just long enough for me to do this properly...'

Alex took the ring from his pocket. It wasn't the biggest diamond in his inheritance by a very long way, but it had been carefully chosen and was one of the best in quality, flawless and slightly blue in colour.

'I'm starting a new tradition.'

Her eyes widened. 'What? Tell me!'

'My tradition is that when the King of Belkraine wants to marry he takes one diamond from the royal diadem, replacing it with another gem.'

'That's...from a crown?' She pointed at the diamond

ring. It was modern and simply fashioned, made to Alex's exact specifications.

'Will you make it yours? We'll take our inheritance and mould it into something that we're proud to pass on to our children.'

She held out her hand and Alex slipped the ring onto her finger. Suddenly everything fell into place. Their love... his inheritance. All that they wanted to do with their lives. It was all one.

She laid her hand on the book filled with pictures of him as a child. 'I want a baby that looks just like you.'

Alex chuckled. 'And I'd like one that looks like you. We can work on that.'

She hugged him close. 'Can we run away together now? To the seaside.'

Alex kissed her. 'There's nothing I'd like better.'

Alex took Marie to the old manor house in Sussex a few weeks after their engagement. She recognised the carefully laid out gardens and the brickwork around the massive doorway from the photographs in the book he'd made for her. She held on to his hand tightly as he showed her around.

'What do you think?' His brow creased a little as he asked the question.

'It's...okay...'

She loved the Victorian knot garden, the Elizabethan rooms with their nooks and crannies and large, deep fireplaces, the massive banqueting hall which had been turned into a sitting room, big enough to hold a beautiful grand piano at one end. The decor left a lot to be desired—it was far too ostentatious for Marie's taste—but the house was a pure delight.

'You love it, don't you?' He shot her a knowing look.

'A house with a maze in the garden? I'm sure there'll be lots of interest when you put it up for sale.'

It was a wonderful, magical place. But Alex had been so unhappy here when he was a child.

'What if *we* live in it? The location's perfect—it's only an hour out of London by train. We can keep the flat for when we're working late and make this our home.'

'But…you don't want this, do you?' Marie looked around the large sitting room. She could almost see their children playing here. 'The decor…'

'The decor can be changed. You could make this into a wonderful room. We could keep the piano.'

That would be nice…

'And there would be loads of space here to set up an office. We could convert the west wing and run the main charity from here.'

This place could be a wonderful family home. The kind Alex had always wanted and Marie had always dreamed of.

'What do you say to this? We'll bring some of our things down and camp out here for a while. It'll give us time to go through everything, and then you can decide how you feel about living here.'

He wrapped his arms around her, holding her close. 'That would be perfect. Where do you want to camp first?'

'The summer house?'

They should start with the place he liked the best. Alex had written about the summer house as the one place where he had been able to get away from the stifling hold of his family.

He chuckled. 'That sounds wonderful. I'll wake up and make love to you in the morning sunshine.'

'How do you feel about a trial run now?' Marie smiled up at him. 'The afternoon sunshine might do just as well?'

He grabbed the richly upholstered cushions from an ugly sofa, loading half of them into her arms.

'I'll race you there…'

EPILOGUE

The first weekend in February

FOR THE FIRST time in twelve years the plan had changed. Only half the group had arrived at Alex and Marie's home on Friday afternoon; the rest were due the following day. They'd spent a relaxed evening around a roaring fire in the sitting room, celebrating the eve of a wedding.

In the morning Alex had walked to the old church in the village, surrounded by family and friends and with Marie's mother on his arm. After Zack had left home to go to art college she'd moved to be near her other son in Sunderland, and she loved village life there and the cottage Alex had bought for her.

He sat nervously in the front pew, waiting for Marie. 'Have you got the ring, Zack?'

Marie's three brothers had fought over who was to give her away, and in the end her two elder brothers had been given the task, and would both accompany her up the aisle. Alex had claimed Zack as his best man.

'No.'

'What?'

'You've already asked me a hundred times. I thought I'd try a different answer and see how that went.' Zack patted the pocket of his morning suit. 'I've got the ring.'

'Don't do that to me, Zack.' Alex tried to frown, but

today wasn't the day for it. 'You're supposed to be a calming influence, not frightening me to death.'

Zack's laughing reply was lost in the swelling sound of the organ as it struck up the 'Wedding March'. Alex turned and saw Marie and his heart leapt into his throat. He was marrying the most beautiful woman in the world.

Her dress was the simplest part of her attire, the soft lines complementing the riot of flowers in her bouquet. The Amour de Coeur hung at her throat, its sparkle dimmed by her smile.

'You're sure about this?' Zack leaned over, whispering in his ear. 'You've still got time to run…'

'Be quiet, Zack. Of course I'm sure.'

The day had been wonderful—one delight after another: the warmth of family and friends, the way Marie had looked at him as they said their vows… Marie was the most precious thing in his life, and he knew she felt the same about him.

Their reception had taken place back at the home Alex had thought he would never return to, which Marie had made into the place he loved most in the world. Zack had come up with a surprisingly short but touching speech, blushing wildly as he'd sat down to a round of hearty applause.

'I'm so happy, Alex. I love you so much.' Marie whispered in his ear now, as they danced together.

'I love you too.'

That was all he needed to say. It made everything complete. His life and hers were woven together now, and it was a bond that couldn't be broken.

He led her over to the table where their ten oldest friends were sitting with their families. Hugs and kisses were exchanged, and Sunita whispered in Marie's ear.

She laughed, her fingers moving to the Amour de Coeur. 'Yes, it's real.'

Sunita's eyes widened, and Will laughed. 'It's your own fault, Sunita. If you *will* insist on marrying a farmer and burying yourself in the countryside, then you're going to miss some of the gossip. Don't you read the papers? We're in the presence of royalty.'

'You're joking! I *knew* I should have come last night and not this morning. Which one of you is it?'

Alex chuckled. 'Well, technically speaking, it's both of us now. But actually I'm just Marie's loyal and faithful servant.'

'Stop it.' Marie's elbow found his ribs. 'Let's drink a toast, and then Alex will tell the story.'

There were two toasts—the usual one *'to us all'*, and one to the bride and groom. Then Marie sat down next to him.

'Start at the beginning.'

He rolled his eyes. 'Again?'

The story had already been told more than once.

'That's okay. I'll hear it again.'

Will settled himself in his chair and Alex realised that everyone around the table was looking at him.

Marie took his hand, squeezing it. This was no longer his story, it was theirs, and he loved it more each day. They'd rewritten it as a tale of hope—one which would endure in the bricks and mortar of the clinics they planned to build and run, and in the family they'd raise here.

'A hundred and ten years ago...'

* * * * *

VOWS TO SAVE
HIS CROWN

KATE HEWITT

To Cliff, my partner and my prince!

Love, K.

CHAPTER ONE

'I'M SORRY, MATEO.'

On the computer screen, Mateo Karavitis' mother's elegant face was drawn into weary lines of sadness and resignation—sadness for the position she'd put him in, and resignation that it had come to this. A queen who'd had three healthy, robust sons, an heir and *two* spares, and yet here he was, the unneeded third to the throne, now about to be thrust into the unwanted limelight.

'I know you don't want this,' his mother, Queen Agathe, continued quietly.

Mateo did not reply. He knew who didn't want this: his *mother*. How could she? As the third son, and a late surprise at that, he hadn't been prepared for the throne. He'd never been meant to be King, to rule Kallyria with a gentle manner and an iron fist the way his father had for thirty years, as a revered ruler, kind but strong, beloved by his people, feared by his enemies.

It has been his oldest brother Kosmos who had been taken into training from infancy, told from the cradle who he was and what he would become. Kosmos who had gone to military school, who had met dignitaries and diplomats when he was barely out of nappies, who had been crowned Prince and heir to the throne when he was just fourteen, arrogantly assuming the title that would be his. And it was

Kosmos who had died in a sailing accident ten years ago, when he was only thirty.

His oldest brother's sudden death had shocked his family to the core, and rocked its seemingly stable foundations. His father, King Barak, had diminished visibly in what felt like minutes, his powerful frame suddenly seeming smaller, the thick mane of grey hair turning thin and white. Three months after Kosmos' death, Barak had suffered a mini stroke that had affected his speech and movement but kept him on the throne. Four destabilising years after that, he'd died, aged only sixty-eight, and Mateo's older brother Leo, the true spare, had been crowned King.

How had they got here?

'Have you spoken to Leo?' he asked his mother, his tone brusque. 'Has he given an explanation for his unprecedented actions?'

'He…he just can't do it.' Agathe's voice, normally mellifluous and assured, wavered and broke. 'He's not up to it, Mateo. Not up to anything any more.'

'He is *King*.'

'Not any more,' she reminded him gently. 'Not since he abdicated last night.'

Mateo spun his chair around, hiding his face from his mother, a welter of emotions tangled inside him, too knotted up to discern one from the other. He'd never expected this. Even after Kosmos had died, after his father had died, he'd never expected this. Leo had seemed more than ready to assume their father's mantle. Leo, who had always been in Kosmos' shadow, finally ready to shine. He'd been more than ready for it, eager even. Mateo recalled the gleam in his brother's eye at their father's funeral, and it had sickened him. He'd walked away from Kallyria, intent on pursuing his own life here in England, away from the royal family and all its pressures.

And now he had to come back, because Leo was the

one who was walking away. His brother had been King for more than half a decade, Mateo acknowledged with an iron-edged frustration. How could he just walk away from it all? Where was his sense of duty, of honour?

'I don't understand,' he ground out through gritted teeth. 'This is coming from nowhere.'

'Not nowhere.' Agathe's voice was soft and sad. 'Your brother…he has always struggled to assume his royal duties.'

'Struggled?' His brother hadn't struggled when he'd practically snatched the crown from their father's head. 'He seemed more than ready to become King six years ago.'

Agathe's mouth tightened. 'The reality was far more challenging than the dream.'

'Isn't it always?' If his brother had acted as if being King was a licence to indulge whatever pleasures and whims he had…but Mateo didn't know if he had or not, because he'd chosen to distance himself from Kallyria and all it meant, and that had been fine by everyone, because until now he'd never been needed. 'How has he struggled, exactly?' He turned back to face Agathe, wanting to see the expression on her face.

She shrugged her slim shoulders and spread her manicured hands, her face drawn in lines of weary sorrow. 'You know Leo has always been a bit more highly strung than Kosmos. A bit more sensitive. He feels things deeply. He hides behind his pleasures.' Mateo made a dismissive sound. Leo was thirty-eight years old and had been reigning as King for nearly six. Surely it was more than time to put such boyish indulgences behind him, and act like a man. Like a king. 'With the insurgency in the north of the island,' Agathe continued, 'and the economic talks coming up that are so important…' She sighed sadly. 'He fell apart, Mateo. He simply fell apart. It was a long time coming, but I should have seen this was going to happen. He couldn't handle the pressure.'

Leo was now, according to his mother, in a very private, very expensive clinic in Switzerland, leaving his country rudderless at a critical time. Leaving Mateo as the only one to step up and do his duty. To become King.

But Mateo had never been meant to be King.

Outside, the chapel bells of one of Cambridge's many colleges began to peal, a melodious sound so at odds with the bleak conversation he was having with his mother. His life was here, in the hallowed halls of this university, in the modern laboratories where he conducted important research into chemical processes and their effect on the climate.

He and his colleagues were on the brink of discovering how to neutralise certain chemical emissions and potentially reverse their effect on the climate. How could he leave it all behind, to become King of a country most people hadn't even heard about?

A country that was the linchpin in important economic talks, a country that was, if his mother was to be believed, on the brink of war.

'Mateo,' Agathe said softly, 'I know this is hard. Your life has been in Cambridge. I understand that I am asking so much of you. Your country is.'

'You are not asking any more of me than you asked of my brothers,' Mateo said roughly. Agathe sighed.

'Yes, but they were prepared for it.'

And he wasn't. The implication was glaringly obvious. How could he be a good king, when he'd never been shown or taught? When no one had expected anything of him, except to live his own life as he pleased?

And he had done exactly that—going to Cambridge, becoming a lecturer and researcher, even living under a false name so no one knew he was a prince, eschewing the usual security and privileges to be his own man, free from all the encumbrances of royalty.

But all along he'd belonged to Kallyria.

'Mateo?' Agathe prompted and he gave a terse nod of acceptance.

'I'll fly back to Kallyria tonight.'

Agathe could not hide her relief; it shuddered through her with an audible sound. 'Thank you. Thank you.' Mateo nodded, knowing he was doing no more than his duty, even if it chafed bitterly. Of course he would still do it. There had never been any question of that.

'We must move quickly, to secure your throne,' Agathe continued and Mateo stared at her, his blue-green eyes narrowed to aquamarine slits, his chiselled jaw bunched with tension.

'What do you mean?'

'Leo's abdication was so sudden, so unexpected. It has led to some…instability.'

'You mean from the insurgents?' A tribe of nomadic rabble, as far as he could tell, who hated any innovation or threat of modernity.

Agathe nodded, her forehead creased in worry. 'They are growing in power, Mateo, as well as number. Without any-one visible on the throne, who knows what they may do?'

Mateo's gut clenched at the thought of a war. It was so far from his experience, his *life*, that it was almost laugh-able. Tonight he was meant to be speaking at a fundraising dinner, followed by drinks with some university colleagues. Now those plans seemed ephemeral, ridiculous. He had a country to rule. A war to avoid, and if not, then win.

'I will do my best to put a stop to them,' he said, his tone assured and lethal. He might never have been meant to be King, but heaven knew he would step up to the role now. He would do whatever he had to secure his family, his country, his kingdom.

'I know you will,' Agathe assured him. 'But there is more, Mateo.' His mother looked hesitant, and Mateo frowned. What more could there be than what she had already said—his brother abdicating, his country on the verge of ruin, and the necessity for him to leave his entire life behind? How on earth could there be *more*?

'What do you mean?' he demanded. 'Mitera, what are you talking about?'

'Your rule must be made stable as quickly as possible,' Agathe explained. 'With your father and brothers...so much uncertainty...there must be no doubt, Mateo, that our line will rule. That our house will remain established, through all the foibles and fortunes of war.'

'I am travelling to Kallyria tonight,' Mateo answered, with an edge to his voice that he tried to moderate. His mother looked so worn down, so worried. He didn't want to hurt her or cause her any more concern. 'What else can I do?'

'You must marry,' Agathe told him bluntly. 'As quickly as possible, with an heir as soon as possible after that. I have drawn up a list of suitable brides...'

Mateo jerked upright, his mouth dropping open before he snapped it shut, his teeth grinding together. 'Marry? But Leo never married.' Six years his brother had been King, and he'd never even entertained the thought of a bride, as far as Mateo knew. There had certainly been no whispers of a potential match, never mind an engagement or a wedding. Leo had had numerous affairs with unsuitable women, many of them splashed across the tabloids, none of the fleeting relationships leading anywhere.

'It is different now,' Agathe said with bleak, regal honesty. 'There is no one else left.'

A bride.

He resisted the notion instinctively, with an elemental aversion both to marriage itself, and to marriage to a woman he didn't know or care about, a woman who would no doubt be so very *suitable*.

'And what women are on this list of brides?' he asked, a sardonic note entering his voice. 'As a matter of curiosity.'

'Admittedly, not very many. Your bride will play an important role, Mateo. She must be intelligent, not easily cowed, of the right birth and breeding…'

'So no vacuous socialites need apply?' Thank God. He could not stand the thought of being married to some grasping, faint-hearted miss who only wanted his money or title. Yet what kind of woman would agree to marry a man she'd never met? Not, Mateo suspected, one he wanted to share his life with.

'No, of course not.' Agathe gave him a severe look that reminded him of his childhood, of the days when he'd been unrepentantly unruly, testing all the boundaries to make sure they were there. 'You need a bride to suit your station, Mateo. A woman who will one day become Queen.' As she was. Yet no woman could match his mother for strength, elegance, or grace.

Mateo looked away. He couldn't bear to think about any of it. 'So who is on the list?' he asked after a moment.

'Vanessa de Cruz…a Spanish socialite who has started her own business. Women's wear.'

He made a scoffing sound. 'Why would she want to give all that up and become Queen?'

'You're a catch, Mateo,' Agathe said, a hint of a smile in her voice, despite all her sadness.

'She doesn't even know me,' he dismissed. He did not want to marry a woman who would only marry him for his title, her station in life. 'Who else?'

'A French heiress…a Turkish daughter of a CEO…in today's modern world, you need a woman who is her own person by your side. Not a princess simply waiting for the limelight.' His mother reeled off a few more names Mateo had barely heard of. Strangers, women he had no interest in knowing, much less marrying. He'd never intended to marry at all, and he certainly didn't want to love the woman whom he did, but neither did he want such a soulless arrangement as this.

'Think about it,' Agathe pressed gently. 'We can discuss it more when you arrive tonight.'

Mateo nodded his terse agreement, and a few minutes later he ended the video call. Outside the bells had stopped ringing. Mateo looked around his cluttered study, the research paper he'd been writing discarded on his desk, and accepted that his entire life had changed for ever.

'Something's come up.'

Rachel Lewis looked up from the microscope she'd been bending over to smile a greeting at her closest colleague. Mateo Karras' dazzlingly good looks had stopped stealing her breath years ago, thank goodness, but the academic part of her brain still couldn't help but admire the perfect symmetry of his features every time she saw him—the close-cropped blue-black hair, the aquamarine eyes the exact colour of the Aegean when she'd gone on holiday there a few years ago, the straight nose and square jaw, and of course the lithe and tall powerful figure encased now in battered cords and a creased button-down shirt, his usual work attire.

'Come up?' She wrinkled her nose, noting his rather terse tone, so unlike his usual cheerful briskness as he came into the lab, eager to get started. 'What do you mean?'

'I...' He shook his head, let out a weary breath. 'I'm going to be away for...a while. I'll have to take a leave of absence.'

'A leave of absence?' Rachel stared at him in shock. She and Mateo had been pioneering research on chemical emissions and climate change for the better part of a decade, since they'd both received their PhDs here at Cambridge. They were close, *so* close, to discovering and publishing the crucial evidence that would reduce toxic chemicals' effect on the climate. How could he be walking away from it all? It was too incredible to take in. 'I don't understand.'

'I know. I can't explain it all now. I'm afraid I have a family emergency that has to be dealt with. I… I don't know when I'll be back.'

'But…' Shock was giving way to dismay, and something even deeper that Rachel didn't want to consider too closely. She didn't *feel* anything for Mateo, not like that. It was just that she couldn't imagine working without him. They'd been colleagues and partners in research for so long, they practically knew each other's thoughts without needing to speak. When discussing their research, they'd completed each other's sentences on many occasions, with wry smiles and a rueful laugh.

They had a symmetry, a synchronicity, that had been formed over years of dedicated research, endless hours in the lab, as well as many drinks in pub gardens by the river Cam where they discussed everything from radioactive isotopes to organic compounds, and raced each other as to who could recite the periodic table the fastest. Unfortunately, Mateo always won. He *couldn't* be leaving.

'What's going on, Mateo? What's come up?' After nearly ten years together Rachel thought she surely deserved to know, even as she acknowledged that she and Mateo had shared next to nothing about their personal lives.

She didn't really have one, and Mateo had always been very private about his. She'd seen a few women on his arm over the years, but they hadn't stayed there very long—a date or two, nothing more. He'd never spoken about them, and she'd never dared ask.

She'd also never dared consider herself a candidate for that vaunted position—they were poles apart in terms of their appeal, and she was pragmatic enough to understand that, no matter how well they got along, Mateo would never, ever think of her that way. And, Rachel had reminded herself more than once with only a small pang of loss, it wasn't likely that any man would. She certainly hadn't found one yet, and she'd accepted her single state a long time ago, not that she'd ever admitted as much to Mateo.

Over countless conversations, they'd stuck to chemistry, to research, maybe a bit of university gossip, but nothing more. Nothing personal. Certainly nothing *intimate*. And that had been fine, because their work banter was fun, their research was important, and being with Mateo made her happy.

Yet now Rachel knew she needed to know why he was leaving. Surely he couldn't walk away from it all without giving her a real reason.

'It's difficult to explain,' he said, rubbing a hand wearily over his face. Gone was his easy charm, his wry banter, the glint in his aquamarine eyes that Rachel loved. He looked remote, stony, almost like someone she didn't even know. 'All I can say is, it's a family emergency...'

Rachel realised she didn't know anything about his family. In nearly ten years, he'd never mentioned them once. 'I hope everyone is okay,' she said, feeling as if she were fumbling in the dark. She didn't even know if there was an *everyone*.

'Yes, yes, it will be fine. But...' He paused, and a look of such naked desolation passed over his face that Rachel had the insane urge to go over and give him a hug. Insane, because in nearly ten years she had never touched him, save for a brush of the shoulder as they leaned over a microscope together, or the occasional high five when they had a breakthrough in their research. But they'd never *hugged*. Not even close. It hadn't bothered or even occurred to her, until now.

'Let me know if there's something I can do to help,' she said. 'Anything at all. Are you leaving Cambridge…? Do you need your house looked after?' Although she'd never been to his house, she knew it was a sprawling cottage in the nearby village of Grantchester, a far cry from the terraced garden flat by the railway station that she'd scraped and saved to afford and make a cosy, comfortable home.

'I'm leaving the country.' Mateo spoke flatly. 'And I don't know when I'll be back.'

Rachel gaped at him. 'This sounds really serious, then.'

'It is.'

It also sounded so *final*. 'But you will come back?' Rachel asked. She couldn't imagine him not returning *ever*. 'When it's all sorted?' Whatever it was. 'I can't do this without you, Mateo.' She gestured to the microscope she'd been looking through, encompassing all the research they'd embarked on together, and a look of sadness and regret flashed across Mateo's face like a lightning strike of emotion, before his features ironed out and he offered her a nod.

'I know. I feel the same. I'm sorry.'

'Are you sure there isn't something I can do? Help in some way?' She didn't know what to do, how to help, and she hated that. She wanted to be useful, had spent her entire life trying to be necessary to people, if not actually loved. But Mateo was already shaking his head.

'No, no. You…you've been amazing, Rachel. A great colleague. The best I could ask for.'

She grimaced, struggling to make a joke of it even as horror stole over her at the thought of him leaving in such a final way. 'Don't, you make it sound as if you're dying.'

'It feels a little bit that way.'

'Mateo—'

'No, no, I'm being melodramatic.' He forced a smile to that mobile mouth that had once fascinated Rachel far more than it should have. Thankfully she'd got over that years ago. She'd made herself, because she'd known there was no point. 'Sorry, it's all just been a shock. I'll try to explain when I can. In the meantime…take care of yourself.'

He stepped forward then, and did something Rachel had never, ever expected him to do, although she'd dreamed it more times than she cared to admit. He leant forward and brushed her cheek with his lips. Rachel drew in a shocked breath as the sheer physicality of him assaulted her senses—the clean, citrusy smell of his aftershave, the softness of his lips, the sharp brush of his stubbled cheek against hers. One hand reached out, flailing towards him, looking for purchase, but thankfully her mind hadn't short-circuited quite that much, and she let it fall to her side before she actually touched him.

With a sad, wry smile, Mateo met her gaze and then stepped back. He nodded once more while Rachel stared dumbly, her mind spinning, her cheek buzzing, and then he turned around and left the lab. A second later Rachel heard the door to the block of laboratories close, and she knew he was gone.

CHAPTER TWO

MATEO STARED OUT at the idyllic view of his island home—
sparkling sea, pure white beach, and the lovely, landscaped
gardens of the royal palace stretching down to the sand, the
flowers as bright as jewels amidst all the verdant green. A
paradise, which he now knew was rotting at its core.

Everything was worse, far worse, than he'd thought. As
soon as he'd arrived in Kallyria, he'd had briefings from
all of his cabinet ministers, only to discover that Leo had
been running the country—*his* country—into the ground.
The economy, the foreign policy, even the domestic affairs
that should have ticked over fairly smoothly had suffered
under his brother's wildly unstable hand, with decisions
being made recklessly, others carelessly reversed, world
leaders insulted…the list went on and on, as his brother
pursued pleasure and took an interest in affairs only when
it suited him.

Mateo didn't know whether to be furious or insulted that
no one had informed him what was happening, and had
been going on for years. As it was, all he felt was guilt. He
should have known. He should have been here.

But then, no one had expected him to be. Certainly no
one had ever asked. He turned from the window to glance
down at the desk in the palace's study, a room that still
reminded him of his father, with its wood-panelled walls
and faint, lingering smell of cigar smoke—unless he was

imagining that? His father had been gone for six years. Yet the room bore far more of an imprint of him than of Leo, who had, Mateo had discovered, spent more time on his yacht or in Monte Carlo than here, managing the affairs of his country.

Mateo's narrowed gazed scanned the list his mother had written out in her copperplate handwriting—the list of prospective brides. His mouth twisted in distaste at the mercenary nature of the venture; it seemed incredible to him that in this day and age, in a country that professed to be both progressive and enlightened, he was meant to marry a woman he didn't even know.

'Of course, you will get to know her, in time,' Agathe had assured him that morning, a tentative smile curving her mouth, lines of tension bracketing her eyes.

'And then impregnate her as quickly as possible?' Mateo queried sardonically. '*That's* not a recipe for disaster.'

'Arranged marriages can be successful,' his mother stated with quiet dignity. She should know; her own marriage had been arranged, and she'd striven tirelessly to make it work. Mateo knew his father had been a proud and sometimes difficult man; he'd had a great capacity for love and generosity, but also for anger and scorn. Mateo loved his mother; he'd admired his father. But he didn't want to emulate their marriage.

'I know they can, Mitera,' he said with a conciliatory smile, as he raked his hand through his hair. He'd arrived on Kallyria at ten o'clock last night, and only snatched an hour or two of sleep as he'd gone through all the paperwork his brother had left behind, and attended one debriefing meeting after another.

'Is it love you're looking for?' Agathe asked tentatively. 'Because love can grow, Mateo…'

'I don't want *love*.' He spoke the word with a sneer, because he had to. How else was he meant to think of it? 'I've already been in love, and I have no desire to be so again.'

'You mean Cressida.' Mateo didn't bother to reply. Of course he meant Cressida. 'That was a long time ago, Mateo.'

'I know.' He tried not to speak sharply, but he never talked about Cress. Ever. He tried not even to think about her, about the grief and guilt he still felt, like bullets embedded under his skin, a knife sticking out of his back that he couldn't twist around enough to pull out. If he didn't think about it, he didn't feel it, and that was his preferred way of managing the pain.

Agathe was silent for a moment, her hands folded in her lap, her head tilted to one side as she pinned Mateo in place with her perceptive gaze. 'Considering your aversion to that happy state, then, I would think an arranged marriage would suit you.'

Mateo knew she was right, and yet he still resisted the unpalatable notion. 'I want an agreement, not an arrangement,' he said after a moment. 'If I'm going to have my wife rule alongside me, bear and raise my children, be my partner in every way possible... I don't want to trust that role to a stranger who looks good on paper. That seems like the epitome of foolishness.'

'The women on this list have been vetted by several cabinet ministers,' Agathe countered. 'Everything about them is suitable. There is no reason to think they wouldn't be trustworthy, dutiful, admirable in every way.'

'And willing?' Mateo said with a curl of his lip. Agathe shook her head slowly.

'Why is that wrong?'

Mateo didn't answer, because he wasn't sure he could explain it even to himself. All he knew was, after a lifetime of being told he would never be king, he didn't want a woman to marry him only because he finally was. But that felt too complicated and emotional to explain to his mother, and so he straightened his shoulders and reached for the piece of paper with its damned list.

'I'll look it over.'

Several hours later he was no closer to coming to a decision regarding any of the oh-so suitable candidates. He'd searched for information about them online, scanned their social media profiles, and found them all as duly admirable as his mother had insisted. One of his advisors had cautiously told him that initial overtures had been made, and at least four of the women had expressed their interest, despite knowing nothing about him. Having never spoken to him. Knowing only about his wealth and title, his power and prestige. Why did that bother him so much? Why did he *care*?

The whole point was, he didn't want to care. He wouldn't care. Yet he still hated the thought of it all.

His mobile buzzed and Mateo slid it out of his pocket. In the eighteen hours since he'd arrived on Kallyria he hadn't spoken to anyone from his former life, but now he saw with a ripple of undeniable pleasure that the call was from Rachel.

He swiped to take it. 'Yes?'

'Mateo?' She sounded uncertain.

'Yes, it's me.'

'You sounded so different there, for a second,' Rachel told him with an uncertain laugh. 'Like some... I don't know, some really important person.'

Mateo's lips twisted wryly. That was just what he'd become. Of course, he'd been important in his own way before returning to Kallyria; he held a fellow's chair at one of the world's most prestigious universities, and he'd started his own tech company as a side interest, and made millions in the process. Last year he'd been named one of Britain's most eligible bachelors by some ridiculous tabloid. But he hadn't been king.

'How are you?' Rachel asked. 'I've been worried about you.'

'Worried?' Mateo repeated shortly. 'Why?'

'Because you left so suddenly, for a family emergency,' Rachel said, sounding both defensive and a bit exasperated. 'Of course I'd be worried.'

'You needn't be concerned.' Too late Mateo realised how he sounded—brusque to the point of rudeness, and so unlike the usual way he related to his colleague. His *former* colleague. The truth was, he was feeling both raw and uncertain about everything, and he didn't want to admit that to anyone, not even Rachel.

Rachel. She'd been a good friend to him over the years, his closest friend in many ways although she knew little about his life, and he knew less about hers. They'd functioned on an academic plane, both enjoying the thrill of research, of making discoveries, of joking in the lab and discussing theories in the pub. Mateo didn't think he'd ever asked her about her personal life, or she about his. The thought had never occurred to him.

'I'm sorry,' he apologised, for his tone. 'But it's all under control.'

'Is it?' Rachel sounded hopeful. 'So you'll be back in Cambridge soon?'

Realisation thudded through Mateo at the assumption she'd so blithely made. The leave of absence he'd been granted was going to have to become a termination of employment, effective immediately, and yet he resisted the thought. Still, he steeled himself for what he knew had to be both said and done.

'No, I'm afraid I won't. I'm resigning from my position, Rachel.' He heard her soft gasp of surprised distress, and it touched him more than he expected it to. They might have been close colleagues, even friends, but Rachel would be fine without him. She'd find another research partner, maybe even move up in the department. It wasn't as if they'd actually *cared* about each other.

'But why?' she asked softly. 'What's going on, Mateo? Can't you tell me?'

He hesitated, then said, 'I need to take care of the family business. My brother was in charge but he's stepped down rather suddenly.'

'The family business...'

'Yes.' He wasn't ready to tell her the truth, that he was now king of a country. It sounded ridiculous, like something out of some soppy movie, and it made a lie of his life. Besides, she would find out soon enough. It would be in the newspapers, and rumours would ripple through the small, stifling university community. They always did.

'I can't believe it,' Rachel said slowly. 'You're really not coming back at all?'

'No.'

'And there's nothing I can do? No way I can help?'

'No. I'm sorry.' The words sounded so final, and Mateo knew there was no more to say. 'Goodbye, Rachel,' he said, and then he disconnected the call.

Rachel stared at her phone in disbelief. Had Mateo just *hung up* on her? Why was he acting as if he'd *died*?

And yet it felt as if he'd died. In truth, Rachel felt a far greater grief than she'd ever expected to, to have Mateo walk out of her life like that. She knew they hadn't actually been close in the way that most friends were, no matter how much they'd shared together. She suspected they wouldn't keep in touch. Mateo probably wouldn't even think of it. Typical scientist, existing on a mental plane rather than a physical one.

And yet Mateo Karras was a very physical man. Rachel

had noticed it the moment she'd been introduced to him, when they'd both been obtaining their PhDs. Mateo had been in his third year while she'd been in her first, and the rumours had already been swirling around him, with the few female students in the department pretending to swoon whenever his name was mentioned.

Still, Rachel hadn't been prepared for the sheer physical presence of him, the base, animal attraction that had crashed over her, despite the glaring obviousness of their unsuitability. She was plain, nerdy, a little too curvy, with no fashion sense. Mateo might be a brilliant scientist, but he didn't fit the geeky stereotype as so many of his colleagues did.

He was devastatingly attractive, for a start, with close-cropped dark hair and those amazing blue-green eyes, plus a physique that could grace a calendar if he chose. He was also charming and assured, his easy manner and wry jokes disguising the fact that no one actually knew anything about him. Some people wondered at the aloofness under his easy exterior; some had called him a snob. Rachel had felt something else from him. Something like sadness.

In the intervening years, however, she'd disabused herself of that fanciful notion and accepted that Mateo was a man, and a law, unto himself. Charming and urbane, passionate about his work, he didn't need people the way most others did. The way Rachel had, and then learned not to, because it hurt less.

'Rachel? Is that you?' Her mother's wavery voice had Rachel slipping her phone into her pocket and plastering a smile on her face. The last thing she wanted to do was worry her mother about anything, not that she would even be worried. Or notice.

Carol Lewis had been diagnosed with Alzheimer's two years ago, and since then her decline had been dispiritingly steady. She'd moved into the second bedroom of Rachel's flat eighteen months ago. After living on her own since she was eighteen, Rachel had struggled to get used to her mother's company, as well as her many needs…and the fact that her mother had never actually seemed to *like* her very much. Neither of her parents had, and that had been something Rachel had made peace with, or thought she had. Having her mother here tended to be an unwelcome reminder of the lack in their relationship.

'Hey, Mum.' Rachel smiled as her mother shuffled into the room, squinting at her suspiciously.

'Why were you making so much noise?'

She'd been talking quietly, but never mind. 'Sorry, I was on the phone.'

'Was it your father? Is he going to be late again?'

Her father had been dead for eight years. 'No, Mum, it was just a friend.' Although perhaps she couldn't call Mateo that any more. Perhaps she never could have called him that. 'Do you want to watch one of your shows, Mum?' Gently Rachel took her mother's arm and propelled her back to the bedroom, which had been kitted out with an adjustable bed and a large-screen TV. 'I think that bargain-hunter one might be on.' Since being diagnosed, her mother had developed an affinity for trashy TV, something that made Rachel both smile and feel sad. Before the disease, her mother had only watched documentaries, the obscurer and more intellectual the better. Now she gorged herself on talk shows and reality TV.

Carol let herself be settled back into her bed, still seeming grumpy as Rachel folded the blanket over her knees and turned on the TV. 'I could make you a toastie,' she suggested. 'Cheese and Marmite?'

Another aspect of the disease—her mother ate the same thing over and over again, for breakfast, lunch, and dinner. Rachel had gone through more jars of Marmite than she'd ever thought possible, especially considering that she didn't even like the stuff.

'All right,' Carol said, as if she were granting Rachel a favour. 'Fine.'

Alone in the kitchen, Rachel set to buttering bread and slicing cheese, Mateo's strangely brusque call weighing on her heavily. She was going to miss him. Maybe she shouldn't, but she knew she was. She already did.

Looking around the small kitchen—the tinny sound of the TV in the background, the uninspiring view of a tiny courtyard from her window—Rachel was struck with how *little* her life was.

She didn't go out. Her few friends in the department were married with children, existing in a separate, busy universe from her. Occasionally they invited her to what Rachel thought of as pity dinners, where they paraded their children in front of her and asked sympathetically if she wanted to be set up. Rachel could endure one of those about every six months, but she always left them with a huge sigh of relief.

The truth was, she hadn't felt the need or desire to go out, to have a social life, when she'd been working with Mateo for eight hours every day. Their banter, their companionable silence, their occasional debates over drinks… all of it had been enough for her. More than enough, since she'd dealt with the stupid crush she'd had on him ages ago, like lancing a wound. Painful but necessary. Thank goodness she'd made herself get over that, otherwise she'd be in real trouble now.

'Rachel? Is my sandwich ready?'

With a sigh Rachel turned on the grill.

Three days later it was bucketing down rain as Rachel sprinted down the street towards her flat. She was utterly soaked, and even more dispirited by Mateo's disappearance from her life. She'd tried to be cheerful about gaining a new research partner, but the person put forward by the new chair was a smarmy colleague who liked to make disparaging comments about women and then hold his hands up, eyebrows raised, as he told her not to be so sensitive. Work had gone from being a joy to a disaster, and, considering the state of the rest of her life, that was a blow indeed.

She fumbled with the key to her flat, grateful that she'd have half an hour or so of peace and quiet before her mother came home. Carol spent her weekdays at a centre for the memory impaired, and was brought home by a kindly bus service run by the centre, which made Rachel's life a lot easier.

She was just pushing the door open when someone stepped out of the alleyway that led around to the back courtyard and the bins. Rachel let out a little scream at the sight of the figure looming out of the gloom and rain, yanking her key out of the door, ready to use it as an admittedly feeble weapon.

'Rachel, it's me.' The low thrum of his voice, with the faintest hint of an accent, had Rachel dropping her keys onto the concrete with a clatter.

'Mateo...?'

'Yes.' He took another step towards her and smiled. Rachel stared at him in wonder and disbelief.

'What are you doing here?'

'I wanted to see you.'

Rachel shook her head, sending raindrops splattering, too shocked even to think something coherent, much less say it. She realised just how glad she was to see him.

'May I come in? We're both getting soaked.'

'Yes, of course.' She scooped her keys up from the floor and pushed open the door. Mateo followed her into the flat, and as Rachel switched on the light she realised how small her flat probably seemed to him, and also that she had three ratty-looking bras drying over the radiator, and the remains of her jam-smeared toast on the coffee table, next to a romance novel with a cringingly lurid cover. Welcome to her life.

She turned to face Mateo, her eyes widening at the sight of him. He looked completely different, dressed in an expertly cut three-piece suit of dark grey, his jaw closely shaven, everything about him sleek and sophisticated and rich. He'd always emanated a certain assured confidence, but he was on another level entirely now. The disparity of their appearances—her hair was in rat's tails and she was wearing a baggy trouser suit with a mayonnaise stain on the lapel—made her cringe.

She shook her head slowly, still amazed he was in her flat. *Why?*

'Mateo,' she said questioningly, as if he might suddenly admit it wasn't really him. 'What are you doing here?'

CHAPTER THREE

THAT, MATEO REFLECTED, was a very good question. When the idea had come to him twenty-four hours ago, after his initial disastrous meeting with Vanessa de Cruz, it had seemed wonderfully obvious. Blindingly simple. Now he wasn't so sure.

'I wanted to see you,' he said, because that much was true.

'You did?' Rachel pushed her wet hair out of her eyes and gave him an incredulous look. 'Why?'

Another good question. In his mind's eye Mateo pictured Vanessa's narrowed gaze of avaricious speculation, the pouty pursing of her lips that he'd instinctively disliked. She'd been sleek and beautiful and so very cold.

'Of course we'll have a prenup,' she'd said.

He'd stiffened at that, even though he'd supposed it made sense.

'I believe marriage is for life.'

'Oh, no—you're not old-fashioned, are you?'

Mateo had never considered himself so before. In fact, he had always thought of himself as progressive, enlightened, at least by most standards. But when it came to marriage? To vows made between a man and a woman? Then, yes, apparently he was old-fashioned.

'Hold on,' Rachel said. 'I'm soaking wet and I think we could both use a cup of tea.' She shrugged off her sopping jacket, revealing a crumpled white blouse underneath that was becoming see-through from the damp, making Mateo uncomfortably aware of how generously endowed his former colleague was. He looked away, only to have his gaze fasten on some rather greying bras draped over the radiator.

Rachel tracked his gaze and then quickly swept them from the radiator, bundling them into a ball as she hurried into the kitchen. A few seconds later Mateo heard the distinctive clink of the kettle being filled and then switched on.

He shrugged off his cashmere overcoat and draped it over a chair at the small table taking up half of the cosy sitting room. The other half was taken up with a sofa covered in a colourful throw. He glanced around the flat, noting that, despite its smallness, it was a warm and welcoming place, with botanical prints on the walls and a tangle of house plants on the wide windowsill.

He scanned the titles in the bookcase, and then the pile of post on a marble-topped table by the front door. These little hints into Rachel's life, a life lived away from the chemistry lab, made him realise afresh that he didn't know anything about his former research partner.

Yes, you do. She worked hard and well for ten years. She can take a joke, but she knows what to take seriously. You've had fun with her, and, more importantly, you trust her.

Yes, he decided as he lowered himself onto the sofa, he knew enough.

The kettle switched off and a few minutes later Rachel came back into the sitting room with two cups of tea. She'd taken the opportunity to tidy herself up, putting her damp hair back in a ponytail, although curly tendrils had escaped to frame her face. She'd also changed her wet trouser suit for a heather-grey jumper that clung to her generous curves, and a pair of skinny jeans that showcased her just as curvy legs.

Mateo had never once looked at Rachel Lewis with anything remotely resembling sexual interest, yet now he supposed he ought to. At least, he ought to decide if he could.

'Here you are.' She handed him a cup of tea, black as he preferred, and then took her own, milky and sweet, and went to perch on the edge of an armchair that had a tottering pile of folded washing on it. 'Sorry for the mess,' she said with a wry grimace. 'If I'd known you were coming, I certainly wouldn't have left my bras out.'

'Or this?' He picked up the romance novel splayed out on the table, his lips quirking at the sight of the heaving bosom on the cover. '"Lady Arabella Fordham-Smythe is fascinated by the dark stranger who comes to her father's castle late one night…"'

'A girl's got to dream.' Humour glinted in her eyes again, reminding Mateo of how much fun she could be, although her cheeks had reddened a little in embarrassment. 'So why are you here, Mateo? Not that I'm not delighted to see you, of course.' Another rueful grimace, the glint in her eyes turning into a positive sparkle. 'Despite the lack of warning.'

'And the underwear.' *Why* were they talking about her underwear? Why was he imagining, not the worn-out bras she'd bundled away, but a slip in taupe silk, edged with ivory lace, one strap sliding from her shoulder…

The image jolted Mateo to the core, forcing him to straighten where he sat, and meet Rachel's laughing gaze once more.

Her eyes were quite lovely, he acknowledged. A deep, soft chocolate brown, with thick lashes fringing them, making her look like a gentle doe. A doe with a good sense of humour and a terrific work ethic.

'Have you heard who has taken over as chair?' she asked, her grimace without any humour this time, and Mateo frowned.

'No. Who?'

'Supercilious Simon.' She made a face. 'I know I shouldn't call him that, but he is *so* irritating.'

Mateo's lip curled. 'That was the best they could do?' He was insulted that Simon Thayer, a mediocre researcher at best and a pompous ass to boot, had been selected to take his place.

'I know, I know.' Rachel shook her head as she blew on her tea. 'But he's always played the game. Cosied up to anyone important.' The sparkle in her eye had dimmed, and Mateo didn't like it. 'Working with him is going to be hell, frankly. I've even thought about going somewhere else, not that I could.' For a second she looked so desolate Mateo had a bizarre and discomfiting urge to comfort her. *How?* 'Anyway, never mind about that.' She shook her head, cheer resolutely restored. 'How are you? How is the family emergency?'

'Still in a state of emergency, but a bit better, I suppose.'

'Really?' Her eyes softened, if that were possible. Could eyes soften? Mateo felt uncomfortable just thinking about it. It was not the way he normally thought about eyes, or anyone. 'So why are you here, Mateo? Because you haven't actually said yet.'

'I know.' He took a sip of tea, mainly to stall for time, something he wasn't used to doing. When it came to chemistry, he was decisive. He knew what to do, no matter what the scientific conundrum. He saw a problem and he broke down the solution into steps, taking them one at a time, each one making sense.

So that was what he would have to do here. Take her through his reasoning, step by careful, analytical step. Rachel raised her eyebrows, a little smile playing about her generous mouth. Her lips, Mateo noticed irrelevantly, were rosy and lush.

And instead of starting at the beginning, and explaining it

all coherently, he found himself doing the exact opposite—blurting out the end point, with no lead-up or context.

'I want you to marry me,' he said.

Rachel was sure she'd misheard. It had almost sounded as if Mateo had just asked her to marry him. In fact, that was *exactly* what it had sounded like, which couldn't be right. Obviously.

Unless he'd been joking…?

She gave him a quizzical little smile, as if she was un-fazed, perhaps a bit nonplussed, rather than completely spinning inside and, worse, suddenly deathly afraid that he *was* joking. That it was so obviously a joke…as it had been once before. She'd been able to take it from Josh all those years ago, but she didn't think she could take it from Mateo, someone she both liked and trusted. *Please, please don't make me the butt of your joke.* 'Sorry,' she said lightly. 'Come again?'

'I didn't phrase that properly.'

Was there another way to phrase it? Rachel took a sip of her tea, mostly to hide her expression, which she feared was looking horribly hopeful. This was starting to feel like something out of the novel on the coffee table, and she knew, she *knew* real life wasn't like that. Mateo Karras did not want to marry her. No way. No how. It was impossible. Obviously.

'I want you to marry me,' he said again. 'But let me explain.'

'O…kay.'

'I'm not who you think I am.'

Now this was really beginning to seem melodramatic. Rachel had a sudden urge to laugh. 'Okay,' she said. 'Who are you?'

Mateo grimaced and put down his cup of tea. 'My full

name and title? Prince Mateo Aegeus Karavitis, heir to the throne of the island kingdom of Kallyria.'

Rachel stared at him dumbly. He *had* to be joking. Mateo had liked to play a practical joke or two, back in the lab. Nothing serious or dangerous, but sometimes he'd relabel a test tube with some funny little slogan, and they had an ongoing contest of who could come up with the worst chemistry joke.

If H2O is the formula for water, what is the formula for ice? H2O cubed.

Was that what he was doing here? Was he making fun of her? Her cheeks stung with mortification at the thought, and her heart felt as if it were shrivelling inside her. Please, no…

'I'm sorry,' she said stiffly. 'I don't get it.'

Mateo frowned, the dark slashes of his brows drawing together. Why did he have to be so handsome? Rachel wondered irritably. It didn't make this any easier, or less painful. 'Get it?'

'The punchline,' she said flatly.

'There's no punchline, Rachel. I mean it. I accept this comes as a surprise, and it's not the most romantic proposal of marriage, but please let me explain.'

'Fine.' She put down her tea and folded her arms, feeling angry all of a sudden. If this was some long, drawn-out practical joke, it was in decided poor taste. 'Explain.'

Mateo looked a little startled by her hard tone, but he continued, 'Five days ago my brother Leo abdicated his throne.'

'Abdicated? He was King of this Kall—?'

'Kallyria, yes. He's been king for six years, since my father died.'

He spoke matter-of-factly and Rachel goggled at him. Was he actually serious? 'Mateo, why did you never say anything about this before? You're a *prince*—'

'I didn't say anything because I didn't want anyone to

know. I wanted to succeed on my terms, as my own man. And that's exactly what I did. I used a different name, forewent any security protocols, and established myself on my own credentials.' His voice blazed with passion and purpose. 'No one at Cambridge knows who I truly am.'

'No one?'

'No one.'

For a terrible second Rachel wondered if Mateo was deluded somehow. It had happened before to scientists who spent too much time in the lab. They cracked. And the way he'd left so suddenly, this family emergency...what if it was all some weird delusion?

Her face crumpled in compassionate horror at the thought, and Mateo let out an exasperated breath. 'You don't believe me, do you?'

'It's not that...'

Mateo said something in Greek, most likely a swear word. 'You think I'm actually making it up!'

'Not making it up,' Rachel soothed. 'I think you *believe* you're a prince...'

Mateo swore again, this time in English. He rose from her battered sofa in one fluid movement of lethal grace. 'Do I look or act like someone who is insane?' he demanded, and Rachel cringed a little.

No, he most definitely did not. In fact, with his eyes blazing blue-green fire, in a suit that looked as if it cost more than she made in a month, he *did* look like a prince. She sagged against the back of her chair, causing the pile of laundry to fall in a heap to the floor, as the realisation thudded through her.

'You really are a prince.'

'Of course I am. And in a week's time I am to be crowned king.'

He sounded so assured, so arrogant, that Rachel wondered how she could have doubted him for a minute. A second. And as for being deluded…of course he wasn't. She'd never seen a more sane, focused, determined individual in her life.

'But what does this have to do with me?' she asked shakily, as she remembered what he'd said. He wanted to *marry* her…

Surely not. *Surely not.*

'As King of Kallyria, I'll need a bride,' Mateo resumed his explanation as he paced the small confines of her sitting room. 'A queen by my side.'

Rachel shook her head slowly. She could not reconcile that statement with him wanting to marry her. Not in any way or form. 'Maybe I'm thick, Mateo, but I still don't understand.'

'You are not thick, Rachel.' He turned to face her. 'You are the smartest woman I know. A brilliant scientist, an incredibly hard worker, and a good friend.'

Her cheeks warmed and her eyes stung. He was speaking in a flat, matter-of-fact tone, but his words warmed her heart and touched her soul. She couldn't remember the last time she'd been given so much sincere praise.

'Thank you,' she whispered.

'I must marry immediately, to help stabilise my country. And produce an heir.'

Wait, what? Rachel stared at him blankly, still unable to take it in. She must be thick, no matter what Mateo had just said. 'And…and you want to marry *me*?' she asked in a disbelieving whisper. Even now she expected him to suddenly smile, laugh, and say of *course* it was a joke, and could she help him him to think of anyone suitable?

Yet she knew, just looking at him, that it wasn't. He'd come back to Cambridge; he'd come to her flat to find her. He looked deadly serious, incredibly intent.

Mateo Karras—no, Karavitis—Prince—no, *King* of a country—wanted to marry her. *Her.* When no man had ever truly wanted her before. Still, she felt uncertain. Doubtful. Josh's words, spoken over a decade before, still seared her brain and, worse, her heart.

How could any man want you?

'Why?' Rachel whispered. Mateo didn't pretend to misunderstand.

'Because I know you. I trust you. I *like* you. And we work well together.'

'In a chemistry lab—'

'Why not in a kingdom?' He shrugged. 'Why should it be any different?'

'But…' Rachel shook her head slowly '…you're not offering me the vice-presidency, Mateo. You're asking me to be your *wife*. There's a huge difference.'

'Not that much.' Mateo spread his hands. 'We'd be a partnership, a team. I'd need you by my side, supporting me, supporting my country. We'd be working together.'

'We'd be *married*.' An image slammed through her head, one she had no business thinking of. A wedding night, candles all around, the slide of burnished skin on skin…

Like something out of the book on the table. *No*. That wasn't real. That wasn't her. And Mateo certainly didn't mean that kind of marriage.

Except he'd mentioned needing an heir. As soon as possible.

'Yes,' Mateo agreed evenly. 'We'd be married.'

Rachel stared at him helplessly. 'Mateo, this is crazy.'

'I know it's unexpected—'

'I have a *job*,' she emphasised, belatedly remembering the life she'd built for herself, just as Mateo had, on her own terms. She'd won her place first at Oxford and then Cambridge, and finally her research fellowship, all on her own merit, not as the daughter of esteemed physicist, William Lewis, with his society wife Carol. She'd made no mention of her parents in any of her applications, had made sure nobody knew. She'd wanted to prove herself, and she *had*.

And Mateo was now thinking she might leave it all behind, everything she'd worked so hard for, simply to be his trophy wife, a mannequin on his arm? She started to shake her head, but Mateo forestalled her, his voice calm and incisive.

'I realise I am asking you to sacrifice much. But you would have limitless opportunity as Queen of Kallyria—to promote girls' involvement in STEM subjects; to fund research and support charities and causes that align with your interests; to travel the world in the name of science.'

'Science? Or politics?' she asked, her voice shaking with the enormity of it all. She couldn't grasp what he was asking her on so many incredible levels.

'Both,' Mateo replied, unfazed. 'Naturally. As king, one of my priorities will be scientific research. Kallyria has a university in its capital city of Constanza. Admittedly, it is not on the same level as Cambridge or Oxford, but it is esteemed among Mediterranean countries.'

'I don't even know where Kallyria is,' Rachel admitted. 'I'm not sure I've ever heard of it before.'

'It is a small island country in the eastern Mediterranean Sea. It was settled by Greek and Turkish traders, over two thousand years ago. It has never been conquered.'

And he was asking her to be its *Queen*. Rachel felt as if her head were going to explode.

'I don't...' she began, not even sure what she was going to say. And then the front doorknob rattled, and her mother shuffled into the house, looking between her and Mateo with hostile suspicion.

'Rachel,' she demanded, her voice rising querulously. 'Who is this?'

CHAPTER FOUR

MATEO STARED DISPASSIONATELY at the old woman who was glaring back at him.

'Mum,' Rachel said faintly. 'This is...' She glanced uncertainly at Mateo, clearly not sure how to introduce him.

'My name is Mateo Karavitis,' Mateo intercepted smoothly as he stepped forward and offered his hand. 'A former colleague of your daughter's.'

Rachel's mother looked him up and down, seeming unimpressed. 'Why are you visiting here?' She turned back to Rachel. 'I'm hungry.'

'I'll make you a toastie,' Rachel said soothingly.

She threw Mateo a look that was half apology, half exasperation. He gave her an assured, blandly unfazed smile in return.

So Rachel had a mother who was clearly dependent on her care. It was a surprise, but it did not deter him. If anything, it offered her an added incentive to agree to his proposal, since he would be able to offer her mother top-of-the-line care, either here in England or back in Kallyria.

Not, Mateo reflected as Rachel hurried to the kitchen and her mother harrumphed her way to her bedroom, that she needed much incentive. Judging from everything he'd seen so far of her life outside work, there was nothing much compelling her to stay.

He fully anticipated, after Rachel had got over the sheer

shock of it, that she'd agree to his proposal. How could she not?

He came over to stand in the doorway of the kitchen. Rachel was looking harassed, slicing cheese as fast as she could.

'How long has your mother been living with you?' he asked.

'About eighteen months.' She reached for a jar of Marmite and Mateo stepped forward.

'May I help?'

'What?' Rachel looked both frazzled and bewildered, her hair falling into her eyes. 'No—'

Deftly he unscrewed the jar of Marmite she seemed to have forgotten she was holding. Plucking the knife from her other hand, he began to spread the Marmite across the bread. 'Cheese and Marmite toastie, yes?'

'What?' She stared at him blankly, then down to the bread he was preparing. 'Oh. Er… Yes.'

Mateo finished making the sandwich and placed it on the hot grill. 'Shouldn't be a moment.'

'I don't understand,' Rachel said helplessly. Mateo arched an eyebrow.

'How to make a toastie? You did seem to be having trouble mastering the basics, but I was happy to step in.'

A smile twitched her lips, and Mateo realised how much he'd missed their banter. 'Thank goodness for capable males,' she quipped. 'What on earth would I have done if you hadn't been here?'

His lips quirked back a response. 'Heaven only knows.'

'I shudder to think. Careful it doesn't burn.' She nodded to the grill. 'I'll make my mother a cup of tea—do you want another one?'

'Not unless it has a generous splash of whisky in it.'

'Sorry, I'm afraid that's not possible. Not unless you want to nip out to the off-licence on the corner.'

He stepped closer to her. 'What I really want is to take you to dinner to discuss my proposal properly.'

A look of fear flashed across Rachel's face, surprising him. He didn't think he'd ever seen her actually look afraid before. 'Mateo, I don't think there's any point—'

'I think there is, and, considering how long we have known each other, I also think it's fair to ask for an evening of your time. Assuming your mother can be left for a few hours?'

'As long as she's eaten and the TV's on,' Rachel answered with clear reluctance. 'I suppose.'

'Good. Then I will make arrangements.' He slid his phone out of his pocket and quickly thumbed a text to the security guard he had waiting outside in a hired sedan.

Smoke began to pour out of the oven. 'I think you've burned my mother's toastie,' Rachel said tartly, and with a wry grimace Mateo hurried to rescue the sandwich from the grill.

Half an hour later, Carol Lewis was settled in front of a lurid-looking programme, a toastie and cup of tea on her lap tray.

'I'll be back in about an hour, Mum,' Rachel said, sounding anxious. 'If you need anything, you can always knock on Jim's door.'

'Jim?' Carol demanded. 'Who's Jim?'

'Mr Fairley,' Rachel reminded her patiently. 'He lives in the flat upstairs, number two?' Her mother harrumphed and Rachel gave Mateo an apologetic look as she closed her bedroom door. 'Do I need to change?'

Mateo swept his glance over her figure, noting the way the soft grey cashmere clung to her breasts. 'You look fine.'

Her lips twisted at that, although Mateo wasn't sure why, and she nodded. 'Fine. Let's get this over with.'

Not a promising start, but Mateo was more than hopeful. The more he saw of Rachel's life, the more he was sure she would agree…eventually.

Outside the drenching downpour had tapered off to a misty drizzle, and an autumnal breeze chilled the air. Rachel had shrugged on a navy duffel coat and a rainbow-colored scarf, and Mateo took her elbow as he led her to the waiting car.

'We're not walking?'

'I made a reservation at Cotto.'

'That posh place in the Gonville Hotel?' She pulled her arm away from him, appalled. 'It's so expensive. And I'm not dressed appropriately—'

'You'll be fine. And we're in a private room, anyway.'

She shook her head slowly, not looking impressed so much as uncertain. 'Who *are* you?'

'You know who I am.'

'You never did this before. Private rooms, hired cars—'

'I need to take necessary precautions for my privacy and security, as well as yours. Once it becomes known that I am the King of Kallyria—'

'I can't help but think you're deluded when you say that,' Rachel murmured.

Mateo allowed himself a small smile. 'I assure you, I am not.'

'I know, I really do believe you. I just…don't believe this situation.'

The driver hopped out to open the passenger door of the luxury sedan. Mateo gestured for Rachel to get in first, and she slid inside, running one hand over the sumptuous leather seats.

'Wow,' she murmured, and then turned to face the window.

Mateo slid in beside her, his thigh brushing hers. She moved away. He thought about pressing closer, just to see, but decided now was not the time. The physical side of their potential arrangement was something that would have to be negotiated carefully, and there were certainly other considerations to deal with first.

They didn't speak as the driver navigated Cambridge's traffic through the dark and rain, and finally pulled up in front of the elegant Georgian façade of the Gonville Hotel. A single snap of his fingers at the concierge had the man running towards him, and practically tripping over himself to accommodate such an illustrious personage as the Crown Prince, soon to be King.

Rachel stayed silent as they were ushered into a sumptuous private room, with wood-panelled walls and a mahogany table laid for two with the finest porcelain and silver.

'I've never seen you like this before,' she said once the concierge had closed the door behind them, after Mateo had dismissed him, not wanting to endure his fawning attentions any longer. She shrugged off her coat and slowly unwound her scarf.

'Seen me like what?' Mateo pulled out her chair and she sat down with murmured thanks.

'Acting like…like a king, I suppose. Like you own the place. I mean, you were always a little *arrogant*,' she conceded as she rested her chin in her hand, 'but I thought it was just about your brain.'

Mateo huffed a laugh. 'I'm wondering if I should be offended by that.'

'No, you shouldn't be. I'm basically telling you you're smart.'

'Well, then.'

'Except,' Rachel continued, 'I don't think you're making a very smart decision here.'

Mateo's gaze narrowed as he flicked an uninterested glance at the menu. 'Oh?'

'No, I don't. Really, Mateo, I'd make a terrible queen.'

* * *

Rachel eyed him mischievously, her chin still in her hand. It was actually a bit amusing, to see this self-assured man, who was kind of scaring her in his fancy suit, look so discomfited. It helped her take her mind off the fact that he'd asked her to marry him, and she still had absolutely no idea how to feel about that. Flattered? Furious? Afraid? Appalled? All four, and more.

'I disagree with that assessment,' Mateo said calmly.

'I can't imagine why.'

He frowned, and even when he was looking so ferocious, Rachel couldn't help but acknowledge how devastatingly handsome he was. The crisp white shirt and cobalt-blue tie were the perfect foil for his olive skin and bright blue-green eyes. He'd looked amazing in rumpled shirts and old cords; he looked unbelievably, mouth-dryingly gorgeous now. And it was yet another reminder that they couldn't possibly marry each other.

'I don't understand why you are putting yourself down,' he said, and Rachel squirmed a bit at that. It made her feel pathetic, and she wasn't. A long time ago she'd accepted who she was…and who she wasn't. And she'd been okay with that. She'd made herself be okay, despite the hurt, the lack of self-confidence, the deliberate decision to take potential romance out of the equation of her life.

On the plus side, she had a good brain, a job she loved— or at least she'd *had*—and she had a few good friends, who admittedly had moved on in life in a way she hadn't, but *still*. She'd taken stock of herself and her life and had decided it was all good.

'I'm not putting myself down. I'm just being realistic.'

'Realistic?' Mateo's dark eyebrows rose, his eyes narrowed in aquamarine assessment. 'About not being a good queen? How would you even know?'

'I'm terrible at public speaking.' It was the first thing

she could think of, even though it had so little to do with her argument it was laughable.

Mateo's eyebrows rose further. 'You are not. I have heard you deliver research papers to a full auditorium on many occasions.'

'Yes, but that was research. Chemistry.'

'So?'

She sighed, wondering why she was continuing this ridiculous line of discussion, even as she recognised it was safer than many others. 'I can talk about chemistry. But other things...'

'Because you are passionate about it,' Mateo agreed with a swift nod. Rachel felt her face go pink at the word passionate, which was embarrassing. He wasn't talking about passion in *that* way, and in any case she couldn't think about that aspect of a marriage between them without feeling as if she might scream—or self-combust. 'So you will have to find other things you are passionate about,' he continued calmly. 'I am sure there are many.'

Now her face was fiery, which was ridiculous. Rachel snatched up her menu. 'Why don't we order?'

'I have already ordered. The menu is simply so you can see their offerings.'

'You ordered for me?' Her feminist principles prickled instinctively.

Mateo gave a small smile. 'Only to save on time, since I know you are concerned about your mother, and also because I know what you like.'

'I've never even been to the restaurant.' Now she was a bit insulted, which was easier than feeling all the other emotions jostling for space in her head and heart.

'All right.' Mateo leaned back in his chair, his arms folded, a cat-like smile curling his mobile mouth. A mouth she seemed to have trouble looking away from. 'Look at the menu and tell me what you would order.'

'Why? It's too late—'

'Humour me. And be honest, because if you order the black truffle and parmesan soufflé, I'll know you're lying. You hate truffles.'

How did he know that?

One of their seemingly innocuous conversations in the lab or the pub, Rachel supposed. They might not have shared the intimate details of their personal lives, but food likes and dislikes had always been a safe subject for discussion.

She glanced down at the menu, feeling self-conscious and weirdly exposed, even though they were just talking about choices at a restaurant. Across the table Mateo lounged back in his chair, that small smile playing about his lips, looking supremely confident. He was so sure he knew what she was going to order.

Rachel continued to peruse the offerings, tempted to pick something unlikely, yet knowing Mateo would see through such a silly ploy.

'Fine.' She put the menu down and gave him a knowing look. 'The beetroot and goat cheese salad to start, and the asparagus risotto for my main.'

His smile widened slightly as his gaze fastened on hers, making little lightning bolts run up and down her arms. Now, *that* was alarming. She'd inoculated herself against Mateo's obvious attraction years ago. She'd had to.

You couldn't work with someone day in and day out, heads bent close together, and feel sparkly inside while the person next to you so obviously felt nothing. It was positively soul-deadening, not to mention ego-destroying, and Rachel had had enough of both of those. And so she'd made herself not respond to him, not even *think* about responding to him.

Yet now she was.

'So is that what you ordered for me?' she asked, a little bolshily, to hide her discomfort and awareness.

'Let's find out, shall we?' As if on cue, a waiter came quietly into the private room, two silver-domed dishes in his hands. He set them at their places, and then lifted the lids with a flourish. Rachel stared down at her beetroot and goat cheese salad and felt ridiculously annoyed.

'You just like winning,' she told him as she took her fork. The salad did look delicious. 'I mean, how many hours did you practise reciting the periodic table just to beat me?'

'Practise,' Mateo scoffed. 'As if.'

She shook her head slowly as she toyed with a curly piece of radicchio. 'You might know what I like to eat, but that's all.'

'All?'

'That is not a challenge. I just mean…we don't actually know each other, Mateo.' She swallowed, uncomfortably aware of the throb of feeling in her voice. 'I know we've worked together for ten years, and we could call each other friends, but… I didn't even know you were a prince.'

'No one knew I was a prince.'

'And you don't know anything about me. We've never really talked about our personal lives.'

She felt a ripple of frustration from Mateo, like a wavelength in the air. He shrugged as he stabbed a delicate slice of carpaccio on his plate. 'So talk. Tell me whatever it is you wish me to know.'

'What an inviting prospect. Why don't I just give you my CV?'

'I've seen your CV, but do feel free.'

Rachel shook her head. 'It's not just a matter of processing some information, Mateo. It's *why* we don't know anything about each other. Ten years working together, and you don't even know…' she cast about for a salient fact '… my middle name.'

'Anne,' Mateo answered immediately. And at her blank look, 'It's on your CV.'

Rachel rolled her eyes. 'Fine, something else, then. Something that's not on my CV.'

Mateo cocked his head, his gaze sweeping slowly over her, warming everywhere it touched, as if she were bathed in sunlight. 'I'm not going to know something you haven't told me,' he said after a moment. 'So it's pointless to play a guessing game. But I know more about you than perhaps you realise.'

Which was a very uncomfortable thought. Rachel squirmed in her seat at the thought of how much Mateo could divine from having worked so closely with her for ten years. All her quirks, idiosyncrasies, annoyances... She really did not want to have the excoriating experience of having him list everything he'd noticed over the past decade.

He was a scientist, trained in matters of observation. He would have noticed *a lot*, and she should have noticed the same amount about him, but the trouble was she'd been exerting so much energy trying *not* to notice him that she wasn't sure she had.

Which put him at a distinct and disturbing advantage.

'Look, that isn't really the point,' she said quickly. 'This is not even about you knowing or not knowing me.'

'Is it not? Then what is it about?'

Rachel stared at him helplessly. She wasn't going to say it. She wasn't going to humiliate herself by pointing out the glaringly obvious discrepancies in their stations in life, in their *looks*. She didn't want to enumerate in how many ways she was not his equal, how absurd the idea of a marriage between them would seem, because she'd been in this position before and it had been the worst experience of her life.

'It's about the fact that I don't want to marry you,' she said in as flat and final a tone as she could. 'And I certainly don't want to be queen of a country.'

Something flickered across Mateo's beautiful face and then was gone. His gaze remained steady on hers as he answered. 'While I will naturally accept your decision if that is truly how you feel, I do not believe you have given it proper consideration.'

'That's because it is so outrageous—'

He leaned forward, eyes glinting, mouth curved, everything in him alert and aware and somehow predatory. Rachel tried not to shrink back in her seat. She'd never seen Mateo look so intent.

'I think,' he said, 'it is my turn to give my arguments.'

CHAPTER FIVE

RACHEL'S EYES WIDENED at his pronouncement, lush lashes framing their dark softness in a way that made Mateo want to reach across the table and touch her. Cup her cheek and see if her skin was as soft as it looked. He realised he hadn't actually *touched* his former colleague very much over the last ten years. Brushed shoulders, perhaps, but not much more. But that was something to explore later.

Right now she needed convincing, and he was more than ready to begin. He'd patiently listened to her paltry arguments, sensing that she wasn't saying what she really felt. What she really feared. And he'd get to that in time, but now it was his turn to explain why this was such a very good idea.

Because, after an evening in her presence, Mateo was more convinced than ever that it was. Rachel was smart and focused and, more importantly, he *liked* her. And best of all, he *only* liked her. While he sensed a spark of attraction for her that could surely be fanned into an acceptable flame, he knew he didn't feel anything more than that.

No overwhelming emotion, no flood of longing, desire, or something deeper. And if he didn't feel that after ten years basically by her side, he would never feel it.

Which was a very good thing.

'All right,' Rachel said, her voice wavering slightly although her gaze was sharp and focused, her arms folded. 'I'm waiting for these brilliant arguments.'

'I didn't say they were brilliant,' Mateo replied with a small smile. 'But of course they are.'

Rachel rolled her eyes. 'Of course.'

Mateo paused, enjoying their back and forth as he considered how best to approach the subject. 'The real question, I suppose,' he said slowly, 'is why *wouldn't* we get married?' He let that notion hover in the air between them, before it landed with a thud.

'Why wouldn't we?' Rachel repeated disbelievingly. 'Please, Mateo. You're a *scientist*. Don't give me an argument from fallacy. Neither of us is married. Therefore we should marry. That is *not* how it works.'

'That is not how science works,' Mateo agreed, hiding his smile at her response. She was so fiery. He'd never enjoyed it quite so much before. 'But this isn't science.'

'Isn't it?' she challenged, a gleam in her eye that looked a little too much like vulnerability. 'Because I'm not sure what else it could be.'

She had him on the back foot, and he didn't enjoy the sensation. Mateo took a sip of the wine the waiter had brought—a Rioja because he knew Rachel liked fruity reds—to stall for time. 'Elucidate, please.'

'Fine, I'll *elucidate*.' She lifted her chin slightly, her eyes still gleaming, making Mateo feel even more uncomfortable. Something more was going on here than what was apparent, and it made him a little nervous. 'You came back to Cambridge to convince me to marry you. Considering we've never dated or even thought about dating for an entire decade, it's hardly love or physical attraction that brought you to my doorstep.' She spoke matter-of-factly, which was a relief. He must have been imagining that unnerving note of vulnerability in her voice, of something close to hurt. Yes, he had to have been.

'True,' Mateo was willing to concede with a brief nod.

'So the reasons for wanting me to marry you are scientific, or at least expedient, ones. Let me guess.' She paused, and Mateo almost interrupted her. He wasn't sure he wanted his arguments framed in her perspective.

'All right,' he said after a moment, leaning back in his chair to make it seem as if he were more relaxed than he was. 'Guess.'

Rachel pursed her lips, her gaze becoming distant as she considered. Mateo waited, feeling tense, expectant, almost eager now to hear what she thought.

'We get along,' she said at last. 'We have a fairly good rapport, which I imagine would be important if we were working together to rule a country.' She shook her head, smiling ruefully. 'I can't believe I'm even *saying* that.'

'I take exception to *fairly*,' Mateo interjected with a small smile, willing her to smile back. She did, tightly.

'Fine. We get along well. Very well, even.'

He inclined his head. 'Thank you.'

Rachel let out a breath. 'And we know each other, on a basic level.'

'More than a basic—'

'You said you trust me,' she cut across him.

'I do.' His heartfelt words seemed to reverberate between them, and Mateo watched with interest as her cheeks went pink.

'Still,' Rachel pressed. 'None of that is reason to get married.'

Mateo arched an eyebrow. 'Is it not?'

'If it was, you should have asked Leonore Worth to marry you,' she flung at him a bit tartly.

'Leonore?' She was a lecturer in biology at the university, a pointy woman with a nasal laugh whom he'd escorted to a department function once. He hadn't made that mistake again. But why was Rachel mentioning *her*? 'Why would I do that?' he asked.

'Because she's…' Rachel paused, drawing a hitched breath. Her cheeks were turning red. 'More suited to the role than I am,' she finished.

Mateo stared at her, mystified. 'I am wondering, from a purely scientific view, of course, how you arrived at that conclusion.'

She shook her head, looking tired, even angry. 'Come on, Mateo,' she said in a low voice. 'Stop it.'

'Stop what?'

'Pretending you don't know what I'm talking about.'

'I don't.' Of that he was sure. They were skirting around something big and dark but damned if he knew what it was.

Rachel flung her arms out, nearly knocking her plate of almost untouched salad to the floor. 'I am not queen material.'

'Define your terms, please,' Mateo said. Perhaps it would be easier if they did make this as scientific as possible: What is queen material?

'Oh, this is pointless,' she cried. 'I'm not going to marry you. I'm not going to leave my job—'

'Toadying up to smarmy Simon?' he interjected. 'You've already said you're considering looking elsewhere.'

'I didn't really mean that.'

'Your job has changed, Rachel, and not for the better. I'm offering you a greater opportunity.'

'To hang on your arm?' Her sneer was insulting.

'Of course not. If I wanted a mere trophy wife, I would have picked one of the eminently suitable candidates on the list my mother drew up.'

Rachel nearly choked at that, her soft brown eyes going shocked and wide. 'There's a list?'

'Yes, more's the pity. I don't want a trophy wife, one who ticks all the boxes. I want someone I can trust. Someone who makes me laugh. Someone who, dare I sound so sentimental, *gets* me.'

Tears filled her eyes, appalling him. He'd been trying for humour, but he feared he'd only sounded twee. 'Rachel...'

'Why are you making this so hard?' she whispered, blinking back tears. Her teeth sank into her lower lip, creating two rosy indents he had the urge to soothe away—with his tongue. Mateo forced the unwanted and unhelpful image back.

'I'm making it hard because I want you to agree.'

'And if I did?'

The thrill of victory raced through his veins, roared in his ears. Never mind that she sounded a bit sad, a touch defeated. *She was actually considering it.*

'Then I'd arrange for you to travel back to Kallyria with me as soon as possible. We'd be married as soon as possible after that, in the Cathedral of Saint Theodora. Everyone in the royal family has been married in the Greek Orthodox church. I hope that is acceptable to you.'

'Mateo, I was speaking hypothetically.'

He shrugged, refusing to be deterred. 'So was I.'

'But after the ceremony? What then?'

'Then we live together as man and wife. You accompany me to state functions, on royal tours. You decide on which charitable institutions you wish to pioneer or support.'

'And I give you an heir?' She met his gaze even though her cheeks were fiery now. 'That's a part of this marriage deal you haven't actually mentioned yet.'

'No, I haven't,' Mateo agreed after a moment. He wished he knew why she was blushing—was it just because they were talking about sex? Or was it something else, something more? 'It seemed fairly obvious.'

'That this would be a marriage in...in every sense of the word?'

'If, by that phrase, you mean we'd consummate it, then

yes.' He held her gaze evenly despite the images dancing through his mind. Images he'd never, ever indulged in before, of Rachel in slips of silk and lace, smiling up at him from a canopied bed in the royal palace, her thick, wavy hair spread across the pillow in a chocolate river...

'Don't you think that's kind of a big thing to discuss?' Rachel asked, her voice sounding a little strangled. 'Obvious as it may seem?'

'Fine.' Mateo spread his hands as a waiter came in to quickly and quietly clear their dishes. 'Then let's discuss it.'

What had she got herself into? Rachel sat in silent mortification, willing her blush to recede, as the waiter cleared their plates and Mateo waited, completely unfazed by the turn in the conversation, just as he'd been unfazed by everything that had already been said.

He was like a bulldozer, flattening her every objection, making his proposal seem obvious, as if she should have been expecting it. And meanwhile Rachel felt as if she kept stumbling down rabbit holes and across minefields, dodging all the dangers and pitfalls, as she was accosted by yet another reason why a marriage between them would never work.

'You're not attracted to me,' she stated baldly. It hurt to say it; it humiliated her beyond all measure, in fact, and brought up too many bad memories or, really, just one in particular, but Rachel had long ago realised that confronting the elephant in the room, naming and shaming it, was the only way forward for her dignity. She'd done it before and she'd do it again, and she'd come out stronger for it. That much had been her promise to herself, made when she was a shy and naïve twenty and still holding true today, twelve years later.

She held his gaze and watched his lips purse as an expression flickered across his face that she would have given her eye teeth to identify, but could not.

'Sexual attraction is not a strong foundation for a marriage,' he said at last, and Rachel swallowed, trying not to let the sting of those words penetrate too deeply.

'It's not the most important part, perhaps,' she allowed. 'But it matters.'

Another lengthy silence, which told her just how unattracted to her he had to be. Rachel took a sip of wine, her gaze lowered, as she did her best to keep Mateo from knowing how much he was hurting her.

'I don't believe it will be an obstacle to our state of matrimony,' he said at last. 'Unless you have an intense aversion to me?' He said this with such smiling, smug self-assurance that Rachel had the sudden urge to throw her wine in his face. Oh, no, of *course* it couldn't be the case that she found him undesirable. Of course *that* was a joke.

'It might surprise you,' she said with a decided edge to her voice, 'but I want more from a potential marriage than the idea that my attractiveness, or lack of it, won't be an *obstacle*.'

Mateo's eyes widened as he acknowledged her tone, the rise and fall of her chest. She saw his lips compress and his pupils flare and knew he didn't like her sudden display of emotion. Well, she didn't like it, either.

She was far too agitated for either of their own good, and their reasonable, scientific discussion had morphed into something emotional and, well, *awful*. Because she really didn't want any more explanations about how he was willing to sacrifice sexual attraction on the altar of— what? His duty? Their compatibility? Logic? Whatever it was, Rachel didn't want to know. She'd had enough of being patronised. Enough of being felt as if she'd just about do. She'd had enough of that before this absurd conversation had even begun.

'Please.' She raised one hand to forestall any explanations he might have felt compelled to give, throwing her napkin onto the table with the other. 'Please don't say anything more, because I really don't want to hear it. Any of it. I am not going to marry you, Mateo, end of. Thanks anyway.'

She rose from the table on unsteady legs, her chest still heaving. She had to get out of here before she did something truly terrible, like start to cry.

But before she could even grab her coat, Mateo had risen from his own seat and crossed the small table to take her by the arms, his grip firm and sure.

'If you will not believe my words,' he said in a voice bordering a growl, 'then perhaps you will believe my actions.'

And then he kissed her.

It had been a long time since Rachel had been kissed. So long, in fact, that she'd sort of forgotten she had lips. Lips that could be touched and explored and licked. Lips that Mateo was moving over with his own, his tongue tracing the seam of her mouth before delving inward, making her knees weaken. She'd never known knees to actually do that before. She'd considered it a metaphor rather than scientific fact.

His lips felt both hard and soft, warm and cool. A thousand sensations exploded inside her as she parted her own lips, inviting him in. He reached up and cupped her cheek with his big, warm hand, his thumb stroking her skin, making her both shiver and shudder. Everything felt as if it were on fire.

The kiss went on and on, deeper and deeper, fireworks exploding all over her body. She'd never been kissed like this. She'd never *felt* like this.

Her hands came up of their own accord to clutch at his hard shoulders, fingers clawing at him, begging him for more.

And he gave it, one knee sliding between her own will-ing legs, the length of his hard, taut body pressed against hers for one glorious second before he stepped away, look-ing as composed to Rachel's dazed gaze as if they'd just shaken hands.

While she…she was in pieces. *Pieces*, scattered on the floor, with her mind spinning too much to even start to pick them up.

'I think that proves,' Mateo said in a clipped voice as he straightened his suit jacket, 'that attraction is not an issue.'

He stood there, a faint smile curling his mouth, his eyes gleaming with unmistakable triumph, while Rachel was still gasping and reeling from what had obviously been an unremarkable kiss to him. Meanwhile it had rocked her world right off its axis. Heaven only knew if she'd be able to straighten it again.

Standing in front of her, his arms folded, his eyebrows raised, he looked so confident, so utterly assured of his un-deniable masculine appeal, that Rachel wanted to scream. Claw the face she'd just kissed. Had he really felt it neces-sary to prove how in thrall to him she could be?

While he seemed almost at pains to show how utterly unaffected he was—his expression composed, his breath-ing even, his manner bland.

Damn him.

'If you thought that was meant to win me over, you were wrong,' Rachel choked out, unable to hide the tears of mor-tification that had sprung to her eyes. She couldn't stand another minute of this utter humiliation. When she'd felt it once before, she'd vowed never to expose herself to it again, and so she wouldn't. This meeting was over.

While Mateo looked on, seeming distinctly nonplussed, she grabbed her coat and yanked it on, winding the scarf tightly around her neck, needing as many barriers between him and her as she could get.

'Rachel…' He stretched out one hand, his brows knitted together. He didn't understand. He thought she should be grateful for his attention, for the fact that he could kiss like a cross between Prince Charming and Casanova. And that made Rachel even more furious, so her voice shook as she spoke her next words.

'You might think you're God's greatest gift to women, Mateo Karr—whatever, but that doesn't mean I'm about to fall into your lap like a plum ripe for the picking. As much as you so obviously thought I would.' She jabbed a finger into his powerful pecs for good measure, making his eyes widen.

'So you're handsome. So you're a good kisser. So you're an out-and-out prince. I don't care! I don't care a—a *fig* about any of it. I am *not* marrying you.' And with that final battle cry, the tears she'd tried to keep back spilling from her eyes, Rachel stalked out of the room.

CHAPTER SIX

WELL. THAT HADN'T gone exactly as he'd expected. In fact, it hadn't gone the way he'd expected at *all*—a failed experiment, if there ever was one.

Because if he'd truly been conducting an experiment, Mateo acknowledged with a grimace, he would have first made his aim.

To convince Rachel Lewis to marry him, and that physical compatibility would not be an issue for them.

And his prediction? That she would agree, and it wouldn't. And the variables? Well, how attracted they both would be, he supposed. And those had been *variable* indeed.

In fact, he didn't really like to think how variable their attraction had been. He'd been acting on instinct at first, sensing that Rachel needed proof that physicality between them would not be a problem. And from the moment his lips had brushed hers—no, from the moment he'd put his hands on her arms, felt her warm softness, and drawn her to him—he'd known there was no problem at all.

In fact, the *lack* of problem suggested a problem. Because Mateo hadn't expected that variable, hadn't expected to want more and more from the woman who had become so pliant in his arms.

Well, he told himself now, there had been another variable—the fact that he hadn't had sex in a very long time, and so his response had to have been predicated on that. Explainable. Simple. It didn't *mean* anything. It certainly didn't mean he had some sort of ridiculously overwhelming attraction to Rachel Lewis, when he hadn't looked at her that way even once in ten years.

Which right now felt like a comfort. He could be attracted to her, but it wasn't a force in his life. It wasn't something he would have to keep under control.

Not that it mattered anyway, because she'd stormed out of here as if she never intended seeing him again.

So what should his next step be? Why had she been so offended by his kiss? He'd felt her response, so he knew it wasn't some sort of maidenly revulsion. He thought of her words—*'You might think you're God's greatest gift to women...'*

He hardly thought that, of course. Admittedly, he'd never had trouble finding sexual partners, not that he'd had all that many. He was too focused on his work and too discerning in his companions to sleep around, but it certainly wasn't for lack of interest on women's—*many* women's— part. But Mateo didn't think he was arrogant about it, and he hadn't been proving to Rachel how attractive she found him, but rather how good they could be together.

And the answer was they could be quite surprisingly good indeed.

So why had she been annoyed? Why had she seemed, rather alarmingly, *hurt*?

Mateo was still musing on this when there was a tap on the door. Expecting the waiter back, to deliver the main course they now wouldn't be eating, he barked a command to enter.

The door creaked open slowly and Rachel appeared. Her hair was in damp tendrils around her face, and the shoulders of her coat were wet. The look she gave him was one of abashed humour.

'I think I may have been a little bit of a drama queen there,' she said, and Mateo nearly laughed with the relief of having her back, smiling at him.

'At least you were a queen,' he returned with a small smile. 'I knew you had it in you.'

She laughed ruefully and shook her head. 'This is all so crazy, Mateo.'

'I agree that it seems crazy, but how many experiments have we conducted over the years that others said were crazy? Or pointless? Or just wouldn't work?'

She bit her lip, white teeth sinking into pink lushness, making Mateo remember exactly how those lips had felt. Tasted. 'Quite a few.'

'And this is just another experiment. The ultimate experiment.' It sounded so clever and neat, but a shadow had entered Rachel's eyes.

'And what happens when the experiment fails?'

'It won't.' He answered swiftly, too swiftly. She wasn't convinced.

'We write up the lab results? Draw some conclusions? *Marriages between princes and commoners are not a good idea.*'

'I admit, the experiment analogy only goes so far. And you only have to look at this country's royal family to know that a marriage between a prince and a commoner has an excellent chance of success.'

'Or not.'

'The point is, our marriage can be successful. There's absolutely no reason for it not to be.'

'Isn't there?' There was a note of sorrowful vulnerability in her voice that made Mateo tense. And this had all been starting to look so promising.

'Are you referring to something specific?' he asked in as reasonable a tone as he could manage.

She sighed, shrugging off her wet coat as she sat back

down at the table. It seemed they would be eating their main course, after all. 'Yes and no, I suppose.'

Mateo took his own seat. 'As you know, there are no yes-and-no situations in science.'

'This isn't science. But it may be chemistry.' She met his gaze evenly, her expression determined.

'Physical chemistry,' Mateo stated, because it was obvious. 'You think we don't have it? I thought I proved—'

'You proved you were a good kisser,' Rachel cut across him. 'And that you can…make me respond to you.'

He frowned, wishing he could figure out what was bothering her, and why it was so much. 'And that is a problem?'

'It's not a problem. It's just…an inequality.' She looked away, blinking rapidly, and Mateo realised that no matter her seemingly calm and practical exterior, something about their kiss had affected her deeply, and not on a physical level.

'Why were you a drama queen, Rachel?' he asked slowly, feeling his way through the words. 'What made you respond so…emotionally?'

She was silent, her expression distant as she looked away from him, and Mateo decided not to press.

'When are our main courses coming?' she finally asked. 'I stormed out of here without eating my salad, and I'm starving.'

'So why did you storm out of here, exactly?' Mateo asked, taking the obvious opening. Rachel paused, her once determined gaze sliding away from his. Whatever it was, she clearly didn't want to tell him. 'Rachel,' he said gently, 'if we're going to be married, I need to know.'

She swung back towards him, her face drawn in lines of laughing disbelief. '"If we're going to be married"? A little cocksure, aren't you, Mateo?'

'I meant hypothetically,' he returned smoothly. 'If it's

something you're thinking about even remotely…and you must be, because you came back here.'

'Maybe I came back here because I value your friendship.'

'That too.'

'And I didn't want to look like a prima donna.'

'Three reasons, then.'

She laughed and shook her head. 'Oh, Mateo. If we don't get married, I will miss you.'

Something leapt inside him and he leaned forward. 'Then marry me, Rachel.' His voice throbbed with more intent than he wanted to reveal. More desire.

Her eyes widened as her gaze moved over his face, as if she were trying to plumb the depths of him, and Mateo didn't want that. He held her gaze but he schooled his expression into something calm and determined. How he really felt.

'The reason I might have overreacted,' she said slowly, her gaze still on his face, 'is because I've… I've been burned before. By an arrogant man who thought I'd be grateful for his attentions, and then made a joke of them afterwards.'

Mateo didn't like the sound of that at *all*. Everything in him tightened as he answered levelly, 'Tell me more.'

She shrugged, spreading her hands. 'Sadly there's not much more to tell. He was a doctoral student when I was in my second year at Oxford—he paid me special attention, I thought he cared. He didn't, and he let people know it.' Her lips tightened as she looked away.

What was that supposed to mean? 'He hurt you?' Mateo asked, amazed at how much he disliked the thought. Not just disliked, but *detested*, with a deep, gut-churning emotion he didn't expect or want to feel.

'Emotionally, yes, he did. But I got over it.' Rachel lifted her chin, a gesture born of bravery. 'I didn't love him, not like that. But my ego was bruised, and I felt humiliated and hurt, and I decided for myself that I was never going to let another man treat me that way ever again, and so far I haven't.'

Realisation trickled icily through him and he jerked back a little. 'And you think I did? Was?'

'It felt like that at the time, but, I admit, I probably over-reacted, due to my past experience.' She shrugged again. 'So now you know.'

Yet he didn't know, not really. He didn't know what this vile man had done, or how exactly he'd humiliated Rachel. He didn't know how she'd responded, or how long it had taken her to recover and heal. But Mateo was reluctant to ask any more, to know any more. It was her private pain, and she'd tell him if she wanted to. Besides, information was responsibility, and he had enough of that to be going on with.

'I'm sorry,' he said. 'For what happened. And how I made you feel.'

'You didn't mean to. At least I don't think you did. Which is why I'm still here.' She gave him one of her old grins. 'That, and the risotto that had better be here soon.'

'I assure you, it is.' Mateo reached for his phone and texted the maître d' of the restaurant, whom he'd contacted earlier to make the reservation. Within seconds the waiter was back, with two more silver-domed dishes.

'So if you really are a prince,' Rachel asked after he'd whisked the lids off and left, 'where's your security detail? Why isn't there a guy in a dark suit with a walkie-talkie in the corner of the room?'

'That would be a rather unpleasant breach of privacy,' Mateo returned. 'He's outside in the hall.'

Rachel nearly dropped her fork. '*Is* he?'

'Of course.'

She shook her head slowly. 'Did you have security all the time in Cambridge? Was I just completely blind?'

'No, I didn't. I chose not to. As the third in line to the throne, I had that freedom.'

'But you don't any more.'

His lips and gut both tightened. 'No.'

Rachel watched Mateo's expression shutter with a flicker of curiosity, and a deeper ripple of compassion. 'Do you want to be king?' she asked and he stiffened, the shutter coming down even more.

'It's not a question of want. It's my duty.'

'You didn't actually answer me.'

His mouth thinned as he inclined his head. 'Very well. I want to do my duty.'

Which sounded rather grim. Rachel took a forkful of risotto and chewed slowly. It was delicious, rich and creamy, but she barely registered the flavour as her mind whirled. Was she really thinking seriously about saying yes to Mateo's shocking proposal?

It had struck her, as she'd stormed away from the restaurant and got soaked in the process, that she was a little too outraged. It was easier to feel outraged, to wrap herself in it like a cloak of armour, than to think seriously about what Mateo was suggesting.

And yet the farther she'd walked, the more she'd realised she had to be sensible about this. She had to be the scientist she'd always been. She couldn't sail on the high tide of emotion, not for long. It simply wasn't in her nature.

And so she'd gone back, and now she was here, thinking seriously about saying yes.

'So what would a marriage between us look like?' she asked. 'On a day-to-day basis?'

'We'd live in the royal palace in Constanza,' Mateo answered with calm swiftness. 'It is a beautiful place, built five hundred years ago, right on the sea.'

'Okay...'

'As I said before, you could choose your involvement in various charities and initiatives. Admittedly, there would be a fair amount of ribbon cutting and clapping, that sort of thing. It's unavoidable, I'm afraid.'

'I don't mind that. But I don't exactly look the part, do I?' She had to say it.

Mateo looked distinctly nonplussed. 'So you've intimated before. If you mean clothes, I assure you, you will be provided with a complete wardrobe of your choice, along with personal stylists and hairdressers as you wish.'

'So like Cinderella.' She didn't know how she felt about that. A little excited? A little insulted? A little afraid? All three, and more than a little.

Mateo shrugged. 'Like any royal princess—or queen.'

'And what about children?' Rachel asked. Her stomach quivered at the thought. 'You mentioned needing an heir as soon as possible.'

'Yes.'

'That's kind of a big thing, Mateo.'

'I agree.'

'You don't even know if I want children.'

'I assume we would not be having this discussion if you were completely averse to the idea.'

Rachel sighed and laid down her fork. Her stomach was churning too much to eat. 'I don't even know,' she admitted. 'I haven't let myself think about it.'

Mateo frowned, his gaze searching her face. 'Let yourself?'

'I'm thirty-two, and I haven't had a serious relationship since university. I assumed it wasn't likely to happen.'

'Well, now you can assume differently.'

'Assuming I can get pregnant in the first place.'

He shrugged. 'Is there any reason you believe you cannot?'

'No.' She couldn't believe they were talking about having a baby together so clinically, and yet somehow it didn't surprise her at all. Mateo was approaching the whole matter of their marriage in as scientific a way as possible, which she didn't mind, not exactly.

'What about love?' she asked baldly. 'I know you didn't approach me because of love, but is it something that could happen in time? Something you'd hope for?' A long silence ensued, which told her everything.

'Is that something you would wish?' Mateo asked finally. 'Something you would hope for?'

Which sounded pathetic, and was the exact reason why she'd thought this whole idea was ridiculous in the first place. Well, that and a lot of other reasons, too.

And yet…was it? Did she want the fairy-tale romance, to fall head over heels in love with someone? With *Mateo*? Falling head over heels sounded painful. And from her limited experience with Josh, it had been. Did she really want that again, just because everyone around her—on TV, in books—seemed to assume it was?

When she and Mateo had first started working together, she'd had a bit of a crush on him and she'd worked to get over it. And she *had*. Did she really want to feel that soul-pinching, gut-churning sensation of liking someone more than he liked you, and in this case to a much more serious degree? Wouldn't it be easier if they just both agreed to keep that off the table for ever?

'Honestly, I don't know,' she said slowly. 'It's what everyone assumes you should want.'

'Maybe between the pages of a book like the one on your coffee table, but not in real life. Feelings like that fade, Rachel. What we have—what we could have—would be real.'

'You don't need to sound quite so dismissive about the whole idea,' Rachel returned.

'Not dismissive,' Mateo countered. 'Sensible. And I think you're sensible, as well.' He held her gaze, his aquamarine eyes like lasers. Not for the first time, Rachel wondered why he had to be so beautiful. It would be so much easier if he was more normal looking. Average.

'So you're not interested in falling in love?' she asked, unsure if her tone was pathetic or joking or somewhere in between. 'I just want to make sure.'

Mateo was silent for a long, painful moment. 'No,' he said finally. 'I am not.'

She nodded, absorbing that, recognising that at least then the whole issue would be off the table. Not something to be discussed or hoped for, ever. Could she live with that? Was she *sensible* enough? 'I have my mother to consider,' she said at last, hardly able to believe they were now talking about real practicalities. 'She has Alzheimer's. She needs my care.'

'That is not a problem. She can accompany us to Kallyria, where she will receive top medical care, her own suite of rooms, and a full-time nurse.'

'I don't know if she could cope with that much change. She struggled to move here from Sussex.'

'If it is preferable, she could stay in Cambridge. I can arrange her care at the best residential facility in the area immediately.'

Rachel sighed. Thinking of her mother made her feel anxious—and guilty. Because the thought of escaping the mundanity of her life with her mother, the constant complaining and criticism that she'd faced her whole life and that had become only worse with her mother's disease, was wonderfully liberating.

'I don't know,' she said at last. 'I suppose I could discuss it with her.' A prospect that made her stomach cramp.

'If it helps, I could do that with you,' Mateo said, and for a second Rachel felt as if she'd put on a pair of 3D glasses. She could see the whole world in an entirely different dimension.

If she married Mateo, she wouldn't have to do everything alone. She'd have someone advocating for her, supporting her, and backing her up. Someone to laugh with, to share life with, to discuss ideas and sleep next to. What did love have on any of that? Suddenly, blindingly, it was obvious. Wonderfully obvious.

'Thank you,' she said after a moment, her voice shaky, her mind still spinning.

'It's not a problem at all.' Mateo paused, his hands flat on the table as he gave her a direct look. 'While I recognise the seriousness of your decision, and the understandable need for time to consider, I am afraid matters are quite pressing. The situation in my country is urgent.'

'Urgent?'

'The instability of rule has led to a rise in insurgency. Nothing that cannot be dealt with, but it means I need to be back in Kallyria, firmly on my throne, my wife at my side, as soon as possible.'

'How soon as possible do you mean?' Rachel asked as she grappled with the whole idea of insurgency and Mateo needing to deal with it.

'Tomorrow would be best.'

'*Tomorrow...?*' She gaped at him. 'Mateo, I'd have to give at least a term's notice—'

'That can be dealt with.'

'My mother—'

'Again, it can be dealt with.'

'My flat…'

'I can arrange for it to be sold or kept, as you wish.'

She'd worked hard to save for that flat. Prices in Cambridge had skyrocketed over the last decade and, even on a researcher's salary, buying the flat had been a stretch. Rachel took a quick, steadying breath. 'I don't know. This is a lot quicker than I expected.'

'I understand.' Yet his tone was implacable. He understood, but he would not change the terms. And that, Rachel realised, was an attitude she would encounter and have to accept again and again if she said yes.

'I don't know,' she said at last. 'Can I think about it for a little while, at least? A night, and I'll tell you first thing in the morning?'

Mateo hesitated, and Rachel knew even that felt like too long to him. Then he gave a brief nod. 'Very well. But if you do say yes, Rachel, I will have to put things in motion very quickly.'

'I understand.'

He hesitated, then reached over and covered her hand with his own, his palm warm and large and comforting on hers. 'I know this all seems quite overwhelming. There are so many different things to consider. But I do believe, Rachel, I believe completely, that we could have a very successful and happy marriage. I wouldn't be here if I didn't believe that absolutely.'

She nodded, pressing her lips together to keep them from trembling. Already she knew what her answer would be.

CHAPTER SEVEN

RACHEL PEERED OUT of the window as the misty grey fog
of an English autumn grew smaller below and the plane
lifted into a bright azure sky. It was the day after Mateo's
proposal, and they were on the royal Kallyrian jet, for an
overnight flight to Constanza.

Rachel's head was still spinning from how quickly everything had happened. Mateo had escorted her home,
kissed her cheek, and told her he would ring her at seven
in the morning for her answer.

Back in her flat, with her mother parked in front of a
television on highest volume and the burnt smell of her
toastie still hanging in the air, Rachel had felt the smallness of her existence descend on her like a thick fog. When
she'd opened a patronising email from Supercilious Simon,
it had been the push she hadn't even needed.

She was going to say yes. As crazy as it seemed, as risky
as it might be, she believed in her heart that life was meant
for living, not just existing, and without Mateo in it that was
what hers had become. A matter of survival.

She spent a sleepless night trying to imagine her future
and unable to come up with anything more than hazy, vague
scenes out of a Grace Kelly film, or maybe *The Princess
Diaries*. When her mobile buzzed next to her bed at seven
o'clock precisely, her stomach whirled with nerves—but
also excitement.

'Mateo?'

'Have you decided?'

She took a breath, let it fill her lungs. She felt as if she were leaping and twirling into outer space. 'Yes,' she said softly. 'I say yes.'

Mateo had sprung instantly into action. He'd disconnected the call almost immediately, saying he would come over within the next half-hour to begin arrangements.

'My mother...' Rachel had begun, starting to panic. 'She doesn't do well with change...'

'We will make her transition as smooth as possible,' Mateo promised her, and it had been. He'd left her mother speechless and simpering under the full wattage of his charm, and that very afternoon the three of them had toured the high-end nursing home on the outskirts of Cambridge that had a private facility for memory-impaired residents.

Carol had seemed remarkably pleased with it all—the private room was far larger and more luxurious than the one she currently had, and the nursing home had a full schedule of activities. And when Rachel had explained she would be moving away, her mother hadn't been bothered in the least. Not, Rachel acknowledged with a sigh, that that had been much of a surprise.

Still, it all seemed so incredibly, head-spinningly fast. Her mother was already settled in the nursing home; Rachel and Mateo had moved her over that very evening. A lump had formed in Rachel's throat as she'd hugged her mother goodbye. Who knew when or if she'd see her again? Yet her mother had barely seemed aware of her departure; she'd turned away quickly, intent on investigating the lounge area with its large flat-screen TV. As she'd watched her mother shuffle away, it had seemed hard to believe that she'd once been the sophisticated and erudite wife of a prominent academic.

'Bye, Mum,' she'd whispered, and then she'd walked away without looking back.

Back at her flat, Rachel had packed her things up in a single suitcase, since Mateo had assured her she would not need anything once she was in Kallyria; all would be provided. He advised only to take keepsakes and mementoes, of which she had very few.

It felt a little sad, a bit pathetic, to leave an entire life behind so easily. She'd email her friends once she reached Kallyria, and Mateo had promised her that he would pay for anyone she wished to attend the wedding to be flown over. He'd dealt with her job situation, and she'd felt a flicker of sorrow that, after ten years, she could both walk away and be let go so easily. But Cambridge was a transient place; people moved in and out all the time. Even after ten years, she was just one more.

Still, Rachel told herself as the royal jet levelled out, there was no point in being melancholy. She was about to embark on the adventure of a lifetime, and she wanted to enjoy it.

She glanced at Matteo, who was sitting across from her in a sumptuous seat of white leather, frowning down at his laptop. Since securing her hand in marriage, he had paid very little attention to her, but Rachel hadn't minded. He had much to attend to, a country to rule and, besides, she wasn't one to want to be fussed over.

Still, she wouldn't have minded a bit of conversation now.

'I feel like we should have champagne,' she said a bit playfully, and Mateo looked up from his screen with a frown.

'Champagne? Of course.' He snapped his fingers and a steward materialised silently, as if plucked from the air.

'Yes, Your Highness?'

That was something that was going to take a lot of getting used to. Despite Mateo's obvious and understated displays of both wealth and power, she realised she hadn't fully believed in the whole king thing until she'd stepped on the royal jet, and everyone had started bowing and curtseying and 'Your Highnessing' him. It had been weird.

The steward produced a bottle of bubbly with the kind of label Rachel could only dream of, popped the cork and poured two crystalline flutes full.

'Cheers,' Rachel said a bit tartly. During this whole elegant procedure, Mateo hadn't so much as looked up from his screen.

She took a large sip of the champagne, which was crisp and delicious on her tongue. Another sip, and finally Mateo looked up.

He took in the open bottle chilling in a silver bucket, his untouched flute, and Rachel's expression with a small, rueful smile.

'I apologise.' He reached for his glass and touched it to hers, his gaze warm and intent. 'As we say in Kallyria, *yamas.*'

'I don't even know what language that is,' Rachel confessed, wrinkling her nose. 'Or what language you speak in Kallyria.'

'It is Greek, and it means health or, more prosaically, cheers.'

'Do you speak Greek?'

'Yes, and Turkish.'

'Wow.' She realised how little she knew about, well, *anything.* 'I should have done an Internet search on you last night.'

He arched an eyebrow. 'You didn't?'

'I was too busy thinking about whether or not I was going to marry you.' Although really she'd already decided. She'd spent most of the evening walking around in a daze, doing nothing productive.

'You can ask me what you like. There will be a lot to learn.'

'Yes.' Rachel could see that already. 'What's going to happen when we land?'

'I've had our arrival at Constanza embargoed—'

'What does that mean?'

'I am not alerting the media and no press will be allowed.'

'Okay.' She tried to process that for a moment, and failed. 'Why?'

'Because I want to control all the information,' Mateo answered swiftly. 'When we arrive at the royal palace, I will take you to meet my mother.'

Rachel swallowed. 'Have you told her about me?'

'Yes, she is greatly looking forward to making your acquaintance.'

'That's nice,' Rachel said faintly. She didn't know why she was starting to feel so alarmed; she'd known this was the kind of thing she was signing up for. And yet now it was starting to feel so very *real*. 'And then what?'

'Then you will meet with your stylist and hairdresser,' Mateo answered. 'They are temporary only, as I am sure you will like to select your own staff when the times comes.'

'I've never had staff before,' Rachel said with a nervous laugh. She took a gulp of champagne to steady her nerves.

'You do now.' Mateo nodded towards the stewards in the front cabin of the aircraft. 'Everyone who works for me works for you.'

'Right.' Something else she could not get her head around.

'When you have finished with the stylists, you will be introduced to Kallyria.'

'Introduced to a country? How is that meant to happen?' Already her mouth was drying, her heart beginning to hammer at the thought.

'There is a balcony from where royalty has traditionally made all such announcements. I shall introduce you, we will wave, and then retire into the palace. Some time in the next week we will hold an engagement ball where you will meet all the dignitaries and statesmen you need to, and then we will marry next Saturday.'

'Wait, what? That's only a week from now.'

Mateo's brows snapped together as he regarded her evenly, his flute of champagne held between two long, lean fingers. 'Is that a problem? You are aware of the urgency of the situation.'

Rachel swallowed dryly. 'It's not a problem. Just…give me a moment to get my head around it.'

'Very well.' Mateo turned back to his laptop, and Rachel sipped the last of her champagne, her mind feeling like so much buzzing noise. After a few moments she excused herself with a murmur and went to the back of the plane, where there was a sumptuous bedroom with a king-sized bed and an en suite bathroom all in marble.

Rachel sank onto the bed and looked around her in as much of a daze as ever, if not more. What was she doing here, really?

Mateo straightened the cuffs of his suit as he waited for Rachel to emerge from the bedroom where she was changing into a fresh outfit to exit the plane.

He'd spent the majority of the flight working, grabbing an hour of sleep in his seat while Rachel had retired to the bedroom as soon as she'd drunk her champagne, and she hadn't come out again until an hour before landing.

Mateo had checked in on her halfway through the flight, and seen her still in her clothes, curled up on top of the covers, fast asleep. Her hair was spread across the pillow just as he'd once imagined, and as he gazed at her he realised he'd never seen her sleep before, and yet from now on he would many times over.

The thought had brought a shaft of—something—to him. Something he wasn't sure he wanted to name, because he couldn't discern how it made him feel.

He'd rushed into marriage because he'd had to, and he'd done it with Rachel because at least he knew and trusted her. But watching her sleep, he was accosted by the realisation of how intimate their lives together would have to be, no matter how much he kept a certain part of himself closed off, a part that he hadn't accessed in fifteen years, since Cressida.

No matter how physically intimate they might be, no matter how close they might become, Mateo knew there was only so much he could ever offer Rachel. Only so much he knew how to give, and he had to trust that it would be enough. It certainly would be for him, and it had better be for her, because he didn't have anything else.

Straightening his tie, he gave his reflection one last glance before he went to knock on the bedroom door.

'We're landing in twenty minutes, Rachel. We need to take our seats.'

'All right.' She opened the door, throwing her shoulders back as she gave him a smile that bordered on terrified. 'Do I look all right?'

'You look fine,' Mateo assured her, because the media wouldn't be there and so it didn't matter. In truth he acknowledged that she would benefit from the help of a stylist. The shapeless trouser suit and plain ponytail that had served her so well for over ten years in academia were not exactly the right look for a queen, something he suspected Rachel was completely aware of. She certainly seemed aware of any potential deficiencies in her persona, and Mateo was determined to assuage her concerns.

'Did you sleep well?' he asked as he took her elbow

and escorted her to the front of the plane. She gave him a strange look, and he realised it wasn't something he would have normally done...*touch* her. Yet he acknowledged he needed to start acting like a husband, not a colleague, and in any case he found he wanted to do it, his fingers light on her elbow, her breast brushing his arm as they walked. Was she aware of it? She didn't seem to be, but he most certainly was.

'Better than I expected,' Rachel answered with a little laugh. 'I think I was so exhausted because I didn't sleep a wink the night before!'

'Didn't you?'

She gave him a wry, laughing look. 'No, I most certainly did not. I stayed up the entire night wondering if I was going to marry you, and trying to imagine what that would look like, because frankly I still find it impossible.'

'Yet very soon you will find out.'

'I know.' She fiddled with the seat buckle, her gaze lowered so her ponytail fell forward onto her shoulder, like a curling ribbon of chocolate-brown silk. For some reason he couldn't quite understand, Mateo reached forward and flicked it back. Rachel glanced at him, startled. He smiled blandly.

'Tell me about your mother,' she blurted.

'My mother? Her name is Agathe and she is a very strong and gracious woman. I admire her very much.'

'She sounds completely intimidating.'

Mateo frowned. 'She isn't.'

'I don't believe you. You're intimidating.' Rachel gave him a teasing smile, but Mateo knew she was serious—and scared. He could see it in her eyes, in the way she blinked rapidly, her lush lashes fanning downwards again and again as she moistened her lips with the tip of a delectably pink tongue.

'You've known me for ten years, Rachel,' he pointed out reasonably. 'How can I be intimidating?'

'You're different now,' she answered with a shrug. 'Until yesterday, I never saw you snap your fingers at someone before.'

Mateo acknowledged the point with a rueful nod. 'I don't think I had, at least not while at Cambridge.'

'You seem so used to all this luxury and wealth. I mean, I suppose you grew up with it, and I knew you had a fancy house in Cambridge because of some investments or something…'

He raised his eyebrows. 'Is that courtesy of the university gossips?'

Rachel smiled, unabashed. 'Yes.'

'Well, it wasn't investments. It was a company I founded. Lyric Tech.'

'What, you just *founded* a company in your spare time?'

He shrugged. 'I had an idea for a music app and it went from there.'

'As it does.' Rachel pursed her lips, looking troubled. 'See, when you say stuff like that, I feel as if I really don't know you at all.'

'You know me, Rachel.' He hadn't meant his voice to sound so low and meaningful, or to caress the syllables of her name quite so much, but they did. Her eyes widened and a faint blush touched her cheeks as she stared at him for a second before looking away.

'Maybe we should talk about molecular electrocatalysis or something?' she suggested shakily. 'Just to feel like our old selves again.'

'If you like.' Mateo relaxed back into his seat. He was always happy to talk shop. 'What are your thoughts on the metal-to-metal hydrogen atom transfer?'

Rachel looked surprised that he was playing along, but then a little smile curved her mouth and she considered the question properly. 'I suppose you're talking about iron and chromium?'

'Indeed.'

'There are some limitations, of course.' They spent the next fifteen minutes discussing the potential benefits of the new research on various forms of renewable energy, and she became so engrossed in the discussion that Rachel didn't even notice the plane landing, or taxiing along the private airstrip. It was only when she glanced out of the window and saw several blacked-out sedans with a small army of people in front of them that her face paled and she gulped audibly.

'Mateo, I don't know if I can do this.'

'Of course you can,' he answered calmly. He meant it; he'd seen her handle a dozen more demanding situations back at Cambridge. All she had to do now was walk out of the plane and into a waiting car. 'You are going to be my queen, Rachel. The only one who doubts whether you are up for the role is you.'

She gave him a wry look. 'Are you sure about that?'

'Positive.' If anyone else doubted it, he would make sure they stopped immediately. He would not allow for anyone to doubt or deride his chosen queen.

Rachel glanced back out at the sedans, and the flank of waiting security, all looking suitably blank-faced, and Mateo watched with pride as the iron entered her soul. She nodded slowly as she straightened her shoulders, her chin tilting upward as her eyes blazed briefly with gold.

'All right,' she said. 'Let's do this.'

Moments later the security team were opening the door to the plane, and Mateo reached for Rachel's hand. Hers was icy-cold and he twined his fingers through hers and gently drew her closer to his side. Her smile trembled on her lips as she shot him a questioning look. This closeness was new to both of them, but Mateo didn't mind it.

'Ready?' he asked softly, and, setting her jaw, she nodded.

Then together they stepped out of the plane, onto the stairs. They walked side by side down the rather rickety stairs to the waiting car, and Mateo nodded at the security team, who all bowed in response, their faces remaining impressively impassive. Mateo did not explain who Rachel was; they would find out soon enough. They could almost certainly guess.

Pride blossomed in his soul as she kept her chin tilted and her back ramrod straight as she walked from the bottom of the stairs to the waiting car. She was, Mateo acknowledged with a deep tremor of satisfaction, fit to be his queen.

CHAPTER EIGHT

THE WORLD BLURRED by as Rachel sat in the sedan and it sped along wide boulevards, the sea glittering blue on the other side of the road, palm trees proudly pointing to an azure sky.

Since exiting the plane, Rachel had felt as if she were disembodied, watching everything unfold as if from far above. She couldn't possibly be sitting in a luxury sedan with blacked-out windows, an armed guard travelling before and behind and a man set to be king brooding next to her, on her way to an actual palace?

It had been utterly surreal to walk down those steps and see the guards bowing to Mateo—and her. She'd seen their impassive faces and recognised the look of people well trained to keep their expressions to themselves. Had they guessed she was Mateo's bride, their next queen? Or did they assume she was some dowdy secretary brought along to take dictation? That was what she would have assumed, if she'd been in their place.

As much as she was trying to keep from getting down on herself, Rachel had to acknowledge the struggle was real. Her trouser suit was five years old and bought on the bargain rack, because she'd never cared about clothes. She had no make-up on because when she tried to use it, she looked like a clown. Her hair hadn't been cut in six months at least. Yes, she was definitely feeling like the dowdy secretary rather than the defiant queen.

'If I'd known I was going to become a queen this week,' she quipped to Mateo, 'I would have had my hair cut and lost a stone.'

He turned to her, his expression strangely fierce, his face drawn into stark lines of determination. 'Neither is necessary, I assure you.'

She eyed him sceptically. 'Didn't you mention a team of stylists and beauticians waiting at the palace to turn me into some kind of post-godmother Cinderella?'

'It doesn't mean you need to change.'

Rachel glanced down at her trouser suit. 'I think I might,' she said. 'At least this outfit.' She didn't want to dwell on all the other ways she might need to change, and so she chose to change the subject. 'So what is the royal palace like? Besides being palatial, naturally.'

A small smile twitched the corner of Mateo's mouth. 'And royal.'

'Obvs.'

'It's five hundred years old, built on the sea, looking east. It has magnificent gardens leading down to the beach, and many beautiful terraces and balconies. You will occupy the Queen's suite of rooms after our marriage.'

'You need to stop saying stuff like that, because I feel like I'm living in a fairy tale.'

His smile deepened as he glanced down at her, aquamarine eyes sparkling. 'But it's true.'

'And where will I be before our marriage?' Which was now in six *days*, something she couldn't let herself think about without panicking.

'A guest suite. But first, remember, my mother wishes to meet you.'

'Right away?' Rachel swallowed hard. 'Before anything else?'

'It is important.'

And terrifying. Rachel tried to moderate her breathing as the car sped on, past whitewashed buildings with terracotta roofs, flowers blooming everywhere, spilling out of pots and window boxes. She gazed at a woman with a basket of oranges on her head, and a man with a white turban riding a rusty bicycle. Kallyria was a place where the east and west met, full of history and colour and life. And it was now her home.

The reality of it all, the enormity of the choice she had made, slammed into her again and again, leaving her breathless.

After about ten minutes, the motorcade drove through high, ornate gates of wrought iron, and then down a sweeping drive, a palace of sparkling white stone visible in the distance. It was a combination of fairy-tale castle and luxury Greek villa—complete with terraces and turrets, latticed shutters and trailing bougainvillea at every window, and Rachel thought there had to be at least a hundred.

'Welcome home,' Mateo said with a smile, and she nearly choked. She felt as if she were caught up in a riptide of officialdom as she was ushered out of the car and into the soaring marble foyer of the palace, a twisting, double staircase leading to a balcony above, and then onwards. A cupola high above them let in dazzling sunlight, and at least a dozen staff, the royal insignia on their uniform, were lined up waiting to bow or curtsey to Mateo.

'My mother is waiting upstairs, in her private parlour,' Mateo murmured, and, taking her by the elbow, he led her upstairs.

'Mitera?' he called, knocking on the wood-panelled door once, and when a mellifluous voice bid them to enter, he did.

Rachel followed, her knees practically knocking together. What if Mateo's mother didn't like her? What if she looked at her and wondered why on earth he'd chosen her as his bride? His queen?

The woman rising from a loveseat at one end of the elegant and spacious room was exactly what Rachel had expected, even though she had never seen a photograph of Agathe Karavitis.

She was tall and elegant, her dark blonde hair barely streaked with silver drawn back in a loose chignon. She wore a chic silk blouse tucked into wide-leg trousers and as she came forward, a welcoming smile on her face, her arms outstretched, she moved with an unconscious grace. Rachel felt like the dowdiest of dowds in comparison, and she tried not to let it show in her face as Agathe kissed both her cheeks and pressed her hands between her own.

'Rachel. I am so very delighted to make your acquaintance.'

'As I am yours,' Rachel managed to stammer. She felt woefully and wholly inadequate.

'I must check on a few things before we appear publicly,' Mateo informed her. Rachel tried not to gape at him in panic. He was leaving?

'She is in safe hands, I assure you,' Agathe said.

'We will appear on the balcony at two…' Mateo gave his mother a significant look.

'She will be ready.' She waved at him with an elegant hand. 'Go.'

Mateo gave Rachel a quick smile that did not reassure her at all and then strode out of the room.

'I have called for tea,' Agathe said once he had left, the door clicking firmly shut behind him. 'You must be exhausted.'

'I'm a bit tired, yes,' Rachel said carefully. She realised she had no idea how to handle this meeting. Despite Agathe's air of gracious friendliness, she had no idea how the woman really thought of her. According to Mateo, Agathe had drawn up a list of suitable brides, and Rachel had most certainly not been on it.

'Come sit down,' Agathe invited, patting the seat next to her. 'We have little time today to get to know one another, but tomorrow I have arranged for us to have breakfast together.'

'That's very kind.' Rachel perched on the edge of the loveseat while Agathe eyed her far too appraisingly. Rachel knew how she looked—how limp her ponytail, how creased her suit, how pasty her skin. She tried to smile.

'I suppose you are surprised,' she said finally, because as always she preferred confronting the truth rather than hiding from it. 'I am not the expected choice for your son's bride.'

'You are not,' Agathe agreed with a nod. 'And yet I think you might be exactly right.'

That surprised Rachel, and for the first time in what felt like for ever she actually started to relax. 'You do?'

'Don't sound so surprised,' Agathe returned with a tinkling laugh. 'Did you think I would not approve?'

'I wondered.'

'More than anything, I wish my son to be happy,' Agathe said quietly. 'And the fact that he chose you, that he knows you and calls you his friend...that is important. Far more important than having the right pedigree or something similar.' She shrugged slim shoulders. 'It is a modern world. We are no longer in the days of princes and kings needing to marry young women of suitable social standing, thank goodness.'

Rachel wasn't sure how to reply. Her father had been a well-regarded academic, if a commoner, but she doubted that held much water in the world of royalty. 'Thank you for your understanding,' she said at last.

An attendant came in with a tea tray, and Agathe served, her movements as elegant as ever. 'I am afraid we have only a few moments, if we wish you to be ready for the announcement.'

Rachel's stomach cramped as she took a soothing sip of the tea. Swallowing, she said, 'I don't think I'll ever be ready.'

'Nonsense,' Agathe said briskly. 'You just need the right tools.'

Mateo felt the weight of responsibility drop heavily onto his shoulders as he took a seat at his father's desk. His desk now. How long would it take him to think of it like that? To think of himself as King?

Two days away had taken their toll, and now his narrowed gaze scanned the various reports that had come in during his absence. Increased unrest in the north of the country; the important economic talks on a knife edge; domestic policy careening towards a crisis. An emergency on every front, and in just three hours he and Rachel would step in front of the waiting crowds and he would announce his choice of bride.

At least he did not regret taking that decision. Although she clearly had doubts about her suitability, Mateo did not. His only concern was making sure their relationship did not veer into the overly emotional or intimate. As long as they stayed friends, they would be fine. He would make sure of it.

Mateo spent an hour going over reports before he decided to check on Rachel's progress with the stylists he'd engaged. After a member of staff informed him of their whereabouts, he strode towards the east wing of the palace, where the guest suites were housed. From behind the first door on the corridor he heard the accented trill of the woman who dressed his mother.

'Of course we will have to do something about those eyebrows…' Mateo stopped outside the door, frowning.

'And that *chin*...' The despair, bordering on disgust, in the woman's voice tightened his gut. 'Fortunately some—how do they say in the English?—contouring will help. As for the clothes...something flowing, to hide the worst.'

The worst?

Furious now, as well as incredulous, Mateo flung open the door. Four women, matchstick-thin and officious, buzzed around Rachel, who sat in a chair in front of a mirror, looking horribly resigned. At his entrance the women turned to him, wide-eyed, mouths open.

'What is going on here?' Mateo demanded, his voice a low growl of barely suppressed outrage.

The women all swept panicked curtsies that Mateo ignored.

'Your Highness...'

'What is going on?'

'We were just attending to Kyria Lewis...'

'In a manner I find most displeasing. You are all dismissed at once.' A shocked intake of breath was the only response he got, followed by a frozen silence.

'Mateo,' Rachel said softly. He turned his gaze to her, saw her giving him one of her wonderfully wry smiles. 'Remember when I was being a drama queen? Don't be a drama king. They're just doing their job.'

'They insulted you,' he objected, his voice pulsating with fury. 'I will not have it.'

'They were just being pragmatic, and in any case they weren't saying anything I haven't said myself a thousand times before. I really don't like my chin.'

'Your chin is fine.'

Rachel's mouth quirked. 'Shall we argue about it?'

'Their comments and attitude are *not* acceptable.' He would not back down, no matter what damage mitigation Rachel felt she needed to do.

'Your Highness,' Francesca, the main stylist, said in a

hesitant voice. 'Please accept my deepest apologies for my remarks. I was thinking out loud…but you are right, it was unacceptable.' She bowed her head. 'If you will give me this opportunity to style Kyria Lewis, I will do my utmost to help her succeed.'

'She will succeed with or without you,' Mateo snapped. 'You are not here to make her succeed, but simply to provide her with the right clothes and make-up.'

Francesca's head dipped lower. 'As you say,' she murmured.

'Mateo.' Rachel's voice was gentle. 'Honestly, it's okay.'

But it wasn't. He saw so clearly how she accepted being belittled, how she thought because she was curvy and dressed in shapeless clothes she wasn't worth the same as a woman with a wasp-like waist and a similar attitude. Mateo hated it.

'You will dress and style Kyria Lewis,' he instructed the women, his eyes like lasers on the penitent Francesca. 'I will review the terms of your contract with the palace myself before the day is out.'

The women murmured their thanks and he strode out of the room, still battling an inexplicable fury. Why did he care so much? Rachel didn't. Why couldn't he just let it go? Yet he found he couldn't.

He'd never considered Rachel's feelings in such a specific way before he'd decided to marry her. He'd never considered *anyone's* feelings, he acknowledged with wry grimness, not really.

Not since Cressida, whose feelings he had considered both far too much and not nearly enough. The paradox of his relationship with her, the manic highs and terrible lows, was something he knew he wasn't strong enough to experience again. And even though Rachel was entirely different, he feared the root cause of those emotions was the same. *Love.* Best to avoid.

And yet now, despite his determination to keep a certain aloofness, and for reasons he did not wish to probe too deeply, he felt as if he was changing. Now he cared—admittedly about something relatively small, but still. It mattered. It mattered to him.

Wanting to leave such disturbing thoughts behind, Mateo went to meet with the palace press officer and arrange the last details of their appearance on the main balcony. All the country's press would be assembled in the courtyard below, along with most of Europe's and some of Asia's.

Kallyria was a small country, but since the discovery of oil beneath its lands, it had become a major player on the world stage. The whole world would be waiting for and watching this announcement. Mateo wanted to make sure everything was ready—and perfect.

At quarter to two, the door to the reception room whose French windows opened onto the main balcony opened, and Francesca ushered Rachel in, beaming with pride.

Mateo gave her a level look, still unimpressed by her behaviour, before turning his attention to his soon-to-be wife…and then trying not to let his jaw drop.

Rachel looked…like Rachel, yet more. Her hair had been trimmed and was styled in loose waves about her face, soft and glossy. She wore minimal make-up, but it highlighted everything Mateo liked about her—her lush and rosy lips, her dark eyes with their luxuriant lashes, and cheekbones that he hadn't actually noticed before but now couldn't tear his gaze away from.

She wore a simple wrap dress in forest-green silk—a dress that clung without being too revealing and made the most of the generous curves Mateo longed to touch and explore. Her shapely calves were encased in sheer tights, and accentuated by a pair of elegant black heels.

'Well?' Her voice held a questioning lilt that bordered on uncertainty. 'Will I pass?'

'You will more than pass.' Mateo gave Francesca a grudging nod. 'I meant what I said earlier, but I will admit you have done well.'

'Thank you, Your Highness.' She bobbed a curtsey and then was gone. Rachel walked slowly towards him, grimacing a little.

'I'm tottering. I know it. I'm not used to heels.'

'All you'll have to do is step through those doors and stand still.'

She shot a worried look towards the gauze-covered windows. 'How many people are out there?'

Mateo knew there was no point in dissembling. 'Quite a few.'

Rachel nodded and ran her hands down the sides of her dress. 'Okay.' She threw back her shoulders and lifted her chin, as she'd done before when she was gathering her courage. He loved to see it.

'I don't look ridiculous, do I?' she asked in a low voice. 'You know, silk purse, sow's ear...'

'Rachel.' Mateo stared at her incredulously. 'You look amazing. Gorgeous, vibrant, full of life, *sexy*.' The words spilled from him with conviction; they *had* to be said.

She stared at him for a moment, her lips parting, her eyes widening. Belatedly Mateo realised how intent he'd sounded, how involved. He cleared his throat, but before he could say anything more the press officer stepped forward.

'If we could go over the schedule, Your Highness?'

'Yes, in a moment.' He waved the man aside before drawing the small black velvet box out of his jacket pocket. 'You need one more thing to complete your outfit.' Her eyes had widened at the sight of the box, and she didn't speak. Mateo opened it to reveal a blue diamond encircled with smaller white diamonds, set on a ring of white gold. 'This is the Kallyrian Blue. It has been in the royal family for six hundred years.'

'Oh, my goodness…' She looked up at him with genuine panic. 'Can I please wear a fake? I cannot be responsible for a jewel that size.'

'It is heavily insured, don't worry. And it belongs to you now. It has always been the Queen's engagement ring.'

'Your mother…'

'Was more than happy to pass it on.'

Rachel let out a shaky breath. 'Whoo, boy.' She held out her hand, and Mateo slipped the ring onto her finger.

'There. Perfect.'

'It's so heavy.' She let out a breathy, incredulous laugh. 'I feel like I'm doing finger weights, or something.'

'You'll get used to it.' Mateo gestured to the press officer, and he stepped forward. 'Now, the schedule?'

The next ten minutes passed quickly as they rehearsed their brief performance—step out on the balcony, smile and wave, and then Mateo would introduce Rachel as his queen, with their wedding and joint coronation on Saturday to be celebrated as a national holiday.

'That's *insane*,' Rachel murmured, and the press officer gave her an odd look.

'It's quite normal for royal weddings,' Mateo remarked calmly.

'Your Highness, it's time!'

Mateo glanced at Rachel, who had suddenly morphed into the proverbial deer snared by headlights. She threw him a panicked look.

'I can't…'

'You can.' His voice was low and sure as he reached for her hand. 'All you have to do is take a single step, smile and wave.'

She nodded rather frantically. 'Smile and wave. Smile and wave.'

'That's it.'

Two attendants threw open the French windows that led out to the balcony, the massed crowd visible below in a colourful blur.

'Oh, my heavens,' Rachel whispered. 'There are thousands of people down there.'

And even more watching the live video stream, but Mateo chose not to enlighten her.

'Let's do this,' he said, echoing her words from before. She gave him a small smile of recognition, and then he drew her out onto the balcony, the applause crashing over them in a deafening wave as they appeared. He turned to Rachel, his mouth curving in pleasure and pride as she offered the crowds below a radiant smile and a decidedly royal wave.

After a few moments of cheering and clapping, Mateo made his announcement, which was met with even more applause and excited calls. Then a cry rose up: *'Fili! Fili!'*

Rachel's forehead wrinkled slightly as she gave him a questioning look. She didn't know what they were calling for, but Mateo did.

Kiss.

And it seemed like the most natural thing to do, to take her in his arms, her curves fitting snugly against him, and kiss her on the lips.

CHAPTER NINE

RACHEL GAZED DOWN at the list of potential charities to support and marvelled for about the hundredth time that this was now her life.

The last three days had felt like a dream. She had, quite deliberately, chosen to enjoy all the good and ignore the worrisome or flat-out terrifying. And there was a lot of good—not least the people who surrounded her, who were determined to help her to succeed.

The day after her arrival and the announcement on the balcony, Agathe had invited Rachel to her private rooms for breakfast. Eighteen hours later, Rachel's lips had been practically still buzzing from the quick yet thorough kiss Mateo had given her, to the uproarious approval of the crowds below. He'd given her a fleeting, self-satisfied smile afterwards, his eyes glinting with both knowledge and possession, while Rachel had tottered back into the palace on unsteady legs that had had nothing to do with her heels.

She and Agathe had chatted easily over croissants and Greek yogurt withsweet golden honey and slices of succulent melon.

'I can see now more than ever that my son has made a good choice,' Agathe said with a little smile and Rachel blushed as she recalled that kiss yet again.

'It's not like that,' she felt compelled to protest. 'We're only friends. What I mean is, that's all we've been.'

'And it is a good, strong foundation for a marriage. Much better than—' She stopped abruptly, making Rachel frown in confusion.

'Much better than what?' she prompted.

'Oh, you know.' Agathe laughed lightly as she poured them both more of the strong Greek coffee. 'The usual fleeting attraction or empty charm.'

Yet as Agathe dazzled her with a determinedly bright smile, Rachel couldn't shake the feeling that she'd been about to say something else, something she'd decided not to.

Despite that brief moment of awkwardness, the rest of the conversation was easy and comfortable, and Rachel's initial concerns about being intimidated by Mateo's elegant mother proved to be as ill-founded as she might have hoped.

After breakfast, the over-the-top unreality of her situation continued as her personal assistant Monica—a neatly efficient woman in her late twenties—introduced herself and put herself entirely at Rachel's disposal.

Then came another session with Francesca, who was becoming a firm friend. Rachel knew, despite Mateo's outrage, that the stylist had been merely pragmatic in her assessment of Rachel's looks, although she apologised yet again when they met to discuss her wardrobe, and in particular her evening gown for the ball in a few days' time, and also for her wedding in less than a week.

Rachel's head continued to spin as she was outfitted beyond her wildest imaginings—yet with an eye to what she liked and felt comfortable in. Instead of shapeless trouser suits, she had chic separates in jewel-toned colours that Francesca assured her highlighted her 'flawless skin' and 'gorgeous eyes and hair'. Rachel had never heard herself described in such glowing terms, and some battered part of her that she hadn't let herself acknowledge began to heal...just as it had when Mateo told her she was gorgeous and sexy.

But surely he couldn't have meant that...?

Whether he did or not was not something Rachel let herself dwell on for too long, because either way they were getting married. She'd already told herself she could manage without love, and that included desire, too. At least the kind of head-over-heels, can't-live-without-you desire she knew Mateo didn't feel for her, no matter what he had said.

The trouble was, she felt a little of it for him. Looking at him was starting to send shivery sparks racing along her nerve-endings, and sometimes when she was watching him she had an almost irresistible urge to touch him. Run her hand along the smooth-shaven sleekness of his jaw, or trail her fingertips along the defined pecs she saw beneath the crisp cotton of his shirt.

She didn't, of course, not that she had any opportunity. In the three days since she'd arrived on Kallyria, she'd barely seen Mateo at all. Which was fine, she reminded herself more than once, because he had a country to run and she had a wedding—a whole life—to prepare for.

Rachel made a few ticks next to charities she was interested in supporting before laying the paper aside. She was in her private study, on the ground floor of the palace, a spacious and elegant room with long, sashed windows open to the fragrant gardens outside. Even though it was autumn, the air was still warm, far balmier than the best British summer.

Despite all the beauty and opulence surrounding her, Rachel felt a little flicker of homesickness that she did her best to banish. As wonderful as all this was, as kind as people were, it was still all incredibly unfamiliar. She kept feeling as if she were living someone else's life, and as small as her own had been, at least it had been hers.

At least she'd been able to email her friends and have regular updates about her mother. Her friends had been amazed and thrilled by her change in circumstances; apparently her and Mateo's kiss had been on the cover of several British tabloids. Rachel hadn't felt brave enough to look at any of it online. The thought of seeing herself splashed on the covers of national magazines was both too surreal and scary even to contemplate, much less actually inspect.

Several of her friends and former colleagues from Cambridge were coming to the wedding, all at Mateo's expense, a prospect that lifted her spirits a bit. She wasn't completely cut off from her old life, even if sometimes she felt as if she were.

Rachel rested her chin on her hand as she gazed outside. A bright tropical butterfly landed on a crimson hibiscus blossom, the sight as incredible as anything she might find in the pages of a nature magazine, and yet commonplace in this new world of hers.

She supposed she was bound to feel a bit uncertain and out of sorts, at least at the start. Everything had happened so fast, and the change had been so enormous. She wished she'd seen more of Mateo, because she recognised that he grounded her, and his reassurance would go a long way. But when she'd asked that morning, one of the palace staff had informed her he'd left for the north of the country last night, and wouldn't be back until this evening. He hadn't even told her he was leaving. And she kept telling herself not to mind.

But that didn't mean she had to sit and do nothing about it.

Rachel was busy for the rest of the afternoon, between fittings for her evening gown and wedding dress, and lessons on comportment that Agathe had gently advised her to attend. Rachel hadn't even known what those were until she'd shown up for her first one, and Agathe had begun to explain how to both sit and stand in public; how to make small talk with strangers; how to navigate a table setting with six separate forks, knives, and spoons.

At first Rachel had bristled slightly at the instruction; she wasn't a complete yokel, after all. She knew how to behave in public, surely, and she'd made small talk with plenty of people over her years in academia. Still, it hadn't taken her long to realise, when it came to royalty, she was out of her element, and Agathe was here to help her. She had only a week to become royalty-ready, and she—and Agathe—were determined to make the most of every moment.

As evening fell, the sky scattered with stars, Rachel heard the sound she hadn't even realised she'd been waiting for—the loud, persistent whirr of a helicopter. From the window of her bedroom she watched the royal helicopter touch down on the palace's helipad.

Mateo was back…and she was going to find him.

Mateo scrubbed his gritty eyes as he tried to refocus on the report he was reading. He'd barely slept last night, having spent the last forty-eight hours on the move in the north, trying to arrange a meeting with the leader of the insurgents gathering there.

Despite the unrest, the realisation of his marriage and ascension to the throne had made them more willing to consider a compromise, thank heaven. His marriage to Rachel was already paying dividends.

Rachel. He hadn't seen her in several days, and barely before that. Barely since the kiss on the balcony, when they'd as good as sealed the deal. He wondered how she was now, if she was coping with all the change and busyness. He told himself she was too sensible to have cold feet, but he wished he could see her. He'd make time tomorrow, he promised himself. At least, he'd try to.

A soft footfall outside had him tensing. The palace was nearly impregnable and teeming with security. He wasn't nervous, not exactly…just conscious that he'd spent the last few days negotiating with desperate men who were little more than terrorists, and if they wanted to put an end to him, before his wedding would be the time to do it.

'Mateo…?' The voice was soft, low, and wonderfully familiar.

'In here.'

The door creaked open and Rachel peeked her head in, smiling with relief when she saw him. 'I've been wandering around in my nightgown, which I realised is probably not the best idea. Certainly not queenly behaviour.'

'Well, you're not a queen yet.' Mateo smiled, pleasure at seeing her like honey in his veins. She was wearing an ivory dressing gown that was all silk and lace and hugged her sweet curves lovingly.

She caught him looking at her and, grimacing, spread her arms wide. 'Isn't this the most ridiculous thing ever? Francesca insists it's perfectly appropriate night-time attire for a queen, but I feel a bit like—I don't know—Lady Godiva.'

'As I recall, Lady Godiva was meant to be naked, as well as on a horse.'

'Right.' Rachel laughed huskily. 'Well, you know what I mean.'

Yes, he did. Just as he knew that with the lamplight behind her and her arms spread, Rachel might as well be naked. Out of decency he knew he should inform her of the fact, but he didn't want to embarrass her—and he was enjoying the view.

'Anyway.' She dropped her arms and moved towards him, so the robe became seemly again, more was the pity. 'Where have you been? How *are* you? I haven't seen you since—well, since the balcony.'

She blushed at that, which Mateo liked. He might have been trying to keep Rachel at arm's length, but the memory of that kiss was scorched onto his brain. And after several days of having her much farther away than his arm, he was enjoying her company far too much to put up the usual barriers.

'I know, I'm sorry. I'm afraid I have had much to command my attention.'

'You don't have to apologise.' She perched on the edge of his desk, giving him a small smile. 'You were up north?'

'Trying to set up some peace talks, yes.'

'And were you successful?'

'I believe so.'

'And now?' She nodded towards the stack of files on his desk. 'What are you working on now?'

He paused, because he had already developed the instinct to keep his royal work private, and yet this was the woman he'd hashed out every potential problem with for a decade. They'd wrangled and wrestled with countless theorems and difficulties, had debated the best way forward on countless experiments, had worked side by side most days. He'd wanted to marry her for just those reasons, and yet sharing this work did not come naturally to him.

'Mateo?'

'I'm trying to decide who to place in my cabinet of ministers,' he said at last. 'When a new king ascends to the throne, it is his privilege and right to choose his own cabinet.'

'Is it? That's a lot of power to hand to one person.'

'Indeed, but his choices must be ratified by sixty per cent of parliament, which helps to keep things balanced.'

'So what's the problem?'

Mateo gestured to the stack of files, each one containing information on potential ministers. 'I don't actually know any of these people. I've been away from Kallyria for too long.' He could not keep the recrimination from his voice. This was his fault.

'Then you can get to know them, surely.' Rachel edged closer, so her hip was brushing Mateo's hand. She leaned over so she could glance at the files, and gave him a delightful view down the front of her dressing gown.

'I can, but it's a matter of time. I need things settled and stabilised as quickly as possible.' With what was surely a herculean effort, he dragged his gaze away from Rachel's front.

'You must have some top contenders.' She reached for the first file, her narrowed gaze scanning it quickly. Mateo leaned back and watched her work, enjoying the sight—her hair spilling over her shoulders, her breasts nearly spilling out of her nightgown. He could practically hear her brain ticking over. Smart *and* sexy.

'You're looking at one of them.'

'Mm.' She continued to read the file before tossing it aside. 'No.'

'No?' Mateo repeated in surprise. 'Why not?'

'Look at his voting pattern.' She gestured to the third sheet of the file. 'Entirely inconsistent. He can't be trusted.'

Mateo leaned forward to glance at the relevant part of the document. 'I wouldn't say it's entirely inconsistent. I think it was more of knowing which way the wind was blowing.'

'You want people with principles. Otherwise they will be swayed—sometimes by you, and sometimes not.'

'True,' Mateo acknowledged. He realised how much he appreciated her input, and how much he was enjoying the sight of her. 'What about the next one?'

Over the next few hours, they went through every single file, creating piles of yes, maybe, and definitely not. Mateo was grateful for Rachel's input, and as they discussed the different candidates they fell into a familiar pattern of bouncing ideas off one another, along with the banter between them that he'd always enjoyed.

'You just like him because he went to Cambridge,' Rachel scoffed. 'You are so biased.'

'And you're not?'

'Of course not.' She smiled at him, chocolate eyes glinting, and quite suddenly as well as quite absolutely, Mateo found he had to kiss her.

'Come here,' he said softly, and Rachel's eyes widened as he reached for the sash of her robe and tugged on it.

'I'm afraid that's not going to do it,' she said with a husky laugh. 'Silk isn't strong enough.'

'But I am.' He anchored his hands on her hips as he pulled her towards him—and she came, a little breathlessly, a little nervously, but she came.

Mateo settled her on his lap, enjoying the soft, silky armful of her. Her hair brushed his jaw as she placed her hands tentatively on his shoulders.

'This feels a bit weird,' she whispered.

He chuckled. 'Good weird or bad weird?'

'Oh, definitely good.' Her anxious gaze scanned his face. 'Don't you think?'

'I definitely think,' Mateo murmured, 'that we should stop talking.'

Rachel's mouth snapped shut and Mateo angled his head so his lips were a breath away from hers. He could feel her tremble. 'Don't you think?' he whispered.

'Oh, um, yes.'

That was all he needed to settle his mouth on hers, her lips parting softly as a sigh of pleasure escaped her. Her hands clenched on his shoulders and he drew her closer so he could feel the delicious press of her breasts against his chest.

He deepened the kiss, sweeping his tongue inside the velvet softness of her mouth. She let out a little mewl, which enflamed his senses all the more. The need to kiss her became the need to possess her, with an urgency that raced through his veins and turned his insides to fire.

He slid his hand along the silky length of her thigh, spreading her legs so she was straddling him, the softest part of her pressed hard against his arousal. He flexed his hips instinctively, and she moaned against his mouth and pressed back.

He was going to explode. Literally. Figuratively. In every way possible. Mateo pressed against her once more as his brain blurred. Her hands were like claws on his shoulders, her breasts flattened against his chest. He slid his hands under her robe to fill them with those generous curves, everything in him short-circuiting.

If he didn't stop this now, he was going to humiliate himself—and her. They couldn't have their wedding night in a *chair*.

Gasping, he tore his mouth away from hers and with shaky hands set her back on the desk. Her lips were swollen from his kisses, her hair in a dark tangle about her flushed face, her nightgown in delicious disarray. Mateo dragged his hands through his hair as he sought to calm his breathing.

'We need to stop.'

'Do we?' Rachel asked shakily. She pulled her robe closed, her fingers trembling.

'Yes. This isn't…' He shook his head, appalled at how affected he was. The blood was still roaring through his veins, and he most definitely needed an ice-cold shower. He couldn't remember the last time he'd felt this way about a woman.

Yes, you can.

Abruptly he rose from the chair and stalked to the window, his back to Rachel. 'I'm sorry,' he managed to choke out. 'I shouldn't have taken such advantage.'

'Was that what you were doing?' Rachel asked with a husky yet uncertain laugh.

'We're not married yet,' Mateo stated flatly.

'I'm a grown-up, Mateo, and we're getting married in

three days. I think it was allowed.' She sounded wry, but also confused. He still couldn't look at her.

Their relationship wasn't supposed to be like this. Yes, he enjoyed their camaraderie, and the physical attraction was an added bonus he hadn't expected. But the way his need for her had consumed him? The way it had obliterated all rational thought?

No, that wasn't something he was willing to feel. He could not sacrifice his self-control to his marriage.

'You should go to bed,' he said, his voice brusque, and a long silence ensued. He waited, not willing to turn, and then finally he heard the swish of silk as she slid off the table.

'Goodnight, Mateo,' she said softly, and then he heard the click of the door closing as she left the room.

CHAPTER TEN

RACHEL GAZED AT her reflection anxiously as the flurry of nerves in her stomach threatened to make their way up her throat. In just fifteen minutes she was going to enter the palace ballroom on Mateo's arm, and be presented to all Kallyrian society as his bride-to-be.

Their wedding was in less than forty-eight hours, a fact that kept bouncing off Rachel's brain, refusing to penetrate. In forty-eight hours they would be *married*, and then crowned King and Queen in a joint ceremony.

A fact which would have filled her with excitement last night, when she and Mateo had worked together on the list of potential cabinet ministers, and then he'd kissed her.

Oh, how he'd kissed her. Rachel had never been kissed like that in her life, and she'd been in a ferment of desire since, longing to be kissed again—and more. So much more. To feel his hands on her, his mouth possessing her, his gloriously hard body beneath her...

But since he'd rather unceremoniously pushed her off his lap, Mateo had avoided her like the proverbial plague. At least, it felt that way. Rachel told herself he had to be busy, but she knew it was more than that, after the way he'd ended their kiss and turned his back, quite literally, to her.

She had no idea what had made him back off so abruptly, but the fact that he had filled her with both disappointment and fear. Was she a clumsy kisser? Heaven knew, it was perfectly possible. It wasn't as if she'd had loads of experience. Or maybe he'd gone off her for some reason—when he'd touched her? She knew she was a little overweight. Maybe Mateo now knew it too.

The thought made her stomach clench as she frowned at her reflection, all her old insecurities, the ones she'd fought so hard to master, rising up in her again. Whatever it was, he'd ended the kiss and then avoided her ever since, so she hadn't seen him from that moment to this. At least, she hoped she'd see him in this moment—they were meant to enter the ball together, after all, in just a few minutes.

Taking a deep breath, Rachel ran her hands down the sides of her gown, a fairy-tale dress if there ever was one. Made of bronze silk, it was strapless with a nipped-in waist and a delightfully full skirt that shimmered every time she moved. The dress was complemented with a parure from the Kallyrian crown jewels—a tiara made of topaz and diamonds, with a matching necklace, bracelet, and teardrop diamond earrings. She truly was Cinderella; the only question was when and if midnight would strike.

A knock sounded on the door of her bedroom, and, with her heart fluttering along with her nerves, Rachel croaked, 'Come in.'

The door opened and Mateo stood there, looking devastatingly handsome in white tie and tails. They were the perfect foil for his olive skin and black hair, his eyes an impossibly bright blue-green in his tanned face.

'Well?' Rachel asked shakily as she straightened her shoulders. 'Will I do?'

'You look stunning.' The compliment, delivered with such quiet sincerity, made a lump form in her throat.

Why did you push me away? She longed to ask, but didn't dare. She wasn't brave or strong enough to hear the answer.

'These jewels are stunning,' she said, nervously touching one of her earrings. 'When Francesca showed them to me, I couldn't believe I was meant to wear them.'

'Who else should wear them?' Mateo countered. 'You are Queen.'

'Technically, I'm not. Not for another forty-eight hours.'

'It is as good as done. Tonight, in the eyes of the world, you are my Queen.'

Rachel shook her head slowly. 'I feel like I'm living in a dream.'

'Is that a bad thing?' Mateo asked, his gaze fastened on hers.

'No, but the thing with dreams is…you have to wake up.'

'Maybe with this one you don't. Maybe it will go on for ever.'

She laughed uncertainly. 'No dream lasts for ever, Mateo.'

He acknowledged her point with a nod. 'True.'

What, Rachel wondered, were they really talking about? She felt an undercurrent to their conversation, to the tension tautening the air between them. He extended his hand, and she took it, the feel of his warm, dry palm under hers sending little shocks along her arm. She would never stop responding to him, and yet it seemed he could turn his physical response to her off like a tap.

She pushed the thought away. She had enough insecurity to deal with already, appearing in public, knowing there would be whispers and rumours, criticisms as well as compliments. It was the nature of being a public figure, which, amazingly, she had now become.

'Ready?' Mateo asked softly, and she nodded.

They walked in silence from her bedroom in the palace's east wing, along the plushly carpeted corridor to the double staircase that led down to the palace's main entrance hall. The hall had been cleared for their entrance, save for a few security men flanking the doors to the ballroom, where a thousand guests were waiting.

Dizziness assailed Rachel and she nearly stumbled in the heels she still wasn't used to wearing.

'Breathe,' Mateo murmured, his hand steady on her elbow.

'You try breathing when you're wearing knickers that are nearly cutting you in half,' Rachel returned tartly, and was gratified to see his mouth quirk in a smile. No matter how Mateo did or did not feel about her physically, Rachel didn't want to lose his friendship. As he'd said before, it was a good foundation for a marriage. She needed to remember that. She needed to remind herself of how important it was.

'Here we go,' Mateo said, and two white-gloved footmen opened the double doors to the ballroom. Taking a deep breath, Rachel held her head high as she sailed into the room on Mateo's arm.

The crowd in the ballroom parted like the Red Sea as they entered under the glittering lights of a dozen chandeliers. The guests naturally formed an aisle that Mateo and Rachel walked down, hands linked and held aloft.

'We'll have to dance,' Mateo murmured. 'The first waltz. It is expected.'

'Dance?' Rachel whispered back as she nearly tripped on the trailing hem of her gown. 'No one told me that! I don't dance.'

'It's a simple box step. Follow my lead and you'll be fine.' They were almost at the end of the aisle, and panic was icing Rachel's insides.

'No, really,' she said out of the side of her mouth, her gaze still straight ahead. She felt like a bad ventriloquist. 'I. Don't. Dance. At all. Two left feet would be a kind way of putting it.'

Why hadn't Agathe covered this in her comportment lessons? Or had she just assumed that Rachel could dance?

She risked a glance at Mateo's face; he wore the faint smile he'd had on since they'd entered the ballroom. He was so handsome it hurt. And she was about to humiliate herself publicly in front of a thousand people, and, really, the whole world. She was wearing a dress worthy of Beauty in *Beauty and the Beast*, but in this case she felt like the beast.

'Mateo—'

'Just follow my lead.'

'I *can't*—'

'Trust me.' The two words, simply spoken and heartfelt, were enough to allay her fears, or almost. Whatever he had planned, she knew she would follow along.

The crowds parted to reveal an empty expanse of gleaming parquet, a string orchestra poised at the other end. As Mateo escorted her to the centre of the floor, they struck up a familiar waltz tune: 'Gold and Silver'.

Rachel stared at him in blind panic.

'Put your feet on top of mine,' Mateo murmured, so low she almost didn't hear the words.

'On top? I'll kill your feet—'

'Do it.'

She did, and Mateo didn't even wince as she practically crushed his toes.

'Hold on,' he said, slipping one hand around her waist, and the next thing Rachel knew she was flying around the dance floor, her skirt swinging out in an elegant bell as Mateo moved them both around in a perfectly elegant waltz.

'Are you in agony?' she whispered as he arced around, carrying her easily without even seeming to do it.

'Smile.'

She did. Two more minutes of soaring music and graceful moves when she felt as if she were flying, and then finally, thankfully, the waltz was over. The crowd erupted into applause and Mateo looked at Rachel and winked.

* * *

His feet were killing him, it was true, but the sight of Rachel looking at him in wonder and admiration and maybe even something more made it worth it. More than worth it. The look she gave him could have powered a city. Or perhaps the feeling inside him could have.

Whatever it was, Mateo felt like a king—of the whole world.

'Your Highness.' A local dignitary, someone whose name Mateo had forgotten, approached him with a bow. 'That was exceptional. Please let me introduce you to my wife...'

The next hour passed in a blur of introductions and small talk. Just as he'd known she would, Rachel shone. She wasn't one to give tinkling laughs or arch looks; she was far too genuine for that. But she talked to everyone as if she wanted to, and she listened as if she was really interested in what they had to say. Mateo was proud to have her on his arm and, more importantly, she seemed happy to be there. The evening, he knew, would be deemed a great success.

He didn't think anything of it when Rachel was escorted into dinner by Lukas Diakis, a senior minister from his father's cabinet. Nor when she listened politely to his Aunt Karolina, her gaze darting occasionally to him. He smiled back every time, but her own smiles became smaller and smaller until they were barely a stretching of his lips, and then they weren't there at all, because she'd stopped looking at him.

Mateo told himself not to be concerned. What on earth could a doddering retired minister or an elderly spinster aunt possibly say to Rachel to make her seem so thoughtful and pale?

Still Mateo couldn't shake his unease through the six-course meal. Even though they were at opposite ends of the table, he felt her disquiet. Or was he just being fanciful? It wasn't as if they had some sort of mental or, heaven forbid, emotional connection. He didn't even want that.

At the end of the meal Rachel left first, arm in arm with Diakis. Mateo watched them go, but by the time he'd made it back to the ballroom she was lost in the crowd and annoyance bit at him. She was his wife. He'd already told her they would spend much of the evening apart, mingling and chatting, but now he wanted her by his side.

He needed her there, which would have alarmed him except right now he didn't care. He just wanted to find her.

Another hour of mingling passed, endless and interminable. Occasionally Mateo glimpsed Rachel across the room, but it would have been impolite, if not downright impossible, to storm through the crowds and approach her. Besides, as the minutes ran into hours, Mateo managed to convince himself that nothing was amiss…and he certainly didn't *need* anything or anyone. He breathed a sigh of relief at the thought.

Finally the evening came to an end. It was two in the morning, the sky full of stars, as the guests departed in a laughing stream, while Mateo, Rachel, and his mother all stood by the door, saying their official farewells. Rachel looked ready to wilt.

'Such a success!' Agathe kissed Rachel on both cheeks. 'You were marvellous, my dear. Absolutely marvellous.' She turned to Mateo. 'Wasn't it a success, Mateo? An absolute triumph!'

'It was.' He glanced searchingly at Rachel, but her gaze flitted away. What was going on?

'I must say goodnight,' Agathe said on a sigh. 'I am absolutely exhausted, as you both must be.' She kissed Mateo's cheek. 'You've done so well.'

'Thank you, Mitera.'

His mother headed upstairs, and the staff melted away

to clean up after the ball. They were alone in the great entrance hall, the space stretching into shadows under the dimmed lights of the chandelier high above. From outside someone laughed, and a car door slammed before an engine purred away.

'You really were wonderful,' Mateo told her.

'Your feet must be killing you.' Rachel reached up and took out the teardrop earrings. 'These are lovely, but they're agony to wear. I haven't worn earrings since my uni days.'

'You look amazing.'

'Thank you.' She still wasn't looking at him, and Mateo bit back his annoyance. What game was she playing?

'I think I'll go to bed.' Rachel let out a little laugh that sounded brittle as she started towards the staircase. 'I think I could fall asleep right here.'

'It's been a long evening.'

'Yes.' She glanced back at him, like a beautiful flame in her bronze gown with the topazes and diamonds glinting in her hair and at her throat and wrists. 'Goodnight, Mateo.' She almost sounded sad, and that irritated him further.

They'd had a brilliant evening, they were getting married the day after tomorrow, and she was playing some passive-aggressive game of showing him she was sad without actually saying it.

'Why don't you just tell me what's going on, Rachel?' His voice came out hard, harder than he'd meant it to, but he'd never liked these games. Not with Cressida, when he'd so often had to guess the reason for her pique, and not with Rachel. Not with anyone.

Her eyes widened as she stilled, one hand on the banister. 'What…what do you mean?'

'You know what I mean.'

She stiffened, her eyes flashing with affront at his tone. 'I really don't.'

'Are you sure about that?' Mateo knew he was handling this all wrong, but hours of wondering and worrying that something was amiss had strung him tighter than he'd realised. He was ready to snap now, and it was hard to pull back.

'Yes, I'm quite sure. I'm tired, Mateo, and I want to go to bed.'

So he should let her go. He knew that, and yet somehow he couldn't. 'Why did you keep giving me looks all evening?'

'Looks?'

'During dinner. As if...' He struggled to put a name to the expression in her eyes. 'As if you were disappointed in me.' The realisation that that was indeed what her look had been was a heaviness in his gut.

Recognition flashed in Rachel's eyes, and Mateo knew he was right. Something was wrong...and she didn't want to tell him what it was. She wanted him to guess, and beg, and plead. He'd been here before, and he hated it. He wouldn't play that game.

'You know what? Never mind.' He shook his head, the movement abrupt, dismissive. 'I don't care what it is. If you can't be bothered to tell me, I can't be bothered to find out.'

'Why are you so angry?' She sounded bewildered, and rightly so. He was overreacting, he knew it, and yet he still couldn't keep himself from it. Because this was bringing back too many old, painful memories, memories he'd suppressed for fifteen years. He really didn't want them rising up now.

'I'm not angry.' His tone made his words a lie.

She gave a little shrug, as if the point wasn't worth arguing, which it probably wasn't. His hands balled into fists at his sides.

'Rachel...'

'Fine, Mateo, if you want to do this now.' She let out a weary sigh that shuddered through her whole body before she gave him a look that was both direct and sorrowful. 'Who is Cressida?'

CHAPTER ELEVEN

SHE HADN'T WANTED to confront him. She'd told herself there was no point. And yet Mateo had forced an argument, much to her own shock, because he'd never acted in such an emotional and unreasonable way before. And now they were here, and she'd asked the question that had been burning on her tongue since Karolina had patted her hand at dinner and said in a dreamy way, *'You're so much better for him than Cressida, my dear.'*

When Rachel had smiled politely in return, the conversation had moved on, but then the man who had escorted her from the table had said something similar.

'Thank God he didn't marry Cressida.'

And Rachel had started to feel…unmoored. She couldn't have explained it better than that, that the sudden emergence of this unknown woman that Mateo must have considered marrying had left her feeling entirely and unsettlingly adrift. And so she'd asked, and now she wasn't sure she wanted to know the answer.

Who is Cressida?

Mateo stared at her unsmilingly, his hands still in fists by his sides. 'Where did you hear that name?' he asked tonelessly, but with a seething undercurrent of anger that Rachel sensed all the way from the stairs.

'Does it matter?'

'Where?'

She stiffened at his tone. She'd never seen Mateo like this, and it frightened her. It made her wonder if she knew him at all.

Who *was* Cressida?

Did she really want to know?

'Karolina told me,' she said. 'And then Lukas Diakis, the minister.'

'What did they say?'

She stared at him, willing the fierce mask to crack. Why was he looking so terribly ferocious? She shrugged, deciding to play it straight, as she played everything. She was never one for machinations, manipulations, a sly tone, a leading question, no matter what Mateo had just accused her of.

'Karolina said she thought I was better for you than Cressida, and Lukas said he was glad you didn't marry her.' Mateo's face darkened, his brows drawing together in a black slash. Rachel took a step backwards on the stairs and nearly stumbled on her gown.

'They should not have spoken of her.'

His icy tone should have kept her from saying anything, but Rachel sensed that if they didn't talk about Cressida now, they never would.

'Who is she, Mateo? Why have you never mentioned her before?'

'Why should I have?'

'She's obviously someone important to you.' Rachel struggled to keep her tone reasonable even though she had an almost uncontrollable urge to burst into tears.

It was past two in the morning, she'd had the longest and most stressful night of her life, wonderful as it had been, and she knew she was feeling far too fragile to handle a big discussion right now…just as she knew they needed to have it. 'You dated her,' she said, making it not quite a question.

'Yes.' Mateo's mouth thinned to a hard, unforgiving line. 'It was a long time ago. It's not important.'

Not important? Was he serious?

'She seemed like someone important to you, judging from your reaction now.'

'My reaction,' Mateo informed her in as chilly a tone as she'd ever heard from him, 'was because my relatives and civil servants were gossiping about me like a bunch of fishwives.'

'It wasn't like that—'

'It was exactly like that.' Mateo strode past her, up the stairs. Rachel watched him go with a sense of incredulity. This was so unlike Mateo, it was almost funny. He wasn't this cold, autocratic, ridiculous dictator of a man. He just *wasn't*.

And yet right now he was.

'Why won't you tell me about her, Mateo?' she called up the stairs. 'We're about to be *married*—'

He did not break his stride as he answered. 'It is not to be discussed.'

Rachel watched him disappear up the stairs, dazed by how quickly things had spiralled out of control. Alone in the soaring entrance hall, she strained her ears to hear the distant sound of Mateo's bedroom door closing.

She glanced around the empty hall and swallowed hard. She felt numb inside, too numb to cry. Had they just had their first argument?

Or their last?

Slowly she walked up the stairs. She was still in her gown and jewels, but the clock had definitely struck midnight. The party was over.

Francesca was waiting for her in her bedroom, eager to hear about the party as she helped her undress.

'You wowed them all, I am sure,' she exclaimed. 'So beautiful…'

Rachel forced a smile as she bent her head and allowed Francesca to undo the clasp of her necklace. She remained quiet as she took off the rest of her jewels, and the stylist put them away in a black velvet case that would be returned directly to the vault where all the crown jewels were kept.

Then Francesca undid the zip of her gown, and Rachel carefully stepped out of it, and into the waiting robe.

'I drew you a bath,' Francesca said as she swathed the dress in a protective bag. 'I know it's late, but I thought you might want to relax.'

'Thank you, Francesca, you're a saint.' Since their first meeting, when Mateo had glowered at and almost fired her, Francesca had proved to be a stalwart stylist and a good friend. Rachel was grateful for the other woman's support.

With the dress draped over one arm, Francesca frowned at her. 'Is everything all right?'

Rachel managed another wan smile. 'Just tired. Exhausted, really.' She considered asking Francesca if she knew who Cressida was, but she could imagine Mateo's reaction if he discovered she was asking around. Clearly, for him, the woman was off-limits to everyone, even Rachel. Especially Rachel.

'Have a bath and get some sleep,' Francesca advised. 'It's a big day tomorrow.'

'Another one?' Every day had been a big day.

'We have the final fitting for your dress, a rehearsal for the ceremony, and a dinner in the evening with about thirty guests.'

Rachel's head drooped at the thought of it. 'Right. Okay.'

'You're sure everything is all right?' Francesca looked at her, worry clouding her eyes.

For a second Rachel wanted to confide in the other woman. She wanted to confess to all the doubts that were now crowding her heart and mind.

*I don't know if I can cope with this. I'm not sure I'm
queen material after all. I'm afraid the man I'm about to
marry is still in love with another woman.*

'I'm fine,' Rachel said as firmly as she could. 'Thank
you.'

Francesca patted her on the shoulder and left the room,
and Rachel sagged visibly once the woman had gone, unable to put up a front any longer.

She nearly fell asleep in the bath, the hot water doing
its best to loosen the knots tightening her shoulder blades.
When she finally got out of the bathroom, dripping wet
and aching with both tiredness and sorrow, she fell across
the bed, pulling the duvet across her, her hair still in a wet
tangle, and didn't stir until bright autumn sunshine was
pouring through the windows whose shutters she'd forgotten to close.

In the morning light, everything seemed a little better. At least, Rachel felt more resolved. Last night she'd
been blindsided by Mateo's sudden change in attitude, the
way he'd morphed from the charming, easy-going man
she'd known into some parody of a cold, frosty stranger.
She knew the pressures of his kingship weighed on him
heavily, but he'd never taken that tone with her before,
and Rachel had no intention of setting some sort of awful
precedent now.

She showered and dressed, blow-dried her hair into art-
ful waves and chose one of her new outfits to boost her
confidence—a pair of wide-leg trousers and a cowl-necked
topped in soft maroon jersey. Her engagement ring glinted
as she moved, reminding her of the promises they'd already
made to each other. They'd get through this. They were getting married tomorrow, after all.

Finding Mateo, however, was not as easy as Rachel
hoped. After a buffet breakfast in the palace dining room

by herself, she was whisked away by Monica, her personal assistant, to the final fitting of her wedding gown.

Rachel loved the pure simplicity of the white silk gown, with its edging of antique lace on the sleeves and hem, and the long veil of matching lace. When she wore it, she truly felt like a princess. A queen.

After the fitting, Monica met with her in the study Rachel was to call her own, going over the schedule of events on tomorrow's big day. Rachel scanned down the list— wedding ceremony and coronation in the cathedral across the square, and then a walkabout through the plaza to greet well-wishers before returning to the palace for a wedding breakfast. Then a turn around the city in a horse and carriage before returning to the palace for a ball, and finally spending their wedding night there in a private suite. Considering Mateo's responsibilities, there would be no honeymoon.

'That looks like a very full day,' Rachel said with a smile, trying to ignore the butterflies swarming in her middle. Even though she was getting a little bit used to being in the public eye, the thought of all those events made her feel dizzy with anxiety. What if she tripped and fell flat on her face? What if she was sick? Considering how nervous she was, she knew it was perfectly possible. She could utterly humiliate herself in front of thousands of people, not to mention those watching from their homes, since everything was to be broadcast live.

Don't think about it, she instructed herself. *When the times comes, you'll just do it. You'll have to.*

She turned to Monica with as bright a smile as she could manage. 'Do you know where the king is?'

The wind streamed by him, making his eyes water, as Mateo bent low over the horse and gave it its head. The world was a blur of sea, sand, and sky as the stallion raced over the dunes.

When he'd woken up that morning after a few hours of restless sleep, he'd known he needed to get out of the palace. Out of his own head. And riding one of the many horses in the royal stables was the perfect way to do it.

Mateo hadn't been on a horse in years, but as soon as he'd settled himself atop Mesonyktio, the Greek word for midnight, he'd felt as if he were coming home. And feeling the world fall away, even if just for a few minutes, was a blessed and much-needed relief.

He was still angry with himself for the way he'd handled the altercation with Rachel. He was also angry with his meddling relatives and colleagues for mentioning Cressida; he'd only brought her to Kallyria once, fifteen years ago, but they remembered.

He remembered. He'd been so besotted. So sure that she was the only, the ultimate, woman for him.

Of course she hadn't been. His gut tightened and he leaned farther over Mesonyktio's head, letting the wind and speed chase away the last of his tumultuous thoughts.

By the time he arrived back at the stables, he was tired enough not to have to think too much about last night, or how he regretted the way he'd handled that tense and unexpected situation with Rachel.

He slid off Mesonyktio's back and led him by the reins into the dim coolness of the palace stables, only to stiffen when he heard a familiar voice say quietly, 'Mateo.'

He blinked in the gloom, breathing in the smell of horse and hay, and then focused his gaze on Rachel, standing in front of him, chin tilted, eyes direct.

'What are you doing here?'

'I wanted to talk to you.'

He drew a deep breath, forcing himself to relax. 'All right. Let me see to the horse first.'

She nodded and stepped out of the way as he brought Mesonyktio to his stall and began to unfasten his saddle.

'I didn't even know you rode.'

'Not much time or space for it, back in Cambridge.'

'No, I suppose not.'

She remained quiet as he rubbed the horse down, taking his time to delay the moment when he'd have to face her. He should apologise. He knew that. Yet somehow the words wouldn't come.

Finally there was nothing more to do with Mesonyktio, and Mateo knew he could not delay the inevitable. He turned around and faced his bride-to-be. She looked lovely in a pair of tailored trousers and a soft top in burgundy that made the most of her curves. Her hair was loose about her shoulders, her eyes wide and dark and fastened on him.

'I want to talk about last night,' she said without preamble. Rachel was no shrinking violet, never had been. She had always been willing to be confrontational at work, politely so, but still. Mateo should have known she wouldn't let last night go, no matter how foreboding he might have seemed.

'I'm sorry if I seemed a bit abrupt,' he said. 'It's a sensitive subject.'

Her eyebrows rose. 'You seemed a bit abrupt? Nice try, Mateo, but I'm not having that.'

Despite the tension coiling inside him, he almost smiled. 'You're not?'

'No. We're about to be married.' She glanced at her watch, an elegant strip of diamond-encrusted gold that was part of her trousseau. 'In less than twenty-four hours. I'm not having you go all glowery on me and refuse to discuss something that is clearly important. The whole point of marrying me, or so you said, was because we were friends, and we liked and trusted one another. So don't pull the Scary King act on me, okay?'

'I don't think "glowery" is actually a word.'

'Well, it should be. And if it was in the dictionary, you'd be next to the definition.' She blew out a breath. 'So, look. Just tell me what the deal with Cressida is.'

Even now, when she'd played her hand straight, the way she always did, he was reluctant to reveal the truth, and what details he gave her he would do so sparingly.

'I told you all you need to know, Rachel. I dated her back in university. We were both young. The relationship ended.'

'There must be more to it than that.'

'I don't ask you about your relationship with that man who broke your heart,' he retorted, and she flinched.

'He didn't break my heart. I told you that. I said I was never in love with him.' She paused, seeming to weigh whether she wanted to ask the question he already knew was coming. 'Were you in love with her? Cressida?'

Mateo stood still, doing his best to keep his face bland, his body relaxed. It took effort. 'I suppose I was. Yes.'

She nodded slowly, as if absorbing a blow. 'I wish you had told me before.'

'Before? When, exactly?'

'When you asked me to marry you.' A crumpled note of hurt entered her voice, and she took a breath, clearly striving to hold onto her composure.

'Would it have made a difference?'

'I don't know, but you know as well as I do, Mateo, that when a scientist does not have all the relevant information regarding an experiment, they cannot draw an accurate conclusion.'

Mateo folded his arms and attempted to stare her down. He should have known he wouldn't succeed. Rachel had never been one to be cowed. 'What happened before has no relevance on the present or the future, Rachel. Our future. It was a long time ago. Fifteen years.'

'Yet you can't say her name,' she said softly. 'You haven't said it once since we've started talking about her.'

Everything in him tightened. 'I admit, it was a painful time. I do not wish to revisit it.'

'So fifteen years on, you still have trouble speaking about it? About her?' She shook her head sorrowfully. 'That does make a difference, Mateo.'

'Why?' he demanded. 'It ended a long time ago, Rachel. It doesn't matter any more.'

'Is she the reason you want a loveless marriage?' Rachel asked stonily.

'I didn't say that—'

'You as good as did. One based on friendship and trust, rather than love. That's been clear all along, Mateo. You told me you weren't interested in falling in love. I just... I didn't realise it was because you'd been in love before.'

He flinched at that, but did not deny it.

'So.' Rachel nodded slowly. 'That's how it is.'

'This really doesn't need to change things, Rachel. Like I said, it was a long time ago.'

'What happened?' Rachel asked. 'I deserve to know that much. How did it end? Did she leave you?'

Mateo struggled to keep his expression even, his voice neutral. 'She died.'

'Oh.' The sound that escaped her was soft and sad. 'I'm so sorry.' He nodded jerkily, not willing to say more. To reveal more. 'So if she hadn't died...' Rachel said quietly, almost to herself, and Mateo did not finish that thought. She nodded again, then looked up at him. 'You should have told me,' she stated quietly. 'No matter how long ago it happened. I should have known.'

'I didn't realise it mattered.'

'Then you are not nearly as emotionally astute as I thought you were,' she retorted with dignity. 'You talked about how you trusted me, Mateo, but what about whether I can trust you?'

'This is not about trust—'

'Isn't it?' The two words were quiet and sad, and she didn't wait for his answer as she walked out of the stables.

CHAPTER TWELVE

TODAY WAS HER wedding day. Rachel gazed into the mirror at her princess-like reflection and tried to banish the foreboding that fell over her like a dark cloud.

Ever since her confrontation with Mateo in the stables yesterday, she'd felt as if she were walking under it, blundering forward in a storm of uncertainty, trying to make peace with this new knowledge of her husband-to-be, and what it might mean for their marriage.

So he'd had his heart broken. He'd been deeply in love with a woman, and she'd died. It wasn't a deal-breaker, surely, but Rachel would have appreciated knowing and adjusting to the fact before she was about to walk down the aisle.

No matter what Mateo might insist, it made a difference knowing he'd loved and lost rather than believing he'd never been interested in loving at all.

All through yesterday, as she'd gone through the motions of their wedding rehearsal, and chatted over dinner with dignitaries whose names she couldn't remember, a battle had been raging in her head.

Should I? Shouldn't I?

But at the end of the day, when she'd gone up to her suite of rooms and seen her wedding gown swathed in plastic and ready for her to wear in the morning, she'd known there wasn't a battle at all.

Her wedding was the next day. Her marriage was already set in motion. She had a *coin* with her name minted on it, as Mateo had informed her that evening. She couldn't walk away from this, just because the situation was a little bit messier than she'd anticipated. There was far, far more riding on this marriage than her own happiness.

And yet…it caused a pain like grief deep inside her to know that Mateo had loved another woman, loved her enough to not want to love someone else ever again. It was, she told herself, a grief she could get used to, and would ultimately have to live with, but a grief, nonetheless.

Since their confrontation in the stables, Rachel had felt a coolness between her and Mateo that definitely hadn't been there before, and it saddened her. It was no way to start a marriage, to say vows, with this tension between them.

And yet that was how it seemed it was going to be.

She'd woken that morning to bright sunshine and pealing bells—apparently they would ring all morning, until the wedding. Rachel tried to tune them out as Francesca helped her dress, giving her understated make-up and sweeping her hair into an elegant up-do.

'This feels crazy,' Rachel murmured numbly as she stood in front of the mirror and gazed at the vision she beheld. 'That can't be me.'

'It is,' Francesca said with a wide smile. 'You look utterly fabulous.'

'All thanks to you.'

'Not all,' the stylist answered with a wink. 'But I'll take a *tiny* bit of credit.'

Rachel moved to the window that overlooked the front of the palace and the large square that stretched to the cathedral on the other side, already crowded with spectators even though it was still several hours until the ceremony.

Many looked as if they had set up early, with camping

chairs and flasks of coffee, and others were waving flags or banners. All for her…her and Mateo.

Since coming to Kallyria, Rachel had been too busy and overwhelmed to look online and find out what the media was saying about her and Mateo, and in truth she wasn't sure she wanted to know. Now, however, as she eyed a banner that said simply *True Love*, she wondered.

'Francesca,' she asked slowly. 'What are they saying about Mateo and me?'

The stylist, who was tidying away the many cosmetics she'd used to create Rachel's natural look, glanced up with an arched eyebrow. 'Hmm?'

'What are they saying about us? Are they asking why we're marrying?' Rachel caught sight of a sign that read *A Real-life Fairy Tale*!

'Well…' Francesca paused as she mentally reviewed all she'd heard and read. 'Nothing bad, if you're worried about that. Everyone thinks it's incredibly romantic that you've worked together for so long and that now he's king Mateo wants you by his side. I mean, it *is* romantic, right?'

Rachel forced her lips upwards in what she suspected was a parody of a smile. 'Right.'

'I mean, Mateo could have chosen anyone…but he wanted you. People are saying you're the luckiest woman in the world.'

'Right,' Rachel said again. She turned back to the window, not wanting Francesca to see the expression on her face.

The luckiest woman in the world.

Why did she not feel that way right now? Why did she feel as if she were living a lie?

A short while later, it was time to go. Francesca arranged her veil to spread out behind her as Rachel headed down the staircase to the palace's entrance hall, for a round of official photographs.

Her cheeks ached from smiling, and the heavy satin of the dress felt as if it was weighing her down, as Rachel posed for photograph after photograph. This was what she'd agreed to, she reminded herself. She was lucky, even if she was filled with doubts right now. Mateo was a good man, a man she liked and trusted, even if love was never going to come into their particular equation. She had more, so much more, than most women of the world. She certainly wasn't going to complain.

But her heart felt as heavy as her dress as she prepared to make her official exit from the palace, and walk alone across the crowd-packed square to the cathedral where her groom—and a thousand guests—awaited.

As the doors were flung open, the bright sunlight streamed in, making Rachel squint. Francesca's hand was at her back, her voice a murmur in her ear.

'Chin up, eyes straight ahead. Nod, don't wave, in case you drop your bouquet.'

Rachel glanced down at the magnificent selection of white roses and lilies she'd been given for the photos. She gulped. 'Okay.'

'Walk slowly—right foot forward, feet together, and so on. It will feel a lot slower than you're used to. Count it in your head.'

'Okay,' Rachel said again. She wished they'd rehearsed this part, and not just what happened in the church, but it had sounded simple when the square was empty. All she had to do was walk across it.

'Go,' Francesca urged, and gave her a little push. Rachel stepped through the palace doors. The noise greeted her first, like a towering wave crashing over her. They were cheering. She, the nobody who had been overlooked by everyone for most of her life, even by her parents, now had what felt like the entire world screaming their approval. It was daunting, terrifying even, but also, surprisingly and amazingly, wonderful.

'Go,' Francesca whispered, and Rachel started down the shallow steps towards the square, her gown fanning behind her in an elegant arc of lace-edged satin. She knew she was meant to keep her gaze straight ahead, on the path that had been cleared through the crowd, with crowd barriers keeping everyone at bay, but she couldn't help but meet the gazes of some of the people who had queued for hours simply to be here, to see her.

'Queen Rachel!' someone called, and she nearly jerked in surprise. Queen Rachel. If that didn't sound crazily weird…

'You're so beautiful!' someone else shouted, and she let her gaze move amidst the crowd, settling on as many faces as she could and offering them her smile. Her bouquet was too heavy for her to free one hand to wave, and she hoped her smile was enough.

'Thank you,' she heard herself saying. And then, *'Efharisto. Efharisto!'*

The cheers continued all the way across the square, which felt like a hundred miles instead of the equivalent in metres. On impulse, at the doors to the cathedral, she handed her bouquet to a waiting attendant and lifted her hand in a wave that sent the crowd cheering even more wildly. Then she reached for her bouquet and headed into the cool, hushed interior of the cathedral.

She blinked in the candle-flickering gloom, the brightly painted icons of saints visible high in the shadows of the huge cathedral. She took in the pews and pews filled with guests in their wedding finery, and there, at the start of a very long aisle, Mateo, standing by himself, looking devastating in a white tie and tails, bright red and blue royal regalia pinned to his chest. A king. *Her* king. Waiting to escort her down the aisle and to the ceremony.

For a second, poised on the threshold of her entire life, Rachel hesitated as a thousand thoughts tilted and slid through her mind. Her hands tightened on the bouquet as organ music crashed and swelled.

This was happening. She was doing this. *They* were doing this. And she hoped and prayed that somehow it would be the right thing for them both.

Mateo's gaze was fixed on his bride as she turned to face him. Her veil flowed over her shoulders in a lace river, her dress belling out behind in her in a floaty arc of satin. He reached out a hand and, with her gaze fixed on him, she took it. Her fingers slid across his and then tightened. The moment felt suspended, stretching on in significance, before Mateo turned and together they began to walk down the aisle.

He glanced at her as they walked—her chin tilted proudly, her shoulders back, her gaze straight ahead. She was elegant. Regal. Magnificent. Mateo's heart swelled with pride and something else, something dangerously deeper, as they walked towards the altar. All the unspoken tension and coolness that had existed between them for the last two days fell away in that moment. They were walking towards their future together, and she would soon be his.

The ceremony passed in a dazed blur. As was tradition, every vow was repeated three times, and wedding crowns of laurel placed on their heads, rings slipped onto their right hands, the hand of blessing. The music swelled and Mateo lifted her veil. She smiled at him tremulously, everything she felt and more in her eyes. He kissed her, barely a brush of her lips, but it felt like fireworks exploding in his head.

How was he going to stand this? How was he going to maintain that necessary distance for his own safety, as well as hers?

The questions fell into the tumult of his mind and were

lost as the ceremony continued, into their coronation. Now husband and wife, they ascended the steps of the cathedral and knelt, hand in hand, before the two thrones there.

The bishop placed the historic crowns on their heads; the weight was surprising, and Mateo glanced at Rachel, a tremor rippling through him at the beautiful sight of her—wearing both a crown and a wedding dress. His bride. His Queen.

Then the ceremony was over, the crowns removed, and the music started again. After helping her to rise, Mateo escorted her back down the aisle. They were married. Husband and wife, for ever.

'Did that actually happen?' Rachel asked shakily as they stood on the steps of the cathedral, blinking in the bright sunlight.

'It most certainly did.' Mateo glanced down at the ring sparkling on his hand. He felt changed in a way he hadn't expected, on a molecular level. His whole *being* was changed, as if he'd undergone a chemical reaction without realising. He could never go back, and neither could Rachel.

'What do we do now?' Rachel asked. 'I know I've been told, but everything feels different now.'

'It does, doesn't it?' He felt a rush of gratitude and even joy that she felt the same as he did. They were *changed*.

'I mean, there's people, for one.' She gestured to the crowds who had been waiting for them to emerge. 'It's completely different, to walk across that square when it's filled with people.'

'Of course.' Mateo looked away, annoyed with himself for rushing to such a stupid, sentimental conclusion. They were changed. Right.

'So should we go? Or do we wait?'

'We can go.' His jaw tightened as he reached for her hand. 'Might as well get this over with.'

Hurt flashed in her eyes as she looked at him. 'Is that really how you see it, Mateo?' she asked quietly.

'I didn't mean anything by it,' he said a bit shortly, even though he had. He'd been reminding himself as well as her of what their marriage was really based on, and it wasn't some stupid rush of emotion.

'This is our wedding day,' Rachel stated with quiet dignity. 'The only one we'll ever have, God willing. Can't we enjoy it?'

He felt like a cad then, a real joy-stealing jerk. 'I'm sorry,' he said. 'Of course we can. Why don't we give them a kiss?'

'Wait—what?'

'A kiss,' he said more firmly, and took her into his arms. She came willingly, and as he settled his mouth on hers he felt a deep sense of satisfaction as well as a rush of desire. This part of their marriage, at least, didn't have to be so complicated.

Rachel's mouth opened like a flower under his and she reached up to cup his cheek with one hand, in an unsettlingly tender gesture. The crowd roared and stamped and whistled their approval. Reluctantly Mateo broke the kiss. His breathing was ragged and so was Rachel's.

'That's a deposit towards later,' he said, and she let out a little breathless laugh.

'Good to know.'

They started the traditional wedding walk across the square to the palace, where they would have a formal wedding breakfast, followed by the carriage ride and then later by a ball. People continued to cheer, reaching their hands across the barriers. It was usual royal protocol to ignore such gestures, but Rachel broke ranks and starting shaking people's hands, and Mateo started to restrain her before he saw how people were responding to her—with both devotion and joy.

Mateo had always intended to model his kingship on his father's, to be dignified, a bit austere and remote, but also sincere and hardworking. His father would never have shaken a commoner's hand, never mind posing for a selfie as Rachel was now doing. And yet when Mateo saw the reaction of his people, their unfettered delight, he realised that this might be what was needed.

His father had kept the public at a distance, thinking he was above them, and Leo had ignored them in pursuit of his own private pleasure. Maybe it was time for Mateo to be different. For the King and Queen to engage with their people, to love them as their own.

The thought was novel, a bit alarming, and yet also strangely exciting.

'They love you,' Mateo murmured as they finally cleared the crowds and entered the palace. 'They really love you.'

'It's so strange,' she murmured, shaking her head, looking dazed. 'I've never...' She stopped, but something in her tone made Mateo turn to her.

'You never what?'

She paused, biting her lip as she gazed at him uncertainly. 'I've never been loved before,' she confessed with a shaky laugh. 'By anyone. But I think I could get used to it.'

It was such a dramatic statement that Mateo shook his head instinctively. 'Of course you've been loved.'

'No, not really.'

'Your mother. Your parents—'

'No. Not like that, anyway.'

He frowned, searching her face, looking for self-pity but finding only her usual good-humoured pragmatism. 'What are you talking about, Rachel?'

'My parents didn't love me,' she said simply. 'Or at least, they didn't like me. Which is worse, do you think?' She posed it like an academic question.

'Of course your parents loved you.' Even though he'd

rebelled as a youth, even though he'd resented being seen as unnecessary in the line to the throne, and walked away from everything as a result, he'd never doubted his parents' love. *Never.* Yet Rachel spoke about her loveless parents as if she was simply stating facts.

'I suppose they loved me after a fashion,' she said after a moment. 'I mean, they provided for me, certainly. But they didn't act as if they loved me, or wanted me in their lives, so I didn't feel loved.' She shrugged. 'But why on earth are we talking about this now? We need to go into the wedding breakfast.'

'They must have loved you.' Mateo didn't know why he was labouring the point, only that he really hated the idea that Rachel had grown up unloved. Disliked, even. *Rachel.* 'Maybe they were just reticent...'

She rolled her eyes. 'Okay. Sure. That's what they were. Can we go now?'

It was obvious she wanted to drop it, and now was hardly the time or place for some sort of emotional discussion—the kind of discussion he'd never really wanted to have—and yet Mateo was realising what a fool he'd been, to think he could separate parts of his life—his heart—like oil and water, never mixing. Marriage wasn't like that. It was a chemical reaction, just as he'd felt in himself; two separate entities combining and becoming something new. Hydrogen and oxygen turning into life-giving water. Or perhaps caesium and water, causing a life-threatening explosion. *Which was it?*

Only time would tell. And whichever it was, Mateo knew he couldn't take the affection and the trust and the physical desire and compartmentalise them all, neatly labelled, put away in a drawer and never causing him any bother. As much as he wanted to, needed to, he couldn't.

And that was when Mateo knew he was in big trouble.

CHAPTER THIRTEEN

RACHEL'S HEART FLUTTERED like a wild thing in her chest as Mateo closed the door of the bedroom. They were in the honeymoon suite, tucked away in a tower in a far wing of the palace, with a view of the sea shimmering under the moonlight from its high windows.

The circular room was something out of another fairy tale—*Rapunzel*, perhaps—with a twisting staircase that led up to this lovely room, a cosy fire crackling in the grate, and a canopied king-sized bed draped in silks and satins of various shades of ivory and taupe taking pride of place.

Rachel released a shuddery breath she hadn't even realised she'd been holding. It had been a long day, an endless day, from the ceremony and coronation this morning to the formal wedding breakfast with speeches and toasts, posing for photo after photo, and then the carriage ride around the old city, and finally a ball to finish. She'd changed into another gown, the one she wore now, a strapless ball gown in taupe satin and a diamanté-encrusted band around her waist.

At least she and Mateo hadn't had to dance in front of everyone, although after three glasses of champagne she'd managed a simple swaying with him to a modern pop song. Mateo had smiled down at her as they had danced, but she hadn't been able to gauge his mood, just as she hadn't been able to all day. Just as she couldn't now.

He turned from the door, his expression inscrutable as he loosened his white tie. Rachel watched him, feeling like a mouse being observed by a hawk, although there was nothing particularly predatory about his cool blue-green gaze. She was just feeling uncertain and vulnerable now that they'd finally reached this moment, the moment when they were alone together. When they would truly become husband and wife.

'It's very late,' Mateo remarked. 'We don't have to do anything tonight.'

Rachel couldn't keep disappointment from swooping inside her. Clearly he wasn't in any rush.

'We might as well get it over with,' she tossed back at him, echoing his words from this morning that had hurt her more than they should have.

'Is that how you view it?' His lips twisted and he tossed his tie aside.

'It's not how I want to view it,' she returned. The last thing she wanted to do was argue *now*. 'I'm not trying to sound snippy, but I have no idea how you feel about this, Mateo.'

'This?'

'Us.' She gestured to the bed. 'You *know*.'

'Sex?' he stated baldly, and for some reason she flinched. He made it sound like some sort of physical procedure they had to perform, rather than the joyful consummation of their marriage.

'Yes,' she muttered, and suddenly found herself fighting tears. She turned away from him, not wanting him to see, but he caught her arm.

'Rachel.'

'What…?' she managed thickly, blinking as fast as she could to keep the tears back. A few fell anyway.

'I'm sorry. I think I'm being an ass.'

'You think?'

'All right. I am. I'm sorry. I don't...' He blew out a breath. 'This is strange for me too.'

'Not as strange as it is for me,' she returned tartly, and he frowned at her.

'What do you mean?'

'I have a feeling that my experience is significantly more limited than yours,' she informed him, knowing it needed to be said even as she wished that it didn't.

'Oh?' Mateo gazed at her appraisingly. 'You might be wrong.'

She almost laughed at that. 'I don't think so.'

'I'm not some Lothario, Rachel. Work has been my mistress more than any woman.' His mouth curved in a crooked smile. 'I've spent far more time with you than anyone else, you know.'

'As gratified as I am to hear that, I still stand by my statement.' She felt her cheeks heat as she confessed, 'I have *very* little experience, Mateo.'

His narrowed gaze scanned her face. 'You're...you're not a virgin,' he stated, not quite making it a question.

'No...but almost.'

'How can you be almost?'

She pressed her hands to her cheeks, willing her blush to fade. 'This is seriously embarrassing, you know?'

'You don't have to be embarrassed with me.' He made it sound so obvious, but it wasn't.

'I do, especially when you turn all brooding and remote on me, and make me feel as if I don't know you at all.'

'Brooding and remote?' The corner of his mouth lifted in a smile. 'Just slap me when I do that.'

'I might.'

'Seriously, Rachel.' He took a step towards her, his shirt open at the throat, his gaze a bit hooded, his eyes so bright and his hair so dark and his jaw so hard... He was just too beautiful. It should have been a crime. It certainly wasn't fair. 'Tell me.'

'Tell you what? How little experience I have when it comes to this?' She gestured to the bed.

'Only if it would make you feel better, to have me know.'

'One time, okay?' The words rang out and she closed her eyes in mortification. 'I've done it one time, and, trust me, it was completely forgettable.' There. It was out. Thirty-two years old and she'd had sex *once*, with a guy who had turned out to be a complete cad. But she didn't want to go into those humiliating details now.

'Okay,' Mateo said after a moment.

'Okay?' Rachel stared at him uncertainly.

'Now I know.' Mateo shrugged. 'It doesn't make any difference to me. I'm not put off, if that's what you're afraid of.'

'Not *yet*.'

'Not ever. A lack of experience isn't a turn-off, Rachel, trust me.'

'That's assuming you're turned *on* in the first place,' she muttered. She felt tears again, and tried to hide it. This was all getting a bit too much.

'Why would you think I wouldn't be?'

'Why would I think I would?' she challenged. 'We've known each other for ten years, Mateo, and you haven't felt anything like that for me in all that time.'

'And nor have you for me,' Mateo countered. Rachel decided to remain silent on that point. There was only so much honesty she could take. 'It's changed now. We're looking at each other differently now.'

'You haven't exactly had trouble keeping your hands off me,' she felt compelled to point out. 'Quite the opposite. We've kissed exactly three times since we've been engaged.'

Mateo's lids lowered as he looked at her meaningfully. 'We've done more than kiss.'

'Barely. And even then you were pretty quick to haul me off your lap.' The humiliation of that moment stung all over again, and a tear fell. She dashed it away hurriedly and Mateo swore under his breath.

'Rachel, I had no idea you felt this way.' He looked flummoxed; the colour leached from his face as he shook his head slowly.

'I'm not expecting you to fall in love with me,' she managed stiltedly. 'Or even be wild with passion for me. I know I'm not exactly—'

'*Don't* say it.' Mateo sounded fierce. 'Don't run yourself down, Rachel. You're amazing. You're beautiful. You're my *wife*.'

'Then show me,' she whispered brokenly. *'Show me.'*

Mateo held her gaze for one blazing second and then he swiftly crossed the room and, cupping her face in his hands, kissed her deeply.

He'd kissed her before, and it had always made her senses spin. Now was no different, as his mouth slanted and then settled over hers and his tongue swept the softness inside, making her body sag and her knees weaken. He kissed her as if he *knew* her. And that made all the difference.

Rachel wrapped her arms around his hard body and he pressed closer, one knee sliding between the billowing folds of her gown as his kiss took possession of her, and her spinning senses started to drown. She was overwhelmed. Overloaded. Undone. And all by one kiss.

When he finally lifted his head to give her a questioning, demanding look, she managed the weakest smile she'd ever given.

'That's a start.'

'A *start*?' he growled, and he kissed her again. Deeper this time, until she was truly and utterly lost, and yet at the same time found. She'd never been kissed like this before. She'd never felt like this before. And she wanted more.

Mateo broke the kiss to give her another one of his burning looks. Then he began to unbutton his shirt. Rachel swallowed hard.

'I've never seen you without your shirt on before,' she remarked conversationally, except her voice came out in a croak.

'You're going to see me with a whole lot less on than that.'

Rachel gulped—and then thought of her wobbly bits that she wasn't sure she wanted Mateo seeing. 'Maybe we should move to the bed,' she suggested. 'Get under the covers.'

Mateo arched an eyebrow. 'Are you trying to hide from me?'

'A little,' she confessed. 'Let's face it, Mateo, when it comes to basic good looks—'

He laid a finger against her lips. 'I don't want to hear it. Not one more disparaging word. This is our wedding night, Rachel, and you are a beautiful, gorgeous, sexy *queen*. Don't ever forget it.'

His finger was still against her lips as she regarded him with wide eyes. 'I won't,' she whispered, and then Mateo lifted his finger from her lips and finished unbuttoning his shirt, shrugging it off his broad shoulders in one sinuous movement.

He was breathtakingly beautiful, all hard, sculpted muscles, pecs and abs burnished and defined, making Rachel long to touch him, but she felt too timid.

Mateo met her shyly questioning gaze. 'Touch me,' he commanded, and so she did.

The trail of Rachel's fingertips along his abdomen had Mateo's muscles flexing involuntarily. Her hesitant caress was positively enflaming, with an intensity he hadn't expected. He *responded* to this woman, and it wasn't just merely physical. Her artless confession, her shy looks, that small smile, *everything...*

It humbled him, that Rachel was so honest. She'd experienced so little in life—so little love, so little desire—and yet she'd still held onto her pragmatic attitude, her good humour. And even though the intensity of his own feeling, as well as the intimacy of Rachel's confession, had Mateo instinctively wanting to throw up all the old barricades, he didn't.

Because this wasn't about him, or at least not just him. It was about Rachel, and showing her how beautiful and desirable she was. It was about making her feel cherished and wanted, because right now Mateo realised he wanted that for her more than anything. More than his instinct for self-protection. He could give her this. He *needed* to give her this.

Her fingers skimmed up his chest and she looked at him with a question in her eyes. 'You can touch me a lot more than that,' he told her. 'But first we need to get some clothes off.'

Her eyes widened and she bit her lip. She was nervous about being naked in front of him. Mateo knew that, and it felt like a gift. He would cherish it. Cherish her.

'Turn around,' he said softly, and slowly she did.

Her ball gown had about a thousand tiny buttons from the middle of her back right down to the base. Mateo began undoing them one by one as Rachel sucked in a hard breath.

'I think there's a lovely nightgown around here somewhere,' she said shakily. 'Francesca picked it out...'

'We'll save it for later.' His fingers skimmed her skin as he slid each button from its hole, revealing the smooth, silky expanse of her back. He spread his hands, enjoying the whisper-soft feel of her skin against his palms. With the last button undone, the dress fell about her waist. The gown had had a built-in bra, and so there was nothing on her top half and Mateo liked it that way.

He reached around and filled his hands with the warm softness of her breasts, and she let out a shocked gasp at his touch. After a second she leaned back against him and he brushed his thumbs across her nipples, making them both shudder. Her gown slithered lower on her hips, and it only took one swift tug to have it falling in a crumpled heap around her calves.

Taking a deep breath, Rachel stepped out of it, and then turned to face him, her heart—and all her fear—in her eyes. She wore nothing but a lacy slip of underwear, and a pair of stockings with lace garters. Her hair had half fallen out of the elegant up-do, and lay in tumbled, chestnut waves over her shoulders. Her cheeks were flushed, her lips bee-stung, her eyes like stars. And her *body*…all the blood rushed from his head as Mateo gazed upon her.

'Rachel,' he said in a voice that throbbed both with sincerity and desire. 'You are truly beautiful.'

'I feel beautiful,' she whispered, sounding amazed, and Mateo reached for her. The press of her breasts against his bare chest was exquisite, but he wanted more. He let her go to briefly shrug out of his clothes, muttering with impatience as he fumbled with his waistcoat, the faff of his trouser buttons. Finally he was free, as nearly naked as she was, and he drew her to the bed.

They fell upon it in a tangle of covers and limbs, and Mateo ran one hand from her ankle to her hip, revelling in the silken sweetness of her skin.

'Touch me, too,' he whispered and she pressed her palm flat against his chest, before an impish smile came over her face and she trailed her hand down and down, wrapping her fingers around the throbbing heat of him.

'I've never done this before,' she whispered as her fingers explored and stroked. 'Am I doing it right?'

Mateo could not keep from groaning aloud. 'Yes,' he told her as she continued her artless, and very effective, caresses. *'Yes.'*

She continued to stroke and explore, her caresses becoming less and less hesitant, making his blood heat and his mind blur. He was going to lose his self-control very, very soon.

'This might surprise you,' he managed as he gently but firmly removed her hand, 'but I am not nearly as experienced as you seem to think I am, and it has been rather a long time since I have been in this type of situation.'

Her eyes widened as she looked at him. 'Really?'

'Really. And if you keep doing what you're doing, our wedding night will be rather short and, I fear, even more disappointing. So let me touch you now.'

A small smile curved her mouth as he gently pushed her onto her back. 'All right.'

Mateo kissed her on her mouth, savouring the sweetness of her lips, before he moved lower, kissing his way from her jaw to her throat, and then taking his time to lavish each of her lovely breasts with his full attention. The mewling sounds she made enflamed him further, and he moved lower, his tongue skimming the gently rounded beauty of her belly to settle happily between her thighs.

'Mateo...' Her fingers threaded through his hair as her hips lifted instinctively and Mateo tasted his fill.

Rachel's cry shattered the air as her body shuddered with her first climax. Mateo intended there to be several.

'Oh, my goodness...' she managed faintly, and Mateo smiled against her skin. 'I've never...'

'Now you have.'

She laughed at that and he rolled on top of her, bracing himself on his forearms, as he looked down at her, flushed and sated, yet clearly ready for more. 'Oh...' she breathed as he nudged at her entrance. She wriggled underneath him, a look of concentration on her face as she angled herself upwards, ever the scientist looking for the perfect conditions for an experiment.

And the conditions were perfect, Mateo acknowledged as he slid slowly, inch by exquisite inch, inside her. Rachel's eyes widened and her lips parted and she hooked one leg around his waist to draw him even deeper, so their bodies felt totally enmeshed, utterly entwined. *As one.*

Here was the ultimate chemical reaction, where something new was created from two separate substances, and could never, ever be torn apart.

Mateo began to move, and Rachel moved with him, hesitant at first but then with sinuous certainty, and they found their rhythm together as easily as if they'd always known it, minds and bodies and hearts all melded.

It was wonderfully strange and yet as natural as breathing, as they climbed higher and higher towards the pleasure that was promised both of them, just out of reach until it burst upon them like a dazzling firework, and then, with a gasp and a cry, they fell apart, reassembling themselves together, as one, their bodies still entwined, their arms around each other as their releases shuddered through them.

Mateo rolled onto his back, taking Rachel with him, their hearts thudding against one another with frantic beats.

He'd meant to offer this—himself—as a gift to her, but it wasn't, he realised now, that simple an exchange. He couldn't give without receiving. He couldn't offer himself and at the same time keep himself separate.

If he'd thought he was in trouble this morning, after the ceremony, he knew he was utterly lost now. Lost—and yet found. And the thought terrified him, not for his own safety or self-protection, but for Rachel's.

He could not hold her heart in his hands. He could not bear to, for he would surely, surely shatter it.

CHAPTER FOURTEEN

'THANK YOU SO much for your contribution, Your Highness.'

Rachel smiled and nodded graciously at the head teacher of the girls' high school in Constanza, where she'd been part of a round-table discussion on encouraging female pupils to study STEM subjects. The conversation had been wide-ranging and invigorating, and she'd enjoyed every minute of it.

'Thank you for inviting me,' she said as she took her leave, pausing for a photo op before shaking hands with everyone at the table. A few minutes later she was in the back of a black SUV, speeding back towards the palace.

It had been a month since her wedding, and Rachel had done her best to fully involve herself as Queen. She'd selected several charities to support, and said yes to almost every engagement at which she'd been asked to appear. Maybe if she kept herself busy enough, she wouldn't notice the empty space in her heart.

She had nothing to complain about, Rachel reminded herself severely. It was a talking-to she had to give herself almost every day. Absolutely nothing to complain about, because she'd agreed to this; she'd known what she was getting into; she'd accepted the deal with full understanding of what it had meant.

She just hadn't realised how it would *feel*.

Since their wonderful and frankly earth-shattering wed-

ding night, Rachel had had hopes that something more—
something a lot like love—would blossom between them,
in time. When Mateo had held her to him, moved inside
her, buried his face in her hair…

She'd been so sure. Everything had felt possible.

But in the month since that night, that incandescent sense
of possibility had begun to fade, day by day and night by
night. Mateo wasn't cruel, or cold, or even cool. He was
exactly what he'd said he'd be—a trusted friend, an affectionate partner. But he didn't love her, Rachel knew that
full well, and while she'd agreed in theory to a marriage
based on friendship rather than love, she'd assumed it would
mean that neither of them loved the other.

Not, Rachel acknowledged hollowly as she watched the
streets of Constanza slide by, that she would fall in love
with a man who was determined not to love her. Who kept
part of his heart clearly roped off, who had a shadow in his
eyes and a certain distance in his demeanour that even a
passionate night of lovemaking—not that she could even
call it lovemaking—could banish.

And meanwhile she felt herself tumbling headlong into
something she was afraid was love. The kind of soul-deep,
long-abiding love she had never expected to feel for anyone. But Mateo had been so kind…had made her feel so
valued…had held her like a treasure and laughed with her
and given her joy. Of course she'd fallen in love with him.

It was just he hadn't fallen in love with her, and had no
intention of ever doing so, as far as Rachel could see.

The SUV drove through the palace gates and then up
to the front doors. A footman hurried out to open Rachel's
door, bowing as she stepped out. Four weeks of this kind
of treatment and it still felt surreal. Rachel thanked him
and then walked into the palace, heading for her private
suite of rooms. It still felt strange, to live in a palace rather
than her own home.

Although Mateo had assured her she could redecorate her suite as she liked, Rachel hadn't dared touch any of the antiques or oil paintings, the silk hangings and fine furnishings. As a result she felt as if she lived in a five-star hotel rather than a home, which was sometimes nice and sometimes a bit disconcerting.

'Your Highness, you're back.'

Rachel turned to give her personal assistant a smile. 'Yes, I am.'

'The discussion was productive?'

'Very much so, I believe. Do I have anything scheduled for the rest of the day, Monica?'

'I don't believe there is anything on your schedule until a dinner tomorrow night.'

'Right.' Rachel paused as she took off the heels she still hadn't got used to wearing. 'And do you happen to know where the King is?' she asked casually.

Monica's face was carefully blank. 'I believe he is out.'

'Thank you.' She dismissed her assistant with a smile and a small wave.

Alone in her suite Rachel drifted around, grateful for an unscheduled afternoon and yet still feeling a bit lost. She'd seen very little of Mateo in the last month, besides formal events and nights—nights which were seared on her mind and made her body tingle. Still, she missed spending time with him, missed the easy friendship they'd once had, when it hadn't been complicated by the demands of royalty—and marriage. Even if he would never love her, she wished he'd spend time with her.

She had just changed into comfortable clothes and settled on a sofa by the window with her laptop, hoping to catch up on some emails to friends, when a light knock sounded on her door.

'Yes?'

'Hello.' Mateo popped his head around the door, giving her a wry smile. 'Are you busy?'

'Busy? No.' Rachel closed her laptop, trying to temper the feeling of delight that was spreading through her like warm, golden honey. Perhaps he just had a quick question to ask, and then he'd be on his way...

'I thought we could spend the afternoon together,' Mateo said, an unusual note of hesitation in his voice. 'If you wanted to.'

If? The smile that bloomed across Rachel's face was impossible to suppress, not that she even wanted to. 'I'd love that.'

'Good.'

'What did you have in mind?'

'I thought we could go sailing, just the two of us.'

'On our own?' After being shadowed by security and staff for the last month, the prospect was wonderfully liberating.

'We'll leave the security on the shore. They can't live in my pocket all the time.'

Rachel frowned. 'Are you sure it will be safe?'

'No one's knows where we're going.' Mateo shrugged. 'It would be good to get away.'

Yes, it would. And the fact that Mateo wanted to spend time alone with her was intoxicating. 'All right,' Rachel said. 'When do you want to go?'

'How long until you're ready?'

She laughed. 'Five minutes.'

And it was only five minutes later that they were driving in a dark green convertible, a palace car Rachel hadn't seen before, but much preferred to the heavy SUVS with their blacked-out windows.

With the sky bright blue above them and the sea sparkling below, the day felt full of promise.

'Where are we going, exactly?' Rachel asked.

'A private marina where there's a sailboat.'

'I didn't even know you could sail,' she said with a laugh. Mateo threw her a glinting smile.

'There's a lot of things you don't know about me.'

Today, with the sun shining and the sky so blue, that felt like a promise rather than a warning. Rachel smiled back.

Half an hour later they were on a small sailing raft heading out into the shimmering blue-green waters of the Mediterranean Sea, with not a security officer or staff member in sight.

'Where are we going now?' Rachel asked as she tilted her face to the sun. 'Do you have a destination?'

'As a matter of fact, I do. There is a small island out here—not much more than a speck of land, but it has a nice beach. I used to go here when I was younger.'

'To get away from it all?' Rachel teased, and Mateo gave a grimacing nod.

'Actually, yes. When I was out here, I could forget I was a prince.'

'Was that something you wanted to forget?' Rachel asked softly. She was aware, not for the first time, of all she didn't know. She didn't know about Mateo's family, really, only that he was the youngest of three brothers. One had died, and one had walked away. Both, she realised now, must have left scars.

'Sometimes it was,' Mateo answered after a moment, his narrowed gaze on the glinting sea. 'I'd always get punished for trying to escape. Sent to my room with no dinner. I suppose I deserved it.'

'Your parents must have been worried about you.'

'I suppose.'

'You don't sound convinced.'

He shrugged. 'As the third son, and a later surprise at that, I was a bit of an afterthought.'

Rachel frowned. 'Were you neglected?'

'No, not at all. In some ways, it was a blessing—I had so much more freedom than either Kosmos or Leo.'

'Tell me about your brothers,' she said. 'I've never heard you speak of them before.'

'I suppose I haven't had much to say.' He nodded towards the sea ahead of them, and the shape of an island now visible. 'Let me get us to the shore.'

They spent the next few moments navigating the waters, and then mooring the boat in an inlet of a postage-stamp-sized island, no more than a strip of beach and a bit of scrub. With the sea stretching in every direction, Rachel couldn't imagine a lonelier or lovelier spot.

'I brought a picnic,' Mateo told her as he reached for a wicker basket. 'Or rather, I had the kitchen make one for me.'

'Isn't that how kings always do things?' Rachel teased as she took his hand and he helped her out of the boat. She couldn't remember when they'd last talked so much, or when she'd felt so happy. This was what she'd imagined, what she'd longed for—their friendship back, but something more as well.

They strolled hand in hand onto the beach, and Mateo spread out a blanket before opening the picnic basket and setting out a variety of tempting goodies—strawberries, smoked salmon, crusty bread, a ripe cheese, and, of course, champagne.

It was perfect, Rachel thought as he popped the cork on the bottle and poured them both glasses.

Everything was perfect.

Mateo hadn't planned any of this. It was strange, but his own actions were taking him by surprise. It felt as if one moment he'd been sitting in his study, staring out at the blue sky, and the next he'd jumped into a boat and sailed for the blue yonder.

Not that he regretted what he'd done. In fact, he couldn't remember the last time he'd felt so relaxed, so free. He took a sip of champagne and closed his eyes, enjoying the sunlight on his face.

He realised he didn't even mind talking to Rachel about things he tried never to think about, never mind discuss—his family, his brothers, the deep-seated desire he'd had not to be a prince—or even a king. Yet somehow it felt different out here, sipping champagne on the sand, the barriers gone or at least a little lowered, the whole world wide open.

'When did your older brother die?' Rachel asked quietly, her generous mouth curved downwards, her eyes as soft as a bed of pansies.

'Ten years ago. A sailing accident.'

'Sailing…' Those soft eyes widened and she glanced instinctively at the little boat bobbing gently on the waves.

'Kosmos was a risk-taker. He loved living dangerously. He took a boat out during dangerous conditions, and sailed through a storm.' Mateo remembered the shock of hearing the news, the sudden fury that his older brother, more of a distant, admired figure than someone he'd felt truly close to, could be so careless.

'That was right when we started working together.' Rachel frowned. 'You never told me.'

'We barely knew each other then.'

'It's more than that, Mateo.' She paused, seeming to weigh her words. 'Why did you never confide in me? I don't mean about the royalty thing, which I actually do understand keeping to yourself. But other things. Your brother's death. Your father's death.'

Mateo considered the question for a moment, rather than dismiss it out of hand, as he normally would have, saying, *I never talk about myself.* Or, *There was never a good time.*

'I don't know,' he said at last. 'I suppose because, in doing so, I would have revealed something about myself.'

As soon as he said the words, he felt weirdly vulnerable, and yet also relieved.

Rachel kept her soft gaze steady on him. 'Something you didn't want others to see?'

He shrugged. 'I was never that close to Kosmos or Leo. I looked up to them, but they were both older than me and they were very close themselves. They had a similar set of experiences—the heir and spare preparing for a life in the royal spotlight, while I was left to do more or less as I pleased.'

'That sounds lonely.'

'Like I said before, it had its benefits.'

'Even so.' Her quietly compassionate tone was nearly the undoing of him. Emotions he hadn't even realised he'd been holding onto, buried deep, started to bubble up. Mateo took a sip of champagne in an effort to keep it all at bay. 'It must have been a shock, when you were told you had to be King.'

'It was,' he agreed. He thought his voice was neutral but something must have given him away because Rachel leaned forward and laid her hand over his.

'You're doing an amazing job, Mateo. *You're* amazing. I know I don't even know a tenth of what you do, and with the talk of insurgency and this economic thing...' She laughed softly. 'I don't know much about it, but I know you are doing the best job you can, giving two hundred per cent all the time.'

'As a scientist, you should know better than to use the erroneous phrase two hundred per cent,' he quipped, because to take her seriously would be to very nearly weep.

'I'm a scientist, not a mathematician,' she retorted with a smile. 'And I'm not taking back any of it.'

He shook his head, smiling to cover how much her words meant, how thankful he was for her. He wanted to tell her as much, but he couldn't manage it because he felt too much and he wasn't used to it.

For fifteen years he'd kept himself from deep relationships, from love, because he was afraid of being hurt the
way he'd been before, but more importantly, more deeply,
because he was afraid of hurting another person. He
couldn't live with that kind of guilt and grief again, and
yet here he was, treading on the thinnest of ice, in telling
Rachel these things. In starting to care, and letting her
care about him.

He should stop it right now, but the truth was he didn't
want to. It felt too much, but part of that was good. It was
wonderful.

'I know you don't want to hear anything soppy,' she
continued with an uncertain smile, 'but I'm going to tell
you anyway.'

'I consider myself warned,' he said lightly, although his
heart gave an unpleasant little lurch. Was she going to tell
him she loved him? He would not know how to handle that.

'You've given me such confidence, Mateo,' Rachel said
quietly. 'I haven't told you much about Josh except that he
didn't break my heart. And he really didn't. But he broke
my confidence—not that I had that much to begin with.'

'How…?' Mateo asked, although from what Rachel had
already told him, he thought he could guess. She sighed.

'He was older than me, worldly and sophisticated. I had
a crush on him. I suppose it was obvious.'

'So what happened, exactly?' Mateo asked, although
judging by Rachel's tone, the look of resignation and re-
membrance in her eyes, he wasn't sure he wanted to know.

'I suppose if it had been a romance novel, I would have
said he seduced me. But if it was a romance, he wasn't the
hero.'

'The one time?' Mateo surmised.

She nodded. 'And the worst part was, afterwards he
acted as if he didn't know me. I bounced into class the next
day, full of hope, of certainty. I thought we were a couple.

He acted as if he couldn't remember my name. Literally.'
She tried to laugh but didn't quite manage it. 'And then I
overheard him joking to his friends, about how it would
have to be a really desperate guy who was willing to…you
know…with me.'

'Oh, Rachel.' Mateo couldn't get any other words out.
He hated the bastard Josh for what he'd done—the careless, callous disregard he'd shown for someone as lovely
and genuine and pure as Rachel.

'Anyway, I was telling you all this not to throw myself a pity party, but because you've changed that, Mateo.
You've changed *me*. I used to always feel about myself—
my body, my looks—the way he did. As if I was beneath
notice. Easily forgettable. But when you look at me…' Her
voice trailed off and blush pinked her cheeks as she tremulously met his gaze. 'I feel different. I feel…desirable. For
the first time in my life. And that's been wonderful.' She
gave an uncertain little laugh and Mateo did the only thing
he could do, the only thing he wanted to do. He leaned forward and kissed her.

Her lips were soft and tasted of champagne and she let
out a breathy sigh as he deepened the kiss. She grabbed
his shoulder to steady herself but even so they ended up
sprawled on the sand, the kiss going on and on and on.

He slipped his hand under her T-shirt and revelled in
the warm softness of her body. As he tugged on her capri
bottoms she let out a little laugh.

'Here…?'

'Why not? It's not as if anyone can see.' He smiled down
at her and she blinked up at him, a look of wonder in her
eyes. She cupped his face with her hands and for a second Mateo's heart felt like a cracked vessel that had been
filled to the brim—overflowing and leaking, going everywhere. She'd done this to him. She'd awakened the heart
he'd thought had been frozen for ever behind a paralysing

wall of grief and fear. Love was too dangerous to consider, and yet here he was. Here *they* were.

'Rachel…' He couldn't bring himself to say the words, but he *felt* them, and he thought she saw it in his eyes as she brought his face down to hers and kissed him with both sweet innocence and passionate fervour. With everything she had. And Mateo responded in kind, moulding his body to hers, wanting only to keep this moment between them for ever.

CHAPTER FIFTEEN

RACHEL WAS HAPPY. It was a frail, fragile thing, like gossamer thread or a rose just about to bloom—all it would take was a gentle breeze to blow it all away. But, still, she was happy.

Since their afternoon on the island, Rachel had sensed a shift in Mateo, a softening. He'd willingly talked about his family, his emotions—things that Rachel had sensed had been off-limits before. The aloofness she'd felt from him since their marriage—the shadow lurking in his eyes, the slight repressiveness of his tone—had gone. Mostly.

Mateo, Rachel suspected, was a man at war with himself. He was starting to fall in love with her—if only she really could believe that!—but he didn't want to. At least, that was her take on the matter, and Agathe surprised her by agreeing.

They'd been having lunch in one of the palace's many salons when Agathe had said quite out of the blue, 'You must be patient with him, my dear.'

Rachel had nearly choked on a scallop. 'Pardon?'

'Mateo. I know he can be…difficult. Remote. It's his way of coping.'

Rachel absorbed that remark, tried not to let it hurt. 'What is he coping with?' she asked even as she thought, *Me?* Was his marriage something her husband had to *cope* with?

'Everything,' Agathe answered with a sad little sigh. 'The pressures of the kingship, certainly. His father was the same.'

'Was he?' Once again Rachel realised how little she knew about the Karavitis family.

'My husband believed he needed to keep a certain distance between him and his people. It was a matter of respect and authority. I don't know if he was right or not, but Mateo feels the responsibility, especially when he was never meant to have any royal role at all. I am afraid we did not prepare him as we should have.'

'Yet he is rising to the challenge,' Rachel returned, a fierce note of pride in her voice.

'Indeed he is, but at what cost?' Agathe smiled sadly. 'But it is more than that. Mateo has lost so many people… if he closes himself off, it's because he doesn't want to risk losing anyone else. Losing you. But it doesn't mean he doesn't love you.'

'You don't know that,' Rachel said after a moment. She paused, deliberating whether she should mention the person who was still utterly off-limits. 'Sometimes I wonder if he has any more room to love, after…' she took a quick breath '…after Cressida.'

Agathe's face softened into sympathetic lines. 'Of course he does. His relationship to Cressida…that was no more than schoolboy infatuation.'

'He doesn't talk about it like that,' Rachel said, even though she desperately wanted to believe it. 'He won't talk about it at all.' Agathe nodded slowly, and Rachel looked down at her plate. 'I shouldn't be talking to you about this. I know Mateo wouldn't like it.' He'd feel as if she'd betrayed him, and she couldn't stand that thought.

'Give him time,' Agathe said by way of answer. 'Be patient…and believe.'

Rachel was still holding onto those words, praying they

were a promise, when she got ready for an engagement in Constanza one foggy afternoon in November. She and Mateo had been married for six weeks, and winter had finally hit the island country, with thick, rolling fog and damp, freezing temperatures.

Mateo remained as busy as ever, but not as aloof, and Rachel continued to feel she had reason to hope. To believe. And, she reminded herself, she was happy.

A knock on her bedroom door had her turning, expecting Monica to tell her the car was ready to take her into the city. To her surprise, Mateo stood there, stealing her breath as he always did, wearing a navy-blue suit with a dark green tie that brought out the brightness of his eyes.

'You have an engagement?' he asked and she nodded as she fastened the second of her pearl earrings. 'Yes, at the bazaar in the city. Supporting women stallholders.'

'In the bazaar?' Mateo frowned. 'That's not the safest place.'

'I'll have my usual security.' Rachel glanced at him in concern. 'Has something happened? Are you worried?'

'No, I just don't like you being in such an exposed, rough place.'

'It's a market, not a Mafia den,' Rachel told him with a little laugh. 'I'm sure I'll be fine.'

Mateo nodded slowly, still looking less than pleased. 'I suppose so.'

He didn't sound convinced and Rachel laid a hand on his arm. 'Is there something you're not telling me, Mateo?'

He hesitated, his lowered gaze on her hand still resting on his arm. 'The insurgents are still active,' he admitted after a moment.

'But in the north…'

'Yes, but it isn't that far away.'

Nerves fluttered in Rachel's stomach at his grim tone.

'Surely they're not in the bazaar?' she asked, trying for a light tone and almost managing it.

Mateo was silent for a long moment, his gaze still lowered. 'No,' he said at last. 'Of course not.'

'Then I'll be fine.' She looked at him directly, willing him to meet her gaze. When he did, the look on his face—a mixture of resolution and despair—made her want to put her arms around him. Tell him she wouldn't go.

But then his lips curved in a quick smile and he nodded. 'It will be fine, I'm sure. I'll see you later today, for dinner.'

'All right.' He gave her a quick kiss on the cheek and as Rachel watched him walk away she had a strange, tumbling sensation that she forced herself to banish. Mateo's worries were just that—worries. Worries of a king who cared too much, who had lost people before. She was just going to the city's bazaar; she'd be surrounded by security. And really, she should be pleased that Mateo cared so much. Another sign, she wondered, that he was coming to love her? Or just wishful thinking?

An hour later Rachel had banished all her concerns as well as Mateo's as she entered the colourful bazaar with its rickety stalls and colourful banners. She spent an enjoyable hour meeting with the female stallholders and chatting about the goods they sold—handmade batik cloth; small honey cakes dotted with sesame seeds; hand-tooled leather wallets and purses.

She was impressed by their ingenuity and determination, and charmed by their ready smiles and cheerful demeanour. They faced far more challenges than she ever had, and yet they'd kept their heads as well as their smiles.

She was just saying goodbye when she felt the heavy hand of one of her security guards, Matthias, on her shoulder.

'Your Royal Highness, we need to go.'

'We're not in a rush—' Rachel began, only to have Matthias grip her elbow firmly and start to hustle her through the crowds and alleyways of the bazaar.

'There is a disturbance.'

'A disturbance—?' Rachel began, craning her neck to see what he meant.

In her six weeks as a royal, she'd become used to being guarded, even as she'd believed it to be unnecessary. There had never been any 'disturbances', and the unrest Mateo spoke of in the north was nothing more than a vague idea.

Now, as she saw Matthias with one hand on her elbow, one hand on the pistol at his hip, she felt a flicker of the kind of fear she'd never experienced before.

This couldn't be happening. This couldn't be *real*. It felt as impossible as Mateo's proposal, as her arrival in Kallyria, as her over-the-top wedding. Just another moment that she couldn't compute in this crazy life of hers.

'Get her in the car,' Matthias growled into his mouthpiece, and Rachel saw another guard emerge from behind an SUV with blacked-out windows, and Matthias started to hand her off.

Then she heard a sizzle and a crack and the next thing she knew the world had exploded.

Mateo could not ignore the tension banding his temples and tightening his gut as he tried to focus on the briefing one of his cabinet ministers was giving.

There was no reason to feel particularly anxious about Rachel's visit to the bazaar, but he did. Maybe it was a sixth sense. Maybe it was just paranoia. Or maybe it was the fact that he was finally acknowledging to himself that he cared about Rachel. Hell, he might even love her, and this was the result. This gut-twisting fear. This sense that he could never relax, never rest, never even breathe.

Love was fear. Love was failure. Love was dealing with both for ever, and it was why, after his experience with Cressida, he'd chosen never to pursue that dangerous, deadly emotion again. Yet like the worst of enemies, it had come for him anyway.

'Your Highness…'

Mateo blinked the minister back into focus, realising he'd stopped speaking some moments ago, and everyone was waiting for him to respond.

'Thank you,' he said gruffly, shuffling some papers in front of him, hating how distracted he was. How he couldn't stop thinking of Rachel, for good or ill, for better or worse. Just like the marriage vows he'd made.

But it wasn't supposed to be this way.

He'd been so sure, when he'd first come up with his great plan, that with Rachel he'd be immune. He'd had ten years of inoculation, after all. How could he possibly fall in love with her after all that time together? How could he barely keep his hands off her, when for an entire decade he hadn't even considered touching her?

How had everything changed since their vows had been spoken, most of all himself? Because loving Rachel felt both as natural as breathing, as terrifying as deliberately stepping off a cliff.

He was already in free fall, because he knew it was too late. He already loved her. He'd been fighting it for weeks now, fighting it and revelling in it at the same time, to his own confusion and despair.

He knew Rachel saw the struggle in him, just as he knew she was patiently waiting for him to resolve it. He saw the hope in her eyes when she looked at him, and that made everything worse, because he knew he was going to disappoint her, no matter what.

'Your Highness.'

He'd stopped listening to the conversation again. Irritated with himself beyond all measure, Mateo made himself focus on the minister again, only to realise he wasn't the one speaking.

A guard who had entered the stateroom was, and Mateo suddenly felt as if he'd been plunged underwater, as if everything were at a distance and he could only hear every third word. *Bazaar...bomb...wounded.*

He lurched up from the table, panic icing his insides, making it hard to breathe. Impossible to think. Rachel was in danger...and it was his fault. He'd been here before. He knew *exactly* how this felt.

'Is she alive?' he rasped.

'She's being taken to the hospital—'

'Get me there,' Mateo commanded, and he strode out of the room.

Half an hour later he was at the Royal Hospital on the outskirts of the city, the wintry fog obscuring the view of the terracotta roofs and onion domes of his city, his kingdom, so all was grey.

On the way there Rachel's security team had briefed him on what had happened—a clumsy, homemade bomb thrown into the bazaar; the explosion had hurled Rachel in the air and she'd hit her head on a concrete kerb. Two other people had received non-life-threatening injuries, including her personal bodyguard, Matthias; they were both being treated.

'And the Queen?' Mateo demanded. 'How is she?'

'She sustained an injury to the head,' the doctor, an olive-skinned man with kind eyes, was telling him, although Mateo found it hard to listen to a word he said. His mind kept skittering back to other doctors, other sterile rooms, the awful surreal sensation of hearing what had happened and knowing he was to blame. Just him.

There was nothing we could do...so sorry...by the time she made it to the hospital, it was too late.

'Is she in a coma?' Mateo asked brusquely. 'Is there… brain damage?'

The doctor looked at him strangely and Mateo gritted his teeth. He couldn't bear not knowing. He couldn't bear being in the same place, knowing the life of the woman he loved was hanging in the balance, and it was all because of him. 'Well?' he demanded in a throaty rasp.

'She is conscious, Your Highness,' the doctor said, looking unnerved by his sovereign's unprecedented display of emotion. 'She regained consciousness almost immediately.' Mateo stared at him, not comprehending. Not possibly being able to understand what this meant. 'She needed to have six stitches to a cut on her forehead,' the doctor continued, 'but other than that she is fine.'

'Stitches?' Mateo repeated dumbly.

'She might have a small scar by her left eyebrow,' the doctor said in an apologetic tone, and Mateo just stared.

Stitches? Her *eyebrow*?

'She's…?' He found he could barely speak. 'She's not…?'

The doctor smiled then, seeming to understand the nature of Mateo's fear. 'She's fine. I will take you to her, if you like.'

Mateo found he could only nod.

A few minutes later he walked into a private room where Rachel was sitting up in bed, looking tired and a bit exasperated.

'I'm quite sure I don't need to stay overnight,' she was telling one of the nurses who fussed around her. *'Den… Chei… Efharisto…'*

He almost smiled at her halting attempts at Greek, which the nurses resolutely ignored with cheerful smiles, but he felt too emotional to manage it. He stood in the doorway and simply drank her in, his heart beating hard from the adrenalin rush of believing, of being so *certain*, she was in danger. Of thinking he was to blame.

Rachel turned and caught sight of him, smiling wryly. 'No one seems to be listening to me,' she said with a little shrug of her shoulders. Her gaze clouded as she caught the look on his face, although Mateo didn't even know what it was. 'Mateo…'

He didn't answer. He simply walked over to her and kissed her hard on the mouth. The nurses scattered like a flock of sparrows.

Mateo eased back and studied the six neat stitches by her eyebrow.

She was all right.

'I'll have quite a cool scar,' Rachel joked uncertainly, looking at him with worry in her eyes.

'I thought you were dead.'

Her lovely, lush mouth turned downward as she realised what he'd gone through, although of course she didn't re-alise at all. 'Oh, Mateo…'

He shook his head, the remembered emotion, the abso-lute terror of it, closing his throat. 'Dead,' he forced out, 'or in a coma. A traumatic brain injury…'

'Barely more than a graze.' Her fingers fluttered on his wrist. 'I'm okay, Mateo.'

Now that he knew she was all right, he couldn't escape the awful knowledge that this could have been so much worse…just as it could have been avoided. 'I knew it was dangerous.'

She shook her head. 'It wasn't the rebels. Just some poor deranged man acting on his own. No one could have predicted—'

'This time.'

'Mateo—'

'You should never have gone to the bazaar. I shouldn't

have let you.' The words came out savagely, a rod for his own back.

'You can't keep me in a cage, you know.' Rachel's voice was deliberately light as her concerned gaze scanned his face. Mateo had no idea what she saw there. He felt as if he were a jumble of disparate parts; he'd been so terrified, and then so relieved, and now, inexplicably, he felt possessed by a fearsome, towering rage. He wanted to shout at the doctors. He wanted to tear apart the lone assailant with his bare hands. He wanted to hold Rachel and never let her go.

As the feelings coursed through him, each one more powerful and frightening than the last, he knew he couldn't handle this tempestuous seesaw of emotions any more. He couldn't live with the endless cycle of fear, relief, hope and guilt that had been his two years with Cressida. It had left him a husk of a man fifteen years ago, and he couldn't bear to have it happen again. He couldn't bear for Rachel to see it…or worse, far worse, for her not to see it, because one time it *wouldn't* be six stitches above her eyebrow.

This was what love wrought—grief and guilt, fear and failure. And he didn't want any part of it. He couldn't.

Rachel pressed her hand against Mateo's cheek and he closed his eyes. 'It's okay, Mateo.'

'It isn't.' He opened his eyes and stared at her, imprinting her on his brain, his heart. 'I can't do this,' he said, and he walked out of the room.

CHAPTER SIXTEEN

IT HAD BEEN raining for over a week. It was late November, and Kallyria was in the grip of the worst weather the island had seen in a century, or so her staff had told Rachel.

She liked the rain; it fitted her mood. It reminded her of England, and of everything she'd left behind. And while she couldn't bring herself to regret the choice she'd made, she still felt sad about it.

Ever since the day in the bazaar, Mateo had changed. When he'd walked out of her hospital proclaiming he couldn't do this—and Rachel was frankly terrified to ask him what 'this' meant—he'd kept his distance. The fledgling feeling that she'd been hoping had been growing between them seemed to have withered at the root, before it had had a chance to blossom.

And yet it had blossomed for her; she was in love with him, had been slowly and surely falling in love with him since their wedding, or, really, before then. Really, Rachel acknowledged to herself, she'd been falling in love with him since she'd first met him, when he'd introduced himself as her research partner and her breath had caught in her chest.

For ten years she'd kept herself from falling, because she knew, of *course* she knew, how impossible a relationship between them could be. Yet he'd asked her to marry him, and made her feel beautiful, and even though the kind of relationship she really wanted still felt impossible, she knew the truth.

She loved him. And he didn't love her back. Worse than that, far worse, was that he was choosing not to love her. Actively. Intentionally. And it was that knowledge, rather than him not loving her at all, that was bringing her closer to true despair than she'd ever felt before.

'So we have a round-table discussion today,' Francesca said, bustling into Rachel's bedroom with a briskly officious air and a quick smile. 'And a private engagement with the head of a girls' school tomorrow...'

'Right.' Rachel managed a tired smile. At least, she hoped she did. She hadn't slept well last night, with Mateo lying so silent and stony behind her, and she wondered if she ever would again. *'I can't do this,'* he'd said two weeks ago. Well, neither could she.

Francesca looked at her closely. 'Is everything all right? You're looking a bit peaky.'

Rachel just shrugged. As close a confidante as her stylist had become, she wasn't willing to share this particular heartache.

'Is it PMT?' Francesca asked sympathetically. 'I think it's that time of the month, isn't it?' Rachel stared at her blankly and she gave her an impish little smile. 'One of the things it helps to keep track of, when considering your wardrobe choices.'

Rachel's mind ticked over and she shook her head. 'I don't have PMT.'

'No?' Francesca was already in the enormous walk-in wardrobe that was now filled with clothes for a queen.

'I'm late,' Rachel said quietly. And she was never late. Of course, it shouldn't surprise her. She and Mateo had not been using any birth control, since he'd been upfront for his need for an heir as soon as possible. And yet somehow, in the midst of all the busyness of being, Rachel had forgotten she could fall pregnant. Mateo seemed to have forgotten it as well, for he'd certainly never mentioned it.

And yet here she was, just two months into her marriage, and her period six days late. She shouldn't be shocked, and yet she was.

'I was thinking something bright today,' Francesca said. 'To make you stand out in this endless rain...' She brandished a canary-yellow coat dress Rachel had never worn before. 'What do you think?'

Could she really be pregnant? And how would she find out? Rachel's mind raced. She couldn't exactly pop out to the nearest chemist's, at least not without a security detail and half the palace staff knowing what she was up to.

She glanced at Francesca. 'Francesca, can you be discreet?'

Her stylist didn't miss a beat as she answered, 'My middle name.'

'Could you go to the chemist for me?'

'The chemist?' Francesca's eyes narrowed. 'What for?'

Rachel swallowed dryly. 'A pregnancy test.'

Francesca, to her credit, merely gave a swift nod. 'Of course.'

Just twenty minutes later, Rachel knew. It felt strangely surreal to perch on the edge of the sunken marble tub in the adjoining bathroom and wait the requisite three minutes to read the test. She'd never taken one before, and she'd spent ten minutes studying the instructions before she'd done what she'd needed to do.

And now she had turned over the little stick, seen the two blazing pink lines, and knew. She was pregnant.

'This is good news, yes?' Francesca asked cautiously as Rachel came out of the bathroom. She knew the expression on her face wasn't one of undiluted joy. 'The King needs an heir...'

'Yes, it's good news.' Her voice sounded a bit wooden.

'You want to be a mother?' the stylist pressed.

'Yes.' Rachel was sure of that. She might have given up on the hope of motherhood years ago, when her romantic possibilities had been nil, but one of the reasons she'd said yes to Mateo's unconventional proposal had been for the possibility of children.

'So…' Francesca waited for Rachel to fill in the blanks, but she couldn't. She didn't want to talk of something so private and sacred to anyone—but Mateo. And she didn't know what she was going to say to him.

She spent all afternoon in a daze, going through the motions of her meetings, her mind elsewhere. Mateo was engaged on other business until the evening, so it wasn't until dinner that she had the chance to talk to him, and by that time she was resolved.

Agathe was otherwise engaged, which meant it was just her and Mateo in one of the palace's smaller dining rooms, the curtains drawn against the night and the rain, candles flickering on the table between them.

A member of staff served them the first course and withdrew. They were seated at opposite ends of the table that seated twelve, a dozen silver dishes between them along with all that hadn't been said.

Rachel gazed at her husband's face and felt an ache of longing for how she'd hoped for things to be. Oh, how she'd hoped. And yet one glance at Mateo's set jaw forced her to acknowledge that those were all they'd ever be. Hopes. Disappointed hopes.

They ate the first course in silence, as had become their habit in recent weeks, and Rachel tried to work up the courage to say what was on her mind—and heart.

Finally, when their main course had been delivered, she forced herself to speak.

'Mateo, I need to talk to you.'

He looked up, his expression already guarded. 'Yes?'

'Two weeks ago you left my room at the hospital, saying, "I can't do this."' She paused, waiting for him to respond, or say anything, but he simply remained silent, his jaw tense, his eyes narrowed. 'What was it you couldn't do, Mateo?'

'Why are you asking?'

'Don't I have a right to know?'

He sighed, the sound impatient. 'Rachel...'

'You've been shutting me out ever since then,' Rachel stated with quiet, trembling dignity. 'Did you expect me not to notice? Not to *care*?' Her voice caught on a wavering note and she sucked in a quick breath, determined to stay composed.

Mateo laid his hands flat on the table. 'No, of course not. I'm sorry. I know... I know I'm not being fair to you.'

'But you'll do it anyway?'

'The truth is, I don't know how to be.' The look of naked vulnerability on his face seared her heart. 'I don't... I don't know how to love someone. And if that's what you want...'

'Don't know? Or don't want to?'

He hesitated, a familiar, obdurate cast on his features. 'Both, I suppose.'

'Why?'

'I don't want to hurt you—'

'You already have,' Rachel cut across him, trying to sound matter-of-fact and not bitter. 'So if that's your only reason...'

'Why can't we be happy the way we were?' Mateo said. 'As friends.'

'Because you're not acting like my friend, Mateo. You're acting cold and stony and basically a big, fat jerk.' He let out a huff of surprised laughter and Rachel squared her shoulders, knowing what more she needed to say, even if saying it would break her heart clean in half.

'I've been thinking about this quite a lot lately,' she said quietly. 'About you and me, and whether I'd be happy to live without love.'

'I do care for you—'

'But the thing is,' Rachel interjected sadly, 'you don't want to. You're fighting it. Fighting me. Maybe it's because you loved someone before and it hurt. I understand that, Mateo. You've lost a lot of people in your life. Your father, your brother.' She paused. 'Cressida.' Mateo did not reply, but his eyes flashed and his jaw tightened. Even now he couldn't bear to have her name mentioned, and that felt like the saddest thing of all.

'What I'm saying is, I'm not going to fight you back. Part of me wants to, a large part. To fight for you, for *us*. But the funny thing is…' her voice wavered and almost caught on a sob that she managed to hold back '… I'm not going to, because you made me feel I was worth more than that. All my life I've tried to make myself useful or needed, because I'd convinced myself that was almost as good as being loved. I told you my parents didn't love me, and I made myself not mind, because it was easier that way. They weren't bad people, really. They loved their jobs and their social life and they didn't really want an awkward, nerdy girl messing it all up.'

Mateo opened his mouth and Rachel held up a hand to keep him from interrupting. 'I'm not saying this to gain your pity. I really don't want that. I'm just trying to explain. Between them and the whole thing with Josh…well, you were the first person in my life who made me feel I was worth loving.'

'Rachel…'

'You made me feel beautiful and lovely and lovable. And you woke me up to the reality that I shouldn't have to settle for anything less.'

Mateo's eyes widened as he stared at her. 'What are you saying?'

'Don't worry,' she said calmly. She felt empty inside, now that it was all being said. 'I'm not going to leave you. I made vows, and I know my duty. I will stay by your side, as your Queen.' Another breath, to buoy her. This felt like the hardest part. 'But I'm not going to try any longer, Mateo. I'm not going to try to make you love me, and I'm going to do my best not to love you back. It's too hard to handle the ups and downs—the days when you decide to relax enough to let me in, and then the days when you don't.'

'I don't…' Mateo began helplessly, shaking his head. He looked shell-shocked.

'It's not fair on me,' Rachel stated, 'and it wouldn't be fair on our child. Because that is something else I've realised. I don't want a child of mine growing up thinking one of their parents doesn't love them.'

'I would love my child,' Mateo declared in a near growl.

'Would you? How can I possibly believe or trust that?'

'Because—'

'You don't have a great track record,' Rachel cut across him. 'But I accept that you will be involved in our child's life.'

'Of *course* I will—'

'But as for us, I want us to live separately. I'll still live in the palace, but in a separate wing. I'll continue with my own interests and charitable causes, and I'll appear with you in public, but privately we won't spend time together or have a relationship.'

'What…?' Mateo's mouth gaped open as he stared at her. 'But…'

'I think you'll find this works best for both of us,' Rachel said firmly, even though she felt as if her heart were being torn into little pieces and then stamped on. How could this be better? And yet how could she survive otherwise?

'We're married, Rachel—'

'A marriage of convenience only.'

'I still need an heir—'

'That's no longer an issue,' Rachel told him woodenly. 'Because I'm pregnant.'

Mateo stared at Rachel, his mind spinning uselessly, as she told him she was expecting his child and then rose from the table and walked out of the dining room with stiff, wounded dignity.

He slumped back in his chair, hardly able to take it all in. Rachel living separately from him. Trying not to love him. *Pregnant with his child...*

A sound close to a moan escaped him as he raked his hands through his hair. How had this happened? And why did he not feel relieved—that Rachel was suggesting exactly the sort of arrangement that should suit him? No complications. No messy emotions. No danger, no risk, no guilt or grief.

This should be exactly what he wanted, but in that moment Mateo knew it wasn't. It wasn't what he wanted at *all*. Instead of feeling relieved, he was gutted. Eviscerated, as if the heart of him had been drawn right out, replaced by an empty shell, the wind whistling through him.

He didn't know how long he sat there, his mind and heart both empty, but eventually a member of staff came to clear the plates, and Mateo stumbled out of the room.

He must have fallen asleep at some point in the night, although time seemed to have lost all meaning. He spent most of those endless hours simply staring into space, his mind empty of coherent thought and yet full of memories.

Memories of Rachel...ones he hadn't even realised he'd had, and yet now held so dear. The way she'd stick a pencil in her messy bun as she was working, and then forget she had it there and search for one uselessly around her until Mateo drew the stub out of her hair and handed it to her with a laugh.

Evenings at their local pub, him with a pint and her with a shandy—such a funny, old-fashioned drink—testing each other on the periodic table. She'd come up with the game first, insisting she could name all the elements faster than he could. Even though he'd won that first time, they'd continued to play the game, finding it funnier with each playing.

And then later, far sweeter memories—Rachel in her wedding gown, her heart in her eyes, and then Rachel with nothing on at all, her hair spread out in a dark wave against the pillow as she looked up at him with so much trust and desire and love.

Yes, love. She loved him. He knew that; he felt it, just as he felt his own love for her, like a river or a force field, something that couldn't be controlled. Why didn't he just stop fighting it?

'Mateo.' His mother's gentle voice broke into his thoughts, and Mateo looked up, surprised to see his mother in the doorway of his study. Had he gone to bed? He couldn't even remember, but sunlight was now streaming through the windows, the fog finally breaking apart.

'What time is it?' he asked as he scrubbed his eyes and tried to clear the cobwebs from his mind.

'Seven in the morning. Have you slept at all?'

'I don't know.'

Agathe came into the room, her smile sorrowful and sympathetic as her gaze swept over her son. 'Is it Rachel?' she asked quietly.

'How did you know?'

'I have been watching you both all this time, and seeing how you love one another. Knowing you would fight it.'

'I made such a mess of my last relationship,' Mateo said in a low voice. 'My love was toxic.' He choked the words, barely able to get them out.

'Mateo, that wasn't your fault.'

'Wasn't it?' He stared at her hopelessly. '*She* said it was.'

'Cressida was a fragile, damaged individual,' Agathe said gently. 'Her death was not your fault. And,' she continued firmly, 'Rachel is not Cressida. She's strong, and she knows her own mind.'

'She's leaving me.'

'What…?'

'Not properly,' he amended as he scrubbed his eyes. 'We'll remain married. But she wants us to live separate lives.'

'Ah.' Agathe nodded slowly. 'I was afraid of something like this.'

'Were you?' Mateo dropped his fists from his eyes to look at his mother, the weariness and memory etched into every line of her face.

'It's not easy to love someone who doesn't love you back quite as much, or even at all.'

It took Mateo a moment to make sense of his mother's meaning. 'Do you mean Father…?'

'The Karavitis men are strong and stubborn. They don't want to need anybody.'

'But you had such a successful marriage.'

'There are different definitions of success. I choose to believe in one that is about love and happiness, as well as duty and service.'

'I'm sorry,' Mateo said after a moment. 'I never knew.'

'We were happy, in our way,' Agathe said. 'I learned to be happy. But I want more for you…and for Rachel.'

'So do I,' Mateo said, his voice throbbing with the strength of his feeling. 'That's why…'

'Oh, Mateo. Do you honestly think she'd be happy without you?'

'She doesn't know—'

'Then tell her,' Agathe urged, her voice full of sorrow and love. 'For heaven's sake, tell her.'

* * *

He found her in the gardens. The fog had finally lifted, and the day was crisp and clear, the sun surprisingly warm as it shone down on the rain-washed gardens.

Mateo had gone to her suite of rooms first, and everything in him had lurched at the sight of several blank-faced members of staff moving her things out.

'Where are you putting those?' he'd demanded hoarsely, and someone had told him Queen Rachel was intending to reside in the south wing, about as far from him as possible. He felt both angry and lost, and yet he couldn't blame her.

So he'd left her rooms and gone to the south wing, but she wasn't there either, and when Francesca had told him, a look of naked pity on her face, that Rachel had wanted some fresh air, he'd come out here, and now he'd found her, in a small octagonal-shaped rose garden, the branches now pruned back and bare.

'Rachel.' His voice sounded hoarse and he cleared his throat. 'Rachel,' he said again, and she looked up.

'Mateo.'

'You're having your things moved.' It wasn't what he wanted to say, but he couldn't manage anything else right then.

'I told you I would.'

'I know.' He took a step towards her. She was sitting on a stone bench by a fountain that had filled with autumn leaves. Her hair was back in a plait and she was wearing a forest-green turtleneck in soft, snug cashmere and a grey skirt. She looked every inch the Queen, every bit his wife, and so wonderfully beautiful. *His.* She had to be his.

'I don't want you to,' he said and she started to shake her head. 'Please. Hear me out. I heard everything you said last night, and I've been thinking about nothing else since. But now…now I want a turn to tell you about what I've been thinking.'

A guarded expression came over her face, and she nodded. 'All right.'

Mateo moved to sit down next to her on the bench. 'You told me how your parents shaped how you felt about yourself. Well, in a fashion, mine did as well. I knew I was loved—I never doubted that. But I didn't feel important.'

'Because you weren't the heir?'

'My parents thought they were doing me a kindness, and I suppose in a way they were. They shielded me from all the intensity and pressure of the royal life. They gave me the freedom to pursue my own dreams—which led me to chemistry, and Cambridge, and you.' He swallowed hard. 'But I suppose I struggled with feeling a bit less than. I rebelled as a child, and then I turned away from all things royal. And then I met Cressida.'

Rachel's eyes widened as she gazed at him. 'You're going to tell me about her?'

'Yes, I'm going to tell you about her.' He took a deep breath, willing himself to begin, to open the old wounds and let them bleed out. 'Cressida was…fragile. She'd had a difficult if privileged upbringing and she liked—she needed—people to take care of her. I liked that at first. When I was with her, I felt important. I was eighteen, young and foolish, and Cressida made me feel like I was essential to her well-being. I craved that feeling of someone needing me absolutely. It stroked my ego, I'm ashamed to say.'

'That's understandable,' Rachel murmured. Her gaze was still guarded.

'But then she became unstable.' He shook his head, impatient with himself. 'Or, more to the point, I realised she was unstable. I should have seen it earlier. The warning signs were all there, but I thought that was just Cressida. How she was.'

'What happened?' Rachel asked softly.

'Her moods swung wildly. Something I said, something

seemingly insignificant, could send her into a depression for days. She wouldn't even tell me what it was—I had to guess, and I usually got it wrong.' He paused, the memories of so desperately trying to make Cressida feel better, and never being able to, reverberating through him. 'I tried so hard, but it was never enough. She spiralled into severe depression on several occasions. I'll spare you some of the more harrowing details, but she started hurting herself, or going days without speaking or even getting up from bed. Her grades started to suffer—she was studying English— and she was close to being sent down from university.'

'That sounds so difficult,' Rachel murmured. Mateo couldn't tell from her tone whether she truly empathised with him or not. She looked cautious, as if she didn't know what was coming.

'It was incredibly complicated. I wanted to break up with her, but I was afraid to—both for her sake and mine. We'd become so caught up in one another, so dependent. It wasn't healthy, and it didn't make either of us happy, and I don't think it was really love at all.' Even though it had felt like it at the time, and made him never want to experience it again. 'But it consumed us, in its way, and then…' A pause while he gathered his courage. 'In our third year, Cressida killed herself.'

Rachel let out a soft gasp. 'Oh, Mateo…'

'She left a note,' he continued in a hard voice he didn't recognise as his own. Hard and bleak. 'I found it. I found *her*. She'd overdosed on antidepressants and alcohol—I rushed her to the hospital, but it was too late. That's why, I think, I acted so crazily when you were at the hospital. I was right back there, fearing Cressida was dead, and then knowing she was.'

'I'm so sorry…'

'But you know what the note said? It said she was killing herself because of me. Because I made her so unhappy.' His throat had thickened but he forced himself to go on. 'And you know what? She was right. I did make her unhappy. I must have done, because when she was gone, for a second I felt relieved.' His voice choked as he gasped out the words, 'How could I have felt that? What kind of man feels that?' He'd never told anyone that before. Never dared to reveal the shameful secret at the very heart of himself, but Rachel didn't recoil or even blink.

'Oh, Mateo.' Her face softened in sympathy as her arms came around him and he rested his face against her shoulder, the hot press of tears against his lids.

'I'm so sorry,' she whispered, one hand resting on his hair. 'So, so sorry.'

'I'm the one who's sorry,' Mateo said raggedly, swallowing down the threat of tears. He eased back, determined to look at her as he said these words. 'You're right, Rachel, I have been fighting you. I'm scared to love you, scared *for* you. I don't want to make you unhappy, and I don't want to feel the guilt and grief of knowing that I did.'

'Love is a two-way street, Mateo,' Rachel said gently. 'You don't bear the sole responsibility for my happiness. What you had with Cressida...'

'I know it wasn't really love. It was toxic and childish and incredibly dysfunctional. I know that. I've known that for a long time. But you can know one thing and feel something else entirely.'

'Yes,' Rachel agreed quietly. 'You can.'

'But when you left me last night—left me emotionally if not physically—I felt as if you'd died. I felt even more bereft than when I lost Cressida, and without that treacherous little flicker of relief. I was just...grief-stricken.'

Rachel stared at him, searching his face. 'What...what are you saying?' she finally asked.

'That I love you. That I've been falling in love with you for ten years without realising it, and then fighting it for the last few weeks when I started to understand how hard I'd fallen. But I don't want to fight any more. I know I'll get things wrong, and I'm terrified of hurting you, but I want to love you, Rachel. I want to live a life of loving you. If… if…you do love me.'

Rachel let out a sound, half laugh, half sob. 'Of course I love you. I think I fell in love with you a long time ago, but I tried to stop myself. Maybe we're not so different in that respect.' She gave a trembling laugh as she wiped the tears from her eyes.

'Maybe we're not.' Mateo took her hands in his. 'Can you forgive me, Rachel? For fighting you for so long, and hurting you in the process? I was trying not to hurt you, but I knew I was. I'm a fool.'

'As long as you're a love-struck fool, I don't mind,' she promised him as she squeezed his hands.

'I am,' Mateo assured her solemnly. 'Utterly and over-whelmingly in love with you. Now and for always. I know it doesn't mean everything will be perfect, or that we'll never hurt each other, but I really do love you.'

'And I love you,' Rachel told him. 'More than I ever thought possible. Getting to know you these last weeks… it's made me realise how much I love you. And if you love me back…'

'I do.'

'Then that's all that matters. That's what will get us through the ups and downs. That's what will last.'

'Yes, it will,' Mateo agreed, and then leaned forward to kiss her. He settled his mouth softly on hers, and it felt as if he was finally coming home, the two of them together, now and for ever.

EPILOGUE

Three years later

'MAMA, MAMA, LOOK at me!'

Rachel laughed and clapped her hands as her daughter, Daphne, ran towards her, her dark hair tumbling over her shoulders, her blue-green eyes alight with happiness and mischief.

It was a bright, sunny day, the sky picture-postcard-blue, the white sand of Kallyria's famous beaches stretching out before them. They were holidaying at the royal summer palace on the western coast of Kallyria. In the three years since Mateo had taken the crown, he'd dealt with the insurgents, stabilised the country's economy, and been a leader in bringing Kallyria into a modern and progressive world. It hadn't always been easy, but Rachel had been with him every step of the way.

She'd expanded into the role of Queen with energy and grace, not in small part down to Mateo's unwavering support and love. She'd also taken a six-week research position at the university in Athens last year, which he'd wholeheartedly supported.

But her heart was in Kallyria with her King and her family, and she knew there was nowhere else she'd rather be.

A year ago her mother had died, and Rachel had had the privilege of being with her at the end. To her surprise, although her mother hadn't remembered who she was in months, she'd turned to her suddenly, grasping her hand with surprising vigour, and said, 'I'm sorry. Do you know that, Rachel? That I'm sorry?'

And Rachel, with tears in her eyes, had said she had.

Now she scooped up her daughter and pressed her lips to her sun-warmed cheek, revelling in the simple joy of the moment. From behind her she heard Mateo coming through the French windows of the palace that led directly onto the beach.

'This one's up and ready for his mama.'

With a smile Rachel exchanged armfuls with her husband—he took Daphne and she took her three-month-old son, Kosmos, who nuzzled into her neck.

'Come on, *moraki mou*,' he said cheerfully as he tossed Daphne over his shoulder and tickled her tummy. 'Time for lunch.'

'And this one is ready for lunch too,' Rachel said as she followed him inside.

Sunlight streamed across the floor and Mateo caught her eye as he settled Daphne at the table, and Rachel curled up on the sofa to feed Kosmos.

The look he gave her was lingering, full of love as well as promise. Was it possible to be this happy? This thankful? This amazed?

Meeting her husband's loving gaze, feeling the warmth of it right down to her toes, Rachel knew it was, and with her heart full to bursting she smiled back.

* * * * *

EXPECTING THE PRINCE'S BABY

REBECCA WINTERS

I dedicate this book to my angelic grandmother,
Alice Vivia Driggs Brown, who made my childhood
a constant enchantment. She was so romantic
she called the home she and my grandfather
had built 'Camelot.'

CHAPTER ONE

VINCENZO DI LAURENTIS, thirty-three-year-old crown prince of the Principality of Arancia, stood before the camera on the balcony of the royal palace overlooking the gardens to officially open the April Fifteenth Lemon and Orange Festival. This was his first public appearance since the funeral of his wife, Princess Michelina, six weeks ago. He waved to the crowds that had come out en masse.

His country was nestled between the borders of France and Italy on the coast of the Mediterranean. Eighty thousand people lived in the city of the same name. The other thirty thousand made up the population that lived in the smaller towns and villages. Besides tourism, it had depended on the lemon and orange industries for centuries.

For the next two weeks the country would celebrate the mainstay of their economy with marching bands in the streets, food fairs, floats and statuary in the parks decorated with lemons and other citrus fruit.

Vincenzo had just gotten back from a series of visits to three continents, doing business for the monarchy with other heads of state. It felt good to be with his father, King Guilio, again. On his return, he'd forgotten how beautiful Arancia could be in the spring with its orchards in full flower. He felt an air of excitement coming from the people that winter was over. As for himself, the darkness that had consumed him over the last six weeks since Michelina's death seemed to be dissipating.

Their marriage had never been a love match. Though betrothed at sixteen, they'd spent very little time together before their wedding fourteen years later. When he'd walked into their apartment earlier this afternoon, more than any other emotion, he was aware of a haunting sense of guilt for not having been able to love her the way she'd loved him.

Romantic love never grew on his part for her, only respect and admiration for her determination to keep up the image of a happily married couple. They'd suffered through three miscarriages hoping for a child, but it hadn't happened.

His passion had never been aroused when they'd made love because he hadn't been in love with her, but he'd done his best to show her tenderness. He'd known passion with other women before he'd married Michelina. But it had only been a physical response because he was never able to give his heart, knowing he was betrothed.

Vincenzo suspected Michelina's parents had undergone the same kind of unfulfilled marriage. He knew his own parents had struggled. It was the rare occurrence when a royal couple actually achieved marital happiness. Michelina had wanted their marriage to be different, and Vincenzo had tried. But you couldn't force love. That had to spring from a source all on its own.

However there was one thing he *had* been able to do that had brought them their first real happiness as man and wife. In fact it was the only thing that had gotten him through this dark period. Just a few days before she'd died, they'd learned they were pregnant again. Only this time they'd taken the necessary steps to prevent another miscarriage.

Relieved that his last duty for today was over, he left the balcony anxious to visit the woman who'd been willing to be a gestational surrogate for them. Abby Loretto, the American girl who'd become his *friend*. Since twelve years of age she'd been living on the palace grounds with her Italian father, who was chief of security.

Vincenzo had been eighteen, with his own set of friends and a few girlfriends his own age, when Abby had arrived on the scene. Yet Abby had become the constant in the background of his life, more like a younger sister flitting in and out of his daily life. It was almost like having a sibling. In a way he felt closer to Abby than he'd ever felt to his sister, Gianna, who was six years older.

The two of them had played in the sea or the swimming pool. She was fun and bright. He could be his real self around her, able to throw off his cares and relax with her in a way he couldn't with anyone else. Because she lived on the grounds and knew the inner workings of the palace, she already had the understanding of what it was to be a royal. They didn't have to talk about it.

When his mother had died, Abby had joined him on long walks, offering comfort. When he didn't want anyone else around, he wanted her. She'd lost her mother, too, and understood what he was going through. She asked nothing from him, wanted nothing but to be his friend and share small confidences. Because they'd been in each other's lives on a continual basis, he realized it was inevitable that they'd bonded and had developed a trust.

She'd been so woven into the fabric of his life that years later, when she'd offered to be a surrogate mother for him and Michelina, it all seemed part of the same piece. His wife had liked Abby a great deal. The three of them had been in consultation for several months before the procedure had been performed. They'd worked like a team until Michelina's unexpected death.

He'd gotten used to their meetings with the doctor and the psychologist. While he'd been away on business, it had felt like years instead of weeks since he'd seen or talked to Abby. Now that she was carrying Vincenzo's son or daughter, she was his lifeline from here on out. He needed to see her and be with her.

All he could think about was getting back to make certain she and the baby were doing well. But accompanying this need was an uncomfortable sense of guilt he couldn't shake. Less than two months ago he'd lost his wife. While still in mourning over the marriage that had been less than perfect, he now found himself concentrating on another woman, who was carrying the baby he and Michelina had made.

It was only natural he cared about Abby, who'd agreed to perform this miracle. Before long he was going to be a father, all because of her! Yet with Michelina gone, it didn't seem right.

But neither was it wrong.

While he'd been traveling, he hadn't had time to dig deep into his soul, but now that he was back, he

didn't know how to deal with this new emotional dilemma facing him, and he left the balcony conflicted.

Abigail Loretto, known to her friends as Abby, sat alone
on the couch in her apartment at the palace, drying her
hair while she was glued to the television. She'd been
watching the live broadcast of Prince Vincenzo opening the fruit festival from the balcony of the palace.

Abby hadn't known he was back. Her Italian-born
father, Carlo Loretto, the chief of palace security, had
been so busy, he obviously hadn't had time to inform
her.

She'd first met Vincenzo sixteen years earlier, when
her father had been made the head of palace security.
The king had brought him and his American-born wife
and young daughter from the Arancian Embassy in
Washington, D.C., to live in the apartment on the palace grounds. She'd been twelve to his eighteen.

Most of her teenage years had been spent studying
him, including his tall, hard-muscled physique. Instead
of a film star or a famous rock star, she'd idolized Vincenzo. She'd even kept a scrapbook that followed his
life, but she'd kept it hidden from her parents. Of course,
that was a long time ago.

The crown prince, the most striking male Abby had
ever met in her life, had many looks depending on his
mood. From what she could see now, he appeared more
rested since his trip.

Sometimes when he was aloof, those black eyes and
furrowed brows that matched his glistening black hair
made her afraid to approach him. Other times he could
be charming and fun, even a tease. No one was immune

from his masculine charisma. Michelina had been the most fortunate woman alive.

His picture was always on the cover of magazines and newspapers in Europe. The camera loved the handsome thirty-three-year-old son of Arancia, with his olive skin and aquiline features. Dogged by the press, he made the nightly news on television somewhere on the continent every day of the year.

The knowledge that he was home from his travels sent a wave of warmth through her body. Six weeks without seeing or talking to him about the baby had felt like an eternity. She knew he'd get in touch with her at some point. But after being away, he would have so much work to catch up on at home, it might be another week before she heard his voice on the phone.

Now that he'd left the balcony and had gone back inside the palace, the station began showing a segment of the funeral that had been televised on every channel throughout the kingdom and Europe six weeks ago.

She would never forget her father's phone call. "I have bad news. Before Vincenzo and Michelina were due to return to Arancia today, she went for an early-morning ride on her horse. Vincenzo rode with her. While she was galloping ahead of him, the horse stepped in a hole. It tossed her over end. When she hit the ground, she died on impact."

Abby froze.

Michelina was dead?

It was like déjà vu, sending Abby back to that horrific moment when she'd learned her own mother had died.

Poor Vincenzo. He'd seen the whole thing… She

couldn't stand it. "Oh, Dad—he's lost his wife. Their baby will never know its mother."

Before long she was driven to the hospital, where Dr. DeLuca had his office. "My dear Abby, what a terrible shock this has been. I'm glad your father brought you here. I'm going to keep you in the hospital overnight and possibly longer to make certain you're all right. The prince has enough pain to deal with. Knowing you're being looked after will be a great comfort to him. Excuse me while I arrange for a private room."

When he left, Abby turned to her father. "Vincenzo must be in absolute agony."

He kissed her forehead. "I know he is, but right now it's you I'm worried about. Your blood pressure is up. I plan to stay with you and will tell Signor Faustino you've caught a bad cold, but will be back to work in a few days."

"You can't stay with me here, Dad. Your place is at the palace. The king will want you there."

"Not tonight. My assistant is in charge, and Guilio wants to be there for his son. My daughter needs me, and I need you, so let that be the end of the discussion."

Her father's words had been final. Deep down she'd been glad he'd remained with her.

Abby kept watching the funeral she'd lived through once before. It was shocking to see how gaunt and shadowed Vincenzo's handsome features had been back then. His wife's death seemed to have aged him.

The most beautiful man she'd ever known in her life made a striking yet lonely figure in his mourning finery. Once again her soul shuddered to see his somber expression as he walked behind the funeral cortege toward the cathedral. He led Michelina's favorite horse from the palace stable alongside him. The chestnut mare was covered in a throw of his wife's favorite pink roses. The scene was so heart wrenching, Abby felt tears well up once again.

Behind him came the king, in his uniform of state, and his mother-in-law, dressed in a black mantilla and suit. They rode in the black-and-gold carriage with the siblings of both families. When the broadcast moved inside the cathedral, Abby listened once again to the scripture reading and remarks from the archbishop. When it was over and the bells from the cathedral rang out their mournful sound, she was once more a trembling mass of painful emotions.

"For those of you who've just tuned in, you're watching the funeral procession of Her Royal Highness Princess Michelina Cavelli, the wife of Crown Prince Vincenzo Di Laurentis of the Principality of Arancia. Earlier in the week she was killed in a tragic horse-riding accident on the grounds of the royal palace on the island kingdom of Gemelli.

"In the carriage is His Majesty Guilio Di Laurentis, King of Arancia, her father-in-law. His wife, Queen Annamaria, passed away two years ago. Seated next to him is his daughter, Princess Gianna Di Laurentis Roselli and her husband, Count Roselli of the Cinq Terres of Italy.

"Opposite them is Her Majesty Queen Bianca Cavelli, mother of Princess Michelina. Her husband, King Gregorio Cavelli of Gemelli, was recently deceased. Also seated in the royal carriage is His Royal Highness Crown Prince Valentino Cavelli of Gemelli and Prince Vitoli Cavelli, the brothers of Princess Michelina.

"On this day of great sadness for both royal houses,

one has to speculate on the future of the Principality of Arancia. The world has been waiting to hear that their Royal Highnesses were expecting a child after three miscarriages, but tragically the love match between Michelina and Vincenzo ended too soon.

"Should the Princess Gianna and her husband, Count Enzio Roselli, have offspring, then their child will be third in line to—"

Abby shut off the TV with the remote and got to her feet, unable to watch any more. She shouldn't have allowed herself to live through that funeral segment a second time. Vincenzo's trip appeared to have done him some good. It was better to leave the tragic past behind and concentrate on the future.

She walked into the den to do some work at her laptop. Her dinner would be arriving shortly. Except for the occasional meal out with her best friend, Carolena, Abby normally ate in while she worked on one of her law briefs. But she had little appetite tonight.

How hard for Vincenzo to come back to the palace with no wife to greet him. His loneliness had to be exquisite and her heart ached for him.

After receiving an urgent message from his father that couldn't have come at a worse moment, Vincenzo had been given another reason to visit Abby. As he rounded the corner to her suite, he saw Angelina leaving the apartment with the dinner tray.

Angelina was Abby's personal bodyguard, hired to keep an eye on Abby, virtually waiting on her. She was the one who fed Vincenzo information on a daily basis when he couldn't be there himself. He stopped her so he could lift the cover. Abby had only eaten a small portion of her dinner. That wasn't good. He put the cover back and thanked her before knocking on the door.

"Yes, Angelina?"

He opened it and walked through until he found Abby in the den, where he could see her at the desk working on her computer in her sweats and a cotton top. The lamp afforded the only light in the room, gilding the silvery-gold hair she must have just shampooed. He could smell the strong peach fragrance. It fell to her shoulders in a cloud.

Instead of the attorney-like persona she generally presented, she reminded Vincenzo of the lovely teenager who'd once flitted about the palace grounds on her long legs.

"Abby?"

She turned a face to him filled with the kind of sorrow he'd seen after her mother had died. "Your Highness," she whispered, obviously shocked to see him. A glint of purple showed through her tear-glazed blue eyes. She studied him for a long moment. "It's good to see you again."

Because of the extreme delicacy of their unique situation, it frustrated him that she'd addressed him that way, yet he could find no fault in her.

"Call me Vincenzo when the staff isn't around. That's what you used to shout at me when you were running around the gardens years ago."

"Children are known to get away with murder."

"So are surrogate mothers." There was something about being with Abby. "After such a long trip, I can't tell you how much I've been looking forward to talking to you in person."

"You look like you're feeling better."

Though he appreciated her words, he wished he could say the same about her. "What's wrong? I noticed you hardly ate your dinner. Are you ill?"

"No, no. Not at all." Abby got up from the chair, rubbing the palms of her hands against the sides of womanly hips. To his chagrin the gesture drew his attention to her figure. "Please don't think that finding me in this state has anything to do with the baby."

"That relieves me, but I'm still worried about you. Anything troubling you bothers me."

She let out a sigh. "After I watched your live television appearance a little while ago, they replayed a segment of the funeral. I shouldn't have watched it." Her gaze searched his eyes. "Your suffering was so terrible back then. I can't even imagine it."

Diavolo. The media never let up. "To say I was in shock wouldn't have begun to cover my state of mind," he said.

Abby hugged her arms to her chest, once again drawing his attention to her slender waist. So far the only proof that she was pregnant came from a blood test. She studied him for a moment. "Michelina loved you so much, she was willing to do anything to give you a baby. I daresay not every husband has had that kind of love from his spouse. It's something you'll always be able to cherish."

If he could just get past his guilt over the unhappy state of their marriage. His inability to return Michelina's affection the way she'd wanted weighed him down, but he appreciated Abby's words.

Little did Abby know how right she was. In public his wife had made no secret of her affection for him and he'd tried to return it to keep up the myth of a love match. But in private Vincenzo had cared for her the way he did a friend. She'd pushed so hard at the end to try surrogacy in order to save their marriage, he'd finally agreed to consider it.

Needing to change the subject, he said, "Why don't you sit down while we talk?"

"Thank you." She did as he asked.

He subsided into another of the chairs by her desk. "How are you really feeling?"

"Fine."

"Rest assured that during my trip I insisted on being given a daily report on your progress. It always came back 'fine.'"

"It doesn't surprise me you checked. Something tells me you're a helicopter father already," she quipped.

"If you mean I'm interested to the point of driving you crazy with questions, I'm afraid I'm guilty. Since you and I have known each other from the time you were twelve, it helps me to know I can have the inside track on the guardian of my baby. Dr. DeLuca said your blood pressure went up at the time of the funeral, but it's back to normal and he promises me you're in excellent health."

Abby had a teasing look in her eye. "They say only your doctor knows for sure, but never forget he's a man and has no clue."

Laughter broke from Vincenzo's lips. It felt good to laugh. He couldn't remember the last time it had happened. "I'll bear that in mind."

"So what does the crown prince's *personal* physician have to say about the state of the expectant father?"

He smiled. "I was disgustingly healthy at my last checkup."

"That's good news for your baby, who hopes to enjoy a long, rich life with his or her daddy."

Daddy was what he'd heard Abby call her father from the beginning. The two of them had the sort of close relationship any parent would envy. Vincenzo intended to be the kind of wonderful father his own had been.

"You're veering off the subject. I told you I want the unvarnished truth about your condition," he persisted.

"Unvarnished?" she said with a sudden hint of a smile that broke through to light up his insides. "Well. Let me see. I'm a lot sleepier lately, feel bloated and have finally been hit with the *mal di mare*."

The Italian expression for sea sickness. Trust Abby to come up with something clever. They both chuckled.

"Dr. DeLuca has given me medicine for that and says it will all pass. Then in the seventh month I'll get tired again."

"Has he been hovering as you feared?"

"Actually no. I check in at the clinic once a week before going to work. He says everything looks good and I'm right on schedule. Can you believe your baby is only one-fifth of an inch long?"

"That big?" he teased. Though it really was incredible, he found it astounding she was pregnant with a part of him. He wished he could shut off his awareness of her. Michelina's death had changed their world.

Vincenzo suspected Abby was also having to deal with the fact that the two of them were now forced to get through this pregnancy without his wife. No doubt she felt some guilt, too, because they were treading new ground neither of them could have imagined when they'd had the procedure done.

A laugh escaped her lips. "It's in the developmental stage. He gave me two identical booklets. This one is for you. Anatomy 101 for beginner fathers."

Abby...

She reached in the desk drawer and handed it to him. The title said *The Ten Stages of Pregnancy at a Glance.*

"Why ten, not nine?"

"A woman wrote it and knows these things."

He appreciated her little jokes more than she could imagine. Her normally lighthearted disposition was a balm to his soul. Vincenzo thumbed through the booklet before putting it in his pocket. When he went to bed tonight, he'd digest it.

"Thank you. Now tell me about your law cases." A safe subject that intrigued him. "Which one keeps you awake at night?"

"The Giordano case. I have a hunch someone's trying to block his initiative for political reasons."

"Run it by me."

Her arched brows lifted. "You'd be bored to tears."

"Try me." Nothing about Abby bored him.

She reached in one of the folders on her desk and handed him a printout on the case, which he perused.

As has been stated, major constraint to import into Arancia is nothing more than bureaucracy. Import certificates can take up to eight months to be released, and in some cases are not released at all. However, if the procedure is simplified, an increase of imports could particularly benefit Arancia, providing high-value high-season products.

That made even more sense to Vincenzo since talking to important exporters on his trip.

At present, the hyper/supermarket chains do not operate directly on the import market, but use the main wholesalers of oranges and lemons as intermediaries. Signor Giordano, representing the retailers, has entered the import market, thus changing some long-established import partnerships. He's following a different strategy, based on higher competition, initial entry fees and spot purchases, thus bringing more revenue to Arancia.

Vincenzo knew instinctively that Signor Giordano was really on to something.

Signor Masala, representing the importers, is trying to block this new initiative. He has favored cooperative producers and established medium-to long-term contracts, without requiring any entry fee. The figures included in this brief show a clear difference in revenue, favoring Signor Giordano's plan.

I'm filing this brief to the court to demonstrate that these high-quality products for fast-track approval would benefit the economy and unfortunately are not unavailable in the country at the present time.

Vincenzo handed her back the paper. Her knowledge and grasp of their country's economic problems impressed him no end. He cocked his head. "Giuseppe

Masala has a following and is known as a hard hitter on the trade commission."

Abby's brows met in a delicate frown. "Obviously he's from the old school. Signor Giordano's ideas are new and innovative. He's worked up statistics that show Arancia could increase its imports of fuel, motor vehicles, raw materials, chemicals, electronic devices and food by a big margin. His chart with historical data proves his ideas will work.

"I'd like to see him get his fast-track idea passed, but the lobby against it is powerful. Signor Masala's attorney is stalling to get back to me with an answer."

She had him fascinated. "So what's your next strategy?"

Abby put the paper back in the folder. "I'm taking him to court to show cause. But the docket is full and it could be awhile."

"Who's the judge?"

"Mascotti."

The judge was a good friend of Vincenzo's father. Keeping that in mind, he said, "Go on fighting the good fight, Abby. I have faith in you and know you'll get there."

"Your optimism means a lot to me."

She was friendly, yet kept their relationship at a professional distance the way she'd always done. To his dismay he discovered he wanted more, in different surroundings where they could be casual and spend time talking together like they used to. Her suite wasn't the right place.

Her bodyguard already knew he'd stopped by to see her and would know how long he stayed. He wanted to trust Angelina, but you never knew who your enemies were. Vincenzo's father had taught him that early on. So it was back to the business at hand. "The doctor's office faxed me a schedule of your appointments. I understand you're due for your eight weeks' checkup on Friday, May 1." She nodded. "I plan to join you at the clinic and have arranged for us to meet with the psychologist for our first session afterward."

"You mean you'll have time?" She looked surprised.

"I've done a lot of business since we last saw each other and have reported in to the king. At this juncture I'm due some time off and am ready to get serious about my duties as a father-in-waiting."

Laughter bubbled out of her. "You're very funny at times, Vincenzo."

No one had ever accused him of that except Abby. He hated bringing the fun to an end, but he needed to discuss more serious matters with her that couldn't be put off before he left.

"Your mention of the funeral reminds me of how compassionate you are, and how much you cared for Michelina. I've wanted to tell you why we decided against your attending the funeral."

She moistened her lips nervously. "My father already explained. Naturally, none of us wanted the slightest hint of gossip to mar your life in any way. Just between us, let me tell you how much I liked and admired Michelina. I've missed my daily talks with her and mourn her loss."

He felt her sincerity. "She cared for you, too."

"I—I wish there'd been a way to take your pain away—" her voice faltered "—but there wasn't. Only time can heal those wounds."

"Which is something you know all about, after losing your mother."

"I'll admit it was a bad time for Dad and me, but we got through it. There's no burning pain anymore."

When he'd seen Carlo Loretto's agony after losing his wife, Vincenzo had come to realize how lucky they'd been to know real love. Abby had grown up knowing her parents had been lovers in the true sense of the word. Obviously she could be forgiven for believing he and Michelina had that kind of marriage. *A marriage that had physically ended at the very moment there was new hope for them.*

"Did your father explain why I haven't phoned you in all these weeks?"

"Yes. Though you and Michelina had told me we could call each other back and forth if problems arose, Dad and I talked about that too. We decided it will be better if you and I always go through your personal assistant, Marcello."

"As do I."

It would definitely be better, Vincenzo mused. She understood everything. With Michelina gone, no unexplained private calls to him from Abby meant no calls to be traced by someone out to stir up trouble. They'd entered forbidden territory after going through with the surrogacy.

Vincenzo had to hope the gossip mill within the palace wouldn't get to the point that he could no longer trust in the staff's loyalty. But he knew it had happened in every royal house, no matter the measures taken, and so did she.

"I mustn't keep you, but before I go, I have a favor to ask."

"Anything."

"Michelina's mother and brothers flew in for the festival." It was an excuse for what the queen really wanted. "She would like to meet with you and me in the state drawing room at nine in the morning."

His concern over having to meet with his mother-in-law had less to do with the argument Michelina and the queen had gotten into before the fatal accident, and much more to do with the fact that he hadn't been able to love her daughter the way she'd loved him. He was filled with guilt and dreaded this audience for Abby's sake. But his mother-in-law had to be faced, and she had refused to be put off. "Your father will clear it with your boss so he'll understand why you'll be a little late for work."

"That's fine."

It wouldn't be fine, but he would be in the room to protect her. "Then I'll say good-night."

She nodded. "Welcome home, Vincenzo, and *buonanotte*." Another smile broke out on her lovely face.

"Sogni d'oro."

CHAPTER TWO

THE PRINCE'S FINAL words, "sweet dreams," stayed with her all night. Seeing him again had caused an adrenaline rush she couldn't shut off. She awakened earlier than usual to get ready, knowing Michelina's mother would ask a lot of questions.

Abby always dressed up for work. Since the law firm of Faustino, Ruggeri, Duomo and Tonelli catered to a higher-class clientele, Signor Faustino, the senior partner, had impressed upon her and everyone else who worked there the need to look fashionable. Though her heart wasn't in it this morning, she took her antinausea pill with breakfast, then forced herself to go through the motions.

Everyone knew she was the daughter of the chief of security for the palace, so no one questioned the royal limo bringing her to and from work. Except for her boss and Carolena, her coworkers were clueless about Abby's specific situation. That's the way things needed to remain until she took a leave of absence.

After the delivery, the palace would issue a formal statement that a surrogate mother had successfully carried the baby of their Royal Highnesses, the new heir who would be second in line to the throne. At that time Abby would disappear. But it wouldn't be for a while.

Vincenzo had been a part of her life for so long, she couldn't imagine the time coming when she'd no longer see him. Once the baby was born, she would live in another part of the city and get on with her life as a full-time attorney. How strange that was going to be.

From the time she'd moved here with her family, he'd been around to show her everything the tourists never got to see. He'd taken her horseback riding on the grounds, or let her come with him when he took out his small sailboat. Vincenzo had taught her seamanship. There was nothing she loved more than sitting out in the middle of the sea while they fished and ate sweets from the palace kitchen. He had the run of the place and let her be his shadow.

Abby's friends from school had come over to her parents' apartment, and sometimes she'd gone to their houses. But she much preferred being with Vincenzo and had never missed an opportunity to tag along. Unlike the big brothers of a couple of her friends who didn't want the younger girls around, Vincenzo had always seemed to enjoy her company and invited her to accompany him when he had free time.

Memories flooded her mind as she walked over to the closet and pulled out one of her favorite Paoli dresses. When Abby had gone shopping with Carolena, they'd both agreed this one had the most luscious yellow print design on the body of the dress.

The tiny beige print on the capped sleeves and hem formed the contrast. Part of the beige print also drew the material that made tucks at the waist. Her friend had cried that it was stunning on Abby, with her silvery-blond hair color. Abby decided to wear it while she still could. The way she was growing, she would need to buy loose-fitting clothes this weekend.

After arranging her hair back in a simple low chignon with three pins, she put on her makeup, slipped on matching yellow shoes and started out of the bedroom. But she only made it to the hallway with her bone-colored handbag when her landline rang. Presuming it was her father calling to see how she was doing, she walked into the den to pick up and say hello.

"Signorina Loretto? This is Marcello. You are wanted in the king's drawing room. Are you ready?"

Her hand gripped the receiver tighter. It sounded urgent. During the night she'd worried about this meeting. It was only natural Michelina's mother would want to meet the woman who would be giving birth to her grandchild. But something about the look in Vincenzo's eyes had given her a sinking feeling in the pit of her stomach.

"Yes. I'll be right there."

"Then I'll inform His Highness, and meet you in the main corridor."

"Thank you."

Because of Vincenzo, Abby was familiar with every part of the palace except the royal apartments. He'd taken her to the main drawing room, where the king met with heads of state, several times. Vincenzo had gotten a kick out of watching her reaction as he related stories about foreign dignitaries that weren't public knowledge.

But her smile faded as she made her way across the magnificent edifice to meet Michelina's mother. She knew the queen was grieving. Marcello met her in the main hallway. "Follow me."

They went down the hall past frescoes and paintings, to another section where they turned a corner. She spied the country's flag draped outside an ornate pair of floor-to-ceiling doors. Marcello knocked on one of the panels and was told to enter. He opened the door, indicating she should go in.

The tall vaulted ceiling of the room was a living museum to the history of Arancia, and had known centuries of French and Italian rulers. But Abby's gaze fell on Vincenzo, who was wearing a somber midnight-blue suit. Opposite him sat Michelina's stylish sixty-five-year-old mother, who was brunette like her late daughter. She'd dressed in black, with a matching cloche hat, and sat on one of the brocade chairs.

"Come all the way in, Signorina Loretto. I'd like you to meet my mother-in-law, Her Majesty the Queen of Gemelli." Abby knew Gemelli—another citrus-producing country—was an island kingdom off the eastern coast of Sicily, facing the Ionian Sea.

She moved toward them and curtsied the way she'd been taught as a child after coming to the palace. "Your Majesty. It's a great honor, but my heart has been bleeding for you and the prince. I cared for your daughter very much."

The matriarch's eyes were a darker brown than Michelina's, more snapping. She gave what passed for a nod before Vincenzo told Abby to be seated on the love seat on the other side of the coffee table. Once she was comfortable, he said, "If you recall, Michelina and I flew to Gemelli so she could tell the queen we were pregnant."

"Yes."

"To my surprise, the unexpected nature of our news

came as a great shock to my mother-in-law, since my
wife hadn't informed her of our decision to use a surrogate."

What?

"You mean your daughter never told you what she
and the prince were contemplating?"

"No," came the answer through wooden lips.

Aghast, Abby averted her eyes, not knowing what
to think. "I'm so sorry, Your Majesty."

"We're all sorry, because the queen and Michelina
argued," Vincenzo explained. "Unfortunately before
they could talk again, the accident happened. The queen
would like to take this opportunity to hear from the
woman who has dared to go against nature to perform
a service for which she gets nothing in return."

CHAPTER THREE

ABBY REELED.

For Vincenzo to put it so bluntly meant he and his mother-in-law had exchanged harsh if not painfully bitter words. But he was a realist and had decided the only thing to do was meet this situation head-on. He expected Abby to handle it because of their long-standing friendship over the years.

"You haven't answered my question, Signorina Loretto."

At the queen's staccato voice, Abby struggled to catch her breath and remain calm. No wonder she'd felt tension from him last night when he'd brought up this morning's meeting. Michelina's omission when it came to her mother had put a pall over an event that was helping Vincenzo to get up in the morning.

He was counting on Abby being able to deal with his mother-in-law. She refused to let him down even if it killed her. More time passed while she formulated what to say before focusing on the queen.

"If I had a daughter who came to me in the same situation, I would ask her exactly the same question. In my case, I've done it for one reason only. Perhaps you didn't know that the prince rescued me from certain death when I was seventeen. I lost my mother in that same sailboat accident. Before I was swept to shore by the wind, I'd lost consciousness.

"When the prince found me, I was close to death but didn't know it." Abby's eyes glazed over with unshed tears. "If you could have heard the way my father wept after he discovered I'd been found and brought back to the living, you would realize what a miracle had happened that day, all because of the prince's quick thinking and intervention.

"From that time on, my father and I have felt the deepest gratitude to the prince. Over the years I've pondered many times how to pay the prince back for preventing what could have been an all-out catastrophe for my father."

The lines on the queen's face deepened, revealing her sorrow. Whether she was too immersed in her own grief to hear what Abby was saying, Abby didn't know.

"The prince and princess were the perfect couple," Abby continued. "When I heard that the princess had had a third miscarriage, it wounded me for their sake. They deserved happiness. Before Christmas I learned through my father that Dr. DeLuca had suggested a way for them to achieve their dream of a family."

Abby fought to prevent tears from falling. "After years of wishing there was something I could do, I realized that if I could qualify as a candidate, I could carry their child for them. You'll never know the joy it gave me at the thought of doing something so special for them. When I told my father what I wanted to do, he was surprised at first, and yet he supported my decision, too, otherwise he would never have approved."

She took a shuddering breath. "That's the reason

I'm doing this. A life for a life. What I'm going to get out of this is pure happiness to see the baby the prince and princess fought so hard for. When the doctor puts the baby in the prince's arms, Michelina will live on in their child, and the child will forever be a part of King Guilio and his wife, and a part of you and your husband, Your Majesty."

The queen's hands trembled on the arms of the chair. "You have no comprehension of what it's like to be a mother. How old are you?"

"I'm twenty-eight and it's true I've never been married or had a child. But I won't be its mother in the way you mean. I'm only supplying a safe haven for the baby until it's born. Yes, I'll go through the aches and pains of pregnancy, but I view this as a sacred trust."

Her features hardened. "You call this sacred?"

"I do. During my screening process, I met a dozen different parents and their surrogates who'd gone through the experience and now have beautiful children. They were all overjoyed and agreed it's a special partnership between them and God."

For the first time, the queen looked away.

"The prince is a full partner in this. He and the princess discussed it many times. He knows what she wanted and I'll cooperate in every way. If you have suggestions, I'll welcome them with all my heart."

Quiet reigned.

Realizing there was nothing more to say, Abby glanced at Vincenzo, waiting for him to dismiss her.

He read her mind with ease. "I'm aware the limo is waiting to drive you to your office."

"Yes, Your Highness."

At those words Michelina's mother lifted her head. "You intend to work?" She sounded shocked.

"I do. I am passionate about my career as an attorney. After the delivery, I will have my own life to lead and need to continue planning for it."

Vincenzo leaned forward. "She'll stop work when the time is right."

"Where will you live after the baby's born?" The pointed question told Abby exactly where the queen's thoughts had gone.

Nowhere near the prince.

She couldn't blame the older woman for that. How could Michelina's mother not suspect the worst? Her fears preyed on Abby's guilt, which was deepening because she'd found herself missing Vincenzo more than she should have while he'd been away. He shouldn't have been on her mind so much, but she couldn't seem to turn off her thoughts. Not when the baby growing inside her was a constant reminder of him.

For weeks now she'd played games of *what if?* during the night when she couldn't sleep. What if the baby were hers and Vincenzo's? What would he or she look like? Where would they create a nursery in the palace? When would they go shopping for a crib and all the things necessary? She wanted to make a special baby quilt and start a scrapbook.

But then she'd break out in a cold sweat of guilt and sit up in the bed, berating herself for having any of these thoughts. Michelina's death might have changed everything, but this royal baby still wasn't Abby's!

How could she even entertain such thoughts when Michelina had trusted her so implicitly? It was such a betrayal of the trust and regard the two women had for each other. They'd made a contract as binding as a blood oath. The second the baby was born, her job as surrogate would no longer be required and she'd return to her old life.

But Abby was aghast to discover that Michelina's death had thrown her into an abyss of fresh guilt. She needed to talk to the psychologist about finding strategies to cope with this new situation or go crazy.

Queen Bianca had asked her a question and was waiting for an answer.

"I plan to buy my own home in another part of the city in the same building as a friend of mine. My contract with the prince and princess includes living at the palace, and that ends the moment the baby is delivered."

Vincenzo's eyes narrowed on her face. "What friend?"

That was probably the only thing about her plans the three of them hadn't discussed over the last few months.

"You've heard me speak of Carolena Baretti and know she's my best friend, who works at the same law firm with me. We went through law school together at the University of Arancia before taking the bar."

If a woman could look gutted, the queen did. "This whole situation is unnatural."

"Not unnatural, Your Majesty, just different. Your daughter wanted a baby badly enough to think it all through and agree to it. I hope the day will come when you're reconciled to that decision."

"That day will never come," the older woman declared in an imperious voice. "I was thrilled each time she informed me she was pregnant and I suffered with her through each miscarriage. But I will never view surrogacy as ethically acceptable."

"But it's a gestational surrogacy," Abby argued quietly. "Dr. DeLuca says that several thousand women around the globe are gestational surrogates and it's becoming preferable to going with traditional surrogacy, because it ensures the genetic link to both parents. Think how many lives can be changed. Surely you can see what a miracle it is."

"Nevertheless, it's outside tradition. It interferes with a natural process in violation of God's will."

"Then how do you explain this world that God created, and all the new technology that helps people like your daughter and Vincenzo realize their dream to have a family?"

"It doesn't need an explanation. It's a form of adultery, because you are the third party outside their marriage. Some people regard that it could result in incest of a sort."

Tortured by her words, Abby exchanged an agonized glance with Vincenzo. "What do you mean?"

"As the priest reminded me, their child might one day marry another of *your* children. While there would be no genetic relationship, the two children would be siblings, after a fashion."

Naturally Abby hoped to marry one day and have children of her own, but never in a million years would she have jumped to such an improbable conclusion. By now Vincenzo's features had turned to granite.

"There's also the question of whether or not you'll be entitled to an inheritance and are actually out for one."

Abby was stunned. "When the prince saved my life, he gave me an inheritance more precious than anything earthly. If any money is involved, it's the one hundred and fifty thousand dollars or more the prince has paid the doctors and the hospital for this procedure to be done." She could feel herself getting worked up, but she couldn't stop.

"I've been given all the compensation I could ever wish for by being allowed to live here in the palace, where my every want and need is taken care of. I'm so sorry this situation has caused you so much grief. I can see you two need to discuss this further, alone. I must leave for the office."

Abby eyed the prince, silently asking him to please help her to go before the queen grew any more upset. He got the message and stood to his full imposing height, signaling she could stand.

"Thank you for joining us," he murmured. "Whatever my mother-in-law's reaction, it's too late for talk because you're pregnant with Michelina's and my child. Let's say no more. I promise that when the queen is presented with her first grandchild, she'll forget all these concerns."

The queen flashed him a look of disdain that wounded Abby. She couldn't walk out of here with everything so ugly and not say a few last words.

"It's been my privilege to meet you, Your Majesty. Michelina used to talk about you all the time. She loved you very much and was looking forward to you helping her through these coming months. I hope you know that. If you ever want to talk to me again, please call me. I don't have a mother anymore and would like to hear any advice you have to help me get through this."

It was getting harder and harder to clap with one hand and the prince knew it.

"Again, let me say how sorry I am about your loss. She was so lovely and accomplished. I have two of her watercolors hanging on the wall of my apartment. Everyone will miss her terribly, especially this baby.

"But thankfully it will have its grandmother to tell him or her all the things only you know about their mother."

The queen stared at Abby through dim eyes.

Abby could feel her pain. "Goodbye for now." She curtsied once more. Her gaze clung to Vincenzo's for a few seconds before she turned on her low-heeled sandals and left the room. The limo would be waiting for her. Though she wanted to run, she forced herself to stay in control so she wouldn't fall and do something to hurt herself.

The queen had put Abby on trial. No wonder Vincenzo's wife had been frightened to approach her mother with such an unconventional idea. Only now was Abby beginning to understand how desperate *and* courageous Michelina had been to consider allowing a third party to enter into the most intimate aspect of all their lives. Facing the queen had to be one of the worst moments Abby had ever known.

But this had to be an even more nightmarish experience for Vincenzo. Here he was trying to deal with his wife's death while at the same time having to defend the decision he and Michelina had made to use a surrogate. He had to be suffering guilt of his own.

Abby blamed no one for this, but she felt Vincenzo's pain. How he was going to get through this latest crisis, she couldn't imagine. Probably by working. That was how *she* planned to survive.

Twenty minutes later Abby entered the neoclassical building that housed her law firm and walked straight back to Carolena's office. Her friend was a patent attorney and had become as close to Abby as a sister. Unfortunately she was at court, so they'd have to talk later.

Both Carolena and Abby had been hired by the well-known Arancian law firm after they'd graduated. Abby had been thrilled when they'd both been taken on a year ago. She had planned for this career from her junior-high days, and had been hired not only for her specialty in international trade law, but because she was conversant in French, English, Italian and Mentonasc.

Since the Mentonasc dialect—somewhere between Nicard and a dialect of Ligurian, a Gallo-Romance language spoken in Northern Italy—was currently spoken by about 10 percent of the population living in Arancia and its border areas, it gave her an edge over other applicants for the position, which required her particular linguistic expertise.

Abby's parents had cleverly directed her studies from a very young age. Thanks to them her abilities had taken her to the head of the class. However, this morning Abby's mind wasn't on her latest cases.

She felt disturbed by the revelation that Michelina had kept her mother in the dark about one of the most important events in her life. Abby had done her research. Since the death of King Gregorio, Queen Bianca become the ruler of Gemelli and was known to be rigid and difficult. Abby had felt her disapproval and didn't envy Vincenzo's task of winning his mother-in-law over.

Hopefully something Abby had said would sink in and soften her heart. At the moment, Abby's own heart was breaking for all of them.

* * *

Six hours later, Abby finished dictating some memos to Bernardo and left the building for the limo. But when she walked outside, she noticed the palace secret service cars had parked both in front of and behind the limo. One of the security men got out of the front and opened the rear door for her. What was going on?

As she climbed inside and saw who was sitting there waiting for her—in sunglasses and a silky claret-colored sport shirt and cream trousers—the blood started to hammer in her ears.

"Vincenzo—"

His name slipped out by accident, proving to her more and more that he filled her conscious and unconscious mind.

The tremor in Abby's voice made its way to every cell of Vincenzo's body. After she'd bared her soul to his mother-in-law that morning, he'd realized not only at what price she'd sacrificed herself to make their dreams of a baby a reality, but he'd been flooded with memories of that day when she'd lost her mother.

Abby had been a great swimmer and handled herself well in the sea. As some of his friends had pointed out years ago when they'd seen her in the water offshore, she wasn't a woman yet, but she showed all the promise.

By the time she'd turned seventeen, he'd found himself looking at her a lot more than he should have. She was one of those natural-blond American girls with classic features, noted for their long, gorgeous legs. At that point in time Vincenzo had already been betrothed to Michelina. Since the marriage wouldn't be for at least another ten years, he'd had the freedom to date the women who attracted him.

Abby had been too young, of course, but pleasing to the eye. She'd turned into a very beautiful girl who was studious, intelligent and spoke Italian like a native. He enjoyed every moment he spent with her; her enthusiasm for everything surprised and entertained him.

But even if he hadn't been betrothed, Abby had been off-limits to Vincenzo for more reasons than her young age or the fact that she wasn't a princess. Her parents had become close friends with Vincenzo's parents. That was a special friendship that demanded total respect.

Though her periwinkle-blue eyes always seemed to smile at him with interest when they chanced upon each other, there was an invisible boundary between them she recognized, too. Neither of them ever crossed it until the day of the squall...

As Abby had told Queen Bianca earlier, she and her mother, Holly, had been out in a small sailboat off the coast when the storm struck. Nothing could come on as rapidly and give so little time for preparation as did a white squall.

Vincenzo had been in his father's office before lunch discussing a duty he needed to carry out when they'd noticed the darkening sky. A cloudburst had descended, making the day feel like night. They hadn't seen a storm this ferocious in years and felt sorry for anyone who'd been caught in it.

While they were commenting on the fierceness of the wind, a call came through informing the king that the Loretto sailboat was missing from its slip. Someone thought they had seen Signora Loretto and her daughter out sailing earlier, but they hadn't come back in yet. Several boats were already out there looking for them.

Abby—

Vincenzo was aghast. *She* was out there?

The sweet girl who'd always been there for him was battling this storm with her mother, alone?

Fear like Vincenzo had never known before attacked his insides and he broke out in a cold sweat. "I've got to find them!"

"Wait, son! Let the coast guard deal with it!"

But he'd already reached the door and dashed from the room. Driven by fear, he raced through the palace. Once outside, he ran to the dock, where a group of men huddled. He grabbed one of them to come with him and they took off in his cruiser to face a churning sea.

The other man kept in radio contact with the rescue boats. Within a minute they heard that the sailboat had been spotted. Vincenzo headed toward the cited coordinates, oblivious to the elements.

The rescue boats were already on the scene as Vincenzo's cruiser came close to the sailboat. It was tossing like a cork, but he couldn't see anyone on board. "Have they already been rescued?"

"Signora Loretto was found floating unconscious in the water wearing her life preserver, but there's no sign of her daughter yet," replied his companion.

Vincenzo's heart almost failed him.

Abby had drowned?

It was as though his whole life passed before him. She *couldn't* have drowned! He couldn't lose her! Not his Abby...

"We've got to look for her! She knows to wear a life jacket. The wind will have pushed her body through the water. We're going to follow it. You steer while I search."

"It's too dangerous for you, Your Highness!"

"Danger be damned! Don't you understand?" he shouted. "There's a seventeen-year-old girl out there who needs help!"

"Tell me where to go."

He studied the direction of the wind. "Along the coastline near the caves!" Vincenzo knew this coastline like the back of his hand. When a low pressure over the Mediterranean approached the coast from the southeast, the weather could change quickly for the worse and its clear sky change to an east wind. If Abby had been knocked unconscious, too, she could have been swept into one of the caves further up the coast.

When they reached the opening of the largest cave, Vincenzo dove in and swam through to the three hidden grottoes, where he'd been many times with his friends. In the second one, his heart had leaped when he saw Abby's body floating lifelessly, like her mother's. Quickly he'd caught hold of her and swum her out to the boat, where he took off her life jacket and began giving her mouth-to-mouth resuscitation. At first there was no response. Her face was a pinched white. Though terrified she was too far gone, he kept up the CPR.

At the last second there came sounds of life, and her eyelids fluttered. He turned her on her side while she coughed and threw up water.

"That's it, my precious Abby. Get rid of it."

When she'd finished, she looked up at him, dazed. "Vincenzo?"

"*Sì,*" he'd murmured in relief. "You were in a storm,

but I found you in one of the grottoes and you're all right now."

Abby blinked. "My mother?" she cried frantically. "Where is she?"

"With your father." It wasn't a lie, but since he didn't know the whole truth of her condition, he kept quiet.

"Thank God." Her eyes searched his. "I could have died in there. You saved my life," she whispered in awe. In a totally unexpected gesture, she'd thrown her arms around his neck and clung to him.

"Thank God," he'd whispered back and found himself rocking her in his arms while she sobbed.

Vincenzo had never felt that close to another human being in his life. She'd felt so right in his arms. When they took her to the hospital and she learned her mother had died of a blow from the mast, she'd flung herself into his arms once more.

That was the moment when he knew Abby meant more to him that he could put into words. Their relationship changed that day. His feelings for her ran much deeper than he'd realized. To imagine his life without her was anathema to him.

She'd been too inconsolable for him to do anything but let her pour out her pain and love for her mother. His only desire had been to comfort her. He'd held her for a long time because her father, overcome with grief, had to be sedated.

In front of the queen today, they'd both relived that moment. Abby's outpouring of her soul had endeared her to him in such a profound way, he could hardly find expression. Though he knew it was wrong, he'd decided to break one of his own rules and pick her up from work.

Bianca had put Abby through a torturous session.

Despite his guilt in seeking her out for a reason that wasn't a medical necessity, he couldn't let it go until he'd seen for himself that she was all right.

"I came to find out how well you survived the day."

The picture of her in that yellow dress when she'd walked in the room had made an indelible impression of femininity and sophistication in his mind. Bianca couldn't have helped but notice how lovely she was, along with her moving sincerity. It hadn't surprised him his mother-in-law had been so quiet after Abby had left the room to go to work.

"My worry has been for you." She sat down opposite him and fastened her seat belt. "For me, work is the great panacea. But it's evident the queen has been in absolute agony."

"She's flown back to Gemelli with a lot to think about."

"The poor thing. We have to hope she'll let go of her preconceived beliefs so she can enjoy this special time."

There was a sweetness in Abby that touched Vincenzo's heart. "You're the one I'm concerned about. It hurts me that you no longer have your mother to confide in." Until now he hadn't thought about how alone Abby must feel. Bianca's castigations had been like a dagger plunged into her, bringing out his protective instincts.

She flicked him a glance. "But I have my father, and I have you and the doctor. Who better than all of you to comfort me when I need it?" Except that Vincenzo wanted to do more than comfort her, God forgive him.

He held her gaze. "I'm sorry if anything the queen said has upset you, but I promise everything's going to be all right in time."

"I believe that, too. Did she say anything else?"

"No, but her son Valentino and I are good friends."
When he'd gone with the queen and his brothers-in-law
to visit Michelina's grave once, they'd eaten lunch before he'd accompanied them to their jet. "He's promised
to keep in close touch. Now let's change the subject."

"You're taking too great a risk, Your Highness. We
mustn't be seen out together like this."

"The limo protects us." Even as he said it, he was
trying to tamp down his guilt over pressuring her when
it was obvious she was afraid to be seen with him. He
ought to be worried about that, too, but something had
come over him.

"Please, Your Highness. The fact that there are so
many security men will cause the locals to speculate about who is so important, driving around in the
crowded streets. Have the car turn around and take me
back to the office."

"It's too late for that." Vincenzo had no intention of
letting her go yet.

"After my audience with the queen, surely you understand my fears."

"After the way she went after you, I have my own
fears where you're concerned. You didn't deserve that
and I want to make it up to you."

CHAPTER FOUR

"WE'RE GOING IN the wrong direction to the palace."

Vincenzo ignored Abby's comment. "Last night you didn't eat a full meal. This evening I intend to remedy that and take you to a very special place for dinner to celebrate the Lemon and Orange Festival. Don't worry," he said when he saw her eyes grow anxious. "We'll be arriving via a private entrance to a private dining room where my own people will be serving us. All you have to do is enjoy a meal free of caffeine and alcohol, with salt in moderation."

She kneaded her hands. "I know why you're doing this, Vincenzo, but it isn't necessary."

"Has being pregnant made you a mind reader?"

For once she couldn't tell if he was having fun with her or if her comment had irked him. "I only meant—"

"You only meant that you don't expect any special favors from me," he preempted her. "Tell me something I don't already know."

"I've annoyed you. I'm sorry."

"Abby—we need to have a little talk. Because of the sacrifice you've made for me and Michelina, any social life you would normally enjoy has been cut off until the baby's born. At this time in your life you should be out having a good time. I have no doubt there are any number of men who pass through your office wanting a relationship with you. Certainly I don't need to tell you that you're a very beautiful woman. My brother-in-law shared as much with me earlier."

"I've never met Michelina's brother."

"But he saw you this morning after you left the drawing room for the limo."

That was news to Abby. Vincenzo's words had shaken her. "Thank you for the compliment."

"Now you sound vexed with me."

"I'm not!"

"Good. Then try to understand that our relationship isn't one-sided, with me reaping all the benefits while you lie around like a beached whale, barefoot and pregnant, as you Americans tend to say."

Abby burst into laughter.

"I'm glad you think that's funny. We're making progress."

No one could be more amusing than Vincenzo when he revealed this exciting side of his nature. "I can't believe you've ever heard those expressions."

"I graduated in California Girls 101 during my vacation one summer in San Diego."

She rolled her eyes. "*That* school. I don't doubt it." She knew he'd traveled a lot in his twenties. "I guess you didn't need a booklet for the class."

He grinned, revealing a gorgeous white smile. "And the tuition was free. Why do you think most men congregate there when they get the chance?"

"Isn't it interesting that most women congregate in Arancia and Italy to attend Mediterranean Gods 101? They don't need booklets, either."

Vincenzo let go with a belly laugh that resonated throughout the interior of the limo. "You must be dynamite in the courtroom."

"Why don't you come up and see me some time?" she said in her best Mae West impersonation. *Why didn't he come to her apartment and stay...* It was a wicked thought, but she couldn't help it. The other night she hadn't wanted him to leave.

The corner of his mouth lifted. "Who were you imitating just now?"

"Someone you'd never know. She was in American films years ago. My mother loved her old movies."

"Tell me her name."

"I'll give you a hint. They named inflatable life jackets after her in the Second World War. If you still can't think of it, I'll do better and have a DVD sent to you so you can see for yourself."

"We'll watch it together."

No. They wouldn't watch it together. They'd done enough of that when she was much younger. He had his own theater in the palace, where she'd seen a lot of films and eaten marzipan with him. But that time was long gone and this idea of his had to be stopped right now. She was having too much fun and needed his company too much.

Thankfully they'd left the Promenade d'Or along the coast and were following a winding road up the hillsides above the city. In another minute they rounded a curve and pulled up to, of all things, a funicular railway.

Vincenzo got out of the limo and came around to help her. Together with some of his security people, they got on and sat on one of the benches. He told her to buckle up before it started climbing the steep mountain.

"There's a lovely little restaurant two kilometers higher that overlooks the Mediterranean. While we eat, we'll watch the festival fireworks being set off in town."

Once Abby was settled, Vincenzo had to talk to one of his security men, leaving her alone with her thoughts for a second. During her teenage years she'd had ridiculous daydreams about being alone with him, but none of them could match the wonder of such an evening. Without question this was the most thrilling moment in Abby's life.

However, there was one problem with reality intruding on this beautiful dream. While he was trying to give her a special night out to make up for her being denied a social life at present, Abby could never forget she was carrying the child he and Michelina had made. The wife he'd adored was gone, leaving him desolate, just like her father.

She remembered the night of Michelina's funeral, when she'd wandered out onto the patio of her apartment, not knowing where to go with her pain. Before her was the amazing sight of dozens of sailboats and yachts anchored offshore from up and down the Riviera with Arancian flags flying at half-mast in the breeze to pay respect to the prince.

While she stood there, her cell phone had rung, causing her to jump. She hurried inside to check the caller ID, hardly able to see through the tears.

"Carolena?" she'd cried after clicking on.

"Abby? When the announcer started speculating on the future of the monarchy, I had to call and see if you're all right."

She breathed in deeply. "Yes," she'd murmured, wiping the moisture off her cheeks with her hand.

"No, you're not. I don't know how you're handling this."

"Truthfully, not very well."

"Talk to me. I know you told me you can't leave the palace until tomorrow and I can't come over there today, so the phone will have to do. Have you even talked to Vincenzo since the accident?"

"Yes. He came for a minute last evening, worried about my welfare, if you can imagine."

"Actually, I can. To know you're carrying his child is probably the only thing keeping him from going under. I never witnessed anything more touching in my life than the sight of the horse covered in her favorite flowers walking alongside that incredible-looking man. Already I've seen one of the tabloids out in the kiosk bearing the headline The Prince of Every Woman's Dreams in Mourning."

Abby had closed her eyes tightly. "The media will make a circus of this." She could hear it all now: *Who will be the next princess? Will she be foreign? Will he wait a year, or will he break with tradition and take a new bride in the next few months?* Abby had a question of her own: *How will the next woman he chooses feel about the surrogacy situation?* All those thoughts and more had bombarded her.

"You really shouldn't be alone."

"All I have to do is get through tonight, Carolena. Tomorrow I can start living a normal life."

Now, seven weeks later, here Abby was with the prince of every woman's dreams, riding to the top of the mountain. But there was nothing normal about his life or hers. When she and her father had gone through all the *what if*s before she'd made her decision to be a surrogate, the idea of either Michelina or Vincenzo dying had only been mentioned in passing. But she couldn't have imagined anything so horrible and never thought about it again.

"Shall we go in?" sounded the deep, velvety male voice next to her.

"Oh—yes!" Abby had been so immersed in thought she hadn't realized they'd arrived. Night had fallen during their journey here. Vincenzo led her off the funicular and walked her through a hallway to another set of doors. They opened onto a terrace with a candlelit table and flowers set for two.

A small gasp of pleasure escaped her lips when she realized she was looking out over the same view she could see from her own patio at the palace. But they were much higher up, so she could take in the whole city of Arancia alive with lights for the nightly festival celebration.

"What an incredible vista."

"I agree," he murmured as he helped her to sit. Of course it was an accident that his hand brushed her shoulder, but she felt his touch as if she'd just come in contact with an electric current. This was so wrong; she was terrified.

Grape juice from the surrounding vineyard came first, followed by hors d'oeuvres and then a luscious rack of lamb and fresh green peas from the restaurant's garden. Abby knew the chef had prepared food to the prince's specifications.

She ate everything. "This meal is fabulous!"

His black eyes smiled at her. "Tonight you have an appetite. That's good. We'll have to do this more often."

No, no, no.

"If I were to eat here every night, I'd be as big as that whale you referred to earlier."

He chuckled. "You think?"

"I know."

While Abby enjoyed the house's lemon tart specialty for dessert, Vincenzo drank coffee. "Mind if I ask you a personal question?"

How personal? She was on dangerous ground, fearing he could see right through her, to her chaotic innermost thoughts. "What would you like to know?"

"Has there been an important man in your life? And if so, why didn't you marry him?"

Yes. I'm looking at him.

Heat filled her cheeks. "I had my share of boyfriends, but by college I got serious about my studies. Law school doesn't leave time for much of a social life when you're clerking for a judge who expects you to put in one hundred and twenty hours a week."

"Sounds like one of my normal days," he remarked. She knew he wasn't kidding. "You and I never discussed this before, but I'm curious about something. Didn't you ever want to be a mother to your own child first?"

Abby stifled her moan. If he only knew how during her teenage years she'd dreamed about being married to him and having his baby. Since that time, history had been made and she was carrying his baby in real life. But it wasn't hers and that dream had come with a price. How could she be feeling like this when he was forbidden to her?

"Well—" She swallowed hard. "The desire to be a mother has always been rooted in me. I've never doubted my ability to be a good one. Despite the fact that Mother died early, I had a charmed and happy childhood. She was a wonderful mom. Warm and charming. Funny. Still, I never saw raising a child as my only goal.

"I'd always envisioned motherhood as the result of a loving relationship with a man, like my parents had. Carolena has told me many times that it's just an excuse because no man has ever lived up to my father. She said the umbilical cord should have been cut years ago. With hindsight I think she's probably right, but there's no one like him."

In truth, there was no one like Vincenzo and never would be. *He* was the reason she hadn't been able to get interested in another man.

"Your father has been a lucky man to have inspired such fierce love from his wife and daughter."

The comment sounded mournful. "Michelina loved you the same way."

"Yes."

"So will your child."

His eyes grew veiled without him saying anything.

The fireworks had started, lighting up the night sky in a barrage of colors, but she couldn't appreciate the display because of a certain tension between them that hadn't been there earlier. She was walking such a tightrope around him, her body was a mass of nerves.

"Maybe coming out to dinner wasn't a very good idea for you, Your Highness."

"What happened to *Vincenzo?*"

Again she had the feeling she'd angered him, the last thing she wanted to do. But it was imperative she keep emotional distance from him. "You're still mourning your wife. I appreciate this evening more than you know, but it's too soon for you to be out doing the things you used to do with her." *And too hard on me.*

She wiped her mouth with the napkin. "When was the last time you brought her here? Do you want to talk about it?"

That dark, remote expression he could get had returned. "Michelina never came here with me."

She swallowed hard. "I see." She wondered why. "Nevertheless, being out on a night like this has to bring back memories."

His fingers ran over the stem of the wineglass that was still full. "Today as I opened the festival, you could feel spring in the air. You can feel it tonight. It calls for a new beginning." His gaze swerved to hers, piercing through to her insides. "You and I are together on a journey that neither of us has ever taken. I want to put the past behind us and enjoy the future that is opening up."

"With your baby to be born soon, it will be a glorious future."

"There are a few months to go yet, months you should be able to enjoy. I want to help you. How does that sound?"

It sounded as though he didn't want to be reminded of his wife again because it hurt him too much and he needed a diversion. Naturally, he did, but Abby couldn't fill that need! She didn't dare.

"I'm already having a wonderful time enjoying this meal with you. Thank you for a very memorable evening."

"You're welcome. I want us to enjoy more."

"We can't, Vincenzo. The people close to you will notice and there will be gossip. If I've angered you again, I'm sorry."

Silence followed her remarks. They watched the fireworks for a while longer before leaving. The ride down the mountain was much faster than the ride up. It was much like the sensation when Dr. DeLuca had said, "Congratulations, Signorina Loretto. The blood test we did revealed the presence of the HCG hormone. You're pregnant!"

Abby hadn't believed it. Even though she'd wanted to be a surrogate mother and had done everything possible to make it happen, for the doctor to tell her the procedure had worked was like the first time she rode the Ferris wheel at a theme park. The bar had locked her in the chair, filling her with excitement. Then the wheel had turned and lifted her high in the air. That was the way she felt now, high in the air over Arancia. She didn't know if she wanted this descent to continue, but it was too late to get off. She had to go with it and just hang on. Only this time she wasn't on the Ferris wheel or the funicular and this ride would continue for the next thirty-odd weeks.

Abby hadn't been able to tell anyone about her pregnancy except Carolena. But she knew she could trust her best friend with her life, and that news hadn't been something she could keep to herself on that day of all days.

When she went to work on the day she'd found out she was pregnant, Abby visited with her gorgeous, fashionable Italian friend, who stopped traffic when she stepped outside. Carolena had worn her chestnut hair on top of her head in a loose knot. Though she didn't need glasses, she put on a pair with large frames to give her a more professional appearance.

She looked up when she saw Abby and smiled. "*Fantastico!* I've been needing a break from the Bonelli case."

"I'm so happy you said that because I've got something to tell you I can't hold in any longer. If I don't talk to you about it, I'll go crazy." She closed and locked the door behind her before sitting down in the chair opposite the desk.

"This has to be serious. You looked flushed. Have you settled the Giordano case already? Shall we break out the champagne?"

"Don't I wish! No, this has nothing to do with the law." She moved restlessly in the leather chair. In fact there'd be no champagne for her for the next nine months. "What I say to you can't ever leave this room."

Carolena's smile faded before she crossed herself.

Abby leaned forward. "I'm going to have a baby," she whispered.

Her friend's stunned expression said it all before she removed her glasses and walked around the desk in her fabulous designer sling-back high heels to hunker down in front of her. She shook her head. "Who?" was all she could manage to say.

The question was a legitimate one. Though Abby had been asked out by quite a few men since joining the firm, she hadn't accepted any dates. No on-site romances for her. Besides, she wanted to make her place in the firm and that meant studying when she wasn't in the office so she could stay on top of every case.

"Their Royal Highnesses."

Carolena's beautifully shaped dark brows met together in a frown. "You mean…as in…"

"Prince Vincenzo and Princess Michelina."

There was a palpable silence in the room. Then, "Abby—"

"I realize it's a lot to swallow."

A look of deep concern broke out on Carolena's expressive face. "But you—"

"I know what you're going to say," she broke in hurriedly. "It's true that I'll always love him for saving me from drowning, but that was eleven years ago when I was seventeen. Since then he has married and they've suffered through three miscarriages. The doctor suggested they look for a gestational surrogate mother for them."

"What?"

"His logic made total sense. Gestational surrogacy, unlike adoption, would allow both Vincenzo and Michelina to be genetically related to their child. Even better, they would be involved in the baby's conception and throughout the pregnancy, so they'd feel a total part of the whole experience."

"But you can't be a surrogate because you've never had a baby before."

"There are a few exceptions, and I'm one of them."

Carolena put a hand on Abby's arm. "So you just nominated yourself for the position without any thought of what it would really mean and threw yourself into the ring?" She sounded aghast at the idea.

Abby had hoped for a happier response from her friend. "Of course not. But I wasn't able to stop thinking about it. I even dreamed about it. The answer of how to repay him for saving my life came to me like a revelation. *A life for a life.*"

"Oh, Abby—despite the fact that you push men away, you're such a romantic! What if midway through the pregnancy you become deathly ill and it ruins your life? I can't even imagine how awful that would be."

"Nothing's going to happen to me. I've always been

healthy as a horse. I want to give them this gift. I didn't make the decision lightly. Though I had a crush on him from the time I was twelve, it had nothing to do with reality and I got over it after I found out he was already betrothed to Michelina."

Those famous last words she'd thrown out so recklessly had a choke hold on Abby now. She adored him, but had to hide her feelings if it killed her.

By the time she and Vincenzo had climbed in the limousine, she realized her due date was coming closer. In one regard she wanted it to get here as quickly as possible. But in another, she needed to hug the precious months left to her, because when it was over, she wouldn't see Vincenzo again. She couldn't bear the thought.

When Abby's eight-week checkup was over, Dr. De-Luca showed her into another consulting room, where she saw Vincenzo talking with the psychologist, Dr. Greco. Both men stood when she entered. The prince topped him by at least three inches.

Her vital signs had been in the normal range during her exam, but she doubted they were now. Vincenzo possessed an aura that had never made him look more princely. He wore a cream-colored suit with a silky brown sport shirt, the picture of royal affluence and casual sophistication no other man could pull off with the same elegance.

The balding doctor winked at her. "How is Signorina Loretto today, besides being pregnant?" She liked him a lot because he had a great sense of humor.

"Heavier."

Both men chuckled before they all sat down.

The doctor lounged back in his chair. "You do have a certain…how do you say it in English? A certain bloom?"

"That's as good an English term as I know of to cover what's really obvious. I actually prefer it to the Italian term *grassoccia*."

"No one would ever accuse you of looking chubby, my dear."

Vincenzo's black eyes had been playing over her and were smiling by now. The way he looked at her turned her insides to mush. She felt frumpy in the new maternity clothes she'd bought. This morning she'd chosen to wear a khaki skirt with an elastic waist and a short-sleeved black linen blouse she left loose fitting.

The outfit was dressy enough, yet comfortable for work. Her little belly had definitely enlarged, but Carolena said you wouldn't know it with the blouse hanging over the waist.

Dr. Greco leaned forward with a more serious expression. "A fundamental change in both your lives has occurred since you learned the embryo transfer was successful. We have a lot to talk about. One moment while I scroll to the notes I took the last time we were together."

Abby avoided looking at Vincenzo. She didn't know if she could discuss some of the things bothering her in front of the doctor. Up to the moment of Michelina's death, when she'd been through a grueling screening with so many tests, hormones and shots and felt like a scientific experiment, she'd thought she'd arrived at the second part of her journey. The first part had been the months of preparation leading up to that moment.

Abby recalled the smiles on the faces of the hopeful royal couple, yet she knew of their uncertainty that made them feel vulnerable. The three of them had seen the embryo in the incubator just before the transfer.

It was perfect and had been inserted in exactly the right place. The reproductive endocrinologist hugged Michelina and tears fell from her eyes. Vincenzo's eyes had misted over, too. Seeing their reaction, Abby's face had grown wet from moisture. The moment had been indescribable. From that time on, the four of them were a team working for the same goal.

For the eleven days while she'd waited for news one way or the other, Abby had tried to push away any thoughts of failure. She wanted to be an unwavering, constant source of encouragement and support.

When the shock that she was pregnant had worn off and she realized she was carrying their child, it didn't matter to her at all that the little baby growing inside of her wasn't genetically hers. Abby only felt supreme happiness for the couple who'd suffered too many miscarriages.

Especially *their* baby, who would one day be heir to the throne of the Principality of Arancia. Vincenzo's older sister, Gianna, was married to a count and lived in Italy. They hadn't had children yet. The honor of doing this service of love for the crown prince and his wife superseded any other considerations Abby might have had.

But her world had exploded when she'd learned of Michelina's sudden death. The news sent her on a third journey outside her universe of experience. Vincenzo had been tossed into that black void, too.

"Before you came in, Vincenzo told me about the meeting with you and his mother-in-law," said the doctor. "He knows she made you very uncomfortable and feels you should talk about it rather than keep it bottled up."

She bit her lip. "*Uncomfortable* isn't the right word. Though I had no idea the queen had such strong moral, ethical and religious reservations against it, my overall feeling was one of sadness for Vincenzo."

"He feels it goes deeper than that."

Abby glanced at Vincenzo. "In what way?"

The doctor nodded to him. "Go ahead."

Vincenzo had an alarming way of eyeing her frankly. "When we went out to dinner the other night, you weren't your usual self. Why was that?"

She prayed the blood wouldn't run to her face. "Months ago we decided to be as discreet as possible. Since your wife's death I've feared people would see us together and come to the wrong conclusion. But you already know that."

"The queen put that fear in you without coming right out and saying it, didn't she?"

This was a moment for brutal honesty. "Yes."

"Abby—our situation has changed, but my intention to go through this pregnancy with you is stronger than ever. You shouldn't have to feel alone in this. I intend to do all the things Michelina would have done with you and provide companionship. I don't want you to be afraid, even if people start to gossip about us."

She shuddered. "Your mother-in-law is terrified of scandal. I could see it in her eyes. It's evident that's why Michelina was afraid to tell her the truth. The other morning I sensed the queen's shock once she heard you'd saved my life, and that I'd lived on the palace grounds since the age of twelve.

"It wouldn't be much of a stretch for her to believe that not only am I after an inheritance, but that I'm after you. I even feared she believes I've been your mistress and that the baby isn't her grandchild."

"I *knew* that's what you were worried about the other night," Vincenzo whispered.

"I wish Michelina had talked to her mother before the decision was made to choose a surrogate, Your Highness."

"So do I. It grieves me that my wife was always intimidated by her and couldn't admit she hadn't told her mother first, but what's done is done and there's no going back."

Abby was in turmoil. "Vincenzo and Michelina have broken new royal ground with my help, Dr. Greco. Unfortunately it's ground that Queen Bianca isn't able to condone. I'm half-afraid she's going to demand that the pregnancy be…terminated." The thought sickened Abby to the point that she broke out in a cold sweat.

"Never," Vincenzo bit out fiercely. "She wouldn't go that far, not even in her mind, but she's going to have to deal with it since the time's coming when people will know you're the surrogate."

The doctor looked at both of them with concern. "Vincenzo is right. I think it's good you've already felt the fire by dealing with Michelina's mother first. To my knowledge no other royal couple in the known world has undergone the same procedure. The situation involving the two of you is an unprecedented case, but a wonderful one since it means preserving the royal line."

"Here's my dilemma." Vincenzo spoke up once more. "Before Michelina's death I'd planned to keep a lower profile around you, Abby, but that's impossible now and I can't have you feeling guilty. Of course we'll try to be careful, but only within reason. Otherwise I'll be worried about the stress on you and the baby."

"Vincenzo makes a valid point, Abby," the doctor inserted.

She lowered her head. "I know he's right. The moment I decided to go through with this, I realized it would be a risk, but I felt helping them was worth it. But with the princess gone…"

"Yes. She's gone, but you still need to keep that noble goal uppermost in your mind. One day soon you'll be free to live your own life again and the gossip will be a nine-day wonder. Do you have any other issues you'd like to discuss with me in this session?"

Yes. How did she keep her emotional distance from Vincenzo when he'd just stated that he intended to be fully involved with her?

"I can't think of any right now."

"You, Vincenzo?"

He shook his dark, handsome head. "Thank you for meeting with us. I'm sure we'll be talking to you again." Vincenzo got to his feet. "Abby needs to get back to work and so do I."

The three of them shook hands before they left his office and walked out of the building to the limousine. Abby's office wasn't that far away from the hospital. When the limo pulled up in front of the entrance, Vincenzo reached over to open the door for her.

"Have you made plans for the evening, Abby?"

"Yes," she lied. "Carolena and I are going to enjoy the festival before it ends."

"Good. Be careful not to tire yourself out."

She didn't dare ask him what he was doing tonight.

It was none of her business. How on earth was she going to get through seven more months of this?

Vincenzo watched until Abby hurried inside before he closed the door and told his driver to head for the palace. For the moment he had an important meeting with the minister of agriculture. That would keep him occupied until Abby got off work.

If she'd been telling the truth and had plans with her friend, then he was in for a night he'd rather not think about. But she didn't make a good liar. He'd known her too long. He had the strongest hunch she would go straight back to the palace after work and dig into one of her law cases. If he was right—and he would find out later—he'd take her for a walk along the surf.

Incredible to believe that the girl he'd saved from drowning eleven years ago had become a gorgeous woman in every sense of the word, *and* was carrying his child. Even though Michelina had been the biological mother, Abby was now the birth mother.

Though there'd been other candidates, the second he'd heard that Abby was one of them, his mind was made up on the spot. Because she'd always lived on the grounds and they'd developed a special bond, he knew her in all those important little ways you could never know about another person without having had that advantage.

Abby was smart, kind, polite, thoughtful, intelligent, fun. In fact, he knew that he would never have gone through with the surrogacy process if she hadn't been on the list. Michelina had been determined to go through with it because she was desperate to fix their marriage. After her incessant pleading, his guilt finally caused him to cave about turning to the procedure for the answer.

No matter how hard they'd tried, theirs had been a joyless union they'd undergone to perform a duty imposed by being born into royalty. He'd driven himself with work, she with her hobbies and horseback riding. Part of each month she spent time in Gemelli, riding with her friends. They had been counting on a child to bring happiness to their lives.

Thanks to the pregnant woman who'd just left the limo, his baby would be born in November. It would have been the miracle baby his arranged marriage had needed to survive. Now that he was alone, he needed that miracle more than ever. His eyes closed tightly. But he needed Abby, too...

CHAPTER FIVE

"Abby?"

"Yes, Bernardo?"

"You just received a message from Judge Mascotti's court. Your case for Signor Giordano has been put on the docket for June 4."

"So soon?"

"It surprised me, too."

"Wonderful. I'll call my client."

That kind of good news helped her get through the rest of the afternoon. At five-thirty Abby said good-night to Carolena, who was going out on a date with a friend of her cousin, and hurried out to the limousine. She needed to let go of any unwanted feeling of guilt for lying to Vincenzo over her plans for the evening.

Once she reached the palace, she walked to her suite with its exposure to the water. In her opinion, her new temporary home, set in the heart of the coastal city, was the jewel in the crown of the Principality of Arancia.

At a much younger age, Vincenzo had shown her around most of the palace and she'd adored the older parts. Nine weeks ago she'd been moved from her dad's apartment to the palace and installed in one of the renovated fourteenth-century rooms, with every convenience she could imagine. It thrilled her that Vincenzo had remembered this one was her favorite.

The maid had told her he'd had it filled with fresh flowers, just for her. When she heard those words Abby's eyes smarted, but she didn't dare let the tears come in front of the staff.

Her bedroom had a coffered ceiling and was painted in white with lemon walls up to the moldings. The color matched the lemons of the trees clumped with the orange trees in the gardens below. This paradise would be hers until the baby was born. Vincenzo had told her she had the run of the palace and grounds until then.

She'd marveled at his generosity, but then, he'd always been generous. Years earlier, when she'd mentioned that she wanted a bike to get around sometimes and hoped her parents would get her one for Christmas, he'd provided one for her the very next day.

They did a lot of bike riding on the extensive grounds and had races. He let her win sometimes. She wondered what the doctor would say if she went for a bike ride now. If he gave her permission, would Vincenzo join her? It was a heady thought, one she needed to squelch.

After a snack, Abby decided to take a swim in the pool at the back of the palace and told Angelina she wouldn't want dinner until later. She was supposed to get some exercise every day and preferred swimming to anything else in order to unwind.

Once she'd put her hair in a braid and pinned it to the top of her head, she threw on a beach robe over her bikini and headed out wearing thonged sandals. When she reached the patio, she noticed Piero Gabberino pulling weeds in the flower bed.

"Ciao, Piero!"

"*Ehi,* Abby!"

The chief gardener's nice-looking son, who would be getting married shortly, had always been friendly with her. They'd known each other for several years and usually chatted for a while when they saw each other.

When she'd found out he was going to college, she took an interest in his plans. Three weeks ago Saturday she'd invited him to bring his fiancée and have lunch with her on the patio. The young couple were so excited about the coming marriage, it was fun to be around them.

"Only a week until the wedding, right?"

He grinned. *"Sì."*

She removed her robe and got in the pool. The water felt good. She swam to the side so she could talk to Piero. "I'm very happy for you. Thank you for the invitation. I plan to come to the church to see you married." Both she and her father had been invited, but she didn't know if her dad would be able to take the time off.

Piero walked over to the edge of the pool and hunkered down. "Thank you again for the lunch. Isabella always wanted to come to the palace and see where I work."

"It's a beautiful place because you and your father's crew keep the grounds in exquisite condition."

"Grazie."

"Aren't you working a little late this evening?"

"I had classes all day today."

"I know what that's like. Have you and Isabella found an apartment yet?"

"Two days ago. One day soon you will have to come over for dinner."

"That would be lovely."

"*Buonasera,* Piero!"

At the sound of Vincenzo's deep voice, Abby's heart thudded. She flung herself around in the water at the same time Piero got to his feet.

"Your Highness! It's good to see you again. Welcome home."

"Thank you. You look well."

"So do you. May I take this moment now to tell you how sorry I am about the princess. We've all been very sad."

"I appreciate those kind words."

As long as Abby had known Vincenzo, he'd almost always gone swimming in the sea in the evenings and did his early-morning workouts in the pool. Now she'd been caught in the act of lying.

He looked incredible in a pair of black swim trunks with a towel thrown around his broad shoulders. Mediterranean Gods 101 could have used him for their model.

Vincenzo eyed both of them. "Don't let me disturb the two of you."

"I was just leaving. *Scusi,* Your Highness." He gave a slight bow to Vincenzo and walked back to the plot of flowers to get his things before leaving the patio.

Abby shoved off for the other side of the rectangular pool while she thought up an excuse why she hadn't gone out with Carolena. She heard a splash and in seconds Vincenzo's dark head emerged from the surface of the water next to her.

His unreadable black eyes trapped hers. "Why did you tell me you had plans with Carolena when it's obvious you wanted to rush home after work to be with Piero? My apologies if I interrupted something between the two of you. You both looked like you were enjoying yourselves."

Her heart fluttered out of rhythm. Coming from any other man, Abby could be forgiven for thinking he was jealous. But that was absurd.

"Before work was over, Carolena told me she'd been lined up with her cousin's friend, so we decided to do something tomorrow evening instead." That was partially a lie, too, but she would turn it into a truth if at all possible.

She could hear his brilliant wheels turning. "Have you and Piero been friends long?"

"Quite a few years. He speaks Mentonasc and has been a great teacher for me. I, in turn, have been coaching him in one of his first-year law classes, but he doesn't really need help."

His black brows lifted in surprise. "He's going to be an attorney?"

"That's been his hope since he was young. He has been influenced by his father to get a good education. Some kind of business law, probably. I've been helping him review appellate court decisions and analyze the judges' reasoning and findings. He's very bright."

Vincenzo looked stunned. "I'm impressed."

"Six months ago he got himself engaged and is going to be getting married next week. I met his fiancée the other day and we had lunch together out here. They've invited me to the wedding next week. I'm thrilled for them."

Vincenzo raked a hand through his wet black hair. "Apparently a lot has been going on around here, under my nose, that I've known nothing about."

"You have so much to do running the country. How could you possibly know everything? Don't forget I've lived on the grounds for years and am friends with everyone employed here. When I was young the gardeners helped me find my mom's cat, who went out prowling at night and never wanted to come home."

Vincenzo's smile was back, reminding her of what a sensational-looking male he was.

"Sometimes they brought me a tiny wounded animal or a bird with a broken wing to tend. Piero's father used to call me 'little nurse.'"

His gaze played over her features and hair. She saw a tenderness in his eyes she'd never noticed before. "All the same, I should have been more observant."

"Need I remind you that your royal nose has much greater worries, like dealing with your country's welfare?" He chuckled. "The word *multitask* could have been coined on your work ethic alone. Don't you remember the dead starling I found and you helped me plan a funeral for it?"

He nodded. "You were so broken up about it, I had to do something."

"It was a wonderful funeral." Her voice started to tremble. "You even said a prayer. I'll never forget. You said that some angels watched over the birds, but if they couldn't save them, then they helped take away the child's sorrow."

His black brows lifted. "I said that?"

"Yes. It was a great comfort to me." *You've always been a great comfort to me.*

"Your praise is misplaced, but like any man I admit to enjoying a little flattery."

"It's the truth. I have a scrapbook to prove it." Her confession was out before she could prevent it. Feeling herself go crimson, she did a somersault and swam to the deep end of the pool to cool down. When she came up gasping for air, he was right there, without a sign of being winded. If her heart didn't stop racing pretty soon, she was afraid she'd pass out. "Haven't you learned it's impolite to race a woman with a handicap, and win?"

His eyes grew shuttered. "Haven't you learned it's not nice to tease and then run?"

Touché.

"When am I going to see this scrapbook?"

Making a split-second decision, she said, "I plan to send it to you when your child is christened." She couldn't help searching his striking features for a moment. "The pictures showing you and your wife will be especially precious. I can promise that he or she will treasure it."

Abby heard his sharp intake of breath. "How long have you been making it?"

"Since soon after we arrived from the States."

"Clear back then?"

"Don't you know every girl grows up dreaming about palaces and princes and princesses? But my dream became real. I decided I would record everything so that one day I could show my own little girl or boy that I once lived a fairy-tale life.

"But now that you're going to have a little girl or boy, *they* should be the one in possession of it. The story of your life will mean everything in the world to them. If they're like me when I was young and poured over my parents' picture albums for hours and hours, they'll do the same thing."

Vincenzo was dumbfounded. Evening had crept over the palace, bringing out the purity of her bone structure, but he saw more than that. An inward beauty that radiated. It was that same innocent beauty he'd seen in her teens, but the added years had turned her into a breathtaking woman.

He wondered what she'd say if he told her that....

Of course he couldn't, but something earth-shattering was happening to him. As if he was coming awake from a hundred-year sleep. Vincenzo was starting to come alive from a different source, with feelings and emotions completely new to him. Not even his guilt could suppress them.

"I'm looking forward to that day, Abby."

"You're not the only one." But she said it with a charming smile. He liked her hair up in a braid. She wore it in all kinds of ways, each style intriguing.

"Shall we swim a couple of laps before we have dinner? When I talked to Angelina and she told me you hadn't eaten yet, I arranged for us to be served out here on the patio." While she was forming an answer he said, "I promise to let you set the pace."

"Thank you for taking pity on me." On that note, she started for the other side of the pool.

Vincenzo swam beside her, loving this alone time with her. There was no tension. A feeling of contentment stole through him. At the moment he was feeling guilty for *not* feeling guilty. He asked himself if he would feel this way if she weren't pregnant, but it wasn't a fair question. With Michelina gone, he naturally felt more protective toward Abby, who no longer had a female mentor to turn to for support.

To his surprise, he'd been disturbed to find her talking and laughing with Piero. *Why* had he felt that way? Was it the helicopter father coming out in him, as she'd suggested? Vincenzo frowned. Was he already becoming possessive?

Her comment about never finding a man who measured up to her father had been on his mind since they'd eaten at the mountain restaurant. He wondered if she'd ever been intimate with any of her boyfriends. If the answer was no, then in one respect he understood his mother-in-law's remark about the pregnancy being unnatural.

Just how would Vincenzo feel when Abby did get married, knowing she'd carried his child for nine months before she'd known another man? When she did get married one day—he had no doubt about that— how would the man she loved feel to know she'd given birth to Vincenzo's baby? Would that man feel robbed in some way?

His thoughts kept going. What if Vincenzo wanted to marry a woman who'd already given birth through surrogacy? It would mean she'd already gone through a whole history with some other man and his wife. Would that change the way he felt about her?

The more he pondered the subject, the more he couldn't answer his own questions.

While he succeeded in tying himself up in knots, Abby climbed the steps to leave the pool. For a moment he caught a side view of her lovely body. His heart clapped with force to see her stomach wasn't quite as flat as he remembered, but at this stage you wouldn't know she was pregnant. Dr. DeLuca had said that since this was her first pregnancy, it might be awhile.

That didn't matter. *Vincenzo knew.*

The day Abby had given him that pamphlet, he'd studied it and learned she would probably start showing by twelve weeks. Michelina had lost their three babies by that point, so he'd never seen his wife looking pregnant.

His excitement grew to imagine Abby in another month. Since he wasn't the most patient man, the waiting was going to be hard on him. And what about her? She was the one going through the travail that brought a woman close to death. Her patience had to be infinite.

He found himself asking the same question as the queen: What *did* Abby get out of this?

Vincenzo had listened to her explanation many times, but right now he was in a different place than he'd been at Christmas when they'd talked about surrogacy as an answer. His focus hadn't been the same back then. Now that he was no longer desperate for himself and Michelina, he had a hard time imagining this remarkable woman, who could have any man she wanted, being willing to go through this.

How did any surrogate mother who wasn't already a mother or who had never given birth leave the hospital and go back to her old life without experiencing changes, psychologically and emotionally? He could understand why it was illegal in many parts of the world for someone like Abby. He and Michelina must have been so blinded by their own unhappiness that they'd agreed to let Abby go through with this.

Though they'd discussed everything before the procedure, nothing had seemed quite real back then. Those same questions were haunting him now in new, profound ways. A fresh wave of guilt attacked him. He needed to explore his feelings in depth with Dr. Greco, because he was concerned for Abby's welfare. She was having to put off being with other men until the baby was born. That meant putting off any possible marriage. To his dismay, the thought of her getting married brought him no joy. What was wrong with him?

Abby put on her white beach robe over her green bikini and they sat down to dinner. "This cantaloupe is so sweet I can't believe it."

"I hear it's especially good for you."

"You're spoiling me, you know."

He gripped his water glass tighter. "That's the idea. You're doing something no one should expect you to do."

A wounded look entered her eyes. "I didn't *have* to do anything, Vincenzo. It was my choice."

"But you've never been pregnant before. My wife and I were entirely selfish."

Michelina because she'd wanted so much to have a child. Vincenzo because he'd wanted Abby to be the woman if they did decide to go through with it. The perfect storm…

After drinking the rest of his water, he darted her another glance. "Though I know you would never admit it to me, you've probably regretted your decision every day since the procedure was done."

She put down her fork. "Stop it, Vincenzo!" It pleased him she'd said his name again.

"You know the reason I did this and you couldn't be more wrong about my feelings now. Why don't we take Dr. Greco's advice and drop all the guilt? Let's agree that though this is an unprecedented case, it's a wonderful one that's going to give you a son or daughter. We need to keep that goal foremost in our minds."

Vincenzo sucked in a deep breath. "So be it! But I

have to tell you that you're the bravest, most courageous soul I've ever known."

"You mean after you. Let's not forget *you* were the one who dove into that cave looking for my body during the most ferocious storm I'd ever seen after moving to Arancia. It wasn't the men in the coast guard who'd performed that deed.

"Their first duty was to protect you. Instead they let you risk your life to save me. If Father hadn't been so devastated over losing Mother at the time, those men would have faced severe penalties, so I'd say we're equal."

There was no one like Abby when her back got up. "All right." He lifted his water glass.

"Truce?"

She did likewise. "Truce." They touched glasses.

After she drank a little and put her glass on the table, he could tell there was something else on her mind. "What were you going to say?"

"How did you know?" she asked, bemused.

"A feeling."

She was quiet for a moment. "Today a minor miracle occurred when I received word that Judge Mascotti is going to hear the Giordano case in less than a month. I was expecting it to be six at the earliest." She eyed him with blue eyes that sparkled with purple glints in the candlelight. "Who do you suppose was responsible?"

"I have no idea," he said in a deadpan voice.

"Liar." No one had ever dared call him that, but then, no one was like Abby. "I'm very grateful, you know. It's my biggest case so far with the firm."

"You've got a good one. My bet is on you to win it in the end."

"Please don't hold your breath."

He smiled. "In my line of work I'm used to doing it. Don't forget I have to face our constitutional assembly on a weekly basis, and they're *all* stars." Laughter bubbled out of her, but he noticed she'd drawn her beach robe closer around her. "It's cooling off, Abby. Since you have another workday tomorrow, I mustn't keep you up any longer."

She got up from the table before he could help her. "I've enjoyed the company and dinner very much. After your good deed in getting my law case heard sooner, I have to hope my side will prevail. *Buonanotte,* Vincenzo."

Her disappearance left him at a loss. As he walked swiftly to his apartment, Vincenzo phoned Marcello. "My mail included an invitation for the wedding of Luigi Gabberino's son. Can you give me the particulars?"

"Momento." Vincenzo headed for the bathroom to take a shower while he waited.

"Friday at four o'clock, San Pietro Church."

"Grazie. Put that date on my calendar. I intend to go."

"I'm afraid there's a conflict. You'll be in a meeting with the education minister at that time."

"I'll cut it short."

"Bene, Your Highness."

On Friday Abby left work at three-thirty in order to get to the church and be seated by four. She'd worn a new designer dress in Dresden-blue silk to the office. The top of the square-necked two-piece outfit shot with silver threads draped below the waistline. The sleeves were stylishly ruched above the elbow. On her feet she wore low-heeled silver sandals.

She'd caught her hair back in a twist with pins. Once she'd bid her latest client goodbye, she retouched her makeup before pulling the new floppy broad-brimmed hat with the silvery-blue rose from her closet. After putting it on, she grabbed her silver bag and left the office with a trail of colleagues gawking in her wake. Carolena had been with her when she'd bought the outfit, and now gave her the thumbs-up.

Outside the building she heard whistles and shouts of *bellissima* from the ever-appreciative male population of Arancia. She chuckled. What a gorgeous, sunny day for a wedding! There was a delightful breeze off the Mediterranean.

The limo wound through the streets until it came to a piazza fronting the church of San Pietro, where she was let out. Abby followed a group of people inside and found a seat in the assembled crowd of friends and extended family. She recognized several employees from the palace, and of course Piero's immediately family.

Before the Mass began, heads turned as a side door opened. When she saw Vincenzo enter surrounded by his bodyguards, she started to feel light-headed. The exquisitely groomed prince of Arancia wore a dove-gray suit. He was heartbreakingly handsome and took her breath away, along with everyone else's.

He sat off to the side. Piero's parents had to feel so honored. This was the second time Vincenzo had gone out of his way to perform a service that hadn't been on his agenda—the first, of course, being a word put in Judge Mascotti's ear to hasten Abby's court case hearing.

The prince was an amazingly thoughtful man. She'd

worked around a lot of men. No man of her acquaintance could touch him. Abby knew deep in her heart he was so grateful for her being willing to carry his baby, there wasn't enough he could do for her. It was something she would have to get used to. When he dedicated himself to a project, he went all out.

For the next hour Abby sat there eyeing him with covert glances while Piero and his bride took their vows. When the service was over, Vincenzo went out the side exit while she followed the crowd outside to the piazza to give the radiant couple a hug. But when she was ready to walk to her limousine, one of the security men touched her elbow.

"Signorina Loretto? If you would come with me, please."

With heart thumping, she followed him around the side of the church to another limousine, where she knew Vincenzo was waiting inside. The breeze was a little stronger now. As she started to climb in, she had to put her hand on her hat to keep it in place. At the same time, her skirt rode up her thighs. She fought madly with her other hand to push it down.

Vincenzo's dark eyes, filled with male admiration, missed nothing in the process, causing her to get a suffocating feeling in her chest. The hint of a smile hovered at the corners of his compelling mouth. After she sat down opposite him, he handed her the silver bag she'd accidentally dropped.

"Thank you," she said in a feverish whisper.

"Anyone could be forgiven for thinking *you* are the bride. That color is very becoming on you. We can't let such a stunning outfit go to waste. What is your pleasure?"

Her pleasure… She didn't dare think about that, let alone take him up on his offer.

"To be honest, it's been a long day. I'm anxious to get back to the palace and put my feet up. If that sounds ungracious, I don't mean for it to be."

"Then that's what we'll do." He let his driver know and the limo started to move out to the street. His arms rested along the back of the seat. He looked relaxed. "I enjoyed the wedding."

"So did I. Piero was beaming. I know he was a happy groom, but your presence made it the red-letter day in all their lives. That was very kind of you, Vincenzo."

"I have you to thank for reminding me of my duty. Now that it's over, we'll concentrate on taking care of you. When we get back to the palace we'll have dinner in your apartment and watch a movie I ordered."

Ordered? Her pulse raced. "I'm sure you have other things to do."

His black eyes glinted with a strange light. "Not tonight. It will feel good to relax. Tomorrow my father and I are leaving to visit my mother's sister in the French Savoie. We'll be attending another wedding and taking a vacation at the same time."

"That's right. Your father usually goes away this time of year."

He nodded. "I'm not sure how soon we'll be back, but I promise I'll be here for your June appointment with the doctor."

June… He'd be gone several weeks at least. She fought to keep her expression from showing her devastating disappointment.

The limo drove up to his private entrance to the palace. "I'll come to your apartment in a half hour, unless you need more time."

"Knowing that you have a healthy appetite, thirty minutes is probably all you should have to wait for dinner."

The flash of a satisfied white smile was the last thing she saw before he exited the limo. It stayed with her all the way to her suite. Her hands trembled as she removed her hat and put it on the closet shelf. Next came the dress and her shoes.

After Abby had put on jeans with an elastic waist band and a pink short-sleeved top, she redid her hair. While she fastened it with a tortoiseshell clip, she was assailed by the memory of Vincenzo's eyes as she'd climbed in the limo. They'd been alive and there was a throbbing moment when…

No. She was mistaken. The prince was a man, after all, and couldn't have helped looking while she was at a disadvantage. Furious with herself for ascribing more to the moment than was there, she lifted the phone to ring Angelina for her dinner tray, then thought the better of it. Vincenzo had made it clear he was orchestrating the rest of this evening.

If she wasn't careful, she could get used to this kind of attention. But once she'd had the baby, her association with the prince would be over. By November he could easily be involved with another woman, who had the right credentials for another marriage.

Her thoughts darted ahead to his trip with the king. Since Vincenzo had recently returned from a trip that had lasted weeks, she doubted he'd be accompanying his father because he needed another vacation.

In all probability there was someone the king and

his aunt wanted him to meet. With a baby on the way, he needed a suitable wife who was already situated at the palace to take over the duties of a mother the minute Abby delivered. But the thought of another woman being a mother to Abby's baby killed her.

This baby was Abby's baby. She couldn't possibly separate herself from it now. She'd been imagining the day she held it in her arms, the clothes she'd buy, the nursery she'd create. No other woman would love this baby as fiercely as the way Abby already did.

But Vincenzo was the father and he'd been born to fulfill his duties. One of them at the moment was to make certain Abby felt secure while she was pregnant with the next royal heir of Arancia. She knew better than to read anything more into what was going on. He was doing his best while trying to cope with the pain of his loss. There was only one way for her to handle this and keep her sanity at the same time.

He needs a friend, Abby. Be one to him.

A half hour later Vincenzo arrived at her apartment. He'd changed out of his suit into chinos and a polo shirt. He looked so fabulous, she tried not stare at him. He'd tucked a DVD under his arm. She flashed him her friendliest smile. "You're right on time."

"In the business I'm in, you have to be."

A quiet laugh escaped her lips. "Well, tonight you can forget business for once. Come right in and make yourself at home."

"If it's all right with you, I'll put this in the machine."

She closed the door after him and folded her arms. "Aren't you going to show me the cover?"

"I'd rather surprise you." In a minute he'd inserted it

so they could watch it on the living room couch when they were ready.

"All I have to offer you is soda from the fridge in the kitchen."

"I'll drink what you're drinking."

"It's boring lemonade."

"Sounds good."

She didn't call him a liar again. He was probably used to some kind of alcohol at the end of the day, but was going out of his way to make her comfortable. This man was spoiling her rotten.

"Excuse me while I get it." When she came out of the kitchen, she found him on her terrace leaning against the balustrade. "In the States we say 'a penny for them.'" She handed him a can.

He straightened and took it from her. "I'll give you one guess." He popped the lid and drank the contents in one go. Abby was thirsty, too, and followed suit, but could only drink half of hers before needing a breath.

"A name for your baby."

"It has already been picked, whether it's a boy or a girl. Actually, I was thinking about your plans after the baby's born," he said on a more serious note.

So had she… Since that terrible morning with the queen, she'd decided that living anywhere in Arancia wouldn't be a good idea after all. "You're giving me a complex, you know."

A frown marred his handsome features. "In what way?"

"You worry too much about everything, so maybe what I tell you will help. The other night my father came over and we had a long talk. Before Christmas, in fact, before I even knew you were looking for a surrogate,

Dad was planning to resign his position here and move back to the States. He says his assistant, Ernesto, is more than ready to take over."

Stillness enveloped Vincenzo for an overly long moment. "Does my father know about this?"

"Not yet. He plans to tell him soon. We have extended family in Rhode Island, where I was born."

"But your father has family here in Arancia, too."

"That's true, but he's been offered a position at a private firm there I know he will enjoy. He won't leave until after I have the baby. Though I had thoughts of living in Arancia and working at the firm with Carolena, I can't abide the idea of him being so far away. Therefore I'll be moving back with him and plan to study for the Rhode Island and New York bar exams. So you see? That's one worry you can cross off your long list."

During the quiet that followed, she heard a knock on the door. He moved before she did to answer it. Angelina had arrived with their dinner. Vincenzo thanked her and pushed the cart to the terrace, where they could sit to enjoy their meal while they looked out over the view.

Once they started eating, he focused his attention on her. "Are you close with family there?"

"We've all kept in touch. Mom took me for visits several times a year."

"I remember. The grounds seemed emptier then."

Abby wished he hadn't said that. Though it was nice to see family, she lived to get back to Vincenzo.

"After she died, Dad always sent me to stay with my mother's sister and her husband at Easter. I have a couple of fun cousins close to my age. It will be wonderful to live around all of them again. My aunt's a lot like my mom, so nice and kindhearted."

That part was the truth, as far as it went. These years in Arancia were a dream that had to end, but she wouldn't allow herself to think about leaving the country, about leaving *him*. Not yet.

"If you've finished," he said all of a sudden, "shall we go inside and start the movie?"

"Marvelous idea. I can't wait to see what you picked out. Something American and silly, I presume, like *Back to the Beach*."

A mysterious smile appeared to chase away his earlier somber look. She got up from the chair before he could help her and walked in the living room to turn it on.

CHAPTER SIX

ABBY'S REVELATION HAD put Vincenzo off the last of his dinner. He'd meant it when he'd told her he missed her presence during her vacations out of the country. Because of their situation, Abby had always been natural with him and treated him like a friend. No artifice. Though he'd been six years older, she'd been there in the background of his life for years. But when she went away next time, she wouldn't be returning.

The sense of loss was already hitting him. He was staggered by the depth of his feelings. When she'd opened the door to him awhile ago, he'd discovered her in yet another new maternity outfit. This time she wore flattering casual attire. Yet no matter how she played down her assets, nothing could disguise the fact that she was a very desirable woman.

Now that she was carrying his child, how could he not notice her or stop certain thoughts from creeping into his mind without his volition? Abby had become as precious to him as the little life growing inside of her.

Earlier, once he'd entered the church and scanned the guests, he'd spotted the hat and the face beneath it. For the rest of the ceremony he couldn't take his eyes off her. She'd lit up the interior like an exotic orchid among the greenery.

"My Little Chickadee?" The excitement in her voice was all he could have hoped for. She swung around to face him with a brilliant smile. "Trust you to manage getting hold of a copy of it. This was Mom's favorite Mae West film. W.C. Fields is in it, too. This movie is hilarious."

"While you stretch out on the couch and put your legs up, I'll sit in the chair with the ottoman."

"Vincenzo—I didn't literally mean I needed to do that. My feet aren't swollen yet!"

He took his place in the chair anyway. "From what I saw as you got in the limo, I couldn't detect any problem in that department, either, but as you reminded me a week ago, I'm only a man and don't have a clue about a woman."

While the film got underway, she curled up on the end of the couch. He saw her shoulders shaking with silent laughter. "You'll never let me live that down. Apparently you have a photographic memory. I bet Gianna could tell me what a maddening brother you were at times."

He grinned at her. "It's a good thing she's not here to reveal my secrets."

Abby flicked him a narrowed gaze. "Oh, I heard a few."

"Like what, for instance?"

"Like the time you and your friends brought some girls to the palace and sneaked them into the pool at three in the morning to go skinny-dipping. I know it's true because I heard about it from my father later. He'd been awakened in the middle of the night by some of the security men."

He spread his hands. "What can I say? My life has been an open book in more ways than one. Were you scandalized?"

"I was only fifteen at the time and wondered how any girl could be so daring."

"But not the guys?"

"No. It's in your nature, which has been written into your Roman mythology. Wasn't it the goddess Diana, Jupiter's favorite daughter, to whom he swore he wouldn't make her marry and allowed her to hunt by the light of the moon? She loved skinny-dipping, and naturally all the young men came to watch."

The laughter rolled out of Vincenzo. He couldn't help it.

Abby kept a straight face. "But sadly for them, when she caught them, she turned them into stags. Of course, that was centuries ago. Today it's the other way around. The teenaged girls are scandalized by prudes like me."

When he could find his voice, he said, "You mean I couldn't have talked you into it?"

"Not on your life!"

She could always make him laugh, and the film *was* hilarious. He'd been waiting for the famous line she'd impersonated. When it came, he realized Abby had sounded just like the legendary actress.

After the film ended, she got up and turned off the machine. "I wish I'd had an older brother. You and Gianna were lucky to grow up together. One day when you marry again, hopefully you'll be able to have another baby so your first one won't grow up to be an only child."

The thought of taking another wife sent a chill through him. He knew when his father had insisted Vincenzo accompany him on this next trip it had been motivated by an agenda that had little to do with the need for a vacation.

"Were you ever lonely, Abby?"

"Not in the sense you mean, because being the brightest light on my parents' horizon was my only reality. I knew nothing else. But when I think of you and Gianna, especially the two of you growing up in a royal household, I can see how great that would have been for you. She told me she went to bat for you when you got into trouble with your father. There's nothing like the power of sibling love."

With pure grace she curled her leg underneath her again and sat down. "Did you ever have to help her out of a spot?"

"Many times. She wanted money. When I didn't feel like carrying out some official function, I'd bribe her to do it for me."

Abby laughed. "At what cost?"

"Pocket money. Our parents kept us both on a strict allowance."

"Good for them! I always liked them, but that admission puts them on an even higher level in—"

Vincenzo's cell phone rang, breaking in on her. "Sorry." He pulled it out of his pocket and checked the caller ID. "Excuse me for a moment, Abby. I have to take this."

"Of course."

He moved to the terrace, out of earshot. *"Pronto?"*

"I'm sorry to disturb you, but the queen was insistent you call her back immediately."

"Do you have any idea why, Marcello?"

"No, except that she'd been talking to the king first."

He had an idea what this might be about. Something told him he needed to put out another fire, but first he needed to talk to his father. "I'll take care of it. *Grazie.*"

When he walked back inside, Abby was waiting for him near the front door. "Duty calls, right?" She'd given him no choice but to leave. "Thank you for this lovely and unexpected evening."

"I enjoyed it, too. Keep the DVD as a reminder of your mother," he said when she was about to hand it him.

"You're too generous, but I'll treasure it."

"That's the idea," he murmured.

She put a hand to her throat. "As soon as you came in from the terrace, I could tell by your face something was wrong. I hope it's nothing too serious."

If his hunch was right, then it *was* serious. But for once, this had nothing to do with Abby. He could thank the Roman gods for that, at least.

Too bad he couldn't get rid of a certain dangerous vision in his mind of joining Abby the Huntress in that forest pool and making love to her before her father discovered them and *he* turned Vincenzo into a stag.

He ground his teeth absently. "So do I, Abby. I'll see you at the clinic for your next appointment. Though I know you'll follow the doctor's orders, I have to say this anyway. Take meticulous care of yourself." June sounded an eternity away.

Her eyes had gone a smoky blue. "You, too, Your Highness. Your baby's going to need you."

Vincenzo turned from her before he couldn't and took off for the other region of the palace at a fast clip.

When he reached his apartment, he decided it wouldn't do any good to call his father first. Without hesitation he phoned Michelina's mother to get this over with.

"Thank you for returning my call, Vincenzo."

"Of course. How are you getting along, Bianca?"

"How do you think? My world has fallen apart. I didn't believe it could get worse until I talked with your father. He informed me you're going on vacation tomorrow to stay with the *duc de Chambery*. If you hadn't chosen Michelina, you would have married his granddaughter Odile, who's still single. That would be a humiliation for our family if you choose her now. I'm telling you I won't—"

"Bianca?" he broke in on her. He had it in his heart to feel sorry for this woman who was grieving over her daughter. "You don't need to say another word. I know exactly how Michelina felt about her. I never considered marriage to Odile and I'll make you a solemn vow now that I never will. Does that answer your question?"

Her weeping finally stopped and all he heard was sniffing. "But you'll take another bride."

He'd braced his back against the door to his den and closed his eyes. "To be frank with you, I don't plan on marrying again. When Father is no longer alive, I may step down so Gianna can take over the business of ruling Arancia. My first duty is going to be to Michelina's and my child."

Her gasp came over the phone loud and clear. "I don't believe you."

"Which part?" he bit out.

"You don't fool me. We both know the only reason why you'd give up the throne…"

Her insinuation was perfectly clear. She'd all but accused Abby of going after Vincenzo. He'd been waiting for her to start in on him. This was just the first volley.

He heard the click, severing their connection.

"Congratulations, Signorina Loretto. You show no problems so far. It means you've been following directions to the letter." Abby could thank Vincenzo for that. "How is the nausea?"

"I hardly ever notice it anymore."

"Good. Your measurements are fine. Be sure to keep your feet up for a little each day after work."

"I will. How big is the baby by now?"

"Um, three inches. You're growing."

"I know. I already prefer lying on my side."

The doctor smiled. "I'll let the prince know that at your sixteen-weeks' checkup we'll do an ultrasound, which should reveal the gender of that special baby."

Abby didn't know if Vincenzo wanted to be surprised and wait until after the baby was delivered, or if he was anxious to know right away. But it was his business, not hers.

"You can get dressed now and I'll see you in another month. Be sure you keep coming in on a weekly basis for your blood pressure check. I'll give Vincenzo the full report when he's back. He'll be delighted. As for Dr. Greco, he said for you to call him when the two of you can come in."

"Thank you, Doctor."

Abby put on her white sundress with the brown-trimmed white bolero top and left for the office. Her father had told her the king had returned to the palace three days ago. That meant Vincenzo was still in France.

With a woman who might possibly take Michelina's place one day?

Abby was used to him honoring every commitment to her. The fact that he hadn't come today shouldn't have mattered, but it did. She missed him and would be lying if she didn't admit that to herself.

The show-cause hearing at the court yesterday had persuaded the judge to hear the Giordano case in August. Abby was thrilled with the outcome and knew his decision had frustrated Signor Masala's attorney. She wanted to share the good news with Vincenzo and thank him, but it would have to wait.

She was starting to get a taste of what it would be like when he wasn't in her life anymore. Not liking that he'd become the focal point of her thoughts, she phoned her father after she got in the limo and invited him to a home-cooked dinner at her apartment that evening. She planned to fry chicken and make scones, the kind her mom always made. He loved them. But to her disappointment, he couldn't come until the following night.

Once she got to work, she invited Carolena to the palace to have dinner with her at the pool. Abby would lend her one of the bikinis she hadn't worn yet. Thankfully her friend was thrilled to be invited and they rode home together in the limo at the end of the day.

"Am I in heaven or what?"

They'd finished eating and had spent time in the pool. Now they were treading water. Abby laughed at her friend. "I've been asking myself that same question since we moved here years ago." She was tempted to tell Carolena her future plans, but thought the better of it until closer to the delivery date. "I think I'll do one more lap and then I'll be done for the night."

She pushed off, doing the backstroke. When she reached the other side and turned to hold on to the side, she saw blood and let out a small cry.

"What's wrong?" Carolena swam over to her. "Oh—you've got a nosebleed."

"I don't know why." She pinched her nose with her thumb and index finger.

"I'll get a towel."

Abby followed her to the steps and got out.

"Sit on the chair." She handed Abby her beach towel.

After a minute she said, "It's not stopping."

"Keep holding while I call your doctor. Is his number programmed in your cell phone?"

"Yes. Press three."

Angelina came out on the patio to clear the table, but let out an alarmed sound the second she saw the blood on the towel and hurried away.

By now Carolena was off the phone. "The doctor wants you to lean forward on the chair and keep pressing your nostrils together for ten or fifteen minutes. Breathe through your mouth. It should stop. Apparently pregnant women get nosebleeds, so not to worry. If it doesn't stop soon, we'll call him back."

"Okay." Before another minute passed, Vincenzo came running toward her. He was back!

"Abby—" Without hesitation he hunkered down next to her. The fear in his eyes was a revelation to her.

"I'm all right, Vincenzo. My nose started to bleed, but I think it has stopped now."

He reached for his cell phone. "I'm calling Dr. DeLuca."

"Carolena already contacted him for me. I'm fine, honestly!"

She removed the towel to show him the episode was over. Already she felt like a fraud.

"Don't move." He got up to get her beach robe and put it around her shoulders. His touch sent fingers of delight through her body. "It's cooler out here now."

"Thank you. I don't believe you've been introduced to my friend, Carolena Baretti. Carolena, this is His Royal Highness Prince Vincenzo."

"Thank heaven you were here for her, Signorina Baretti. I'm very pleased to meet you."

"The pleasure is mine, Your Highness. Dr. DeLuca said the increased blood flow with pregnancy sometimes produces nosebleeds. She's supposed to stay put for a few minutes so she won't get light-headed when she stands. He'll be relieved to know the bleeding has stopped."

"I'll call him and tell him right now."

While Vincenzo walked out of earshot to make the phone call, Carolena moved closer to Abby. Her brows lifted as she stared at her. "When he saw you holding that towel to your face, I thought he was going to have a heart attack."

"I know he was afraid something had happened to the baby."

Carolena shook her head. "From the look in his eyes, it wasn't the baby he was worried about," she whispered. "If a man ever looked at me like that…"

Abby's heart thudded against her ribs. "You're imagining things." But inwardly she was shaken by the look in his eyes. It was that same look he'd given her after she'd recovered on the boat that black day, as if she'd meant the world to him.

What a time for him to return from his trip! She looked an utter mess.

Vincenzo walked toward her. "If you feel all right, I'll help you get back to your apartment."

"I'm fine. Carolena will help me."

"We'll both help." The authority in his voice silenced her.

Together the three of them left the pool. Carolena brought all their things while Vincenzo stayed at Abby's side. When they reached her suite, her friend changed her clothes and announced she was leaving.

"I'll have a limousine waiting for you at the entrance, *Signorina*. Again, my thanks for your help."

"Abby's the best."

"So are you." Abby hugged her friend.

"Thanks for dinner. See you at work tomorrow."

The minute the door closed, Abby glanced at Vincenzo. "If you'll excuse me, I'll take a quick shower."

"Don't hurry on my account. I'm not going anywhere."

That fluttery sensation in her stomach had taken over again. It happened whenever he came near. She rushed into the bathroom and got busy making herself presentable once more. After drying her hair with a clean towel, she brushed it the best she could and put on a clean blouse and skirt.

The nosebleed had definitely stopped. Just one of the surprises brought on by the pregnancy. She couldn't complain. So far she'd been very lucky.

Again she found him out on the terrace, which was her favorite place, too, especially at night. He looked sensational in anything he wore. Tonight it was a silky blue shirt and khakis. "Did the doctor reassure you?"

He turned and put his hands on his hips, the ultimate male. "To a point. I'm much more relieved now that I see you walking around without further problem."

"Don't do it," she warned him.

Those black brows furrowed. "Do what?"

"Start feeling guilty again because I'm in this situation."

"If you want to know the stark, staring truth, guilt is the last thing on my mind. I'm worrying about the next time you get another one. What if Carolena hadn't been with you?"

"I had the usual nosebleed here and there growing up. They've always stopped on their own, as this one did tonight, even though she was with me. But if I'd been alone and needed help, I would have called out for Angelina. Don't forget that at work I'm never alone."

Her logic finally sank in and his frown disappeared. "I'm sorry I didn't make it back in time for our appointment with Dr. Greco. If I hadn't been detained, I would have been in the pool with you when this happened."

A thrill of forbidden excitement shot through her body to hear that.

"Everything's fine. We'll reschedule when it's convenient for you."

His dark gaze wandered over her. "Dr. DeLuca says you're in excellent health."

"You see?" She smiled.

"He's going to do an ultrasound on you next month."

"Is the helicopter daddy anxious to know if he's going to have a boy or a girl?"

"I'm not sure yet. For the moment all I care about is that you and the baby stay healthy."

"That's my prime concern, too. But maybe by then you'll have made up your mind and want to know if the kingdom can expect a prince or a princess."

"Maybe. Let's go back inside where it's warmer so you'll stay well."

When Abby had told her father that Vincenzo was a worrywart, he'd laughed his head off. If he could see them now...

She did his bidding and walked through to the kitchen, where she opened the fridge. He followed her. "Orange juice all right?" she asked.

"Sounds good."

Abby chuckled. "No, it doesn't. Why don't you have some wine from the cupboard? You look like it might do you some good."

"Soda is fine."

"A warrior to the end. That's you." She pulled out two cans and took them over to the table, where he helped her before sitting down. They popped their lids at the same time. The noise was so loud they both let out a laugh, the first she'd heard come from him tonight. A smiling Vincenzo was a glorious sight. "How was your trip?"

"Which one are you talking about?"

She almost choked on her drink. "You took two trips?"

He nodded. "I only flew in an hour ago from Gemelli."

Abby blinked. "I didn't realize you were going there."

"It wasn't on the schedule, but Bianca slipped on a stair in the palace and broke her hip."

"Oh, no—"

"Valentino phoned me after it happened. It was the day Father and I were scheduled to come home. We agreed I should fly to Gemelli to be with her."

Whatever Abby had been thinking about the reason for his absence, she'd been wrong and promised herself to stop speculating about anything to do with him from now on.

"Is she in terrible pain?"

"At first, but she's going to be fine with therapy. We had several long talks. If there can be any good in her getting hurt, it seems to have softened her somewhat in her attitude about the coming event. Despite her misgivings, the idea of a grandchild has taken hold."

"That's wonderful, Vincenzo."

"She's missing Michelina."

"Of course." Abby took another long drink. "You must be so relieved to be on better terms with her."

He stared at her through veiled eyes. "I am. But when Angelina told me about you—"

"You thought you were facing another crisis," she finished for him. "Well, as you can see, all is well. Did your father have a good vacation?"

Vincenzo finished off his soda before answering her. "No."

"I'm sorry to hear that."

"He brought his troubles on himself."

"Is he ill?"

"If only it were that simple."

"Vincenzo—" She didn't know whether to laugh or cry. "What a thing to say."

"Before I was betrothed, my parents arranged for me

to meet the princesses on their short list of candidates, carefully chosen by the extended family."

Abby lowered her head.

"It came down to two, Michelina Cavelli and Odile Levallier, the granddaughter of the *duc de Chambery*. Both were nice-looking at their age, but of the two, I preferred Michelina, who wasn't as headstrong or spoiled."

"I can't imagine being in your situation."

"When you're born into a royal family, it's just the way it is. You don't know anything else. If I'd had a different personality, perhaps I would have rebelled and run away. I was still a royal teenager at the time and knew I had years before I needed to think about getting married, so I didn't let it bother me too much."

Her head came up and she eyed him soberly. "Were you ever in love?"

"At least four times that I recall."

"You're serious."

"Deadly so. In fact it might have been seven or eight times."

Seven or eight?

"Those poor women who'd loved you, knowing they didn't stand a chance of becoming your wife. Did you spend time with Michelina over the years, too?"

"Some. When my father decided it was time for me to marry, I saw her more often. She had always been good-looking and smart. We enjoyed riding horses and playing tennis. She was a great athlete, and loved the water. I could see myself married to her."

"When did you actually fall in love with her?"

He cocked his head. "Would it shock you if I told you never?"

Never?

Shaken to the core, Abby got up from the table and put their cans in the wastebasket.

"I can see that I have."

She whirled around. "But she loved you so much—"

Quiet surrounded them before he nodded. "Now you're disillusioned."

Abby leaned against the counter so she wouldn't fall down. "The loving way you treated her, no one would ever have guessed."

He got up from the table and walked over to her. "Except Michelina, her mother, my parents and now you... We both wanted a baby to make our marriage work."

She couldn't believe it had never worked, not in the sense he meant. Talk about a shocking revelation....

So *that* was the real reason they'd gone so far as to find a surrogate and flaunt convention. It explained Michelina's desperation and her decision not to tell the queen until it was too late to stop it. No wonder Bianca feared another woman coming into Vincenzo's life. The pieces of the puzzle were starting to come together. She could hardly breathe.

"Obviously we were willing to do anything. Again we were presented with a short list. This time it had the names and histories of the women available and suitable to carry our child."

She lifted pleading eyes to him. "Will you tell me the truth about something, Vincenzo?" Her voice throbbed. "Did Michelina want me?"

"Of course. She'd always liked you. She said you had a wonderful sense of humor and found you charming. When she learned you were on that list of possible surrogates who'd passed all the physical tests, like me she was surprised, but happy, too. Our choice was unanimous."

Unable to be this close to him, she left the kitchen for the living room and sat down on the end of the couch. He again chose the chair with the ottoman. They were like an old married couple sitting around before they went to bed.

Abby wished that particular thought hadn't entered her mind. With Vincenzo's revelation, the world as she'd known it had changed, and nothing would ever be the same again. All these years and he hadn't been in love with his wife? He'd been in love seven or eight times, but they didn't count because they weren't royal. She needed to move the conversation onto another subject.

"You were telling me about your father."

Vincenzo let out a sigh. "He wants me to marry again before the baby is born." He came out with it bluntly, rocking her world once more.

"In the beginning Odile was his first choice, only because of his close association with the *duc*. It would be advantageous to both our countries. She hasn't married yet and he feels she would make a fine mother. If she's there from the moment the baby is born, then she'll bond with it."

Abby sucked in her breath. "Does Odile still care for you?" It was a stupid question. The fact that she was still single was glaring proof, but she'd had to say it.

"She thinks she does, but that's because no one else has come along yet whom her grandfather finds suitable. I told Father I couldn't possibly marry Odile because I don't have the slightest feeling for her."

Unable to stand it, she jumped up from the couch.

"This is like a chess game, moving kings and queens around without any regard for human feeling!"

One black brow lifted. "That's where you're wrong. My mother-in-law certainly has a lot of feelings on the subject."

"She knows why you went to France?"

He sat forward. "Every royal household has its spies. That's why she phoned me before I left to tell me she wouldn't stand for it if I ended up marrying Odile. Michelina had been frightened I'd choose Odile over her in the first place."

Incredible. "What did you tell the queen?"

"That there was no chance of it because I don't plan to marry again. For once I'm going to do what my heart dictates and be a good father to my child, period."

Abby started trembling. "I'm sure she didn't believe you." Abby didn't believe it either. He was too young to live out the rest of his life alone. But if he had to marry another royal he didn't love...

"No, but it doesn't matter, because I've made my decision."

"Don't you have to be married to be king?"

"That has been the tradition over the centuries, but Father's still very much alive. If the time comes when someone else must rule, my sister will do it. So in answer to your question, *that's* how my father's trip went. Why don't we get onto another subject and talk about your court case? How did it go?"

She sat back down, still trying to get her head around everything he'd told her. "You know very well how it went. The judge had it put on his calendar for mid-August."

"Excellent. That relieves some of your stress, which

can only be good for the baby. What other cases are you dealing with?"

"I don't know. I—I can't think right now," Abby stammered. She honestly couldn't.

"Let's watch a little television. There's usually a movie on this time of night." He got up from the chair and reached for the remote on the coffee table.

"You don't need to stay with me, Vincenzo. The doctor assured you I'm all right. I know you must be exhausted after being in Gemelli. Please go."

A fierce look marred his features. "You want me to?"

A small gasp escaped. She'd offended him again. "Of course not. It's just that I don't want you to feel you have to babysit me."

"There's nothing I'd rather do. Everything I care about is in this room, and I've been away for weeks."

Shaken again by his honesty, Abby felt his frustration and understood it before he turned on the TV and sat back down again. One glance and she saw that the prince was a channel grazer. Nothing seemed to suit him. On impulse she got up from the couch.

"I'll be right back. I've got something for you." She made a stop at the bathroom, a frequent habit these days. Then she went to the bedroom and pulled her thick scrapbook out of the bottom dresser drawer. She'd had the leather cover engraved in gold letters: *The Prince of Arancia.* She hoped this might brighten his mood.

"Here." She walked over to him. "I'll trade you this for the remote."

He eyed her in surprise. When he got a look at the cover, he let out an exclamation. "I thought this was going to be a gift for the christening."

"I've changed my mind." Abby had compassion for

him and his father, who wanted his son to be happily married and was trying to make it happen in the only way he could think of as king. "You need to see what an impact you've made on the life of your subjects."

Maybe this album would make Vincenzo realize what an important man he was. To live out his life alone wasn't natural or healthy.

"I know the court has a historian who records everything, but this is more personal, with some of my own photos and articles I've found interesting from various magazines and newspapers coming from the U.S. Dad's been receiving the Stateside news for years and I read everything right along with him."

From the moment Vincenzo opened the cover, he went away from her mentally. While she watched the news, he turned page after page, thoughtfully perusing each one. No sound came out of him for at least an hour.

Eventually he closed it and looked over at her. "For the first time in my life, I know what it feels like to have your life flash before your eyes. I don't know what to say, Abby. I'm speechless."

"You're probably tired from viewing all the good works you've done over the years. I hope you realize you've *never* received negative press. Do you have any idea what a great accomplishment that is?"

He studied her as if he'd never seen her before. "I hope *you* realize I've never received a gift like this. You've touched me beyond my ability to express," he said in a husky voice she felt all the way to her toes.

"I'm glad if you're pleased. I consider it an honor to be a friend of yours, and an even greater honor to be the person you and Michelina chose to carry your child. Only a few more months before he or she is here."

She had the impression he wasn't listening to her. "All these photos of yours. I wasn't aware you'd taken them."

"While I was darting around on the grounds with my little camera, I took a lot of pictures and sometimes you were there."

"You got me on my motorcycle!"

"If you have a boy, he'll be thrilled to find out you didn't always behave with perfect decorum. I daresay he'll love it that you were a daredevil. The skinny-dipping I missed, because I had to be in bed and asleep by eleven."

Low laughter rumbled out of him. "I can be thankful your father was the head of security and made sure his daughter minded him."

She smiled. "Do you think you'll be a strict father if you have a girl?"

He got up from the chair and put the album on the coffee table before staring at her. "Probably."

"But since kindness is part of your nature, she won't mind."

He rubbed the back of his neck, looking tired. "Have you had any feelings yet whether you might be having a boy or a girl, Abby? I understand some women instinctively know."

"I've heard that, too, but since I'm not the mother, that's not going to happen to me." Secretly she didn't want him to know how involved she really was with this baby and that she thought about it all the time. "However, there's no law that says the father can't feel inspiration about his own unborn child."

He shook his head. "No indication yet."

"Well, you've got a month before there's the possibility of your finding out. That is, if you want to."

"If it's a girl, Michelina wanted to name her Julietta after her grandmother on her mother's side."

"That's beautiful. And if it's a boy?"

Their gazes held for a moment. "Maximilliano, after three kings in the Di Laurentis line. I'll call him Max."

"I love that name!" she cried. "We had a wonderful Irish setter named Max. He died before we moved here."

Vincenzo looked surprised. "I didn't know that. Why didn't your father get another one when you settled in your apartment?"

"The loss was so great, neither he nor Mom could think about getting another one. They kept saying maybe one day, but that moment never came. Did your family have a pet?"

He nodded. "Several, but by my later teens I was gone so much, my mother was the one who took care of them and they worshipped her."

"That's sweet."

"Whether I have a boy or a girl, I'll make certain they grow up with a dog. It's important."

"I couldn't agree more. Whether you've had a good or bad day, they're always there for you and so loving. My cousin and I liked little creatures. I once kept a cockatoo, a turtle, a snake and a hamster. When each of them died—not all at the same time, of course," she said with a laugh, "Max helped me get through their funerals. Daddy used to say the best psychiatrist is a puppy licking your face."

"Abby..." There was a world of warmth when he said her name. "No wonder Piero's father called you the little nurse."

"It's a good thing he didn't get together with my father to compare notes. If you got him alone, Daddy would tell you I probably killed them all off without meaning to."

She loved the sound of his laughter so much, Abby never wanted it to stop. But for the sake of her sanity and her heart, it was imperative he leave. Quickly she got up from the couch and handed him the scrapbook.

"This is yours to keep. You once saved my life, and now you're taking such good care of me, my thanks will never be enough. Now it's time someone took care of you. Please don't be mad at me if I tell you to go to bed. You look exhausted." She walked to the door and opened it. If he didn't leave, she was on the verge of begging him to stay the night.

"Good night, Your Highness."

In the weeks that followed, Vincenzo made certain his schedule was packed so tight with work he wouldn't be tempted to spend every free moment at Abby's apartment. Though he phoned her every morning before she went to work to know how she felt, he stayed away from her.

The night she'd given him the album, she'd shown him the door before he was ready to leave. When he'd told her the true situation that had existed between him and Michelina, there'd been a definite shift in the universe. He didn't regret his decision to tell her. At this point in the pregnancy, they shared an intimacy that demanded she understand what his marriage had been like so there'd be honesty between them.

The day of the ultrasound was here. His greatest concern was the health of the baby. If something was wrong, then he'd deal with it. Vincenzo had gone back and forth in his mind on the subject of gender and finally decided he didn't want to know. That way both sides of his family would have to go on speculating until the delivery. As for himself, he preferred to be surprised.

He had the limousine pulled around to his private entrance. When Abby appeared in a kelly-green dress with flowing sleeves and a high waist, he lost his breath for a moment. She was finally looking pregnant and more beautiful than she knew with her silvery-gold hair upswept and caught with a comb.

Dr. DeLuca met them in his office first and smiled. "This is the big day. Are you ready for it?"

"It's very exciting," Abby answered. Though she seemed calm, Vincenzo knew she had to be nervous.

"Will you come in to watch the ultrasound, Vincenzo?"

"Yes!"

Abby looked stunned. "You really want to?"

Vincenzo caught her blue gaze. "I've been waiting for this from the moment we found out you were pregnant."

"I—I'm excited, too," she stammered, rather breathlessly, he thought.

"Excellent," the doctor said. "If you'll come this way with me. It won't take long."

They followed him through another door to the ultrasound room. The doctor told Vincenzo to sit at the side of the bed while Abby lay down. His heart picked up speed to realize this moment had come. He didn't intend to miss a second of this whole process.

Abby's face had blushed when he'd said yes. He knew she'd been trying her hardest to keep her professional distance, but at this point in the pregnancy that was impossible. Having a baby was an intimate experience and she'd never been "just a surrogate" to him.

Over the last few months she'd come to be his whole world. It was miraculous that a sonogram could see inside her gorgeous body, where his baby was growing. The body he'd once rescued from the sea. How could he have known that one day she'd carry his child? He couldn't think about anything else.

Michelina was the mother of his child, but right now his focus was on Abby while the doctor put special gel on her stomach. For several nights he'd had trouble sleeping while his mind thought of all the things that might be wrong with the baby.

She shared a searching glance with Vincenzo as the doctor moved the transducer around her belly. Suddenly they both heard a heartbeat coming from the monitor. The doctor pointed to the screen. "There's your baby. The heart sounds perfect."

"Oh, Vincenzo—our baby! There it is!" In the moment of truth, her guard had come down, thrilling him with her honesty. As for himself, he couldn't believe what he was seeing and reached for her hand. She squeezed it hard. "It looks like it's praying."

The doctor nodded with a smile. "Nice size, coming along beautifully. No abnormalities I can see. So far everything looks good. This test can't detect all birth defects, but it's a wonderful diagnostic tool and tells me the pregnancy and your baby are both on the right track."

Relief poured off Vincenzo in waves. He looked into her tear-filled eyes. Without conscious thought he leaned over and kissed her mouth. "You're a wonder, Abby," he whispered. "You're giving me the world."

"I'm so thankful everything's all right."

The doctor cleared his throat. "Do you two want to know the gender?"

"That's up to Vincenzo," she said first.

He'd already made up his mind. "I'd rather wait and be surprised."

"Very well. Here are some pictures for you to keep." The doctor explained what Vincenzo was seeing, but he didn't have to, because the shape of the baby was self-evident and filled him with awe. If Michelina were here, the tears would be overflowing. "The fetus is four and half inches long and developing well."

Vincenzo put them in his jacket pocket. "Doctor? How's Abby?"

He removed his glasses. "As you can see, she's fine. No more nosebleeds?" She shook her head. "I'd say Abby is in perfect health. If she continues to do what I told her and rest a little more often after her swims, she should get through this pregnancy in great shape."

That was all Vincenzo wanted to hear, though it didn't take away his guilt that she was risking her life to give him this baby. "Thank you, Dr. DeLuca."

After the older man left the room, Abby got up off the table to fix her dress. "Can you believe it? Our baby's fine."

"I'm glad to hear you say *our* baby. It is our baby now, Abby. And I'm overjoyed to know you're fine, too." He got up from the chair. "This calls for a major celebration." As they walked out of the hospital to the waiting limo, he said, "After work, we're leaving for a weekend aboard the yacht. The doctor wants you to rest and swim and do whatever you like. I'll let you decide our destination once we leave port."

She looked startled. "How can you get away?"

"Very easily."

Once inside the limo, she turned to him. "Vincenzo? Do you think this would be wise?"

A dark frown broke out on his face, erasing his earlier happiness. "Obviously you don't."

"When I tell my father where we're going, he'll tell me it's not a good idea. Already he's talking about our move back to the States. I can tell he's getting nervous about you and me spending any more time together that isn't absolutely necessary."

Vincenzo's jaw hardened. "Has he spoken to my father yet about leaving?"

"Yes. Last night."

That was news to Vincenzo. "How did he take it?"

"He wanted to know the reasons and asked him about our extended family back home."

"Was my father upset?"

"No. He said he'd been expecting it for some time."

Vincenzo grimaced. "Then he didn't try to dissuade your father from leaving."

"No, and we both know why." Her voice trembled. "You and I have shared a unique relationship for many years. The baby's on the way and Michelina is gone. Guilio wants you to take a wife ASAP."

Vincenzo's dark head reared. "Father knows my feelings on the subject. I'm not planning to get married again and am already looking into finding a full-time nanny to help me with the baby."

"You're serious—"

His mouth tightened. "Do you think I would make that up? If so, then you don't know me at all."

"I don't think Guilio has any idea you mean it. The situation is even worse than I'd feared," she muttered.

"What situation?"

"You know exactly what I'm talking about. The only reason I felt all right about becoming a surrogate was because you and Michelina were a team. But she's not here anymore and *I* am."

He sat forward. "I still don't understand you."

"Yes, you do, even if you won't admit it."

"Admit what?"

"You and I have shared a unique relationship over the years. With Michelina gone and me carrying your child, our friendship is now suspect. The fact that your father isn't begging Dad to stay on tells me it will please him once we've left Arancia for good. He wants you to take Odile on the yacht, not me."

"You haven't been listening to me," he ground out.

Her heart thudded harder, because she could feel how upset he'd become. "Vincenzo, you're in a very rocky place right now and grabbing at what is easy and familiar because I've always been around. But you're not thinking straight. For us to go on the yacht could spell disaster. That's why I'm not going with you."

He said nothing while her guilt was warring with her heart, but her guilt won. "Your wife has only been gone a few months. Of course you haven't been able to figure out your future yet. You're in a state of limbo and will be until the baby is born."

"Have you finished?" came his icy question.

"Not quite yet." As long as she'd been this brave, she needed to get it all said. When she felt her lips, they still tingled from Vincenzo's warm kiss. She'd felt it to the very marrow of her bones. If the doctor hadn't been in the room, she would have kissed him back and never stopped.

"If you recall, Michelina was the one who wanted me to live at the palace, but without her there, it will be better if I move back home with Dad until I have the baby." It was true she and Vincenzo felt too comfortable together. To her chagrin she knew his visits and plans involving her were a distraction that kept him from doing some of his normal functions. All of it needed to stop. A change of residence was the key.

His next comment surprised her. "I was going to suggest it after we got back from our cruise."

"I'm glad we're in agreement about that. I'll still be living on the grounds and can get room service whenever I want. Living with my father will put the kind of distance needed to ease the king's mind." To ease her own mind.

Abby had been thinking of the baby as *their* baby. When he'd kissed her after the sonogram, it had felt so right. She couldn't delude herself any longer. Abby was painfully in love with Vincenzo and felt as if his baby was her baby, too.

"In that case I'll ask some of my security people to move your things back this evening."

"I don't have anything except my clothes, really."

They'd reached the law firm. Vincenzo opened the door for her. She stepped outside, aware that the good news from the ultrasound had been swallowed up in the tension that had plagued them since Michelina's death.

"I'll see you this evening, Abby. Take care."

* * *

After putting in a full day's work, Vincenzo grabbed his phone and left for a run in the palace gym to work off his nervous energy. After a heavy workout, he returned to his suite to shower and shave. His phone rang while he was putting on a polo shirt over cargo pants. He'd asked the sentry guard to alert him when Abby got home from work.

Moving fast, he reached the door to her suite before she did. He wanted to catch her off guard. The second she came around the corner and saw him she stopped, causing the fetching green dress to wrap around her long legs for a moment.

"H-How long have you been waiting here?" Her voice faltered.

"Not more than a minute. I'll help you get packed and we'll have a last dinner here on your terrace. In a little while some of the security men will be here to take your things over."

"No, Vincenzo. I—"

"No?"

She looked conflicted. "What I meant to say is that I'm virtually halfway through this pregnancy and everything has gone fine so far. You don't need to wait on me hand and foot anymore!"

"I *want* to. There *is* a difference, you know. Since you're the only person on this planet who's going to make my dreams come true, would you deny me the privilege of showing my gratitude?"

"But you do it constantly."

He sucked in his breath. "Three-quarters of the time I've been out of the country or occupied with business, so that argument won't wash. All you have to do is tell me that you don't want my company and I'll stay away."

Her eyes flashed purple sparks. "I've always enjoyed your company, but—"

"But what?" he demanded.

"We talked about it in the limo. For the time being, it's best if you and I stay away from each other."

"Best for you, or for me?"

"Best for everyone! From the beginning we knew there'd be gossip. With Michelina's death everything has changed and I'm sure the king is wary of it. You have to know that, Vincenzo." Damn if she wasn't speaking truth. "My going back to live with Father will quiet a situation that's building, but you shouldn't be here helping."

"We've already covered that ground."

"And we'll keep covering it for as long as I'm underfoot here or on the royal yacht!" she cried.

"You *do* have a temper." He smiled. "This is the first time I've ever seen it."

Her face filled with color. "I…didn't mean to snap at you."

He gave an elegant shrug of his shoulders. "Instead of us standing around arguing, why don't you open the door and we'll get started on moving you—baggage and all—out of sight."

She drew closer to him. "Be reasonable."

"I'm offering my services to help. What's more reasonable than that?"

"Because it's not your job!"

The only person who'd ever dared talk to him like this was his father. Abby was even more alluring when she showed this side of her. "What do you think my job is? To sit on my golden throne all day long and order my subjects to fetch and carry for me?"

"Yes!"

But the minute she said it, he could tell she was embarrassed and he burst into laughter that filled the hallway. In another second she started laughing with him. "You're outrageous, Vincenzo."

"My mother used to tell me the same thing. Come on and let me in. After a workout in my golden gym, I'm dying for a cold lemonade."

"The door's open," she said in a quiet voice. "I only lock it at night, but there's really no need to do it, because you've assigned bodyguards who are as far away as my shadow."

CHAPTER SEVEN

VINCENZO OPENED THE door and waited for Abby to pass before he entered. But when he saw the sway of her hips, he had to fight the urge to wrap her in his arms and pull her body into him.

Never in his marriage with Michelina, let alone with the other women in his earlier years, had he known such an intense attack of desire, and without the slightest hint of provocation on Abby's part. She'd done nothing to bring out this response in him.

Somewhere along the way his feelings for her as a friend had turned into something entirely different. Perhaps it was the knowledge that she was leaving the palace tonight that had unleashed the carnal side of his nature. Maybe it was the reality of the baby now that he had the pictures in his possession, knowing it lived inside her body.

Her father was a red-blooded man who'd probably warned her ages ago not to go out on the yacht with him. Vincenzo's own father, a man with several quiet affairs in his background, had no doubt made it easy for Abby's father to leave his service to be certain no misstep was taken.

Vincenzo got it. He got it in spades. But the ache and

longing for her had grown so acute, it actually frightened him.

While she was in her bedroom, he phoned the kitchen to have some sandwiches and salad brought up to the room. "This is Signorina Loretto's last evening in the palace. Tonight she's moving back to Signor Loretto's apartment on the grounds. You'll be delivering her meals there from now on when she requests them."

"Very good, Your Highness."

Having quieted that source of gossip for the moment, Vincenzo hung up and went looking for Abby. "I ordered some sandwiches to be brought. While we're waiting, what can I do to help?"

She had several suitcases on the bed and had already emptied her dresser drawers. "Well…there's not much to take. I left most of my things at Dad's. Maybe if you would empty my CDs and DVDs from the entertainment center. I'll clean out the things in the den myself. The men will have to bring some boxes to pack all my books and Michelina's paintings." She handed him an empty shoulder bag.

She had an impressive collection of operas, from *Madame Butterfly* to *Tosca*. Her choice of movies was as varied as the different traits of her personality. He packed all but one of them and went back to the bedroom. "You enjoyed this?"

Abby glanced at the cover. "*24?* I absolutely love that series. Have you seen it?"

"Yes, and I found it riveting from beginning to end."

Her eyes exploded with light. "Me, too! Did you see the series about the signing of the peace accord?" He nodded. "That was my favorite. Even my father thought it was good, and that's saying a lot considering the kind of work he's in. He only picked apart half of the things in it that bothered him."

A chuckle escaped Vincenzo's lips. "Shall we watch a few episodes of it tonight while we eat and direct traffic?"

"That sounds wonderful."

"Bene."

"Oh—someone's knocking."

"I'll get it."

He opened the door and set the dinner tray on the coffee table.

After she'd emptied the bathroom of her cosmetics, she started on the den. Abby worked fast and it didn't take long. "There!" She came back in the living room. "It's done. Now all your poor slaves can move everything to Dad's."

With a smile he told her to sit in the chair and put her feet up on the ottoman. It pleased him that he got no argument out of her. With a flick of the switch, he sat back on the couch and they began watching *24*.

Again it gratified him that she was hungry and ate her sandwich with more relish than usual. He'd been afraid their little scuffle in the hall had put her off her food, but it seemed that wasn't the case.

The thought came into his head that she was probably excited to live with her father again and enjoy his company. Which left Vincenzo nowhere.

He craved Abby's company. During his trip to France she was all he ever thought about. To his surprise, it wasn't because of the baby. Perhaps in the beginning the two had seemed inseparable, but no longer.

Abby was her own entity. Lovely, desirable. Her companionship brought him nothing but pleasure.

"Don't you think the queen is fantastic in this series? She was the perfect person to be cast in that part. How could the king want that other woman when he had a wife like her?" Abby was glued to the set. Vincenzo didn't think her remark was prompted by any other thought than the story itself, but it pressed his guilt button.

In his own way he'd been faithful to Michelina, but it hadn't been passionate love. This need for Abby had only come full force recently. His amorous feelings for her had crept up on him without his being aware.

"She's very beautiful in an exotic way," Vincenzo agreed, but his mind was elsewhere.

"How would it be to have been born that exotically beautiful? I can't even imagine it."

He slanted her a glance. "You have your own attributes. There's only one Abby Loretto."

"What a gentleman you are, Vincenzo. No wonder your subjects adore you."

"Abby—"

"No, no." She sat up straight. "Let me finish. All you have to do is look through that scrapbook again to see it."

A burst of anger flared inside him for his impossible situation.

"If you're trying to convince me to continue playing the role I was born to in life, it's not working. I'm no longer a baby who happened to be the child of a king. I've grown into a man with a man's needs. If I've shocked you once again, I'm sorry."

"I'm not a fool," she said quietly. "I can understand why you balk at the idea of marrying someone you don't love, even if it is your royal duty. After your experience with Michelina, it makes more sense than ever. But I can't believe that someday a woman with a royal background won't come along who sweeps you off your feet so you can take over for your father."

The program had ended. Abby got up from the chair to take the disk out of the machine and put it in the shoulder bag with the others.

He eyed her moodily. "Perhaps that miracle will occur. But we're getting ahead of ourselves. At this point, the birth of our child is the only event of importance in my life. It's all I can think about."

"That event isn't far off now."

No... He had less than six months before she left for the States. Getting to his feet he said, "The men should be here shortly. Come with me. If you're up to a walk, I'll escort you back to your old stomping grounds."

A happy laugh, like one from childhood, came out of her. "That sounds like a plan. I ate an extra sandwich half. The doctor would say that's a no-no. Otherwise at my next appointment I'll weigh in like—"

"Don't say it," he warned her. "I prefer my own vision of you."

She was turned away from him so he couldn't see her reaction. "I'll leave a note to tell them everything is here in the living room ready to go."

Vincenzo waited, then led her down another hall outside her apartment that came out at the side of the palace. They passed various staff as they walked down the steps and out the doors into an early evening.

July could be hot, but the breeze off the Mediterranean kept them cool enough to be comfortable. He'd crossed these grounds hundreds of times before, and many of those times with Abby. But this was different.

If he wasn't fearful of giving her a minor heart attack, he'd reach for her hand and hold it tight while they strolled through the gardens. Her father's apartment was in one of the outbuildings erected in the same style and structure as the palace. At one time it had housed certain members of the staff, but that was a century ago and it had since been renovated.

On impulse he stopped by a bed of hydrangea shrubs in full bloom to pick some flowers. "These are for you." He put them in her arms. "The petals are the color of your eyes. Not blue, not lavender, just somewhere in between."

"Their scent is heavenly." She buried her face in them, then lifted her head. "Thank you," she whispered. "You have no idea how many times over the years I've longed to pick these. Mother called them mop heads. These were her favorite flower and color."

"Maybe it's because she was reminded of them every time she looked into her only baby's eyes." Abby now averted them. "Abby, was there a reason your parents didn't have more children?"

She nodded. "Mom and Dad had me five years after they were married, because he'd been in the military. Two years later they decided to get pregnant again, but by that time Dad had been shot while on duty and it turned out he'd been rendered sterile. They weren't keen on adopting right away. I think it's one of the reasons they decided to move to Arancia, where they could make new memories."

Vincenzo was aghast. "I didn't know. Your father was so devastated when he lost her. I'll never forget."

"No. They were very much in love, but they had a great life all the same."

"And they had you." He was beginning to understand why she and her father were so close.

"Their inability to increase the family size was probably another motivating reason for my wanting to be a surrogate for you and Michelina. It's crazy, isn't it? So many women and men, whether in wedlock or not, seem to have little difficulty producing offspring while others…" Abby didn't finish the rest. She didn't have to.

They continued walking until they reached the apartment where she would live until the baby came. She left him long enough to put the flowers in water and bring the vase into the living room. He watched her look around after she'd set it on the coffee table.

This was the first time Vincenzo had been inside Carlo's suite. Family pictures were spread everywhere. He saw books and magazines her father must have read.

"Is it good to be home, Abby?"

She turned to him. "Yes and no. The apartment at the palace has been like home to me for quite a while. Both Dad and I can be semireclusive without meaning to be. We're both insatiable readers and like our privacy on occasion. He's going to have to put up with me invading his space again."

"Oh, I think he can handle it." Vincenzo happened to know her father had been on a countdown to get Abby out of the country from the time Michelina had died. "I'll stay until the men arrive with your things."

Abby sat down on one of the love seats, eyeing him with some anxiety. "I hope you didn't go to too much trouble to get the yacht ready."

"My father pays the captain a good salary to make certain it's able to sail at any time."

She shook her head. "I don't mean the money."

He let out a sigh. "I know you didn't. Frankly, the only person put out is yours truly, because I had my heart set on taking you to Barcaggio, on the northern tip of Corsica."

"I've never been there. You think I'm not disappointed, too?"

Abby sounded as though she meant it. Her response went a long way toward calming the savage beast within him.

"With your love of history, you'd find it fascinating. They had a unique warning system, with sixty guard towers dating from the fifteenth century, to keep the island safe. At least three towers in sight of each other would light fires to give a warning signal of pirates approaching. The Tower of Barcaggio is one of the best conserved and the water around it is clear like the tropics."

"Don't tell me anything more or I'll go into a deep depression."

A rap on the door prevented him from responding. He was glad the men had come. The sooner they left, the sooner he could be alone with her for a while longer. "I'll answer it."

For the next few minutes, a line of security people walked in with bags and boxes. Vincenzo helped to carry some of her law books into the library. What he saw on the desk gave him an idea. After he'd thanked them and they'd left, he called to Abby.

"Is there something wrong?" She hurried in, sounding a little out of breath.

"I think I've found a way we can be together for meals without leaving our suites."

She looked at him with those fabulous eyes. "How?"

"We'll coordinate our meals for the same time every evening and talk on Skype while we eat. That way I can check on you and know if you're lying when you tell me you're feeling fine."

Her lips twitched. "That works both ways. I'll know if you're in a mood."

"Exactly. Is it a deal?"

"Be serious, Vincenzo."

His heart beat skidded off the charts. "When I get back to my apartment, I'll Skype you to make sure everything's working properly."

"You don't mean every night?"

"Why not? Whether I'm away on business, out of the country or in the palace, we both have to stop for food, and we're usually alone. At the end of a hectic day, I'd rather unwind with you than anyone else. It'll save me having to go through Angelina to find out your condition for the day. Shall we say seven?"

"That'll last about two minutes before you're called away to something you can't get out of."

He decided he'd better leave before her father showed up. Together they walked to the entrance of the apartment. "Shall we find out? How about we give this a thirty-day trial? That should keep the gossips quiet. Whoever misses will have to face the consequences."

Amusement lit up her eyes. "You're on, but a prince has so many commitments, methinks *you'll* be the one who will wish you hadn't started this."

Vincenzo opened the door. "Don't count on it. I'll be seeing you as soon as I get back to my apartment." He glanced at his watch. "Say, twenty minutes?"

"I won't believe it till I see you."

With that challenge, he left at a run for the quick trip

back to his suite. There was more than one way to storm the citadel for the rest of her pregnancy without physically touching her. He didn't dare touch her.

It disturbed him that though he'd been in a loveless marriage, he could fall for another woman this fast. He was actually shocked by the strength of his feelings. To get into a relationship was one thing, but for Abby to be the woman, Vincenzo needed to slow down so he wouldn't alarm her. He knew she was attracted to him. It wasn't something she could hide, but she never let herself go.

Because of her control, he had to hold back, but they couldn't exist teetering on the brink much longer. Thanks to cybertechnology, he'd found a way to assuage some of his guilt. Without others knowing, he could be with her every night for as long as he wanted to satisfy his need to see and talk to her while he focused on the baby.

Vincenzo intended to be a good father, but he was struggling with the fact that he'd fallen for the woman who was carrying his child. What did that say about him?

Abby hurriedly put away her clothes and got settled as best she could before heading for the library. Passing through the living room, she picked up the vase of flowers and carried it with her.

After putting it on the desk, she sat down at her dad's computer, ready to answer Vincenzo's call. The big screen rather than her laptop screen would be perfect to see him, *if* he did make contact. She didn't doubt his good intentions, but she knew from her father that the prince followed a tight schedule, one that often ran late into the evenings.

In her heart she knew the decision to move home had been the right one, but when Vincenzo had walked out the door a little while ago, a feeling of desolation swept through her. Her move from the palace had marked the end of the third journey. Now she was embarking on the fourth into the unknown and had the impression it would try her mettle.

She'd lost Michelina, who'd provided the interference. Now it was all on Vincenzo to support her, but he'd made the wise decision to stay at a distance. So had she, yet already she felt herself in free fall.

Trust that clever mind of his to dream up Skyping as a way to stay in touch without distressing their fathers or the queen. As she was coming to find out, Vincenzo's resourcefulness knew no bounds.

Unable to resist, she leaned over to smell the hydrangeas. She'd never see one again without remembering how he'd just stopped and picked an armload for her.

The way to a woman's heart… Vincenzo knew them all, she admitted to herself in an honest moment. He was in there so tightly, she was dying from the ache. There'd never be room for anyone else. The video-call tone rang out, making her jump.

"Good evening, Abby." She'd put the speaker on full volume to make certain she could hear him. The sound of his deep, velvety voice brought her out of her trance-like state.

His looks went beyond handsome. Adrenaline rushed through her veins. "Good evening, Your Highness."

"You've become very formal since I left you."

"I've got stage fright." It was the truth. No one

in Arancia would believe what she was doing, and with whom.

"Our connection is good. We should have no problem communicating tomorrow evening."

"I might have one problem with the time. Dad is going to be home early for a dinner I'm cooking. Would you mind if we said eight-thirty?"

"I'll make a note on my agenda," he teased.

She smiled. "This is fun, Vincenzo."

"It's not the same as being with you in person, but I'm not complaining. Would you answer a question for me?"

"If I can."

"Did Dr. DeLuca let you know the gender of the baby?"

Her lungs froze. "No. He wanted to obey your wishes. I think you're wise not to know yet. Then your father and the queen would either be planning on a future king or future princess. This way everyone's still in the dark."

He chuckled. "I love the way you think, especially when you read my mind so easily. However, there is one thing I'm curious about. You never talk about the baby."

Pain stabbed at her heart. "I've been taking Dr. Greco's advice—don't think about the actual baby too much. Better to stay focused on taking care of yourself rather than dwelling on a child that won't be yours."

His face sobered. "How's that advice working out for you?"

She took a deep breath. "I'm finding it's very hard to carry out. I have to admit that if you hadn't asked me that question just now, I would know you had a stone for a heart."

"Abby," his voice grated, "you've accepted to do the impossible for me. You wouldn't be human if you weren't thinking about the baby day and night."

"You're right. During the talks I had with you and Michelina before I underwent the procedure, I made a decision to be like the postman who delivers the mail without knowing what's inside the letters.

"If a postman were to open one, he'd probably be so affected he would never make it to the next destination. Getting the ultrasound today was a lot like opening that first letter. I can't not think about the baby, whether it's a boy or a girl, if it will look like you or Michelina or someone else in your families."

Vincenzo turned solemn. "I've told you before, but I'll say it again. I'm in awe of you, Abby. You've taken on a weight too heavy to bear."

"You took on a weight, too. Not every man would trust a stranger with the life of his unborn child."

"You're no stranger," he answered in a smoky tone.

"You know what I mean."

"I don't think you know what *I* mean. You were never a stranger to me. A child in the beginning, of course, but from the beginning always a friend. I feel like I've known you all my life. It seemed a natural thing that you became our baby's surrogate mother."

She moistened her lips. "Depending on when the baby decides to come, we could be halfway home right now." Abby didn't want to think about the big event because of what it would mean. The thought of permanent separation was killing her. "Have you bought any things for the baby yet?"

"I'm glad you brought that up. In a few days I'm

going to go shopping and would like your help to set up the well-furnished nursery."

He couldn't know how his comment thrilled her. "I'd love to be involved."

"I'll send you pictures online and we'll decide on things together."

"Do you know where you're putting the nursery?"

"Either in my apartment or the room down the hall next to it."

"What did Michelina want?"

"We never got that far in our thinking. Her concerns over telling Bianca about the pregnancy overshadowed the fun."

Of course. "Well, it's fun to think about it now. If it's in your apartment, you'll have a nanny coming and going out of your inner sanctum." His low chuckle thrilled her. "When you're up all hours of the night with a baby with colic, will you be glad it's near at hand or not?"

"I'll have to think on that one."

"While you do that, what's on your schedule for tomorrow?"

"You really don't want to know."

"Why don't you let *me* decide?"

His smile was wicked. "Remember that you asked. First I'll do a workout in the pool when I get up, then I'll get dressed and eat breakfast with my father, who will tell me what's on his mind. I'll scan a dozen or so newspapers on certain situations in the world.

"At ten I'll visit the Esposito social enterprise to meet the staff and disadvantaged young people working on a building project at Esposito Ricci.

"At eleven-thirty I'll meet representatives of the San

Giovani Churches Trust, the National Churches Trust and restoration workers at Gallo-Conti.

"At noon I'll meet with the different faith communities at Gravina, where I'll be served lunch.

"At one-thirty, in my capacity as president of business, I'll visit the Hotel Domenico, which has been participating in my initiative to promote the meet-and-greet program in all the hotels. I'll visit the shop, which has been created in the meet-and-greet center, and chat with locals.

"At ten to three, as patron of the Toffoli Association, I'll meet staff and residents working at San Lucca Hospital. At four I'll meet pupils and staff at Chiatti Endowed Schools, where I'll tour the school hall and chapel. The pupils have prepared a brief performance for me.

"At ten to five I'll meet local community groups at the town hall in Cozza, as well as some members of the town council.

"At five-thirty, as president and founder of the Prince's Trust, I'll meet with young people who have participated in programs run by the trust, particularly the team program at the Moreno Hotel in Lanz."

Abby tried to take it in, but couldn't. "You made that up."

He crossed himself. "I swear I didn't."

"You mean that's all? That's it? You didn't have time to ride around in your made-for-the-prince sports car?" she exclaimed. "You're right, Vincenzo. I really didn't want to know and never want to think about it again."

Coming over the Skype, his laughter was so infectious she laughed until she had tears, which was how her father found her when he walked in the den. He could see Vincenzo in all his glory on the screen.

"Abby? Why aren't you talking?"

Her father had leaned over to smell the hydrangeas. "I have company."

Vincenzo didn't blink an eye. "Tell your father good evening."

"I will. *Buonanotte,* Your Highness."

She turned off the Skype. Nervous, she looked over at her dad, who had the strangest look on his face.

"Guilio told me his son has always been perfectly behaved. I wonder what could have happened to him."

Abby got up from the desk, needing to think of something quick. "He's going to be a father."

Carlo gave her a hug. "That must be the reason. Welcome home, sweetheart."

CHAPTER EIGHT

REPORTERS BESIEGED ABBY as she and Signor Giordano came out of the Palazzo di Giustizia in downtown Arancia. She'd won the case for him and it meant some big changes for the country's trade policies. Judge Mascotti had summoned her to the bench after announcing his ruling.

"I realize the palace was interested in this case, but I want you to know I made my decision based on the merits you presented."

Abby couldn't have been more pleased to hear those words.

For court she'd pulled her hair back to her nape and used pins to hold a few coils in place.

She'd worn a navy designer maternity outfit with a smart white jacket. The dress draped from a high waistline and fell to the knee. Her bump seemed quite big to her already, but the jacket camouflaged it well. On her feet she wore strappy white sandals.

Mid-August meant she was into her twenty-third week of pregnancy. Two days ago she'd had her first episode of Braxton-Hicks contractions, but the doctor said it was normal because her body was getting ready.

When Vincenzo found out, he had a talk with Dr. De-Luca and they both decided she should quit work.

Abby wasn't ready to stay home yet. Without work to do she'd go crazy, but she'd made an agreement in the beginning and had to honor it. When she got back to her office there was a celebration with champagne, not only because this case was important to their firm, but because it was her last day at work.

Everyone thought she was going back to the States, so she let them think it. Carolena poured white grape juice into her champagne glass when no one was look-ing. That was how she got through the party. If some of them realized she was pregnant, no one said anything.

After Skyping with Vincenzo every night from the start, except for the night she'd gone to the hospital about her false contractions, she told Carolena to Skype her at the apartment. Until the birth of the baby, Abby planned to do research for her friend to help pass the time. Carolena had a backlog of work and had gone crazy over the idea.

They drank to their plan and Abby left the office in brighter spirits than before. She walked out to the limo pretty much depleted energywise after her court appear-ance. Once settled inside, she rested her head against the back of the seat and closed her eyes, still thinking about what the judge had said to her.

She worked hard on every case, but that one had spe-cial meaning because it would benefit Arancia. After listening to Vincenzo's schedule for one day, she real-ized he'd spent his whole adult life promoting the wel-fare of his country. It felt good to know she'd made a tiny contribution toward his goals.

"Signorina?" She opened her eyes to discover they'd

arrived at the harbor. "Your presence is requested aboard the yacht. If you'll step this way, please."

Her heart thundered in her chest as she climbed out and walked with a security man up the gangplank into the gleaming white royal craft. Angelina was there to meet her.

"The palace heard of your victory in court and wishes to honor you with an overnight cruise. A few of your personal things are on board. Come with me and I'll show you to your cabin. Your orders are to relax, swim, eat and wander the deck at will."

"Thanks, Angelina," she murmured, too overcome to manage any more words and followed her. Strange as it was, this meant she'd miss her nightly conversation with Vincenzo. How crazy was that, when anyone else would be jumping out of their skin with joy at such a privilege?

But she'd lived on the palace grounds for years and inside the palace for four months of that time. She'd learned that if Vincenzo wasn't there, it didn't matter if the whole place was paved in gold. Since the judge's ruling, she'd been living to talk to him about everything tonight. Now she'd have to wait until tomorrow night.

"Is there anything else I can do for you?" Angelina asked from the doorway. The separate cabins were on the main deck, with a glorious view of the sea.

"I'm fine, thanks. Right now I just want to lie down. It's been a long day." She checked her watch. Five to six.

"Of course. If you need something, pick up the phone and the person on the other end will contact me. There's food and drink already on the table for you."

She nodded and closed the door after her. The queen-size bed looked good. After closing the shutters over the windows, Abby went to the bathroom, then removed her jacket and sandals. She ate half her club sandwich and some fruit salad before walking over to the bed. She'd undress all the way later. For the moment she was too tired to take off the sleeveless dress before she simply lay down to close her eyes for a little while.

The last thing Abby remembered before she lost consciousness was the movement of the yacht. When she heard someone calling her name, she thought it was the prince talking to her through Skype. She stirred.

"Vincenzo?"

"I'm right here."

"Oh, good. I wanted to talk to you and was afraid we wouldn't be able to until tomorrow night." But as she sat up in the semidark room, she realized something wasn't right. Abby wasn't at the desk. She was on the yacht and there was Vincenzo standing right in front of her in jeans and a sport shirt.

Her pulse raced. "You're here! I mean, you're *really* here."

"I knocked, but you didn't hear me, so I came in the room to check up on you. You didn't eat a lot of the dinner Angelina brought in."

"I was too tired to eat very much when I reached the room." Abby's hair had come unpinned and fell around her shoulders. "How did you get here?"

"I flew aboard on the helicopter. Are you all right?"

No. She wasn't! Abby hadn't seen him in person in about six weeks. The shock was too much and she was totally disoriented.

"Abby?" he prodded.

"Yes," she said too loudly, sounding cross. He was

much too close. She smoothed the hair out of her eyes. "You're not supposed to be here."

"Don't get up," he admonished gently, but she felt at a disadvantage sitting there and stood up anyway. "You're the loser in our contest, remember? This is the penalty I've chosen to inflict, so you're stuck with me until morning."

Her body couldn't stop trembling. "I confess I didn't think you could stick to it."

"Is that all you have to say?"

She'd been caught off guard and didn't know if she could handle this. A whole night together? "What do you want me to say?"

"That you're happy to see me."

"Well, of course I am." But the words came out grouchy.

"You really do look pregnant now. Will you let me feel you?"

If he'd shot her, she couldn't have been more astonished. That's why he kept standing there? It was a perfectly understandable request. It was his baby, after all. But this was one time when she didn't know what to do. To say no to him didn't seem right. But to say yes...

On instinct she reached for his hand and put it on her bump, to make it easier for both of them. It wasn't as if he hadn't touched her before. Heavens, he'd saved her life. She'd sobbed in his arms.

But there had been a whole new situation since then. The warmth of his fingers seeped through the material of her dress, sending a charge of electricity through her body. She held her breath while he explored.

"Have you felt it move?" he asked in a husky voice.

"I've had quickenings, kind of like flutters. At first I

wasn't sure. They only started a few days ago. But when I lay down a few hours ago, I felt a definite movement and knew it wasn't hunger pains."

"It's miraculous, isn't it?" His face was so close to hers, she could feel his breath on her cheek. He kept feeling, shaping his hand against her swollen belly. "I'm glad you're through working and can stay home, where you and the baby are safe."

She bowed her head. "No place is perfectly safe, Vincenzo."

"True, but you were on television today in front of the courthouse. I saw all those steps and a vision of you falling. It ruined the segment for me."

"Signor Giordano had hold of my arm."

"I noticed. He's recently divorced from his wife."

How did Vincenzo know that? But the minute she asked herself the question, she realized how foolish she was. He always checked out everything she did and everyone she worked with.

"I found him very nice and very committed to his fast-track proposal."

"Has he asked you to go out with him?"

Why did Vincenzo want to know? It couldn't be of any importance to him. "He did when he put me in the limo."

His hand stopped roving. "What did you tell him?"

"What I told everyone at my goodbye party. I'm moving back to the States." If she said it long and hard enough, she'd believe it, but his tension heightened. Being barefoot, Abby felt shorter next to his well-honed physique. She took the opportunity to ease away from him before turning on the switch that lit the lamps on either side of the bed.

He gazed at her across the expanse. "Are you still exhausted?"

No. His exploration of her belly had brought her senses alive and no doubt had raised her blood pressure. If he was asking her if she wanted to go up on deck and enjoy the night, the answer was yes. But she could hear her father saying, "I wouldn't advise it."

They'd both crossed a line tonight. His wish to feel the baby was one thing, but she'd sensed his desire for her. Since her own desire for him had been steadily growing for months, there was no point in denying its existence. Once you felt its power and knew what it was, all the excuses in the world couldn't take that knowledge away. Could you die of guilt? She wondered…

But to give in to it to satisfy a carnal urge would cheapen the gift. She'd told the queen this was a sacred trust. So she smiled at him.

"Maybe not exhausted, but pleasantly tired. I need a shower and then plan to turn in. Why don't we have breakfast in the morning on deck and enjoy a swim? That I would love." *Keep him away from you, Abby.*

"We'll be along the coast of Corsica at dawn. If you're up by seven-thirty, you'll see the water at its clearest."

Part of her had been hoping he'd tell her he didn't want her to go to bed yet, but he was a highly principled man and had made a promise to get her safely through this experience. "I'll set my alarm for that time and join you."

"Good night, then." As Vincenzo turned to leave she called his name.

"Thank you for this unexpected surprise."

"You won the court case and deserve a treat. Everyone in the country will benefit."

"Thank you. But I'm talking about more than a night on this fabulous yacht. I want to thank you for our nightly video sessions. I looked forward to every one of them."

His brows lifted. "They're not over."

"I'm so glad to hear that."

"They've saved my life, too, Abby." On that confession, he left her cabin and shut the door.

To read more into those words would be Abby's downfall. They were both waiting out this pregnancy on tenterhooks in a cage no one else could see. It was an unnatural time under the most unnatural circumstances a prince and a commoner could be in. The closer they got to the delivery date, the more amazed she was that she and Vincenzo had made things work this far.

During the early-morning hours, the sun burned a hole through clouds over the Mediterranean. The ray of light penetrated the turquoise water near the guard tower he'd told her about. Abby had thrown on a beach robe and leaned over the yacht's railing to see how far down it went, causing her braid to dangle.

Vincenzo had done several dives and wore his black trunks, so she could see his hard-muscled body clearly. The dramatically rugged landscape continued underwater in the form of more mountains, canyons, needles, peaks and rocky masses. He clung to some huge rocks below the waterline, then moved downward until he was almost out of sight.

Though he swam like a fish, she was nervous until she saw him come up for air. Abby wished she'd brought a camera to capture him on film, but when she'd left the courthouse yesterday, she could never have imagined where she'd end up.

"I'm envious of you!" she shouted to him. Even though it was August, she'd bet the water was cold this morning, but he seemed impervious to any discomfort.

"One day soon you'll be able to do this," he called back to her.

Not this. Not here. Not with him.

"Is there anything dangerous lurking down there?"

"Only a big white."

"Vincenzo!"

A grin appeared on his striking face. With his black hair slicked back, he was the stuff women's fantasies were made of. "Is breakfast ready?"

She giggled. "Have I told you how funny you are sometimes? You know very well your food is always ready!"

"Well, I'm starving!"

"So am I!"

He swam with expertise to the transom of the fifty-two-foot luxury yacht and came aboard. In a minute they were seated around the pool being served a fantastic meal. Once they'd eaten, Abby took off her robe to sunbathe for a little while. Their loungers were placed side by side. Talk about heaven!

The yacht was moving again, this time around the island. By tomorrow evening her idyll would be over, but she refused to think about that yet.

After the intimacy they'd shared last night when he'd reached out to feel the baby, she decided it didn't matter that he could see her pregnant with only her bikini on. Those black eyes slid over her from time to time, but he never made her feel uncomfortable.

The deck steward brought them reading material in case they wanted it. Vincenzo propped himself on one elbow to scan the newspaper. "You made the front page yesterday. I quote, 'A new star has risen in the legal firmament of Arancia.

"'One might take her for a film star, but Signorina Abigail Loretto, a stunning blonde with the law firm of Faustino, Ruggeri, Duomo and Tonelli, has a brain and pulled off a coup for import trade in Judge Mascotti's court that had the attorney for Signor Masala already filing an appeal.'"

Vincenzo handed it to her so she could have a look. "Have I told you how proud I am of you?"

Her body filled with warmth that had nothing to do with the sun. "Am I lying here on the royal yacht being treated like a princess by none other than His Royal Highness?"

"I think we need to start a scrapbook for you."

"It will be a pitiful one, since I quit work yesterday. This was it. My one meteoric rise to fame that came and went in a flash. I hope it's all right with you if I help do research for Carolena at the apartment."

"Your life is your own, Abby. My only concern is that you keep your stress level to a minimum, for your sake as well as the baby's."

"Agreed."

His eyes played over her. "You're picking up a lot of sun, but it's hard to feel it with the breeze."

"You're right. I'll cover up in a minute."

"Abby—" She could tell he had something serious on his mind.

"What is it?"

"When you hear what I have to tell you, it will cause you some stress, but it has to be said."

"Go on."

"We've told Gianna about the situation."

Alarmed, she sat up in the lounger and reached for the beach towel to throw over her. "How long has she known?"

"My sister saw you on the evening news. Since she's known you for years, too, she phoned me about it. I was with Father when her call came through. Now that you've been identified to the public, so to speak, we decided it was time she knew about the baby in case word got out and she hadn't heard it first."

"That makes sense, Vincenzo. She'd be hurt if you hadn't told her." Her heart pounded so hard, it was painful. "Did she have the same reaction as your mother-in-law?"

He sat up to talk. "No. She thinks it's terribly modern of all of us—her exact words—but couldn't believe Michelina would go along with the idea."

"Because of the queen?"

"No," he murmured, sounding far away. Abby supposed she knew the real answer deep down.

"Then it was because *I'm* the surrogate."

Vincenzo's silence for the next minute told its own tale. "It's nothing personal," he said in a grating voice.

"I know that."

"She's afraid of how it's going to look when the news gets out. You and I have already discussed this at length, but I wanted you to be prepared when she and her husband come for a visit."

"How soon?"

"Tonight."

Abby's breath caught.

"If she weren't coming, we could have stayed out another night. You don't have to meet with her if you don't want to, Abby. This is none of her business."

"But it is, Vincenzo. She's going to be your baby's aunt. We'll face her together like we faced the queen. Was she good friends with Michelina?"

He nodded. "They were very close. I know for a fact Gianna's hurt because Michelina never confided in her about this."

"Some matters aren't for anyone's ears except your own spouse. Surely she understands that."

"You would think so." He threw a towel around his shoulders and got up from the lounger. "Come on. You need to get out of the sun."

She pulled on her robe and they walked to the covered bar laid out with cocktail tables and padded chairs. Soft rock played through the speakers. One of the stewards brought them iced lime drinks.

"I'm sorry your sister is upset, but I'm not worried about it, if that's what you're thinking. I had my trial of fire with the queen." A smile slowly broke from her.

Vincenzo saw it and covered her free hand with his own. "Then I won't take on that worry." He squeezed it, then let her go with reluctance and sat back. But she still felt the warmth and pressure of his after it had been removed.

"How long will it take us to get back to port?"

"For you, about five hours."

She groaned inside. "But not you."

"No. Another helicopter will be arriving in a half hour to take me back." The yacht had everything, including a landing pad. "Before I leave, I want to dance with you."

Ignoring her slight gasp, he reached for her and drew her into his arms. He moved them around slowly, pressing her against him.

"Do you know how incredible it is to be holding you in my arms while our baby is nestled right here between us?"

Abby couldn't breathe.

"I've needed to feel you like this for a long time. Don't fight me, Abby." He kissed her cheek and neck, her hair.

She felt as if she would faint from ecstasy. The last thing she wanted to do was push him away. For a little while she let herself go and clung to him. "I wish you didn't have to leave," she whispered.

"It's the last thing I want to do." While she was trying to recover from her severe disappointment that he had to go, he brushed his lips against hers before giving her a man's kiss, hot with desire. It spiked through her like electricity.

Close to a faint, she heard the sound of rotors and saw a speck in the sky coming their way. As it grew larger, she felt her heart being chopped into little pieces. Vincenzo had given her a fantastic surprise, but she wished he hadn't. She couldn't handle being around him like this and being kissed like this, only for him to be whisked away. This was torture.

"I'm afraid it will be better if no one sees us arriving together. The paparazzi will be out in full force. Angelina's going to help you leave with some of the staff from the yacht."

"You've had to go to a lot of trouble for me."

"How could it possibly compare with what you're doing for me?" She averted her eyes. "I'll send for you when it's time. We'll meet in the state drawing room as before. It's the only neutral ground in the palace, if you understand my meaning."

She knew what he meant. They couldn't talk to his sister in either of their apartments or his father's.

Though it was painful, she slowly eased out of his arms. "You need to get ready to go, so I'll say goodbye now and take a shower in my cabin."

He moved fast and accompanied her along the deck to open the door for her. But when she went inside and started to shut it, he stood there so she couldn't. His eyes stared at her. The desire in those black depths was unmistakable. She went weak at the knees. A small nerve throbbed at the corner of the mouth she was dying to taste over and over again.

"I'll see you tonight," he whispered in a raw-sounding voice she hardly recognized.

"Stay safe, Vincenzo. Don't let anything happen to you in that helicopter. Your child's going to need you."

"Abby—the last thing I want to do is leave you."

Then don't! she wanted to cry out. "With family coming, you have to."

His face darkened with lines. "Promise me you won't let Gianna get to you."

"She couldn't."

Abby had the feeling he wanted to warn her about something, then changed his mind.

"It'll be all right, Vincenzo."

His jaw hardened. "I'll Skype you at ten tonight."

She'd be living for it. *"A presto."*

Abby shut the door. After the passion in that kiss, this time it had to be goodbye for good.

When Marcello ushered Abby, wearing her jacketed white dress with the brown trim, into the drawing room, she glowed from the sun she'd picked up on her one day cruise. Her blond hair had been caught back with a dark comb. The newspaper had been right. She was stunning. Vincenzo had never seen her looking so beautiful.

"Gianna and I are glad you're here, Abby," he said, welcoming her to come in and sit down.

"I am, too. It's wonderful to see you again, Gianna." Since they'd all known each other for years, Vincenzo had dispensed with the pretense of formality, hoping to put Abby at ease. But he needn't have worried. She had incredible poise. Her self-possession came naturally to her and served her well in her profession.

Gianna, a tall brunette, smiled at her. "Pregnancy becomes you. You look well."

Vincenzo cringed. His sister wasn't pregnant yet and had gone straight for the jugular. So far the two women in his life who'd insisted on talking to Abby since Michelina's death had managed to show a side that couldn't help but hurt her, though she would deny it.

"Thank you. I feel fine."

His sister crossed her slim legs. "I told Vincenzo I wanted a private word with you. Do you mind?"

"Of course not."

He took that as his cue. "I'll be outside," he told Abby before leaving the room. For the next ten minutes he paced before she came out of the double doors. Despite her newly acquired tan, she'd lost a little color. He was furious with Gianna, but since their father had insisted she be allowed to talk with Abby, Vincenzo had given in, knowing it wouldn't go well.

"Are you all right?"

"I'm fine."

"I'll walk you back to your father's apartment."

"Please don't." It was the first time in their lives she'd ever spoken to him in a cold tone. Gianna had to have been brutal.

"I'll call you as soon as I know you're home." When Abby didn't respond he said, "We have to talk. I want your promise that you'll answer, otherwise I'll show up at your door."

"I—I need to go." Her voice faltered before she hurried down the hall and disappeared around the corner.

Tamping down his fury, he went back inside the drawing room. Gianna was waiting for him. He knew that look. "What in the hell did you say to her?"

Ten minutes later he started for the doors.

"Don't you dare walk out on me!"

Vincenzo wheeled around. "I already did." He strode rapidly through the corridors to the east entrance of the palace and raced across the grounds to Carlo's apartment. Once he arrived, he knocked on the door and didn't stop until Abby answered. After closing the door, he took one glance at her wan face and pulled her into his arms.

"Gianna told me what she unleashed on you. I'm so sorry." He cupped the back of her head and pressed it into his shoulder, kissing her hair. "You have to know it was her pain talking. She had to marry a man she didn't love and so far she hasn't conceived. Though she's attractive, she's not a beauty like you and never was. Her jealousy of you and your association with Michelina finally reared its ugly head."

It was like déjà vu with Abby sobbing quietly against him, the way she'd done after she'd been rescued.

"She used scare tactics on you so you'll leave, but don't you know I'd never let you go?"

After she went quiet, she pulled away from him. Her eyes resembled drenched violets. "Maybe I should."

"Abby—how can you even say that?"

She stared at him, looking broken. "The issues she brought up I've already faced in my mind, except for one."

"Which one?"

"Your child. The thought of it growing up with doubts about who its mother really is breaks my heart."

Vincenzo didn't think he could ever forgive Gianna for planting that absurd fear in Abby's mind. "The baby will be a part of Michelina. Michelina had distinctive genes, like her mother and brother. They don't lie, remember?"

She took a shuddering breath. "You're right. How silly of me."

"Not silly, only human in the face of behavior I haven't seen come out of my sister since she was a teenager and threw a tantrum because she couldn't get her own way. But she'll calm down in time, just like the queen. I left her with the prospect that when Father steps down, she'll be the new ruler of Arancia.

"As Dr. DeLuca reminded us, this is a nine-day wonder that will be over for her soon. The good news is, you've walked through your last fire. From now on, we wait until our baby sends you into labor. Does the prospect make you nervous?"

She nodded and put on a smile for him. "Yes, but I'm not frightened, exactly. How could I be, when hundreds of thousands of babies are born every day? It's just that this baby is special."

"After finding out what it's like to be an expectant father, I've learned every baby is special if it's yours, royal or not. If Gianna had given me the chance, I would have told her you've been a blessing to Michelina and me. She would say the same thing if she were here, so never forget it."

"I won't."

"Do you believe me, Abby? It's imperative you believe it."

Her eyes searched his. "Of course I do."

"Thank you for that." Without conscious thought, he brushed his lips against hers. "I have to go and we'll see each other tomorrow night at seven o'clock. Right?"

"Yes."

Before he went back to the palace, he hurried down to their private beach. After ripping off his clothes, he lunged into the water and swam until he had no more strength before returning to his suite.

His phone registered four messages, from Marcello, his father, Gianna, and Gianna's husband, Enzio.

Not tonight.

Normally he didn't drink except on certain occasions. But right now he needed one or he'd never get to sleep. However, even the alcohol couldn't quiet the adrenaline gushing through his system since he'd held Abby. He'd felt every curve of her body.

Tonight he'd felt the baby move against him, igniting a spark that brought him to life in a brand-new way. It was something he'd never expected to feel. The last thing he remembered before oblivion took over was the sweet, innocent taste of her lips. *Abby, Abby.*

CHAPTER NINE

WHEN ABBY COULDN'T reach her father, she left him a message.

"Hi, Dad. I'm just leaving the doctor's office and wanted to report that my checkup went fine. Can you believe my pregnancy is almost over? I'm meeting Carolena for dinner at Emilio's, then we're going to the concert hall to see Aida. Be sure and eat your dinner. It's in the fridge."

This was one night she wouldn't be Skyping with Vincenzo. Last night she'd told him her plans. He wasn't too happy about her sitting through an opera all evening, but she promised to take it easy during the day.

Since the night when everything had come to a head because of Gianna, he hadn't surprised her by showing up unexpectedly. For the last little while he'd been treating her like a friend. She was doing the same. No contact except for technology. It was much easier this way and relieved her of a lot of guilt.

Gianna had forced Abby to face up to the fact that she was desperately in love with Vincenzo. When he'd kissed her before leaving the apartment, it had taken every ounce of her will not to return it. That kiss from him had been one of affection, not passion. It was his way of trying to comfort her.

She loved him for it.

She loved him to the depth of her soul.

During the last scene of *Aida,* she came close to falling apart. Radamès had been taken into the lower part of the temple to be sealed in a dark vault. Aida was hidden there so she could die with him.

When the tenor cried that he'd never see the light of day again, never see Aida again, she told him she was there to die with him. As they fell into each other's arms, Abby choked up. Tears dripped off her chin onto her program because she could imagine a love like that. It was the way she felt about Vincenzo. Before long she'd have the baby and then she'd be gone for good. Thinking of that goodbye was excruciating.

On the way home in the limousine, Carolena teased her that she was full of hormones. Abby attributed her breakdown to the glorious music and voices, but they both knew it was much more than that.

Her dad was at the computer when she walked in the apartment. He lifted his head. "How was the opera?"

"Fantastic."

"You look like you've been crying."

She smiled at him. "Come on, Dad. You know *Aida* is a real tearjerker." They both loved opera.

"Your aunt phoned me today. They've found a house for us near them and sent an email with pictures. Take a look and see what you think. I like it more than any of the others she's sent."

Abby wandered over and stood next to him to check it out. "That's a darling house. I love the Cape Cod style. Let's do it."

Her response seemed to satisfy him. He turned to look at her. "Did you tell Dr. DeLuca about our plans?"

"Yes. He says he has no problem about my flying back to the States within a week of the delivery, provided I'm not having complications. Since Vincenzo is having us flown on the royal jet with a doctor on standby, Dr. DeLuca is fine with it."

"Good."

"He told me something else. Though he hopes I'll go full-term, I shouldn't worry if I start into labor sooner. The baby has dropped and could be born any time now. He says it would be fine. I was glad for that reassurance. My pregnancy has been so free of problems, it's comforting to know that if there's a complication now, the baby will be all right."

"That reassures me, too."

"Dad? Are you having second thoughts about leaving Arancia?"

Their gazes connected. "Absolutely not. There comes a time when you know you're done. How about you?"

"Naturally I'm going to miss it. I've spent more than half my life here, but we have family in Rhode Island and you'll be there. Once I'm settled in a law practice and take the bar, I know I'll be happy."

"I do, too. You'd better get to bed now, honey."

"I'm going. Good night." She kissed his forehead and left for her bedroom.

While she got ready, her mind was on her father. Abby knew he'd had relationships with several women since her mother died, but he seemed eager to leave Arancia. Since she didn't think it was all because of the situation with Vincenzo, she wondered if there was someone back home he'd known before and was anxious to see again.

Once she got under the covers, there was no comfortable position anymore. Then she got hot and threw them off. She'd had backache for the last week and looked like that beached whale. The doctor said she was a good size. Though she'd tried not to think about having to give up the baby, it had kicked her a lot since her sixth month and made her wonder if it was a boy with Vincenzo's great legs.

Abby knew he would have loved to feel it kicking, but by tacit agreement they'd stayed away from each other. She went swimming when he didn't. He didn't pick her up in the limo. Being able to Skype made it possible for them to talk to each other face-to-face and design the nursery, but that was it. Those days would soon be over.

Everything was planned out. Once Abby delivered, she'd be taken to a private place away from any staff or media before the flight back to the States. The contract she'd made in the beginning was specific: no contact with the baby or the parents. Abby's job would be done. That would be it, the end of her association with Vincenzo.

No meetings, no Skyping, no technology to connect them. It had to be that way for the rest of their lives, for the good of the kingdom, for all of them. Vincenzo would be the prince she couldn't forget, but he could never be a part of her life again.

Carolena was getting ready to go to court with a big law case. The work she'd asked Abby to do while she waited out these last few weeks was heaven-sent. Every time she started thinking about the little life getting ready to come into the world, she'd get busy doing more research. But she couldn't turn off her mind in the middle of the night.

Like Vincenzo, this child would be born into that world never knowing anything else. He'd make a marvelous father. She was excited for him, because his whole world was going to change once the doctor put the baby in his arms.

But to never see the baby, to never see Vincenzo again. She sobbed until oblivion took over.

Dr. DeLuca had given her the phone numbers of several former surrogates, but she hadn't felt the need to talk to them. No matter what, every surrogate's experience giving up a baby was different. Hers most of all, since she loved this royal heir and its father with every fiber of her being.

About five in the morning she woke up with lower-back pain. This was a little stronger than usual. She knew it could mean the onset of labor. Then again, it might be because she'd been to the opera last evening and it had been too much for her poor back.

She went to the bathroom and walked around the apartment for a few minutes. The ache subsided. Instead of going back to bed, she sat on the couch with her legs outstretched to watch a Godzilla film in Italian. Her feet were swollen. So were her fingers.

The film put her to sleep, but pain woke her up again. Whoa. She got up to go to the bathroom. Um. It hurt. It hurt a lot.

She went into her father's bedroom. "Dad? Did Mom have a bad backache before I came?"

He shot up in bed. "She sure did. The pain came around to the front."

"Yup. That's what I've got."

"I'll call the doctor."

"Tell him not to alert Vincenzo and tell him no one at the hospital is to leak this to him on the threat of death!"

"You can't ask him that, honey."

"Yes, I can!" She yelled at him for the first time in her life. "I'm the one having this baby and I'm not Vincenzo's wife. This isn't my child." Tears rolled down her hot cheeks. "If something goes wrong, I don't want him there until it's all over. He's been through enough suffering in his life. If everything's fine, then he ca— O-o-h. Wow. That was a sharp pain.

"Dad? Promise me you'll tell the doctor exactly what I said! I've been good about everything, but I want my way in this one thing!

"And make Angelina swear to keep quiet. If she breathes one word of this to Vincenzo, then—oh, my gosh—you'll fire her without pay and she'll never get another job for as long as she lives. I'm depending on you, Dad. Don't let me down."

He put a hand on her cheek. "Honey, I promise to take care of everything." Then he pressed the digit on his phone.

Vincenzo's life had become a ritual of staying alive to hear about Abby's day, but he was slowly losing his mind.

After a grueling session with parliament, he hurried to his apartment for a shower, then rang for some sandwiches and headed for the computer. It was time for his nightly call to Abby. With the baby's time coming soon, he couldn't settle down to anything. The only moments of peace were when he could see her and they'd talk.

Tonight he was surprised because he had to wait for her to tune in. One minute grew to two, then five. He gave her another five in case she was held up. Still no response.

The phone rang. It was Angelina. He broke out in a cold sweat, sensing something was wrong before he clicked on. "Angelina?"

"I wasn't supposed to let you know, but I think you have the right. You're about to become a father, Vincenzo."

What? "Isn't it too soon?"

"Not according to Abby's timetable. She didn't want you to worry, so she didn't want you to come to the hospital until after the delivery, but I know you want to be there. The limo is waiting downstairs to take you to the hospital."

His heart gave a great thump. "I owe you, Angelina! I'm on my way down."

Vincenzo flew out of the apartment and reached the entrance in record time. "Giovanni? Take me to the hospital, stat!"

Everything became a big blur before one of his security men said, "Come this way, Vincenzo." They took the elevator to the fourth floor, past the nursery to one of the rooms in the maternity wing.

"When did she go into labor?"

"Awhile ago," came the vague response. Vincenzo wanted to know more, but a nurse appeared and told him to wash his hands. Then she put a mask and gown on him before helping him into plastic gloves. He couldn't believe this was finally happening.

"Wait here."

As she opened the door, he saw Dr. DeLuca working with Abby. He was telling her to push. His beautiful Abby was struggling with all her might. "Push again, Abby."

"I'm trying, but I can't do this alone. I need Vincenzo. Where is he?" Her cry rang in the air. "I want him here!"

That was all Vincenzo needed to hear. He hurried into the operating room. The doctor saw him and nodded. "He's arrived."

"I'm here, Abby."

She turned her head. "Vincenzo!" He heard joy in her voice. "Our baby's coming! I should have called you."

"I'm here now. Keep pushing. You can do it."

After she pushed for another ten minutes, before his very eyes he saw the baby emerge and heard the gurgle before it let out a cry. Dr. DeLuca lifted it in the air. "Congratulations, Abby and Vincenzo. You have a beautiful boy." He laid the baby across her stomach and cut the cord.

"A *son,* Vincenzo!" Abby was sobbing for joy. "We did it."

"No, you did it." He leaned over and brushed her mouth.

The staff took over to clean the baby. In a minute the pediatrician announced, "The next heir to the throne is seven pounds, twenty-two inches long and looks perfect!"

He brought the bundled baby over and would have placed it in his arms, but Vincenzo said, "Let Abby hold him first."

The moment was surreal for Vincenzo as together

they looked down into the face of the child he and Michelina had created, the child Abby had carried. His heart melted at the sight.

"*Buonasera,* Maximilliano," she said with tears running down her cheeks. "Oh, he's so adorable."

Vincenzo could only agree. He leaned down to kiss the baby's cheeks and finger the dark hair. Carefully he unwrapped their little Max, who *was* perfect, with Michelina's eyes and ears.

"Look, Vincenzo. He has your jaw and the Di Laurentis body shape."

All the parts and pieces were there in all the right places. Vincenzo was overwhelmed.

Dr. DeLuca patted his shoulder. "You should go with the pediatrician, who's taking the baby to the nursery. I need to take care of Abby."

"All right." He leaned down again, this time to kiss her hot cheek. "I'll be back."

An hour later he left the nursery to be with Abby, but was told she was still in recovery. He could wait in the anteroom until she was ready to be moved to a private room. But the wait turned out to be too long and he knew something was terribly wrong.

He hurried to the nursing station. "Where's Signorina Loretto?" He was desperate to see the woman who'd made all this possible. She'd done all the work. She and the baby were inseparable in his mind and heart.

"She's not here, Vincenzo." Dr. DeLuca's voice.

He spun around. "What do you mean? To hell with the agreement, Doctor!"

Vincenzo felt another squeeze on his shoulder and looked up into Carlo's eyes staring at him above the mask he'd put on. "We all knew this was going to be the hard part. Abby's out of your life now, remember?

"Your boy needs you. Concentrate on him. You have all the help you need and a kingdom waiting to hear the marvelous news about the young prince, especially this bambino's grandfather and grandmother."

Vincenzo didn't feel complete without her. "Where is she, Carlo?"

"Asleep. She had back pain around five in the morning. In total she was in labor about fifteen hours. All went well and now that the delivery is over, she's doing fine."

"Tell me where she is," Vincenzo demanded.

"For her protection as well as yours, she's in a safe place to avoid the media."

He felt the onset of rage. "You mean she's been put in a witness protection program?"

"Of a sort. She fulfilled her part of the bargain to the letter and is in excellent health. You once saved her life. Now she's given you a son. Let it be enough."

Carlo's words penetrated through to his soul. What was the Spanish proverb? *Be careful for what you wish, for you just might get it.*

Vincenzo stood there helpless as hot tears trickled down his cheeks.

"Good morning, honey."

"Dad—"

"I'm here."

"This is a different room."

"That's right. You're in a different hospital. You were transported in an ambulance after the delivery."

"I'm so thankful it's over and Vincenzo has his baby."

"Yes. He's overjoyed. I'll turn on the TV so you can see for yourself." Carlo raised the head of the bed a little for her to see without straining.

Abby saw the flash, "breaking news," at the bottom of the screen. "For those of you who are just waking up, this is indeed a morning like none other in the history of the world. There's a new royal heir to the throne of Arancia. Last night at six-fifteen p.m., a baby boy was born to Crown Prince Vincenzo and the deceased Princess Michelina Cavelli by a gestational surrogate mother who we are told is doing well. The new young prince has been named Maximilliano Guilio Cavelli Di Laurentis."

Vincenzo...

"The seven-pound prince is twenty-two inches long."

"Max is beautiful, Daddy." The tears just kept flowing. "He'll be tall and handsome like Vincenzo!"

"According to the proud grandparents, their majesties King Guilio Di Laurentis and Queen Bianca Cavelli of Gemelli, the baby is the image of both royal families.

"We're outside the hospital now, awaiting the appearance of Prince Vincenzo, who will be taking his son home to the royal palace any minute. A nanny is already standing by with a team to ease Prince Vincenzo into this new role of fatherhood.

"Yes. The doors are opening. Here comes the new father holding his son. We've been told he's not going to make a statement, but he's holding up the baby so everyone can see before he gets in the royal limousine."

Darling. Abby sobbed in joy and anguish.

"This must be a bittersweet moment for him without Princess Michelina at his side. But rumor has it that sometime next year the king will be stepping down and the Principality of Arancia will see another wedding and the coronation of Prince Vincenzo."

Abby was dying for Vincenzo, who was being forced to face this. "I can't stand the media, Dad. Couldn't they let him enjoy this one sacred moment he and Michelina had planned for without bringing up the future?"

"Speculation is the nature of that particular beast. But we can be thankful that for this opening announcement, they played down your part in all this. For such forbearance we can thank the king, who told me to tell you that you have his undying gratitude."

Abby's hungry eyes watched the limo as it pulled away from the hospital escorted by security. The roar of the ecstatic crowds filled the streets. Her father shut off the TV.

She lay there, numb. "It's the end of the fairy tale." Abby looked at him. "I can't bear it. I love him, Dad, but he's gone out of my life."

He grasped her hands. "I'm proud to be your father. You laid down your life for him and Michelina and he has his prize. Now it's time for you to close the cover of that scrapbook and start to live your own life."

"You knew about that?"

Her father just smiled. He wasn't the head of palace security for nothing.

Abby brushed the tears off her face. "I gave it to him months ago when he told me he didn't want to be king. I wanted him to look through it and see all his accomplishments."

Her father's eyes grew suspiciously bright. "You've

been his helpmate all along and it obviously did the trick."

She kissed his hand. "Thank you for keeping him away as long as you could. I didn't want him to have to go through any more grief, not after losing Michelina. Forgive me for yelling at you at the apartment?"

"That's when I knew you meant business. As it so happens, I agreed with you, but a man should be at the bedside of the woman who's giving birth to his baby. Evidently Angelina thought so, too. She's the one who told him to get to the hospital quick."

"Bless her. I needed him there."

"Of course you did."

"Lucky for me I was blessed to have you there, too, Daddy."

"Someday you'll get married to a very lucky man, who will be there when the time comes for your own child to be born. I look forward to that day."

Abby loved her father, but he could have no conception of how she felt. Vincenzo was the great love of her life. There would never be anyone else and she would never have a baby of her own. But she'd had this one and had been watched over by Vincenzo every second of the whole experience.

Through the years she would watch Max in secret, because he was her son and Vincenzo's as surely as the sun ruled the day and the moon the night. No one could ever take that away from her.

"Honey? The nurse has brought your breakfast." He wheeled over the bed table so they could eat together. "Do you feel like eating?"

Abby felt too much pain and was too drugged to have

an appetite yet, but to please her father she reached for the juice.

"We haven't talked about you for a long time." She smiled at him. "I want to know the real reason you decided to step down and move back to Rhode Island. Is there a woman in the picture you haven't told me about? I hope there is."

He drank his coffee. "There has been one, but it was complicated, so I never talked about it."

"You can talk to me about it now." Because if there wasn't, then it meant she and her father had both been cursed in this life to love only one person. Now that she'd lost Vincenzo, both she and her dad would be destined to live out the rest of their lives with memories.

"Can't you guess? There's only been one woman in my life besides your mom. It's been you."

"Don't tease me."

"I'm not."

She frowned. "Then why did you decide you wanted to leave Arancia?"

"Because I could see the hold Vincenzo has had on you. Otherwise you would never have offered yourself as a surrogate. If you hope to get on with your life, it has to be away from here."

Abby lowered her head. "I'm afraid he'll always have a hold on me."

"That's my fear, too. It's why we're getting out of Arancia the moment you're ready to travel."

CHAPTER TEN

VINCENZO HAD SUMMONED Angelina to his apartment as soon as he'd returned to the palace with his son. He'd spent time examining Max from head to toe. After feeding him the way the nurse had showed him, and changing his diaper, Vincenzo gave Max to the nanny, who put him to bed in the nursery down the hall. Now there was no time to lose.

"Tell me what you know of Abby's whereabouts, Angelina."

"I can't, Your Highness. Please don't ask me. I've been sworn to secrecy."

"By whom? Carlo?"

"No."

"The king?"

"No."

"Abby?"

She nodded.

He knew it!

"Tell me which hospital they took her to."

Angelina squeezed her eyes tightly. "I don't dare."

"All right. I'm going to name every hospital in Arancia." He knew them all and served on their boards. "All you have to do is wink when I say the right one. That way you never said a word."

"She'll hate me forever."

"Abby doesn't have a hateful bone in her body. She carried my son for nine months and gave me the greatest gift a man could have. Surely you wouldn't deny me the right to tell her thank you in person."

"But she's trying to honor her contract."

"Contract be damned! She's fulfilled it beyond my wildest dreams. If another person had done for you what she's done for me, wouldn't you want to thank them?"

"Yes, but—"

"But nothing. That may have been the rule when Michelina and I signed on with her, but the baby has arrived. There's no more contract. You're free of any obligation. What if I tell you I won't approach her in the hospital?"

After more silence he said, "I'll wait until she leaves. Surely that isn't asking too much. I swear on my mother's grave she'll never know you told me anything."

Still more silence. He started naming hospitals while holding his breath at the same time. Halfway down the list she winked. His body sagged with relief. San Marco Hospital, five miles away in Lanz. Near the airport and several luxury hotels. It all fit.

"Bless you, Angelina. One day soon you'll know my gratitude with a bonus that will set you up for life."

As she rushed away, he phoned his personal driver. *"Giovanni?"*

"Congratulations on your son, Your Highness."

"Thank you. I need you to perform a special service for me immediately."

"Anything."

He'd been doing a lot of undercover services for Vincenzo since the pregnancy. "I hope you mean that. My red sportscar is yours if you do as I say."

His driver laughed. Giovanni came from a poor family.

"You think I'm kidding?"

"You are serious?"

"Do as I say and you'll find out. I want you to round up all your cousins *pronto* and have them drive to San Marco Hospital in Lanz. Signorina Loretto is there recovering from the delivery. She's being watched by her father's security people. Fortunately they don't know your cousins.

"I want them to cover all the hospital exits leading outside. She'll be leaving there by private limousine. I suspect it will happen by this evening if not sooner. When your cousins spot the limousine, they'll follow and report to you when her limo reaches its destination, which I believe will be a hotel, possibly the Splendido or the Moreno. Then you'll phone me and drive me there. Any questions?"

"No, Your Highness. You can count on me."

"There's a healthy bonus waiting for each of them. My life depends on your finding her, Giovanni."

"Capisci."

Vincenzo hung up and hurried down to the nursery to spend time with his precious son before his father and sister arrived. He had to stop Abby from leaving the country. If she got away, he'd track her down, but it would be much more difficult with the baby. He wanted her here. *Now!*

He played with his baby and took pictures with his phone. While the family took turns inspecting the new arrival, he took a catnap. Bianca and Valentino would be flying in tomorrow morning.

At five in the afternoon, his phone rang. He saw the caller ID and picked up. "Giovanni?"

"We've done as you asked. She was driven to the Moreno under heavy guard."

"I'll be right down." After telling Marcello his life wouldn't be worth living if he told anyone where Vincenzo was going, he put on sunglasses and rushed down to the limo in a Hawaiian shirt, khaki shorts, sandals and a droopy straw hat.

Giovanni took off like a rocket. "You look like all the rich American businessmen walking around the gardens. No one would recognize you in a million years, Your Highness," he said through the speaker.

He bit down hard. "If I can make it to her room before someone stops me, it won't matter."

Carlo had made Abby comfortable on the couch in their hotel suite. This would be their home for a few more days before they left the country. The painkillers they'd given her were working.

"Is there anything you want, honey?"

She kept watching the news on TV to see Vincenzo and the baby. "Would you mind picking up a few magazines for me to look at?"

"I'll get them. Anything else?"

"A bag of dark chocolate bocci balls and a pack of cashews." She'd been starving for foods she couldn't eat during the pregnancy. They wouldn't take away her depression, but she needed to give in to her cravings for some sweets or she'd never make it through the next few days.

"I'll have to go down the street for those."

"Dad—take your time. I'm fine and you need a break. Thank you."

A few minutes after Abby's father left, there was a knock on the door. "Room service."

She hadn't ordered anything, but maybe her father had. "Come in."

"Grazie, Signorina."

Abby knew that deep male voice and started to tremble. She turned her head in his direction, afraid she was hallucinating on the medicine. The sight she saw was so incredible, she burst into laughter and couldn't stop.

Vincenzo walked around the couch to stand in front of her. "What do you think?" he asked with a grin, showing those gorgeous white teeth in that gorgeous smile. "Would you recognize me on the street?"

She shook her head. "Take off the glasses." She was still laughing.

He flung them away and hunkered down next to her. His eyes blazed black fire. "Do you know me now?"

Her heart flew to her throat. "Wh-what are you doing here? How did you find me?"

"You'd be surprised what I had to go through. Giovanni's my man when I need him. Did you really think I was going to let you go?"

Tears stung her eyes. "Don't do this, Vincenzo."

"Do what? Come to see the woman who has changed my entire life?"

She looked away. "You have a beautiful son now. We had an agreement."

"I hate agreements when they don't give me the advantage."

Abby couldn't help chuckling, despite her chaotic emotions. "Is he wonderful?"

"I'll let you decide." He pulled out his cell phone to show her the roll of pictures.

"Oh, Vincenzo—he's adorable!"

He put the phone on the floor. "So are you. I love you, heart and soul, Abby."

The next thing she knew, his hands slid to her shoulders and he covered her mouth with his own. The driving force of his kiss pressed her head back against the pillow. His hunger was so shocking in its intensity a moan escaped her throat in surrender.

A dam had burst as they drank deeper and deeper, but Abby's need for him was out of control. She had no thought of holding back. She couldn't.

"For all my sins, I love and want you to the depth of my being, Vincenzo, but you already know that, don't you? I tried not to love you, but it didn't work. Everything your sister said to me that day in the drawing room was true."

His lips roved with increased urgency over her features and down the side of her neck to her throat. "I fell for you years ago when you almost drowned, but I would never admit it to myself because a relationship with you was out of the question. No matter how hard I tried not to think about you, you were there, everywhere I looked. You're in my blood, *bellissima*."

They kissed back and forth, each one growing more passionate. "It seems like I've been waiting for this all my life," she admitted when he let her up for breath.

"We've paid the price for our forbearance, but that time is over. I'm not letting you go."

Abby groaned aloud and tore her lips from his. "I can't stay in Arancia."

"There's no such word in my vocabulary. Not anymore."

"She's right, Vincenzo."

Her father had just walked in the hotel room, carrying some bags. Her breath caught as she eyed him over Vincenzo's shoulder.

"Carlo." He pressed another kiss to her mouth and got to his feet. "I'm glad you're here so I can ask your permission to marry Abby. She's my heart's blood."

Rarely in her life had she seen her father look defeated. He put the bags on the table and stared at the two of them.

"I don't want an affair with her. I want her for my wife. Since you and I met when I was eighteen, you can't say you don't know me well enough."

Her father moved closer. "That's certainly true." He looked at Abby. "Is this what you want?"

"Yes." Her answer was loud and instantaneous.

Vincenzo reached for her hand and squeezed it. "I have no idea if the parliament will allow my marriage to a commoner and still let me remain crown prince. If not, then I don't intend to be in line for the crown and my sister will take over when the time comes."

"Are you prepared to be the targets of malicious gossip for the rest of your lives?"

"If necessary we'll move to the States with our son. He *is* our son. One way or another, she and I have been in communication whether in person or skyping. Max is every bit a part of her as he is of me and Michelina."

Carlo swallowed hard.

"I love Abby the way you loved your wife. The state

you were in when you lost her altered my view of what a real marriage could be. If Abby leaves me, I'll be as lost as you were."

Vincenzo was speaking to her father's heart. She could tell he'd gotten to him.

"I know the king's feelings on the subject, Vincenzo. He was hoping you would follow after him."

"I was hoping I would fall in love with Michelina. But we don't always get what we hope for. If it's any consolation, Gianna always wished she'd been born a boy so she'd be first in line. She'll make a great ruler when the day comes."

"Are you two prepared to face the wrath of your mother-in-law?"

Vincenzo glanced at Abby. "We'll deal with her. When she sees Michelina's likeness in Max, her heart will melt. I know she'll secretly be full of gratitude to Abby, who put her life on the line for Michelina and me to give her a grandson."

"Dad?" Abby's eyes pleaded with him. "What do you think Mom would say if she were here?"

He let out a strange sound. "She always did say it was sinful that Prince Vincenzo had been born with every physical trait and virtue any red-blooded woman could want. Since she loved films so much, she would probably say yours is one of the greatest love stories of this generation and should be made into a movie. Then she'd give you her blessing, as I give you mine."

"Carlo..."

Vincenzo was as moved as Abby, who broke down weeping. He finally cleared his throat. "I want her to move back into the palace tonight in her old room until we're married. Max needs his mother tonight, not a nanny or a nurse."

"In that case a quiet, private marriage in the palace chapel needs to be arranged within a week or two. Just as soon as you've talked to the king."

"I don't want you to take that job back in Rhode Island, Dad."

He broke into a happy smile. "Since I'm going to be a grandpa, I guess I'm stuck here."

"That'll be music to my father's ears." Vincenzo put his hands on his hips. "Do you feel well enough for the trip back to the palace now?" he asked Abby.

She stared at him. "I feel so wonderful, I'm floating. I want to see our baby."

"Do what you need to do while I help your father get everything packed up. Then we'll go out to my limo for the drive back."

"I'll just run to the restroom and grab my purse." Except she walked slowly and looked back at Vincenzo. "I'm waddling like a goose."

His laughter resonated off the walls.

In a few minutes she was ready. When she came back into the room, she found he'd donned his hat and sunglasses. When she thought he would take hold of her hand, he picked her up like a bride, as if she were weightless.

"You and I have done things differently than most of the world. Now we're about to cross the threshold the other way."

"And me looking such a mess." She didn't have on makeup and her hair hung loose, without being brushed.

"You're the most beautiful sight I ever saw in my life." He gave her a husband's kiss, hot with desire.

"So are you," she murmured, resting her head against his shoulder.

Her father opened the door. "The men have the hallway closed off to the exit. Let's go."

After leaving his stunned father and sister in the king's private living room, where he'd announced he was getting married, Vincenzo headed for the nursery. He found Max sleeping and gathered him in his arms. The nanny left for Abby's apartment, wheeling the bassinet on its rollers down the hall. He followed and carried his son through the corridors of the palace. One day their little boy would run on these marble floors.

The staff all wanted to steal a look at Max, but Vincenzo was careful not to let them get too close. Dr. De-Luca had warned him to keep Max away from people during the next few weeks. He found Abby on top of the bed with her eyes closed. After fifteen hours in labor, she had to be exhausted. She was wearing a blue nightgown and robe and had fastened her gilt hair back at the nape.

Their nanny put the bassinet with everything they would need to one side of the queen-size bed and left the apartment. Since both were asleep, Vincenzo put the baby in the little crib on his back. Then he got on the other side of the bed and lay down facing Abby.

It felt so marvelous to put his arm around her. He'd wanted to do this on the yacht and had been aching for her ever since. While she slept he studied the exquisite oval mold of her face. Her lips had the most luscious curve. He had to pinch himself this was really happening. To have his heart's desire like this was all he could ever ask of life.

Abby sighed and started to turn, but must have felt the weight of Vincenzo's arm. Her eyes flickered open.

"Good evening, Sleeping Beauty." The famous fairy-tale character had nothing on his bride-to-be.

Her eyes looked dazed. "How long have you been here?"

"Just a little while. *Viene qui tesoro.*" She *was* his darling.

He pulled her closer and began kissing her. Abby's response was more thrilling than anything he'd ever dreamed about the two of them. Vincenzo had promised himself to be careful with her. The kind of intimacy he longed for wouldn't happen until her six-week checkup, but he already knew she was an exciting lover.

They didn't need words right now. There'd been enough words expressed to last months, years. The kind of rapture they derived from each other had to come from touch, from her fragrance, from the sounds of her breathing when she grew excited, from the way she fit in his arms as if she were made for him. She was the fire, giving off life-giving warmth. He couldn't get close enough.

In the throes of ecstasy, he heard newborn sounds coming from the other side of the bed. He planted one more kiss to her throat. "Someone's waking up and wants to meet his mama."

With reluctance, he rolled away from her and walked around to the crib. "I've got a surprise for you, *piccolo,* but let's change your diaper first." Practice made perfect.

Abby sat up higher on the bed, her eyes glued to the baby he placed in her arms. "Oh—" she crooned, bending over to kiss his face. "You darling little thing.

You're already a kicker, aren't you? I've been feeling your father's legs for several months and thought you had to be a boy. Are you hungry? Is that why you're getting all worked up?" Her soft laughter thrilled Vincenzo's heart.

He handed her a bottle. She knew what to do. It fascinated him to watch her feed him as if she'd been doing it every day. A mother's instinct. Deep down he knew she'd been thinking about it from the moment she found out she was pregnant.

"Give him about two ounces, then burp him. Here's a cloth."

What took him awhile to learn she seemed to know instinctively. When she raised Max to her shoulder, their little boy cooperated and they both chuckled. She raised a beaming face to him. "I'm too happy."

"I know what you mean," he murmured emotionally.

"I hope you realize I wanted to talk about the baby for the whole nine months, but I didn't dare."

"You think I don't understand?" He sat down on the side of the bed next to her and watched a miracle happening before his eyes. "We'll take care of Max all night and feed him every time he wakes up."

"I can't wait to bathe him in the morning. I want to examine every square inch of him."

Vincenzo leaned over to kiss her irresistible mouth. "Once the doctor gives you the go-ahead, I'm going to do the same thing to *you*."

Blood rushed to her cheeks. "Darling—"

Abby had just put the baby down in the nursery when her cell phone rang. She hurried out of the room, clutching her robe around her, and slipped back in the bedroom she shared with her husband to answer it. "Carolena!"

"You're a sly one."

Her heart pounded in anxiety. "I was just going to call you. I guess the news is officially out."

"Out? It's alive and has gone around the world. I've got the Arancian morning news in front of my eyes. I quote, 'Crown Prince Vincenzo Di Laurentis marries commoner surrogate mother Abigail Sanderson Loretto in private chapel ceremony with only members of the immediate family in attendance. The question of the prince stepping down is still being debated by the parliament.

'The twenty-eight-year-old first-time mother, an American citizen born in Rhode Island, attained Arancian citizenship six years ago. At present she's an *avvocata* with Faustino, Ruggeri, Duomo and Tonelli.

'Her father, Carlo Antonio Loretto, a native of Arancia who served in the Arancian Embassy in Washington, D.C., for a time, is chief of security for the royal palace. His American-born wife, Holly Sanderson Loretto, is deceased due to a tragic sailboat accident eleven years ago on the Mediterranean.

'Prince Maximilliano Guilio Cavelli Di Laurentis, the son of deceased Princess Michelina Agostino Cavelli of the Kingdom of Gemelli, is second in line to the throne.

'The spokesman for the palace reports that Prince Vincenzo's wife and child are doing well.'"

Abby gripped the phone tighter. "This day had to come, the one the three of us talked about a year ago, when I first met with Michelina and Vincenzo.

But I didn't know then that she would die." Her voice throbbed before breaking down in tears.

"I know this is hard, Abby, but you might take heart in the fact that the paper didn't do a hatchet job on you and your husband. They presented the facts without making judgments, something that is so rare in the media world, I found myself blinking."

"That's because of the publisher's long-standing friendship with the king. I shudder to think what the other newspapers have printed."

"I haven't read anything else except the story in one magazine. Do you remember the one after Michelina's death that said The Prince of Every Woman's Dreams in Mourning?"

"Yes." She'd never forget.

"The quote now reads, 'Hopeful royal women around the world in mourning over prince's marriage to American beauty.'"

Abby groaned. "The truth is, that magazine would have been writing about me if he'd decided to marry Princess Odile."

"But he didn't!" Carolena cried out ecstatically. "Listen to this article from that same magazine. 'Enrico Rozzo, a sailor in the coast guard who was at the scene of the terrible death of Holly Loretto, the mother of then seventeen-year-old Abigail Loretto, said, "Prince Vincenzo thought nothing of his own life when he went in search of Signorina Loretto during the fierce storm. He found her body floating lifeless in a grotto and brought her back to life. His bravery, skill and quick thinking will never be forgotten by the coast guard."'"

Abby's body froze. "How did they get hold of that story?"

"How do they always do it? It's a glowing testimonial to your husband, Abby. He's well loved."

"I know." *By me most of all.* She was blinded by tears, still euphoric after knowing Vincenzo's possession for the first time.

"Just think—he married *you* under threat of losing the throne. Talk about Helen of Troy!"

A chuckle escaped despite Abby's angst. "Will you stop?"

"I always thought you were the most romantic person I ever knew. After what you went through to get that baby here, no one deserves a happier ending more than you."

"I'm not looking very romantic right now." She wiped her eyes. "At my six-week checkup yesterday morning, the doctor told me I'm fifteen pounds overweight. I won't be able to wear that gorgeous yellow dress for at least two months! I look like an albatross!" Carolena's laughter came through the phone.

"A stunning albatross," Vincenzo whispered, sliding his arms around her from behind. She hadn't heard him come in. He was in his robe.

At his touch Abby could hardly swallow, let alone think. "Carolena? Forgive me. I have to go, but I promise to call you soon. You've got to come to the palace and see the baby."

"I can't wait!"

He was kissing the side of her neck, so she couldn't talk.

"Your time is coming."

"When the moon turns blue."

"Carolena, you're being ridiculous."

"A presto."

The second Abby clicked off, Vincenzo took the phone and tossed it onto one of the velvet chairs. He pivoted her around and crushed her against him. "Do you have any idea how wonderful it is to walk into a room, any room, day or night, and know I can do anything I want to you?"

She clung fiercely to him, burying her face in his hair. "I found out how wonderful it was yesterday after you brought me home from my checkup." Heat filled her body as she remembered their lovemaking. She'd responded to him with an abandon that would have been embarrassing if he hadn't been such an insatiable lover. They'd cried out their love for each other over and over during the rapture-filled hours of the night.

"I told the nanny we'd look in on the baby tonight, but for the next eight hours, we're not to be disturbed unless there's an emergency."

"We've got eight hours?" Her voice shook.

His smile looked devilish; he rubbed her arms as a prelude to making love. "What's the matter? It *is* our honeymoon. Are you scared to be alone with me already?"

Her heart was racing. "Maybe."

"Innamorata—" He looked crushed. "Why would you say that?"

She tried to ease away from him, but he wouldn't let her. "I guess it's because the news has gone public about us at last. I don't want you to regret marrying me. What if the parliament votes for you to step down? It's all because of me."

He let out a deep sigh. "Obviously you need more

convincing that I've done exactly what I wanted.
Whether I become king one day or not means nothing
to me without your love to get me through this life." He
kissed her mouth. "Sit on the bed. There's something I
want to show you."

While she did his bidding, he pulled the scrapbook
from one of his dresser drawers. "I've been busy filling
the pages that hadn't been used yet. Take a good long
look, and then never again accuse me of regretting the
decision I've made."

With trembling hands she turned to the place where
she'd put her last entry. On the opposite page were the
two ultrasound pictures of the baby. Beneath them was
a news clipping of her on the steps of the courthouse
the day she'd won the case for Signor Giordano. A quiet
gasp escaped her throat as she turned the pages.

Someone had taken pictures of her coming and going
from the palace. Pictures of her on the funicular, at the
restaurant, the swimming pool, the yacht, the church
where she'd worn the hat, pictures on the screen while
they'd Skyped. But she cried out when she saw a close-
up of herself at the opera. The photo had caught her in
a moment of abject grief at the thought of a permanent
separation from Vincenzo.

He'd always found a way to her…

Abby could hardly breathe for the love enveloping
her. "Darling—" She put the album on the bedside table
and turned in his arms. He pulled her on top of him.

"You're the love of my life and the mother of my
child. How can you doubt it?" he asked in that low, velvety voice she felt travel through her body like lava, igniting fires everywhere it went.

"I don't doubt you, sweet prince," she whispered

against his lips. "I just want you to know I'll never take this precious love for granted."

"I'm glad to hear it. Now love me, Abby. I need you desperately. Never stop," he cried.

As if she could.

* * * * *

COMING SOON!

We really hope you enjoyed reading this book.
If you're looking for more romance
be sure to head to the shops when
new books are available on

Thursday 24th
April

To see which titles are coming soon, please visit

millsandboon.co.uk/nextmonth

MILLS & BOON

MILLS & BOON

THE HEART OF ROMANCE

A ROMANCE FOR EVERY READER

MODERN

Prepare to be swept off your feet by sophisticated, sexy and seductive heroes, in some of the world's most glamourous and romantic locations, where power and passion collide.

HISTORICAL

Escape with historical heroes from time gone by. Whether your passion is for wicked Regency Rakes, muscled Vikings or rugged Highlanders, awaken the romance of the past.

MEDICAL

Set your pulse racing with dedicated, delectable doctors in the high-pressure world of medicine, where emotions run high and passion, comfort and love are the best medicine.

True Love

Celebrate true love with tender stories of heartfelt romance, from the rush of falling in love to the joy a new baby can bring, and a focus on the emotional heart of a relationship.

HEROES

The excitement of a gripping thriller, with intense romance at its heart. Resourceful, true-to-life women and strong, fearless men face danger and desire - a killer combination!

From showing up to glowing up, these characters are on the path to leading their best lives and finding romance along the way – with plenty of sizzling spice!

To see which titles are coming soon, please visit

millsandboon.co.uk/nextmonth

LET'S TALK
Romance

For exclusive extracts, competitions and special offers, find us online:

- **f** MillsandBoon
- **X** @MillsandBoon
- **⊙** @MillsandBoonUK
- **♪** @MillsandBoonUK

Get in touch on 01413 063 232

FOUR BRAND NEW BOOKS FROM
MILLS & BOON MODERN

The same great stories you love, a stylish new look!

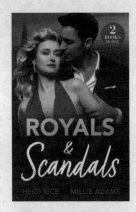

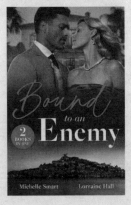

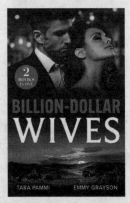

OUT NOW

Eight Modern stories published every month, find them all at:

millsandboon.co.uk

Afterglow Books is a trend-led, trope-filled list of books with diverse, authentic and relatable characters, a wide array of voices and representations, plus real world trials and tribulations. Featuring all the tropes you could possibly want (think small-town settings, fake relationships, grumpy vs sunshine, enemies to lovers) and all with a generous dose of spice in every story.

♪ @millsandboonuk
◎ @millsandboonuk
afterglowbooks.co.uk
#AfterglowBooks

For all the latest book news, exclusive content and giveaways scan the QR code below to sign up to the Afterglow newsletter:

afterglow BOOKS

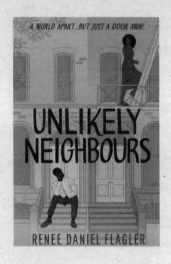

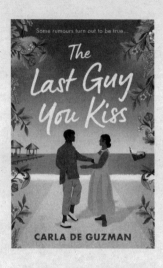

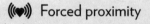

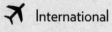

(((♥))) Forced proximity

💻 Workplace romance

🛏 One night

✈ International

⧗ Slow burn

🌶 Spicy

OUT NOW

Two stories published every month. Discover more at:
Afterglowbooks.co.uk